ALLIANCE OF SHADOWS

ALLIANCE OF SHADOWS

LARRY CORREIA
MIKE KUPARI

BAEN

Copyright © 2016 by Larry Correia & Mike Kupari

A Baen Books Original

Baen Publishing Enterprises
P.O. Box 1403
Riverdale, NY 10471
www.baen.com

ISBN: 978-1-4767-8185-3

Cover art by Kurt Miller

First printing, October 2016

Distributed by Simon & Schuster
1230 Avenue of the Americas
New York, NY 10020

Printed in the United States of America

10 9 8 7 6 5 4 3 2 1

ALLIANCE OF SHADOWS

Chapter 1: The Stakeout

VALENTINE
Salzburg, Austria
September 3rd

Bullets pinged off the helicopter's hull as we lifted away from the port. Through the chaos, the scream of the engines and the roar of the machine guns, time seemed to slow to a trickle.

The crew chief ripped off burst after burst from the door gun as the NH-90 maneuvered violently, her pilot trying to avoid the incoming fire. My team leader, Ramirez, was wounded, bleeding out. Tailor was talking into the radio, trying to hide the fear in his voice. Skunky was firing his M14 out one door, while the mysterious Exodus operatives were on the other side of the cabin, huddled protectively around the young girl they'd just rescued. Her hair was silver, almost white. Her face was dirty, and there was fear in her eyes.

We hadn't gone onto the ship with them. That was their op. We were just supposed to provide transportation and security, supposedly the easy part. Exodus performed the extraction—several of them died in the process—but they got the girl. I didn't know who she was. I didn't know why she was so important, why the arms dealer, Federov, kidnapped her in the first place, or why Exodus paid us so much money to help recover her.

The girl's eyes, intensely blue, unnervingly clear, locked onto me, and everything else seemed to fade away. The fear left her face for just a moment, replaced with . . . curiosity? Interest? She cocked her head very slightly to one side as Ling, the Chinese woman who led the

1

Exodus operatives, and their medic looked her over. She was staring right at me.

"Only you can save us."

BANG! *I came crashing back to reality when a large round blasted a hole in the hull of the chopper. The screams of men were joined with the scream of a warning klaxon. I was pinned against my seat as the chopper began rotating. Through the open door I could see Cancun spinning all around us. The ground rushed up to meet us.*

My eyes snapped open. A bead of sweat trickled down my head as I quickly looked around, breathing heavily, trying to remember where I was.

"Are you okay?" Skunky asked. I was sitting in the driver's seat of a car. It was dark out.

I took a moment to catch my breath. "Yeah . . . yeah, I'm fine."

"Did you have a bad dream?"

I closed my eyes for a long moment, trying to will my heart to slow down. "The chopper crash in Mexico again."

Skunky winced. He had been on that op too. His real name was Jeff, and we'd been through a lot together. Riding a helicopter into a swimming pool wasn't the worst thing we'd been through. Not even close.

"How long was I out?"

"About an hour," he said.

"You kept watching the house, right?"

"Naw, man, I zoned out playing *War of Battle Clans* on my phone. Of course I was watching the house. One of us actually has to work." He had a night vision scope in his hands, and a big camera on the dash. We were parked down the road a bit from the target, away from the street lights, in the shadows beneath some trees.

I stretched. "I'm the brains of this operation. I need my rest."

Exodus had sustained terrible losses in the operation at the Crossroads, and was desperately short on manpower. There were only six of us in Austria, trying to prevent the end of the world. I kept telling myself that was the reason I was here, that they needed me.

They say it is good to be needed. I didn't know about that, since the only thing I'd ever been needed for was war.

I shifted uncomfortably in my seat. We had been sitting in this BMW M3 for hours. "Whoever would've thought this is where we'd end up? From a helicopter crash in Mexico to a Beemer in Austria?"

Skunky shook his head. "I think it was meant to be. I don't believe in coincidences like this."

"You know, Ariel told me I was right where I needed to be."

"You should listen to her. She's a smart girl. She knows stuff."

That was an understatement. Ariel was the girl we'd rescued off that ship, the weird one from my dream, only she was all grown up now, and palling around with Exodus—a secret organization dedicated to protecting the weak in all the places the civilized world didn't give a damn about—but which was unfortunately considered a terrorist organization by every law enforcement agency in the world. So she'd come a long way.

"Knowing stuff . . . I can't argue with that."

"I still think she's got psychic powers, man."

"Dude, shut up. She's not psychic." I opened my door. We'd shut off the car's interior light to not give our position away. "I'll be right back. I need some air."

Salzburg is beautiful. It was a clear night, and the city was lovely. Moonlight reflected off of the snow-capped Alps and the Salzach River, which ran through the city. Behind me, at the top of the hill, was Hohensalzburg Castle. The ancient fortress was the most prominent feature of the picturesque city, and was a very popular tourist stop. Narrow, winding streets cut back and forth up the hill leading to the castle. This part of the city was terraced, with houses lining the streets, packed in together. The street I stood on, Nonnberggasse, was at rooftop level with the terrace below me, and I could see down into people's windows. The street was virtually deserted, as the castle was closed at night.

There was some kind of festival going on in the heart of the city. The city center was lit up, and even from where I was, I could hear music. I wondered what it was like to just be able to go to things like that, to live your life without worrying about staying off the radar. I was sick of the cloak and dagger bullshit.

My phone vibrated in my pocket as I made my way back to the car. I had a text message from Ling.

How are you doing?

The phones were a bit of a risk, but as long as we were careful about what we said we were safe. *Cramped,* I texted back. *I had to get out to stretch.*

How are you boys getting along?

Bored. Talking about the old days. How are you?

Same, she wrote back. *S. and A. are up front. I tried to sleep for a while, but got a cramp in my neck.*

Aww. When this is over, I'll massage it out for you.

I can't help but notice that whenever you try to give me a massage, I end up with my clothes off.

I don't see how this is a problem.

I didn't say it was a problem. I just think that, perhaps, with you being as easily distracted as you are, the therapeutic quality of your massages is dubious, at best.

I couldn't help but smile at Ling's judicious use of proper grammar, punctuation, and capitalization in her texts. It was adorable. *I disagree,* I sent back. *Those massages always make me feel great. Hey, you should send me a picture.*

Is that so? Fine. Let me find one you haven't seen yet.

"Val, look," Skunky's tone had changed. It was all business now. "There's a vehicle arriving at the building."

Damn it. I grabbed the radio. "Alpha Team, this is Bravo. We've got a vehicle approaching the building of interest, I say again, vehicle approaching the BOI. Late model Mercedes sedan, four-door, dark color. We're getting it on camera, how copy?"

"*Understood,*" Antoine replied. His deep voice boomed over the radio. "*We're moving now. Keep eyes on until we get to you.*"

"Roger," I said. We had kept our vehicles separate so as to be as discreet as possible, and to watch different paths of entry. Ling's team was in a nondescript Range Rover. This part of Salzburg had too many curvy little streets, so it was impossible to cover all possible routes with just two vehicles, but we had to make do with the assets we had.

"Two people getting out," Skunky said.

"Let me see," I said, taking the camera from him. Resting it on the steering wheel, I zoomed in and studied the two men climbing the steps to the four story house. It was a narrow building, constructed right up against a rocky outcropping on the hill. It didn't have a yard, but it did have an adjacent garage. "Bravo Team, Alpha. I think that's our boy."

"Copy," Antoine said. *"Stefan Varga?"*

Our radios were encrypted and secure, so he could use our target's real name. I studied the zoomed-in image intently, and compared to a picture I had saved on my phone. "Affirmative."

"Are you sure?"

"Sure as I can be. Get up here."

"Copy that," Antoine said. *"We're moving."*

"Roger. As soon as you guys get into position we're going in."

"We need him alive," Antoine reminded me.

"We'll do the best we can. We . . . stand by."

"What's wrong?" Skunky asked.

"Shit," I growled. "Bravo Team, I got a quick look inside when they opened the door. There are more dudes inside. The guy that answered the door had a weapon, submachine gun maybe." We had thought the house to be empty. There was no vehicle parked on the street—though we couldn't see into the garage—and no one had passed by a window in the time we'd been watching the place. They'd kept a low profile. "Security is better than we thought."

"Understood, Alpha," Antoine said. *"Have we been compromised?"*

"I don't think so. I don't know how many guys are in there, though. This could get ugly. How do you want to run this? We got two options. We can kick the door in and do it the hard way, or we can wait until Varga leaves and try to nab him off the street. Either way is risky."

Ling's clear soprano voice came over my radio. *"If Varga gets away, the last two months have been for nothing."*

"Copy that, but if there are six armed dudes in there plus our new arrivals, we're gonna have a bad night. Everything will be for nothing if we all get killed."

"This is your op, Valentine," Ling said, much more formally than she had been via text a minute ago, but she kept our relationship private and separate from our work. *"It is your call. If we try to catch Varga in town, you know what can happen."*

Shit. My mind raced. I'd done this sort of thing before, though door-kicking was not something I was particularly fond of—it's an easy way to get killed—but if this thing turned into a running gun battle downtown, we'd be lucky to avoid getting arrested by the Polizei, and countless innocent people would be endangered.

Skunky started tapping me on the shoulder as I brooded. "Dude. Dude! We've got another vehicle approaching, a motorcycle."

I keyed the radio. "Bravo Team, stand by. We've got a motorcycle rolling up to the house. Bullet bike of some kind. Only the driver. He's wearing riding gear and a full face helmet. He has a messenger bag. Skinny guy, maybe five foot nine, and I'm sorry I can't convert that to centimeters or hectares or whatever for you. He's got a package in his hands, heading up to the door."

"What do you want to do?" Antoine asked.

"Hold up for a moment. Maybe he's just making a delivery or something. It looks like he left the bike running. He'll probably leave in a minute. We'll wait until he's clear before we move in."

"Understood."

I watched on my little screen, recording, as the newcomer walked up the steps to the door of the house. He opened the bag and pulled something out of it.

"Is that a weapon?" Skunky asked.

BOOM! The stranger blasted the door handle with a sawed-off shotgun. He kicked the door open and went inside.

What the hell? There had been no hesitation there. It was roll up and breach. It had taken me by surprise, so it was probably a whole lot worse for our target. I keyed the radio mic. "Bravo, Alpha, shots fired, shots fired!" More gunfire erupted from inside the building as I spoke.

"Say again?"

"There's a goddamn gun battle going on in there!"

"We need Varga alive," Ling said.

"I know!" But I didn't want to jump in the middle of somebody else's gunfight.

"You want to take a look?" Skunky asked.

Seconds ticked by. *Who'd want Varga dead?* Well, besides us? The man worked for a slave trading, arms dealing, drug running, organized crime syndicate. It was probably a long list. More gunfire came from the house. We'd spent months waiting for a chance to grab this guy. "Damn it . . . Come on." I pulled a ski mask over my head and drew my Smith & Wesson 629 revolver. The big .44 Magnum glinted dully in the moonlight as I opened the door. I looked at Skunky. "You ready?"

He got his mask on, drew his Beretta, and nodded.

I hit the radio and warned Ling's team, "We're going in."

"We're on the way."

We moved quickly but cautiously across the cobblestone street, guns drawn, toward the house. The muffled pops of gunfire could still be heard from where we were. This was a sleepy neighborhood, and one of the neighbors was sure to have called the cops by now.

"It sounds like a deathmatch round going on in there, and someone's got a kill streak going."

"I just hope the fuck Varga is still alive," I said as we neared the house.

Skunky pointed toward the top floor. "There's movement in that window."

"What the hell is—" *CRASH!* A body smashed through the fourth-story window and tumbled to the cobblestone below. The man landed with a sickening crunch. I don't know if he'd jumped or been pushed, but that landing was all ribs and skull.

I ran up, saw who it was, lowered my revolver, and sighed. "That, right there, is Stefan Varga."

Skunky knelt next the target whom we had hoped to take alive, probably to take his pulse, but when he saw the brains sliding out, that wasn't really necessary. He looked at the dead man, then at me, then back at the dead man. "Well, crap. What now?"

"Come on," I said, moving past the newcomer's still running motorcycle. "Maybe we can still get some intel from this place."

"It is on the scanner. The police are on the way," Antoine warned. From the tire squealing noise over the radio, he was headed our way fast.

I hesitated. I was still wanted by a shadowy arm of the U.S. government, and they had a long reach. Any involvement with the police would end up with me either being renditioned to a black site or shot in the back of the head. They wouldn't risk letting me escape again. I'd had more close calls than I liked already.

Skunky noticed my hesitation. "Maybe we should just split? He hasn't seen us. We can back off and tail the assassin."

"Unless he's bleeding to death inside." After all, it had only been one man, and he'd shot it out with at least four of them. With Varga dead, our only hope of this operation not being a total bust was to get some answers from *somebody.* I spoke into my radio. "We're going in."

"Understood," Antoine said. *"We'll be there momentarily. Faster, Shen."*

Decision made, I raised my gun, pushed forward, and made it halfway up the house's front stairs when someone flew out the front door and kicked me in the face. Off balance, I lurched backward, crashing into Skunky, and we both tumbled down the stairs. A boot stomped on my chest as the interloper ran right over the top of us. Dazed and still rolling, I saw the shooter running for his motorcycle.

Ling's team came blazing around the corner in their Range Rover, but without slowing the shooter extended a pistol in both hands and cranked off several fast shots. Shen swerved to the side and hit the brakes. The shooter got on his bike, revved the engine, and took off.

I rolled over onto the cobblestone, brought my gun to bear, but it was too late. I didn't have a shot without putting a round into some poor Austrian's house. I pushed myself off the ground, pulled Skunky to his feet, and we sprinted for our car. If we lost sight of him there'd be no way we'd catch up with that bike.

As I buckled myself into the BMW, Shen came back over the radio. *"I tried to ram him. I missed. He's headed down Nonnberggasse. I'll try to go around. Hurry."*

I started the engine, put it in drive, and stepped on it. My face hurt. Blood was trickling from my nose, making a wet spot in the ski mask. Our car was fast, but that bike was faster. And he could fit through things that we couldn't. This would take a miracle, but I intended to catch this son of a bitch.

The rider killed his headlight so it would be harder for us to spot him, but Skunky had a night vision device he couldn't hide from.

"Left, left, left!" Skunky said excitedly. I saw him, but he was still leaving us behind. The motorcycle took a sharp turn, tires squealing, and for a moment I thought he was going to lay it down on the cobblestone street. He recovered and hit the accelerator, having cut a hairpin turn off of Nonnberggasse and onto a street that joined it in a Y-shaped intersection. I nearly spun the BMW out trying to keep up.

"Shit," I snarled, "he's going downtown!" In the heart of the city there would be more lights, but even at this time of night there would still be a lot more traffic. Which he could go through, which I couldn't.

"Do you still have eyes on?" Ling asked.

"Roger, but he's making distance. I'm going to lose him unless he screws up!"

"Do not lose him!" Ling ordered. *"Shen found a shortcut through someone's garden. We're going to try to cut him off."*

I wished I could have seen Shen drive the Range Rover through somebody's garden. An angry motorist in a little hatchback laid on his horn as I swerved around him. I was just trying not to kill anybody.

The short switchback road ended in a T-intersection, which was clogged with traffic. The rider easily picked his way through, probably confident that he was getting away. Suddenly, the Range Rover appeared from the left, speeding out of a narrow alley between buildings. Shen turned hard and flew right in front of the bike. Narrowly avoiding the impact, the rider turned to the side and laid his bike down, hard. One of its mirrors snapped off as it hit the pavement, sliding into the side of a parked Volvo with a crunch. It looked like it hurt. Shen could have had him then, but apparently the Range Rover's brakes weren't that good, and he smashed their front bumper through a plaster planter and killed some shrubbery.

Reaching the intersection, I threw the Beemer into park and jumped out, drawing my gun. Skunky bailed out too. Shen was trying to back up. Motorists honked and cursed at the crazy Range Rover, but the ones who saw two men in ski masks with guns shut their mouths and ducked. The rider had already gotten to his feet. The assassin was small, but he must have been really strong as he dragged the heavy bike upright, mounted up, and took off before any of us was even close to grabbing him. I almost fired, but stopped myself, but there were too many bystanders behind him. I swore aloud and ran back to my car as the motorcycle rider maneuvered through the stopped traffic.

"I didn't have a shot," Skunky grumbled.

"Me either. Get back on the radio, keep telling Shen where he's going."

"Roger! He's turning right onto, uh . . . Erhardg . . . Erhard . . ." Before Skunky could pronounce the name of the street, I jumped the curb, laying on the horn as I sped down the sidewalk, clearing the intersection and keeping eyes on him.

"The police scanner is going crazy. Someone called in the gunshots and the police are en route. Most of them are pulling traffic duty for the festival, but they're being redirected this way."

"Understood." They'd also be calling in our high speed chase now. "We need that diversion!"

"Roger that," Ling said. Our diversion was simple enough: call in emergencies all over the city, spoofing the police. They would have to respond to them all, and it would tie up their resources.

He was still blazing along, getting away from us, but the motorcycle appeared to be wobbling badly. I really hoped he'd damaged it somehow when he'd laid it down. We followed the bike through a roundabout and across a bridge over the Salzach River.

With just that brief straightaway, he nearly lost us, but across the bridge, the motorcycle screeched to a halt. There were two lanes in each direction, but another roundabout on the far side was also jammed with traffic. Just as I was closing in, the bike moved through the tightly packed traffic, and sped off to the northwest. I couldn't afford to lose sight of the faster vehicle for very long, so I cut the wheel to the left, laid on the horn, and Skunky gasped as I drove the BMW onto the sidewalk, sending pedestrians running for their lives, hoping to God I didn't clip somebody. There were police sirens in the distance. A car on the sidewalk would draw attention. I had to get back on the street, blend in, but still keep up with the bike.

The street we were on followed the river northwest. The bike was still a lot faster than my car, and far nimbler, but the rider looked like he was really struggling with it. I was right, it had gotten damaged somehow. I kept him in sight, driving in the margins and on the sidewalk when I had to.

"I think his bike's dying. Get ready for him to bail on foot. Where are you guys?"

"Behind you. We got cut off."

As the river curved to the north, the motorcycle made a hard right, wobbling, nearly wrecking again. The road dipped down and ran under railroad tracks here, but he turned onto a perpendicular street that ran parallel to the tracks. I nearly collided with another car, barely maintaining control, but managed to make the turn and stay with him. The street was separated from the railroad tracks by concrete barriers.

"Where did you go?" Ling called.

"He turned east along Humboldtstrasse! Parallel to the tracks! He's . . . oh, shit!" Riding up an earth berm, the bike jumped the barriers and disappeared on the other side. "He just fucking jumped the fence!"

"What?"

"Val, I lost him!" Skunky said.

"No we didn't!" *There.* There was an access gate in the barriers blocked by a chain link fence a couple hundred yards up the road. "Hang on!" I said, gritting my teeth, and stepped on the accelerator. The car groaned and made a sickening crunching sound as we smashed through the fence. The window cracked. I nearly spun out, but we were through, and I was relieved with the airbag didn't deploy in my face. I stomped on the brakes and launched the chain link gate, which was still on the top of my car, forward onto the tracks.

"Are you okay?"

"There he is!" Skunky pointed. The rider was a short way up the tracks, picking up the bike. He must have lost it on landing. He'd probably been thinking he could get out of sight for a second, and ditch us in here. *Wrong, asshole.* He looked up, saw me, and gunned his accelerator. For a second I thought he was going to crash right into us, but he swerved at the last second, accelerating down the tracks. I cut the wheel to the right, stomped on the gas, and followed.

The car rattled and bounced as we followed the tracks, weaving around parked sets of train cars. It felt like we were going to vibrate our car to death. The bike was producing smoke, and making a lot of noise, but not a lot of speed. His ride was toast.

"I think I can get a shot," Skunky said, Beretta 9mm in hand.

"Hold your fire. Just hang on, I got this."

"Dude, you're going to get us killed trying to catch this asshole and we don't even know if it's worth it!" We flew past a railroad station, under a highway overpass, and the tracks curved to the right. They made a wide loop, turning back to the south. "If we lose sight of him he's gone."

"I know!" I pushed the gas pedal all the way to the floor. The rattling increased so much that I thought the doors were going to fly off. Each bump threatened to send the Beemer out of control as I tried to navigate the tracks by my one remaining headlight. "Okay. Shoot him."

"About time!" Skunky said.

"Try not to make it fatal." Or at least immediately fatal, because we really needed to interrogate this guy.

He leaned out the window a bit, pistol extended in his hand, and popped off shot after shot. "Damn it," he snarled. The car was rattling so badly from driving on the tracks that he couldn't hold his gun steady.

"Holy shit, man, just shoot him!"

"I'm trying! Drive better!" He leaned out the window again, further this time, holding his gun in both hands, and fired again, then again and again. The motorcycle suddenly cut its wheel to the side and fell over, sliding to a stop. "I got him!"

More like Skunky had finally put the bike out of its misery. The rider was on his feet and running away. I cranked the wheel and hit the gas, the BMW bucking over row after row of tracks. The rider sprinted as fast as he could, though obviously hurt. He had nowhere to go. At the edge of the tracks was a metal security fence. *Got him. Wait, what?*

"You have got to be fucking kidding me!" I snarled. The rider scrambled up the eight-foot fence like a monkey and vaulted himself over.

"Dude's got some mad parkour skills," Skunky observed. "Stop the car, you can't crash through that fence. We gotta go on foot!"

I threw the car into park and opened the door. Skunky was already out of the car. He hit the fence, sturdily constructed from steel, and started to climb. "I see him!" he said, at the top. "Come on, hurry!"

"Jesus," I wheezed, hitting the fence as Skunky dropped to the other side. "I'm hurrying!"

Now we were having a foot chase. This really wasn't how I planned my evening to go. The assassin was fast, but Skunky was a damned good runner. I just tried to keep up.

Ling's voice was in my ear as I climbed. *"Where are you?"*

"He wrecked. We're off the tracks now," *pant pant.* "On foot." *pant pant.* I looked at a street sign affixed to a lamp post. "Robinigstrasse, I think." The street was short and ended at what looked like a yard for parking trucks. At least the place was closed down for the night and there weren't any witnesses.

"Come on!" Skunk yelled from down the street. "This way! He went into that building!" Two small warehouses marked the end of the street, which was lit only by a couple amber streetlights.

"He went . . ." *pant pant* ". . . into one of the buildings," I said, relaying it all to Ling. "You got my location?"

"Affirmative." She could track me by GPS, but there was lag when I

was moving. *"We'll be there in a few minutes. Don't enter that building alone!"*

I acknowledged Ling and slowed to a fast walk, breathing hard. *Damn, I'm out of shape.* The warehouse was butted up against some trees. If there was a back door, the rider could get away and I'd never see him.

Skunky was waiting for me at the door. "About time," he whispered.

I flipped him off, still breathing hard. The door of the small warehouse was still open. I took a quick peek around the corner, into the darkness. I didn't see anything, but was immediately answered by shots. I flung myself out of the doorway and pushed Skunky to the ground as a hail of gunfire peppered the corrugated metal behind where I'd been standing. I rolled back over and came to my feet. I transferred my revolver to my right hand, stuck it around the corner, and blindly fired off all six shots.

The gun roared and echoed in the metal building and throughout the neighborhood. I hoped to hell our police diversion was working. I could hear sirens in the distance, but none seemed to be closing in as I twisted a speedloader into my gun's cylinder. I keyed my radio. "Ling, I think I got him cornered in the warehouse. He's armed. Shots fired. What's your ETA?"

"Less than a minute."

"Roger. I'll stall him." I pulled off the ski mask so I could speak more clearly, and so my face could breathe. The sweat was stinging my eyes, making it hard to see, and my face still hurt from him feeding me a shoe on the stairs. "Listen, asshole," I said, shouting into the doorway. "You're trapped. I'm not alone out here, and I've got more backup coming. The cops are coming too. We don't work for the owners of that house. We were doing surveillance. We don't have to be enemies. We just want to talk to you."

There was no response.

I tried to hide the frustration in my voice. "Do you speak English? Can you understand me? I'm not a cop. I just want to talk to you, figure out what the hell is going on. You killed Stefan Varga. We were looking for him. Just come out. I'll put my gun away."

After a long pause, the rider finally spoke. "You have got to be fucking kidding me!"

"What?" I moved away from the doorway when I heard footsteps approaching. I looked over at Skunky and signaled that our guy was coming out.

A moment later the rider stepped out of the shadows. I kept my gun on him, but he came out with his hands up and empty. He ditched his helmet. The face looked familiar, but it still took me a second before I recognized him. Then my heart dropped into my stomach. I knew this man, but he was the last person in the world I'd expected to see here, mostly because he was supposed to be dead.

"Lorenzo?"

Chapter 2: Whispers in the Dark

Lorenzo
Sala Jihan's Fortress
Date Unknown

The shackles bit into my wrists as the soldiers pulled on my chains. I stumbled through the dim hall, pain tearing through me with each halting step, trying to keep up. If I fell, they'd just drag me. I knew from experience that would probably reopen my wounds, but my legs were too weak. When I fell my captors didn't even bother to slow down, and my arms wrenched in their sockets as the chains snapped tight. My stitches pulled, scabs broke and wept blood, but the slave soldiers didn't care. They dragged me until stone turned to soft dirt, and out into the searing daylight.

It really wasn't much light, just a hole in the roof above. I'd been kept in the dark for so long that my eyes were having a hard time adjusting. I couldn't see where I was, but the slaughterhouse smell gave it away.

We were back in the pit.

Time didn't mean anything here, but it had probably been weeks since my last fight. I told time by how healed my wounds were. What would I have to fight today? Slave soldiers? Other prisoners? More vicious dogs?

The soldiers hauled me roughly to my feet and began unlocking my shackles. I didn't struggle. I'd need the energy for whatever was going to come next. My abraded wrists throbbed. My ankles burned where the irons had rubbed off my skin. The soldiers' cheeks had been branded with Sala Jihan's mark. Their eyes were emotionless and vacant as they took the chains away.

There was one other door into the pit, but it was still closed. My opponent hadn't arrived yet. Blinking against the sun, I looked up and tried to see *him.*

As usual, I could see nothing but shadows inside the observers' alcove above. Was the Pale Man here? That was the worst part. Each time I was tortured or made to fight something for Sala Jihan's amusement, I didn't even know if he bothered to watch.

The other heavy door creaked open. More slave soldiers dragged in another prisoner. His tattered rags had once been a North Chinese uniform, but he was fighting the guards, and appeared healthy, so he hadn't been here long. A deserter? A border guard who'd crossed the Pale Man somehow? It didn't matter. Nobody here retained their identity or their sanity for long.

I had nothing against this man. I didn't know him or anything about him, but if I wanted to survive one more day I'd have to kill him.

A slave soldier dropped a knife at my bare feet. "Pick it up," he ordered in Mandarin.

I looked down at the little knife, stuck point first into the dirt. The handle was antler, wrapped in leather strips, stained with dried blood. Last time I'd been forced to fight it had been with bare hands. The time before, I'd been given nothing but a sharpened stick.

I left the knife there. "Why doesn't the Pale Man just kill me and get it over with?"

The soldier backhanded me hard in the face. It barely registered. Blood dripped from my split lip and down my rags. I knew if we didn't fight, they'd just execute other prisoners in front of me until I provided them a good show, women, children, they didn't give a shit. "Pick up the knife."

Instead, I shouted at the alcove. *"Why won't you kill me?"*

Surprisingly, there was movement in the shadows above. "The better question, Lorenzo . . ." Sala Jihan's voice was cold, distant, ominous. "Is why won't you die?"

I picked up the knife.

"I'm Lorenzo," I said through the crack in the wall. "What's your name?"

The prisoner in the next cell didn't respond, but I could hear his labored breathing. I'd heard him in there for the first time today. There were no lights in the cells except for what the guards brought with them, so I'd never seen the man, had no idea who he was, but was extremely thankful for the company anyway.

"I was part of the Exodus mission to assassinate Sala Jihan. We got our asses kicked. Never even saw it coming. I got shot a few times on the mountainside trying to get away. How about you?"

Still no answer. Keeping my voice down, I tried a few other languages. The guards didn't tolerate noise, and I was in no condition to take another beating.

"Do you know what day it is? What month?"

More breathing, sort of wet and gurgley.

"Yeah, me either."

I'd been delirious from blood loss and hypothermia when Jihan's men had carried me off the mountain. I'd woken up in surgery. Well, surgery is an overstatement. No anesthetic. Just some slaves yanking bullets out of me with pliers, and piecing me back together with needles and thread. Even then, barely coherent and half dead, I knew Sala Jihan was keeping me around only because dying quickly was too good for a trespasser.

Healing, I'd spent days in the dark, alone, with no sense of time. Unidentifiable, tasteless food had been shoved into my cell. Occasionally I'd wake up to someone tending my bandages, but asking them questions always ended with a beating. They would give me shots, probably antibiotics, because dying of infected gunshot wounds would be insufficiently painful.

Once I was healed enough to handle the stress, the torture had really begun.

It was purely for sport. They never even asked me any questions. Thankfully they didn't cut any parts off of me, break any bones, or drill any holes. The really invasive stuff tended to kill the subject, so I figured they'd work up to that eventually. It had been things like electrical shocks from a car battery or drowning me in a bucket over and over. Then they'd drag me back to my cell, burned or soaked, and leave me all by myself in the dark for who knew how long. Once I was recovered, they'd do it again.

But the worst part wasn't the torture, it was the noise. I can't explain the sounds in this place, or what made them, but they never stopped. They were always there, just past where you could make sense of what they were saying. Sometimes there was chanting, even singing, but the only sounds I could tell for sure were human were the screams.

"Do they make you fight in the pit too?"

The other prisoner panted and hissed.

"I don't have a choice."

Fighters who refused got shot in the head, and then they'd just haul in the next one. Those that didn't have the will left to put up a fight simply got murdered by their opponent, and I'd seen some savage bastards in the pit. Fighting was the only time I'd interacted with anyone else, but I'd quickly discovered that many of the other prisoners in this place were mentally gone, full-on psycho killers, little more than animals. They'd been here too long, the constant whispering burrowing into their heads, twisting everything. Hell, when I put some poor bastard out of his misery in the pit, I was doing them a favor.

Wheeze, gurgle.

"Don't judge me."

I wouldn't break like the others. I couldn't die, because I had things to do. I was going to find a way out of this hole. I was going to find my brother, stop Katarina, and get back to the woman I love. Love was an alien concept in a place like this, but when the anger and determination ran out, it was all I had left. I'd spent most of my life alone. To survive as a criminal at my level, you had to be willing to abandon everything as soon as you sensed danger. I'd always thought that falling in love was a weakness. Only now, when there was nothing else but the darkness and the whispers and the pain, remembering Jill, imagining her alive and happy somewhere beneath the sun . . . It kept me sane.

The other cell was silent. The breathing had stopped. He'd either died or melted through the floor, I couldn't tell anymore. I was alone again.

Sala Jihan had seen right through my disguise, even recognized what I was, and called me *son of murder.* He'd warned me not to come back here. I should have listened.

Without any sort of reference, it was impossible to keep track of time. When you can't even tell if it is night or day, scratch marks on a wall are pointless. Food came at random times. The temperature never changed. It was always hot and muggy. It stank like a zoo, that kind of cloying, rancid, primal stink of spice and fear and waste. There was a pipe in the floor for waste. When it would rain, water would trickle down through the rock and make a puddle in my cell. That was the closest I came to bathing, well, that and the occasional waterboarding.

Blind, I explored every single inch of my small cell with my fingertips. I knew every crack and bump, but there was no discernible weakness. My chains were heavy-duty and sunk into the rock. I had no tool that could pick the lock on the shackles. It would be virtually impossible to break free, but I picked what I thought was the weakest link, and then I spent most of my time rubbing steel against steel. I had nothing but time. The chains were thick enough to pull a truck, but I worked on them constantly anyway. I did it so often that I could reach down on instinct and immediately find the right link. I'd rub them together until the metal was so hot from friction that it burned my fingers, but I still kept going. I didn't know what would erode first, that metal, or my sanity.

The bad thing about working on the chain was that while my hands were busy I couldn't put my hands over my ears. I was blind, but I wished I was deaf. That damned indescribable background noise never stopped. I tried to make plugs out of scraps from my ragged clothing, but I could still hear it. It was like the noise got inside your head. I slept with my hands clamped over my ears, and if I did it tight enough, the sound of my own pulse would keep the haunted noise out of my dreams. Sometimes.

I seriously contemplated scratching out my own eardrums, but truthfully, part of me was afraid that even then the noises wouldn't stop. I was already mostly deaf in one ear, but even in that one I thought I could hear the whispers. And if I did destroy my hearing, but the voices were still there, then that meant this place had succeeded in driving me crazy.

The only time I saw light was in torture sessions or when they'd drag me into the pit to fight. Even then there was no schedule to it. Strangely enough, I started to look forward to the fights. Despite it being bloody, horrific, and awful, at least I knew it was real. And for a few brief minutes, at least I didn't have to listen to that damned chittering in the walls.

The food was cold slop with chunks in it. It was so devoid of flavor I couldn't tell if the chunks were animal or vegetable. I was so malnourished that I was having a hard time concentrating. I hadn't had much fat on my body to begin with, but there was nothing left now. There were barely enough calories and nutrients in the gruel that I could still fight in the pit, but that meant I was strong enough to get out of here.

After enough time passed for the gunshot wounds to harden into scar tissue, I was ready to escape. The instant I was given an opportunity, I'd take it.

Then one day the chain broke.

When the guards came for me again, I made my move. Their light was blinding, but I was used to not being able to see. I struck the first one in the throat hard enough to crush his windpipe. I beat the second one over the head with his big aluminum flashlight, plunging us all back into the dark. I caught the last one in the hall and choked him to death with my broken chain before he could scream for help.

I swear, as I killed those men, the noises in the walls got louder. I dragged the bodies inside my cell and closed the door. They'd only had the one, now broken, light, so I had to blunder around in the dark, hands on the stone walls, looking for a way out. The prison was a maze. There was no rhyme or reason to the layout. I knew where the pit and the torture room were, and that was it. As I moved through the darkness, I couldn't tell if the voices were cheering me on or ratting me out.

Another guard died by my hand before I found the stairs, but at least now I had another flashlight. The crumbling prison was a maze of passageways. This place had to be ancient, and put to use more recently by the Pale Man. I found rooms filled with nothing but dried blood and scraps of clothing. There was an empty wheelchair in the hall. Eventually I found a set of stairs. The noise seemed to be louder downstairs, so I went up.

The cells on the next floor were separated by iron bars, and each one was packed with people, children mostly. The older males would go to the mines to be worked to death, the younger branded and brainwashed into the ranks of Jihan's army. The females would be sold to vile, horrible men around the world. They stared at my light, fearful, but I was in no position to do anything for them. Exodus had tried to save these people, and gotten themselves slaughtered for it. The only reason I was in here was because I'd been soft and stupid enough to make myself into a distraction to buy time for the Exodus survivors, and I didn't even know if any of them had made it out.

I knew Jill had escaped though. Sala Jihan had seen us together. So if he had caught her, he would have taunted me about it. If he'd killed her, he would have showed me her body. No matter what Jihan did to me, she was beyond his reach, and knowing that was plenty to live for.

They caught me before I could find the way out. I never figured out how they tracked me down, but somehow they knew right where I was. Maybe the whispers told on me. Despite me doing my best to gouge their eyes out, the slave soldiers fought like fanatics and accepted their casualties, determined to take me alive.

It seemed the Pale Man wasn't done with me yet.

Ears ringing from the beating, I woke up chained to a different wall, but from the humidity and the animal stink I knew I was still in the same prison. There was light here though, coming from a bright orange fire burning in a nearby metal tub. There were guards there, and one was holding a metal rod in the fire, the end glowing red hot.

Branding irons. This was new.

I was hanging there, arms stretched overhead. There was no give when I tested the chains. The guards noticed I was awake, but paid me no heed. I was no threat. My body was covered in fresh bruises, cuts, and scrapes. My muscles were cramped and trembling. I was so weak I could barely think. If they were going to burn my face like they did to mark his slaves, there wasn't much I could do about it. The ringing in my ears subsided enough that I could hear the crackle of flames, and then I could barely make out that damnable noise, the whispers and mutters. It was like they were laughing at me.

The door creaked open.

There was one man there, wearing a long black coat, leather and fur, with the hood up. The guards saw who it was and silently bowed their heads. In the shadows beneath the hood I could only make out his jaw, skin deathly white around neatly trimmed black facial hair. He studied the scene for a moment, before pushing back the hood with one gloved hand. His skin was somewhere beyond albino but his eyes were black holes. It was the Pale Man himself.

A feeling of terrible dread formed in my stomach and radiated out through my limbs as Sala Jihan entered. His age was impossible to guess. Neither old nor young, he just *was*. He'd claimed for himself the name of a villain from local folklore and lived at the bottom of an abandoned missile silo. He was a man who had built a kingdom in place where there was no law, reigning over people who believed he wasn't a man at all. The mountain tribes thought of him as a vengeful demon from their past, and feared him accordingly.

The first time I'd met the slave-trading warlord, I tried to tell myself it was all an elaborate act, a mind game to fuck with his opposition. That was before he'd slaughtered the Exodus strike team sent to kill him, and before I'd been exposed to this godforsaken place.

The Pale Man didn't speak for a very long time. He said something to the guards in a language I didn't recognize, but probably meant *leave us.*

The guards closed the door behind them, so it was just me alone with the devil.

"Just kill me already," I croaked, my mouth so dry that I could barely talk at all. "Get it over with." *At least then the whispers would stop.*

He tilted his head a bit to the side, as if listening. "What whispers?"

I didn't remember saying that part out loud.

Sala Jihan came closer, smelling like wet earth. He muttered something else, but it was in no language I recognized, and I'd heard them all. He grabbed me by the hair and violently jerked my head back so he could better see my battered face. Holy shit, he didn't look it, but he was incredibly strong. Somehow I knew he could twist my head off if he felt like it. Those terrible black eyes cut right through me

If I'd had enough saliva, I would have spit in his face. Sala Jihan noted my effort however. The warlord wasn't used to such disrespect, but he refrained from snapping my neck. He spoke in clear, precise English. "What am I to do with you, son of murder?"

"Unlock these chains and fight me like a man."

"I am not merely a man, and you are only a serpent. You invaded my home and killed my servants. You have deserved all of this suffering and more." His words were calm, measured, aloof, yet threatening at the same time. "What you have experienced thus far is nothing compared to the punishments I could inflict next. You exist entirely by my whim."

"Fuck you."

Jihan showed very little reaction, he seemed more curious than anything. "I've known many like you, wretched *hashishin*, wolves who hide among the sheep. Death follows wherever you go. Friend or foe, it does not matter. Yet you are special, a unique variable."

"What the hell are you jabbering about?"

"Fate has not determined a path for you. The son of murder is outside of destiny. Even when captured, you remain defiant, tempting me to end you. I did not because you could still prove useful. If your escape had not failed, what would you have done with your freedom?"

As tempting as it was to talk more shit, I told him the truth. "I'd run as far away from here as I could go."

"And then?"

There was no point in lying. The Pale Man would know. "Find Katarina Montalban and kill her."

"Yes. The woman who was deluded enough to think she could steal my kingdom. Her treachery is the reason you are here. Is it only your desire for vengeance so strong that it has kept you from breaking in this place?"

I clenched my teeth together. The Pale Man could never know what I still lived for, because he'd find a way to take Jill too.

"I know there is more, son of murder. Do not mistake my idle curiosity for caring. Love and hate are equally meaningless to me. I do not care about your motivation, merely the outcome. After you finished killing off the Montalbans, would you return and try to take your revenge upon the great Sala Jihan?"

"No." Even if I managed to survive taking on the Montalban Exchange, I was never coming back to this hell hole. "I swear."

"I believe you mean that, for now." Sala Jihan actually seemed pleased with my answer. "Katarina Montalban did not merely betray you and Exodus, she betrayed me as well."

He had been Exodus' target because he was an evil, slave-trading madman. Kat had nothing to do with that. Exodus was gunning for him no matter what.

"Exodus has tried to destroy me before. They have, and always will be my enemy. Thus, they are irrelevant. Now, I speak only of you. Katarina made you believe it was I who stole your brother. She tried to silence me, to usurp my throne. You were merely her weapon. She was naive enough to think she could use *you* to destroy *me*."

The first time we'd met, the Pale Man had told me that though death had always been my servant, in this place, death only answered to him.

"Yes . . . In this place." Jihan slowly lifted one gloved hand and gestured around the room. "For now my kingdom ends at the borders of the Crossroads. Yet, I desire revenge on Katarina Montalban. I do not like wanting things I cannot have. She must pay for her trespass, only she has moved beyond my reach."

The idea that there was a limit to Sala Jihan's dominion would make me sleep a little easier, at least until the whispers invaded my dreams and turned everything to blood again. "Let me go . . . I'll take care of her for you."

"An intriguing offer, only because the time of her triumph draws near. The Montalbans' plan, this *Project Blue* as you have heard it called, is far more ambitious than you can imagine. Eduard Montalban tried to enlist my aid in this plot. He intended to buy my allegiance with this." The Pale Man pulled a small object from the interior of his coat. There was a slight golden glow between his fingers. "This, too, had once been beyond my reach."

In the palm of his hand was an ancient piece of jewelry. I recognized it immediately. It was the Scarab.

I'd stolen it from a Saudi prince's vault. Being coerced into that heist was what had dragged me back into Big Eddie's world. A lot of people, including two of my best friends, had died to get it. We never even knew what it did. The last time I'd seen the Scarab it had been inside an abandoned building in Nevada as it burned to the ground. How had it survived? *How was it here?*

"That is not your concern." Sala Jihan closed his fist and the Scarab disappeared. "All that matters to you now is that it serves as evidence of your ability to reach that which I cannot. This was kept from me for a very long time, until you freed it."

"You're welcome."

"You would not be so flippant if you understood what you have done." He sneered at me, but I had no clue what that thing was for. "I am patient. I waited a lifetime to retrieve this device. I would do the same to have my revenge on the Montalban family. Only Katarina is too impetuous. She will act soon. If she is triumphant, the balance of power will change. Old orders will fall into chaos. That I will not allow. It appears once again the son of murder must go where the Pale Man is barred, and take for me that which I cannot take myself."

Between the beatings and my overall awful condition, I was having a hard time following the creepy weirdo. Were we cutting a deal? "Take her life?"

The Pale Man nodded slowly. My freedom in exchange for assassinating Kat? That was a no-brainer. Or was he was he dangling freedom in front of me, just long enough to give me hope, only to snatch it away and toss me back in the dark? Was this just a creative new form of torture?

"In exchange, I grant your freedom and declare your punishment fulfilled."

"Agreed." And as soon as I said that, it felt like I'd literally made a deal with the devil.

"I suspected it would come to this. The only reason I did not have hot ash poured down your throat was so that you could still speak your lies. The only reason I have not castrated you was so that you would not lose your will to fight. I left your fingers so you can hold a blade and eyes to find your prey."

Jihan went over to the fire and pulled out the branding iron. He held up the orange glowing metal, the firelight dancing in his black eyes, and satisfied that it was hot enough, turned back to me.

I cringed back as far as I could as he held the hot metal next to my face. So close that it singed my beard and I could smell burning hair. "We have a deal!"

"You still have a face, only because my mark would make it difficult for you to disappear amongst the sheep." Jihan slowly pulled the glowing metal away from my eyes. "You will need all of these things where you are going."

He jammed the branding iron against my chest.

I screamed and thrashed as my flesh sizzled. With shocking force, Jihan held it there, crushing me back against the stone. I screamed until I couldn't scream anymore. When he finally pulled the glowing metal away, a lot of skin went with it.

I must have blacked out, because by the time I came to, Jihan had put the branding iron back into the fire and the whispers had turned to shouts. Hanging there limp, I retched against the stench of my own charred flesh. If there'd been anything inside my stomach, I would have vomited. If I hadn't been so dehydrated, I would have wept.

"Because you would die rather than break, that is not a mark of ownership." The Pale Man returned, crouching next to my sagging body, so we could be eye to soulless black eye. I was flickering in and out of consciousness. "This mark is my final gift. You say you will not return to my kingdom, but I know that in time vengeance would tempt you. Fear would fade. Memories would grow dim. Then you would come back for me, and I would utterly destroy you. Thus I bestow this scar upon you, so wherever you go, for the rest of your days, you will never forget the cost of trespass against Sala Jihan."

Daylight . . . actual daylight.

At first I wasn't sure if I was alive, dead, or back in my cell hallucinating. The pain convinced me it was real. Moving at all caused unbelievable agony as the burnt hole on my chest pulled on the raw red skin around it, but despite the pain, I still had to raise a hand to shield my eyes from the piercing light.

I'll be damned. That really was the sun up there.

I was on an uneven metal floor. There were great jagged tears in the roof above. There were holes—bullet holes—in the walls. Motes of dust swam through the beams of light. When I shifted my weight a bit more, I found that there were shell casings beneath me. Everything was covered in rust, vines, and cobwebs. When I lifted my aching head, there was a human skull watching me. There were mice living inside of it.

I'd been here before. This was the old crashed Russian bomber I'd taken cover in while running from Jihan's soldiers. They'd left me in the exact spot where they had captured me. I listened carefully. There were birds singing and bugs buzzing. The wind rustled and sighed through the trees.

There were no whispers.

I couldn't believe it. For the first time in months, there was quiet. I was out of the prison. It had to be some sort of trick.

Pulling myself up the wall, I saw mountains and trees through the bullet holes. Through the front of the cockpit, I could see the slope I'd climbed up from the river. There was the boulder where I'd been shot in the arm. My eyes weren't used to all this glorious unimpeded vision, so they began to water badly. Okay, maybe part of that was emotion, I'll admit it.

I reached out and touched one of the jagged bullet holes. One of these had pierced my leg. The last time I'd been here, this valley had been covered in snow. Now it was hot. Things had grown, and begun to die. It had to be late summer. That meant I'd been in Jihan's prison for at least four or five months.

It was amazing that I'd survived that long.

Slowly, I dragged myself to the twisted doorway, and flopped through onto the dry grass. Everything hurt, especially the fresh burn on my chest, but I'd been burned before. I'd live. I lay there for a long time, just feeling the sun above and the grass below. Sala Jihan had actually let me go. Either that or this was just a twisted game, and slave soldiers were going to show up any second to take away my last shred of hope.

No . . . If I'd learned anything over the last few months, it was that Sala Jihan was tyrannical and evil, but there was a twisted code of honor in that madness. He'd said he'd set me free in order to stop Kat only because he couldn't. The Pale Man wasn't a liar. He didn't need to be. But he'd also left me miles from civilization, injured, tired, hungry, dehydrated, barefoot, and in rags. So, the Pale Man may have had a peculiar code of honor, but that didn't make him any less of an asshole. I was in no shape to make it out of this forest.

I laughed for a few minutes straight. And then I wanted nothing more than to sleep.

Focus, Lorenzo. Kat and Anders were going to do something horrible, and then they were going to murder my brother and pin it all on him. I couldn't stop them by sitting here on my ass. The Pale Man wouldn't have let me go if there was time to dick around. I didn't just survive a stay in hell to die of exposure on a mountain or get eaten by a fucking wolf, so it was time to man up and get the job done.

Besides, I *really* wanted to murder Kat.

And once that was done, I could find Jill. My time with her had been the best days of my life. Was it possible to actually be happy again? I'd been living off of stubborn determination and hate for so long that I'd forgotten what it felt like to *hope.*

Ignoring the pain, I forced myself to stand up. I knew jack and shit about wilderness survival. I was more of an urban survivalist, but I remembered the maps of the region from when we'd been preparing for the raid. The nearest settlement was Sala Jihan's compound, but I would be avoiding that haunted shithole. If I followed the river, it would take me back to the Crossroads. Once I was back in a town full of criminals I'd be in my element.

I limped toward the Crossroads.

It took two miserable days to reach the Crossroads. When you haven't seen the sun for months, you sunburn like a bitch. After roasting during the day, it still got damned cold at night. There wasn't a security system in the world I couldn't circumvent, but I didn't know how to rub two sticks together to make fire. Bob had been the Eagle Scout, not me. Sure, I'd been a mercenary in Africa, but we'd ridden in trucks to battle, and when we did occasionally have to sleep in the wilderness, I'd had a lighter. So, fireless and miserable, I huddled next to a tree and shivered the night away. Even then it was the best night's sleep I'd had in a long time because of the *real actual quiet.*

In the morning I took what was left of my shirt and wrapped the rags around my feet because I swear the canyon was covered in sharp rocks, just because Mother Nature is a bitch. On the bright side, the horrific burn on my chest was so incredibly painful that it distracted me from torn feet. Yeah, I'm an optimist like that.

There was plenty to drink. The river water was wonderful, colder, clearer, and fresher than the cups of brackish sludge I'd been given in the prison, but I was still weak with hunger. Luckily, I found a fresh animal kill, half eaten. I don't know what killed it, and don't even know what the animal was—what was left had hooves kind of like a little deer—but it wasn't rotten, and that's all I cared about. I used to be a connoisseur of exotic food, the weirder the better, and Carl often said that I could eat things that would make a goat puke, but let me tell you, you've never really vomited until you try to choke down chunks of bloody raw meat after months of eating nothing but gruel. On the second try I kept some inside, and that gave me enough calories to make it the rest of the way. I'd probably get some parasites and microbes or shit, but if I could get back to civilization, they had pills for that.

The Crossroads may have been run by a bunch of criminals acting like competing fiefdoms, but it was a real town. I was going to find some criminal faction to con or suck up to, get myself real food, see a real doctor, then find a way to steal some clothes, shoes, money, and a ticket back to the world. Then I was going to find Kat's people, and torture them until one of them gave me her location, so I could shoot her in the face. Then I was going to find my woman, put this place behind me, and never think about it again. I was really looking forward to my exciting new life plan.

But when I got there, the Crossroads was *gone*.

Well, not gone, but mostly underwater and abandoned. Many of the buildings were still standing, but they were flooded, only the roofs or second stories sticking out of the new lake that had formed where a city had been. There were still people living around it, mostly in yurts and shacks made out of scavenged materials, but the criminal empire, the trading houses, the chaotic businesses, the gun runners and drug dealers, the world's best illicit flea market, it was all gone.

There had been tens of thousands of people in this boomtown just a few months ago, now it was maybe a few hundred, tops. Before, there had been representatives of every regional group. Now they appeared to be mostly nomadic traders. Men with rifles watched me suspiciously as I approached their settlement.

The rail line was on the high ground, and since plants weren't growing over the rails, I assumed trains still passed through here. When I got closer, I saw that the train station had been burned down, and all that remained was an ashen wreck with a collapsed roof. What the hell had happened here? Last I'd heard, the Montalban Exchange was supposed to have made a move against Sala Jihan's garrison in town, but they'd chickened out. Had the Pale Man run everyone out after that? But the Crossroads didn't feel like the victim of a battle, more like a derelict ghost town, and where had this friggin' lake come from?

I hailed the nomads when I got close enough. They didn't shoot me, probably because it was obvious the emaciated scarecrow hobbling in on bloody feet wasn't too much of a threat. I went through a mishmash of languages until they responded with really bad Russian. I had nothing to offer, nothing to trade, but I hoped they'd show some hospitality to a starving man.

When I got close enough that they saw the brand on my chest, they fled in terror.

It wasn't what I expected, but I could work with it. As the nomads retreated toward the other yurts and huddled there for safety, I went to the closest tent and started looting. I was too worn out to run, and if they were going to come back and shoot me, I'd at least die with a full belly. There was a pot of rice, still warm, and I sat down and ate it with my fingers.

While I ate, I looked over the new lake. Though it was leaning to the side now, the Montalban Exchange building was only partially submerged. It had been built to look sort of like a pagoda. My search for my brother had brought me there, and it was only later that I'd learned he'd been prisoner there the whole time, locked in a cell in the basement. I'd thought Bob was in Sala Jihan's compound, and he'd been right there, under my nose the whole time. I'd visited the Montalban Exchange building several times during the preparation and planning for the raid. It wouldn't have surprised me if Anders, being a dick, had taunted Bob about my searching for him the whole time.

Looking at that lopsided pagoda gave me an idea though. Bob was crafty. Everywhere else he'd gone, he'd tried to leave bread crumbs. Why not here?

A few minutes later a single nomad approached. Dressed in lots of wool, leather, and strangely a really faded Chicago Bulls t-shirt, he was probably in his forties, so close to my age, though it was hard to tell because he was so incredibly weathered by the sun, and I couldn't even guess which of the minor regional groups he belonged to. He had an old Mosin Nagant rifle in his hands, but he was polite enough not to point it at me. He stopped near the tent and squatted there. "We are not enemies or friends, but you may eat this meal." His Russian was pretty good, which meant he was probably their leader, or at least their main trader or negotiator.

"Thank you."

He pointed two fingers at my burn. "You are the one *he* freed?" the man asked suspiciously. I hate the pronoun game, but in this case there was no doubt who *he* was.

"I'm guessing that doesn't happen often."

"You are the first. Enjoy our hospitality, and then be gone. You cannot be our guest. We do not want his eyes upon us. Everything he touches is cursed."

"Agreed." I kept chewing. "When does the train pass through?"

"Toward Russia or China?"

"Either."

He pulled back a sleeve and checked his watch. I don't know why it surprised me that a nomad at the ass end of the world had a big fat digital watch. "About three hours." I grunted acknowledgment and kept shoveling rice in my face. I was probably going to get sick, but it was worth it. The nomad seemed happy that I would be leaving. After a minute passed, he got up the courage to ask. "My people tell stories about his prison. Are they true?"

I didn't know what the stories were, but I could guess. "Worse."

He nodded thoughtfully, expression hard to read, but I suspected he might be taking pity on me. He went into the tent and came out with a can of some Russian soda. He tossed it to me. I cracked open the warm can, took a drink of the Motherland's version of Mountain Dew, and it was so magical, it made my teeth hurt. I'd always been a health nut, but I'd missed sugar.

"Oh, man. Thank you. You have no idea. Thank you so much . . ." Right then it felt like the nicest thing anyone had ever done for me. "So what happened to the city here?"

"The night they attacked the Pale Man, they hurt the dam too. A bomb started it leaking. It could not be repaired. The city began to flood. The criminals fought each other. Business slowed. The bazaars moved elsewhere."

Blowing the dam must have been Exodus' backup plan. If they couldn't kill Sala Jihan, at least they could cripple his empire. That explained why Ling and Valentine hadn't been on the raid, too. The sneaky bastards had managed to shut the whole place down and keep the death toll to a minimum. I had to hand it to Exodus, that was clever.

The nomad gestured toward the leaning pagoda. "A year later, it is like this."

A year? It was summer. I'd been captured in spring. That couldn't be right. "What's today's date?"

The nomad looked at me funny, then he checked his giant watch again. Of course it had the date on it. "It is the twenty-second of August."

So I'd been captured five months ago . . . But if the Crossroads had been abandoned too long, that made no sense. "What year?"

He told me. It took a moment for it sink in.

I'd been in prison for almost *a year and a half.* For a long moment, I couldn't even wrap my brain around the number.

"Are you alright?" the nomad asked.

I didn't know. A year and a half . . . *Damn.* What else had I missed? "I will be." I looked toward the leaning Montalban building. I'd noticed something when the nomad opened to tent flap to get the soda can. "Can I borrow that flashlight?"

I swam through the flooded hallway, the borrowed LED flashlight cutting a narrow beat through the dark. Silver fish scattered ahead of me.

This was stupid. Repeatedly diving into the lower floors of a flooded, rotten, collapsing building would have been dangerous with a wetsuit and an air tank. Doing it while freezing and holding your breath, when you were already in bad shape, was suicidal. I swore, not for the first time, that someday I was going to choke the shit out of Valentine. In the most convoluted way possible, he'd once again managed to make my life more difficult. I wasn't going to leave the Crossroads emptyhanded, though, one way or another.

This was my fourth trip down. Most of the lower rooms had been easy to reach, but none of them looked suited for holding someone prisoner. The Montalbans had left all of their furniture behind. It wasn't as if once you betrayed Sala Jihan, there was much time to pack, so it was pretty easy to tell what each room had been used for, and the ones I could reach had been barracks for their employees and hired muscle mostly.

Part of the ceiling had collapsed, so I had to squeeze between the boards. I stuck the flashlight between my teeth, and used my hands to pull myself along. I cut my thumb on a protruding nail, but I got through. I'd have to squeeze back out though, which would take even more time, so I couldn't spare a second in this next room.

It was eerie as hell down here. The water was fairly clear and free of sediment so I wasn't blind, and the flashlight helped a lot. Sadly, nomadic traders in the Golden Mountains didn't stock swim goggles, but I could see well enough to get by. The flood had been so gradual that it hadn't even knocked over chairs. There were still billiard balls on the pool table, though the cues had floated away. Things were starting to decay and the walls were getting fuzzy with moss. There was still a TV mounted on the wall. I'd found the Montalbans' rec room. *Useless.*

My lungs were starting to hurt. I'd been a damned good swimmer, but it had been a long time. By the time I squeezed back through the debris a little bit of panic was starting to build in the back of my mind. I'd pushed too far. I was going to run out of air and die down here. I swam down the hall as fast as I could, passing other rooms I'd already cleared. As the pain grew, I cursed myself. It figured that I'd be the one to survive a prison that no one ever survived, only to drown myself inside a house two days later. Desperate, I reached the stairs, got my hands, then feet on them. The glue had melted so the carpet was a floating bubble, tacked at the edges. I half swam, half walked the last few feet, and gasped in precious air as my face broke the surface.

Dripping and gasping, I stumbled out of the water, sank to my knees, and lay down on the damp floor.

Damn it. That was as far as I could go, yet I'd found nothing.

I began to shiver uncontrollably. We were way up in the mountains, so even in the summer the water was cold as hell, and I had no insulation left. There was a fireplace ten feet away, but no way to light it, and everything here was too soggy to burn.

There was one more room past the rec room, but I couldn't reach it. I knew my brother. If Bob thought there was any way Exodus could find him, he'd leave a clue. He was so dedicated to his investigation, so worried about Project Blue, that he'd been willing to sacrifice his life—and mine—to stop it. Bob had months to piece together more about Blue after those journals of his I'd read, plus he might have learned something from Kat and Anders, or maybe even had an idea of where they would be taking him next. He had to have left something in there. I knew it.

Bob wasn't a quitter. It ran in the family. I'd not given up in the dark for a year and a half—that still boggled my mind—And I wasn't going to give up here either. I was getting into that last room one way or the other, and if there was nothing, then I could get on that train knowing that I'd at least done my best. The Montalban Exchange was big, but it was just a fancy house. I hadn't given up when I was surrounded by solid rock. There was an iron poker next to the fireplace. I got up, went over, and picked it up. It was rusty, but that was fine. I just needed it to last longer than the soggy floorboards.

I made an educated guess about where the last room was, and went to work on the floor. Smashing into the Montalban Exchange gave me a chance to think, and to focus my rage. If there was no clue, no bread crumbs, no answer, then I'd just declare war on the lot of them. I used to work for Big Eddie. I used to know some of his operations and many of his lieutenants. Some of them still had to work for Big Eddie's psychotic little sister. I'd pick them off, one by one, until somebody gave up Kat.

As I pounded the floor into splinters, I had to stop to rest several times. It gave me time to think through the repercussions of going to war with an organized crime family. I'd been elated to get out of the dark, but enthusiasm can only get you so far when you're trying to kill a bunch of professional killers.

There were good odds I'd die. Kat was damned good at her job, and Anders was probably better. Anyone who helped me would be in danger. Kat knew what Jill meant to me. I'd stayed alive for Jill, but once the Montalbans knew it was me, they'd go after her again. I had to keep her out of this. I had to keep Reaper out of it. They were probably still in hiding. They needed to stay that way. Big Eddie had targeted my family to manipulate me once, and if Kat found out I was still alive, she'd do the same thing. Right now, my best defense was them thinking I was dead.

I had to do this the old way, the way I used to operate, back when I truly did not give a shit about anyone or anything. When I was a ghost, faceless and living job to job, doing whatever it took to win, without mercy, without thought, without hesitation. The only way to beat them would be by being worse than them.

Jill had helped me become a better man, and I loved her for it, but being a decent human being was a luxury I couldn't afford. I had to become that perfect killer again, and that meant I had to be alone. If I was going to do this, I could afford no distractions.

In my condition it still took me a while, and by the time I'd pried up enough floor to squeeze through, I was exhausted again. I was going to be cutting it close on catching that train, and if I missed today's, it wouldn't surprise me if one of the nomads just decided to kill me in my sleep to keep life simple. Hospitality is nice and all—until it draws the Pale Man's eye.

Making the hole had at least warmed me up, so it sucked extra when I lowered myself through the moldy insulation and back into the frigid water. I took a deep breath, and dropped into the last room. My vision was blurry, but when I shined the light around, I knew that I'd hit the jackpot.

The four walls were made of solid wooden beams instead of sheetrock like the rest of the place. The door was metal, and looked like it had been looted from an old Russian military bunker when they'd built this place. The only piece of furniture left was a metal bed frame. There were leather straps bolted to the side of the frame. The Montalbans had probably used this room for interrogations. Someone could have screamed their head off in here and the people upstairs would have never known.

If Bob had been here, there hadn't been much to work with in the way of tools, but he would have improvised something. He couldn't have done anything in the open, or they would have seen it when they took him away. I swam down to the bedframe and put the flashlight between my teeth so I could use both hands again. The little flashlight had a yellow plastic body, so at least it was soft enough not to chip my teeth. It still tasted better than Jihan's gruel.

I felt around behind the metal bars. Sure enough. One of the bolts was really loose. That had been his tool. He'd been smart enough to stick it back in the frame so they wouldn't notice. Anders was observant and smart, but Bob was smarter.

My chest was starting to hurt. I felt along the wall. It reminded me of exploring my cell in the dark, looking for any vulnerability I could exploit. *There.* Something was scratched into the wood, placed at an angle that any guard who entered wouldn't see it behind the frame. I had to practically drag myself beneath the bed to get eyes on it. It was too blurry to read, so I had to feel it out with my fingertips. It was rough, and must have taken him forever to do it with the end of a bolt.

Varga.

I knew that name. I swam for the hole. I had a train to catch.

Chapter 3: Rampage

Lorenzo
Budapest, Hungary
September 1st

Ten days later I was in a nightclub in Budapest, looking to take down a Montalban stooge.

Big Eddie's employees loved places like this. Lots of coming and going, big crowds, so much obnoxious music noise that bugging it would be impossible, it was a perfect place to exchange information, collect bribes, plot crimes, and then fade away. The combination of black lights, glowing body paint, and half-naked people was distracting enough that a regular boring criminal—like yours truly—drinking at the end of the bar was practically invisible.

It had taken me a while to get to Hungary. Playing hobo across Siberia isn't as fun as it sounds. I couldn't call in any favors, because I couldn't risk word getting out that I was alive. Once back in the civilized world, I'd stolen money and clothing, and got treated by a shady doctor who'd given me a bottle of antibiotics. Then I'd hotwired a car to get to one of my stashes in Volgostadorsk. That storage locker I had rented years ago had netted me some IDs, a fake passport, and more money. I'd found a Roma caravan. That's how my dad had grown up, before he'd been such a scumbag that they'd tossed his ass. I'd picked up a couple of dialects over the years, and knew how to pay my proper respects—and money—which had bought me a ride to Hungary. Being a passenger had given me time to rest and recuperate. They'd dropped me off in Budapest, I'd stolen a car, and come straight here.

I scanned the crowd for Stefan Varga. Back when I worked for Big Eddie, he'd run this club. It seemed like a legit establishment, but if you knew where to look there were signs and signals to the other criminals that this was Montalban turf. There was still plenty of hired muscle wandering around, partying between their criminal endeavors, but nobody I recognized from the old days. Varga had been a major smuggler for Eddie when I knew him, and smarter than he was tough. Kat had probably promoted him after she took over. She'd always had an eye for talent.

There had to be some reason Varga was important enough that they would have mentioned his name in front of Bob. Unless it was a different crook with the same last name and this was a dead end. Or the right guy, but he'd moved on. But if that was the case, one of these mooks would know where their old boss had gone.

I'd gotten cleaned up in Russia and bought nice clothes so I wouldn't look like the Unabomber. I must have done something right because I got flirted with twice in the last forty minutes, by one woman and one dude. Apparently this scene was into that emaciated, spent a year and a half in a lightless hole chic. I told them that I was waiting for my date and went back to my scotch. I wasn't wearing a disguise, but my hair was longer, my beard was trimmed, and I was probably twenty pounds lighter and a decade older than the last time I'd been here, so I wasn't likely to get recognized by a crew that thought I was dead. However, I probably shouldn't have blown the flirts off, because if I was here alone for too long I'd look suspicious. I couldn't afford to get made. I wasn't even armed. I knew the club would have metal detectors, so the only people in here with guns would be working for Kat.

I got up and walked toward the bathrooms, trying to get a better view of the VIP area. Varga had never been a back office type. He'd always liked to conduct his criminal business out in the lights and music, snorting coke off the table while getting a blow job from an expensive hooker under it. Big Eddie's people were classy like that. If Varga was still here, hopefully he hadn't mellowed with age, because if he was in the offices, I was going to have a hard time getting back there without being seen.

The music was shit. It was better than the horrible noise of Jihan's prison, but that was it. Music had peaked with Black Sabbath. This was just repetitive electronic noise over a bunch of bass and what sounded like a power drill. The DJ looked like a crackhead. The air smelled like pot and sweat. The dancers were sleazy, stoned kids. It made me feel old, but Reaper probably would have loved this place. Damn I missed him. Five minutes on his computer and he'd probably be able to tell me exactly where Varga was right now and what he'd had for breakfast. But I'd made my call. I couldn't risk my old team's lives. This was on me alone.

My target wasn't in the VIP area. In the bathroom I splashed some water on my face and stared at my reflection in the mirror. I was getting stronger, but I still looked like death. The sunburn from the mountains was healing and I was getting my color back. I'd been eating, exercising, and actually sleeping. Sure, the sleep was riddled with nightmares, and I kept waking up in a cold sweat freaking out that I'd imagined my whole escape, but I was getting better. When I woke up now all I had to do was focus on sweet revenge until my pulse slowed down, and then I was fine for another hour or two.

You got this. Satisfied that the hollowed-out, used-up killer staring back at me in the mirror could still do the job, I headed back to the bar.

Back out in the electronic noise and fog machine chaos, for just a moment it felt like someone was watching me. I turned to see a shadowed figure on a balcony above, white skin, black hood. I felt a flash of panic. It was the Pale Man. *He followed me!* But then the spotlights shifted along the rafters, and the figure was gone. It was an illusion. Nothing more than a trick of the lights and smoke. My fear was irrational.

Calm down, you big pussy. I'd been through hell, but that was no excuse. *Focus.* Then, through the dancers, I caught a glimpse of another ghost from my past. Only this one turned out to be real.

Hello, Diego.

It was hard to tell with the flashing lights, but I was certain it was him. The last time I'd seen that lunatic had been at the Crossroads. One of Kat's best men, he was also the asshole she'd sent to try and kill Jill and Reaper during the betrayal, and afterwards Kat had *gloated* about it. Diego had shaved his head since then, but there was no mistaking him for anyone else. See, Diego was one of those guys who was too *pretty.* He stood out, even in a place like this.

Carefully, I followed him, keeping a lot of people between us. Diego was an effeminate crossdresser in his free time, but he was a psychopath and underestimating him would get me killed. From what I'd heard he was a ruthless, efficient killer. Hands on, preferred to work with knives, and good enough at it that most of the Crossroad's resident professional killers had given him a wide berth. It takes a *lot* of skill to build that kind of rep in a place like that.

Diego went past some security guys and up the stairs to the club's offices. I went back to the bar and ordered another drink. Diego was one of Kat's insiders. I might not get another opportunity like this. One of the bartenders had been slicing lemons. There was a little knife on the cutting board. When nobody was looking I snatched it. It was only a skinny, five-inch kitchen knife, with a clumsy square wooden handle. Not exactly a properly balanced killing blade, but it was solid, and when I tested the edge with my thumb I knew it would do.

This asshole had tried to kill my woman. That sort of thing demands retribution.

Normally I liked to plan things out, take my time, look for angles and plan for contingencies, but a few minutes later Diego came down the stairs and headed for the back exit, and I followed him. There was an alley behind the club. He'd probably parked there. I might be able to tail him to someplace quieter, but my car was parked half a block away. By the time I reached it, I might lose him. Diego paused to talk to another security goon in a suit, who handed Diego a motorcycle racing jacket and a helmet. Diego took them and went out the door.

Palming it so the blade was concealed along my forearm, I quickly walked toward the back exit, passing between unsuspecting Hungarians. The big guy in the suit was moving toward the stairs. *Good.* If I'd had to slash his throat in here there'd be too many witnesses. There was a sign that warned opening this door would cause an alarm to sound, but Diego had just proven that was bullshit designed to keep patrons from letting their friends in. I pushed the door open and entered the alley.

The night air was cool. The light was bad. There was a security camera mounted on the bricks high above me. I wouldn't have much time. The annoying techno music faded as the door closed. I looked right. *Clear.* To the left was a green dumpster. I stepped around it. Fifteen feet away Diego was walking toward a parked BMW motorcycle. I'd cripple him, then question him. Simple, nice, fast, and clean.

Making no sound, I flipped the knife around in my hand and started toward him.

Diego must have seen my reflection in the bike's chrome, because he reacted instantly, spinning and hurling the helmet at me. I dodged to the side, but it still caught my forearm, slowing me. I lunged, directing a cut at his face. He blocked my arm with his palm as he moved back. I slashed again. Our arms and hands collided. The man was *quick*.

So much for simple.

Trying to make distance, Diego reached for his side. *Gun!* Kitchen knife flashing back and forth, I followed. His hand came up with a black pistol, but I elbowed it aside, kicked him in the shin, and with the flick of my wrist sliced open his knuckles. The pistol went skittering down the alley. He hit me, but I shoulder checked him into the brick wall. I kept on him, slicing, but I'd lost track of his other hand, and barely avoided getting cut by the blade that had appeared out of nowhere. I leapt back as a six-inch tear appeared in the fabric of my shirt.

We stood there for a moment, a few feet apart, knives pointed at each other. His folder was designed for piercing skin, severing tendons and arteries. Mine was for cutting lemons. But Diego was bleeding and I wasn't. I could still hear that damned techno music. His baby smooth face contorted in rage as he realized I'd already cut him several times. "You realize who I am? You know who you're fucking with, you little bitch?"

"Where's Kat?"

"Lorenzo?" Diego's anger turned to shock. I had a rep too. "But you're dead!"

"Where's Anders?"

Diego rushed me.

The knife was aimed at my eyes, but mostly to steal my attention long enough to nail me with a knee or an elbow. If I'd not had the element of surprise, he might have taken me. He was scary fast, but I was too focused, too angry. All the fights in the Pale Man's dungeon had changed me, honed me. Now? I felt alive. It was amazing the difference food and a purpose could make.

I blocked his knife hand and cut him. I ducked under his fist and cut him. I caught his knee with my forearms and stabbed him. He grunted as the blade punched a hole through his abdominal wall. I shoved Diego back into the dumpster. He left a big streak of blood across the sheet metal.

"Where's Kat?" My voice was cold.

His knife came back around, but I caught his wrist with the edge of my blade. Lemons weren't the only thing it could slice in half. His knife landed at my feet. He punched me in the ribs, but he was losing too much blood and weakening. His next punch was easily dodged, and I stabbed him in the shoulder. I twisted the knife and Diego screamed in my ear. *"Where?"*

"Fuck y—" My elbow knocking out some of his teeth cut that right off.

"Talk." I threw my knee into his side. I felt at least one rib break. As he slid down the metal, I put my palm on his forehead and used his face like a cheese grater on the rusty metal. Back and forth as Diego wailed in agony. He wasn't going to be pretty anymore. I let him fall. "Where's my brother?"

Diego was dazed and hurting, but the important thing was he knew he was beaten. His only hope of survival was my mercy—fat chance of that—or stalling until help arrived. "I don't know," he gasped. "That's Anders' deal."

My eyes flicked to the camera. Any second somebody was going to look at the screen and Montalban goons were going to come out shooting. I retrieved Diego's gun, a Glock 19, then went back and knelt next to him, but kept glancing at the door. "Tell me what I want, and I'll call for an ambulance." Blood loss made you stupid. He might believe me.

He laughed in my face. "Go to hell."

From the amount of blood coming out the hole in the top of his chest, I'd severed his brachial artery. Diego was dying, he just didn't know it yet. I didn't have much time to get answers. "Look at me. Look at me, Diego. I survived Sala Jihan's dungeons. I learned things about suffering you can't ever understand. But I'll share them with you, one by one, until you tell me where they are." I stuck the knife into the meat of his thigh.

Diego bellowed as I turned it. The kicking and thrashing only made the wound worse. "I swear I don't know! There's a number in my phone if we need to speak."

If he was lying, he was damned convincing. "Is Varga still here?"

"No." I pulled the knife out, and moved it to his other leg but he hurried, hoping that giving me something would make the pain stop. "Anders sent him to Austria a year ago."

I pushed the point of the blade into his leg, but stopped short of piercing his skin. "*Where* in Austria?"

"S . . . Salzburg!" he stammered, trying to talk while in agonizing pain.

It felt like the truth. Diego was beginning to fade out. "Hey." I slapped him in the face a few times to bring him back to reality. "What's Project Blue?"

"She took it on after Eddie died. It's like her monument to him. That's all I know. Don't kill me. I don't . . . Please . . ." Diego begged. He must have finally realized how badly he was bleeding out. "Nothing. I know nothing. She kept it secret. Please. I don't want to die."

"Too late." Diego's clock was running down fast. I stood up as he grasped at me uselessly with his ruined hand. "You died when you betrayed us at the Crossroads. You just didn't know it yet."

My trendy new suitcoat was ripped and covered in blood, so I took it off and threw it in the dumpster. The bike was closer and would be a faster getaway than my car. With luck, they'd think that Diego had just driven off and be unaware that anything had happened. By the time I'd taken his wallet, keys, and cellphone, Diego had passed out from blood loss. So I hoisted his body over the side of the dumpster and dropped him inside. He landed with a crash. I took a few seconds to cover him with trash bags. By the time I was done he'd stopped breathing. I smashed the nearest light bulb on the way out to leave the alley in shadows. Hopefully nobody would see all the blood until tomorrow.

The motorcycle racing jacket hid the fresh blood on my shirt and the helmet hid my face. I'd have to get out of Hungary, and Salzburg was on the opposite side of Austria, but I could be there by morning.

The Pale Man had kept calling me the *son of murder*. By the time I got done with the Montalbans I'd earn that title.

LORENZO
Salzburg, Austria
September 3rd

Stefan Varga had been easy for me to find. Criminal scumbags were sort of my peer group. Knowing the right kind of assholes to threaten could get you a list of Montalban hangouts, and there weren't that many. Salzburg wasn't that big. Big Eddie had run a much tighter ship than his little sister. While Eddie had preferred being quietly dreaded, Kat seemed to like flexing the muscles and being openly feared. It seemed like the only thing Kat was tight-lipped about was Project Blue. For the rest of her criminal empire, she liked a bit of flash.

One of the drug dealers I'd kicked the shit out of that morning had told me the top Montalban man in town spent a lot of time at a local freight company. Using legit businesses to cover for smuggling had been Varga's bread and butter, so it fit. I'd lucked out and seen Varga getting into a car there, and tailed him. I'd had to hang back a bit when they'd gotten into these narrow, residential streets, but his Mercedes was parked just ahead of me in front of an old, but very nice, four story house.

Varga had a man with him, probably a bodyguard, not that I'd gotten a good look. There were an unknown number of people inside. The smart thing to do would be to play it cool, plan it out. Despite being a creepy, inscrutable motherfucker, the Pale Man had still acted like time was of the essence, but rushing in would only get me killed. Going after Diego in that alley had been stupid, and I'd been lucky I hadn't gotten hurt, especially in my suboptimal condition. Careful planning was the only reason I'd survived as long as I had in this business. Going head to head against an unknown number of Montalban soldiers was stupid. I needed to wait, study it, find an angle.

Screw it. I got off the bike and walked straight to the front door.

Though I didn't see any on the street, Europeans loved cameras, so I left the helmet on. I had two guns, Diego's Glock, and an old double-barrel shotgun I'd taken off the drug dealer's doorman. The barrels had been hacksawed off just ahead of the forearm. The stock had been cut down so that there was barely anything to hold onto. It would be awkward as hell to shoot, but on the bright side it fit inside a messenger bag. As I walked quickly up the front steps, I pulled the 12 gauge.

First, I tried the doorknob. Of course it was locked, but you never know. So I pressed the shotgun's lopsided muzzle against the lock and pulled the trigger. The buckshot blasted a jagged circle of door and frame into pieces. I kicked it open and rushed inside.

A man in a suit had been sitting not too far from the door, but he'd fallen out of his chair when the shot had gone off. He was fumbling for the subgun slung across his chest, so I simply turned the shotgun on him and gave him the other barrel. With the choke cut off, the pattern was garbage and did more damage to the floor than his body, but he still got hit by a *lot* of double aught buck. He was still thrashing, so I pulled the Glock from my waistband and shut him up with a shot to the brain as I went past.

The helmet muffled sound, so I was lucky I heard the next man coming. He was sloppy, leading with his gun, and the muzzle cleared the corner before he did. I knocked his pistol down with a swing of the shotgun, and as his body followed around the corner I shot him, several rounds fast to the body, and as he stumbled, a final 9mm hollow point through the side of his face. That had been meant for his forehead, but I was out of practice.

I dropped the shotgun and helmet—I'd grab it when I left—and moved down the hall. There was noise above. Thumping, crashing, panicked people taking cover. I took the stairs three at a time. On the second floor landing, somebody started shouting a challenge in German. When I didn't respond, he decided to fire a few rounds through the wall. I knelt down behind an antique table while he put useless holes in the wallpaper around me. He did a real number on the furniture, and the instant I heard panicked swearing as he ran his gun empty, I went through the doorway.

The shooter was an older, overweight, blond man—not Varga—so I shot him four times while he tried to reload his little pocket pistol. I was a little rusty, but shooting was like riding a bicycle, so you might suck, but it isn't like you forget how. He fell across a desk, scattering papers and rubber-banded stacks of euros.

I ran up the next flight. I didn't see anybody on the third floor, and

I didn't have time to look. There was more noise above, from the sound, at least two men, moving in different directions. I moved to the side. If they were smart, they'd hunker down, call for help, wait, and blow my head off if I appeared on the next floor.

Luckily, they weren't tactical geniuses. Instead of waiting, the bodyguard came for me. *Sloppy*. I heard him running down the stairs. I only had to wait a second for his feet and legs to appear, pounding down the stairs. I put the front sight on a knee and fired. Blood flew, and he fell, screaming, momentum taking him face first down the stairs. When he hit the landing, I waited long enough to confirm it wasn't Varga before I shot him a few more times.

The Glock was at slide lock. I'd not realized I'd fired that many rounds already. I picked up the dead man's gun, an FN 57, checked to make sure there was a round chambered, and started up the final set of stairs.

"Whoever you are, there is money and drugs downstairs. It is yours. Take it all. Come any closer and I'll shoot you!" he shouted in German. It had been a long time but I recognized the voice. It was Varga. He repeated much the same thing in Russian, probably because he wasn't sure who the hell had just massacred all his men, but it was clear he thought this was just a robbery.

While he talked, I crept down the hall. He'd placed himself in the back bedroom, probably behind something that would stop bullets. I didn't know if he'd had time to phone for help or not. But I'd just made a lot of noise, and somebody was bound to have called the cops, so time was on his side.

The lower floors had been carpeted and nicely decorated. This floor was all bare and utilitarian. As I passed the other bedrooms, I saw they were filled with bunk beds, each one with handcuff rails and tiedown straps. Then I knew what this house actually was. This was a clearing house. They'd take in runaways or clueless immigrant girls, get them addicted and trained, then ship them off to be pimped out somewhere else. There was a medical cart in the hall, with needles, syringes, and medicine bottles on it. There was huge money in an operation like this. The fact they could get away with shit like this, in a quaint little picturesque neighborhood, extra pissed me off.

I *hate* these people *so much*.

Varga was still shouting, but he'd have a gun trained on the doorway, and there appeared to be only one way in. I needed to get his eyes off the door. If he thought the Russian mafia was moving in on him, I was going to give him Russian mafia. I spoke in Russian, but not to him, but rather like I was speaking to someone right next to me. *"Granata?"* Then I changed the pitch of my voice, and answered myself. *"Da. Granata."* Because of course, the answer to *grenade?* Is always *yes, grenade.* Varga heard that and quit his yapping as he realized he was about to get fragged. Then I tossed one of the medicine bottles through the doorway. It made a very ominous noise rolling across the hardwood.

Since he thought he was about to get blown to hell, Varga instinctively ducked for cover. I used that chance to rush through the door. I found him cowering behind an overturned table. By the time he realized there was no boom and looked up, my stolen pistol was aimed right between his eyes.

Knowing he was screwed, Varga let go of his pistol and slowly raised his hands over his head.

I'd run up four flights of stairs, killed four men, and captured their leader in well under a minute. Not too shabby considering my sorry state and lack of recent practice. I hate to admit it, but it felt good to be *on.* But I couldn't get cocky. I hadn't cleared the place, so there could still be someone else downstairs waiting to fuck me up, or the cops could roll in. I had to make this fast.

I noticed his phone was lying on the floor next to him, and the screen was lit. He'd already called for help. Hell, if they could hear me, anything that might make the Montalban reinforcements hesitate was worth a shot. Keeping the gun on Varga, I picked up his phone and shouted in Russian, *"Vladimir, send ten men to secure the first floor, and another ten to watch the street."* Then I hit End. I switched to English. "I've got some questions."

Apparently, he didn't recognize me. "You think you can rob me, asshole?" Varga hadn't changed much. He was still a thin, heavy lidded, hook nosed scumbag, just a little more gray and with a more expensive suit than the last time I'd seen him. Keeping his hands raised, he got off his knees, and stood up, probably thinking he could bluster or threaten his way out. "This house belongs to—"

I casually raised the pistol and shot him through the palm of his hand.

He flinched, and even managed to blink a few times before the pain hit. The zippy little 5.7 round had blown a perfect hole through his palm, like a high-velocity paper punch. He was lucky it hadn't hit a bone or it probably would have blown up in a meat cloud. He made an awful noise as he clutched his injured hand to his chest, but to his credit, he didn't start screaming. He was tougher than I thought.

"I'm here *because* you work for the Montalbans."

"You shot my hand!" Varga shouted, like I didn't know.

"Each time you don't answer, I put another hole in you. Where's your boss?" I'd settle for either Kat or Anders.

"France!" I moved the gun toward his knee. "Paris! Don't shoot! Katarina is working on something in Paris. I don't know where. She moves from safe house to safe house. Nobody can touch her."

"If Diego had been this forthcoming, he would have lived longer." From the look on Varga's face, they must have found his body in that dumpster. "Yeah, that was me. Don't make the same mistake and force me to bust out my talking knife. Where is Anders holding Bob Lorenzo?"

"Who?" Varga seemed genuinely confused, but I aimed at his knee anyway. "Shit! I don't know who that is! You've got to believe me!"

Good thing he talked fast, there wasn't a lot of slack in this thing's trigger. "Big, bald American. He mentioned your name in the Crossroads." I moved to the window and checked the street. Two figures were moving this way. I couldn't get a good look at them. Maybe Varga's men? Maybe the law? Stupid curious neighbors? Either way it was time to go.

"Anders never told us his name. He was sedated and tied up when I got him. My men flew him to Paris. That's all. Just a package. I move things. That's all I do." I thought about the empty beds down the hall, and resisted the urge to shoot him in the dick. "Anders' men picked him up from my place by the airport. I swear on my mother that's all I know."

I moved back to the door and looked down the stairs. That was my only way out. I couldn't get cut off. I had to make this fast. "Tell me about Project Blue."

Varga was in pain and terrified of me, but when I said those words, his expression slowly changed. I knew that expression well, because every time I'd looked in the mirror since I'd gotten out of the Pale Man's prison, I'd seen it in my own reflection. It was a fatalistic knowledge of certain mortality. As if me simply asking about Blue had sentenced him to death. Just like that, I'd just killed all his hope.

"I moved the cargo for her. As of last week everything is in place, but I never thought Katarina would actually go through with it. She wouldn't," Varga looked wistfully at the window. He'd been willing to give up his employers, but he'd rather try to escape that talk about Blue. "Millions would die!"

Millions? That made me sick to my stomach. "I'm going to stop her."

"Kill her and the plan launches. That's her insurance." Varga looked to the window again, he was doing the math. Four stories onto cobblestones *might* not kill him, but anybody who knew about Blue certainly would.

"Wait—"

Varga went for it.

The glass barely slowed him.

Valentine
Salzburg, Austria
September 3rd

Salzburg was in chaos, the *Polizei* were setting up checkpoints across the city, and we had to get out of town while we still could. We had executed our emergency egress plan, the one we'd put together in case things went sideways. The BMW and the Range Rover had both been doused with gasoline and torched. We switched to backup vehicles we'd prestaged nearby. Months of research and weeks of reconnaissance were all down the drain, thanks to Lorenzo.

Lorenzo who—I was surprised to learn—was somehow still alive.

Four of us were piled into a Mercedes Sprinter van. Antoine and Skunky were in a different vehicle, a tiny little Hyundai i20, leaving the city by an alternate route. Ling and I shared a bench seat behind Shen, who was driving. Behind us, Lorenzo sat by himself, leaning back against the wall of the cabin. His eyes kept darting back and forth, like he thought we were about to come at him.

No one spoke for a few moments. "Well, this is awkward," I said, breaking the uncomfortable silence. "I didn't recognize you for a second there."

Lorenzo watched me, but didn't say anything. His eyes were different than I remembered, sunken into his skull a little more. He looked older. He looked like he'd been through hell. His hair was longer, and he wore a short beard now.

Ling turned around and met Lorenzo's thousand-yard stare. "I'm glad you're still alive, Mr. Lorenzo," she said. "Please don't take this the wrong way, but may I ask how?"

Lorenzo shifted his gaze, staring off into space in silence for a moment. Ling looked back at me; I just shrugged.

"Jill is safe," I said after a moment. That got his attention. "We got her out of the Crossroads and into Mongolia. I think she and Reaper flew home from there. I'm not Facebook buddies with them, but we e-mail once in a while. All encrypted and everything, Reaper set it up. Last I heard they were both doing okay. As okay as they could be, I guess."

Lorenzo looked down at his lap for a moment, then up at me and Ling. "Thank you."

"No, thank *you*," Ling insisted. "Many owe you their lives. We thought . . . we assumed you were dead."

"I thought I was too."

"What happened to you?" Ling began to grill him. "How did you survive? Did you escape? What are you doing here? Why did you kill Stefan Varga?"

Lorenzo shook his head. "Give me a minute, will you? This is a lot to process. Where are we going?"

"Wels. A city just over an hour northeast of here. We have a house there that we've been operating out of, owned by a real estate shell company the organization uses. It's as safe a place as we're going to find."

"It's getting harder and harder to get around Europe," I said. "Police checkpoints are popping up all over. There are riots and mass protests happening all over the place. Terrorist attacks are on the rise, too."

"I heard," Lorenzo said simply. He fell silent then.

"So, uh, listen," I said, struggling to find the right words. "The last time I saw Lorenzo, it was through a rifle scope from several hundred yards away. He was taking cover behind the decaying wreckage of a Soviet bomber as Sala Jihan's forces surrounded him. He'd run some kind of diversion, leading the pursuers off so that the few survivors of the raid on Jihan's compound could get away, and had gotten shot in the process. Ling and had tried to hold them off, but we were running out of ammo and there were just too many of them. I had offered to shoot Lorenzo, then, with the thought that it'd be more merciful than letting Jihan have him. He declined the offer. We had retreated and he'd been captured.

Like a cockroach, you just couldn't kill this guy. Believe me, I had tried.

As if reading my mind, Lorenzo raised a hand. "Don't worry about it. I told you to leave me. You got Jill out. That's all that matters."

"For what it's worth, I'm glad you're alive." It was Shen, looking at us in the rearview mirror.

Lorenzo nodded. Shen never had much to say, but I learned that he and Lorenzo had . . . well, I don't want to call it *bonded*, but they'd understood one another. "I'm glad you guys made it out, too." He looked back at me. "Before I tell you my story, you tell me yours. What the hell are you people doing in Austria? Why were you tailing Stefan Varga?"

"We're trying to track down Katarina Montalban. Our intel suggested Varga knew how to contact her."

Lorenzo simply nodded. "What happened after the Crossroads?"

Ling took a deep breath. "Exodus is . . . not at its strongest right now," she said honestly. "We got our asses handed to us, as you might say. Katarina is a lunatic, and all indications are that Project Blue will have apocalyptic repercussions."

"What the hell *is* Blue?" Lorenzo asked.

"We still don't know," I admitted. "We've tried to find your brother, he probably knows, but haven't had any luck."

"Maybe. Probably. I interrogated Varga. He squealed on Kat's location, no problem, but Blue? He took a swan dive rather than talk." He pointed directly at me. "But what the hell are *you* doing here? These people—Exodus—I get. They're idealistic do-gooders who think they can unfuck the world. No offense, Shen."

"None taken."

"But why you, Valentine?"

"It's a long story."

"Sounds like we've got a long drive ahead of us. Talk. And this time, I want to know everything."

Chapter 4: The Princess in the Tower

VALENTINE

Exodus Compound, Azerbaijan
Several months earlier . . .

"Well? What do you think?"

Dr. Bundt turned off the flashlight he'd been shining in my eyes, and glanced down at his iPad. "Mr. Valentine, you're very healthy. The last time I examined you, you were underweight and injured. You have made a remarkably swift recovery. Aside from some scar tissue and the fact that I performed the procedure myself, I wouldn't have guessed that you had been treated for a traumatic brain injury."

"Okay, that's good, right? So what's wrong?"

"Wrong?"

"Something is obviously bugging you, Doc. What's wrong?"

Dr. Bundt looked at his iPad again. "I'm not sure how to explain this."

"Okay, now you're scaring me. Do I have cancer or something?" That would be a hell of a way to go, after everything I'd been through and survived: fucking *cancer*.

"Cancer? No, no, my boy, you're as healthy as a farm horse. That's just it: you shouldn't be this fit. You should have barely been able to participate in the battle of the Crossroads, given your condition when we recovered you from North Gap."

I couldn't stop myself from wincing at the mention of the black site where I'd been held, interrogated, and had God-knows-what-else done to me.

"Have you read the files on you that we found there?"

I shook my head. "I kept meaning to, but . . . you know."

"I understand." I guess there's no shame in not dredging up unpleasant memories. "Dr. Silvers was conducting certain, ah, procedures on you. The notes we retrieved are vague, but she was working off of a template, a plan of action. The program is called 'XK *Indigo*.' Have you heard of it?"

Now I was scared. "XK what? Was she experimenting on me or something?"

"I wouldn't call it experimenting. She knew exactly what she was doing. I have not been able to find any real specifics on XK Indigo. A search on the internet reveals nothing but rumor and conjecture from conspiracy theorists. As near as I can tell, though, it's a mental and physical conditioning program."

I suddenly felt uncomfortable. I didn't want to talk about this. "Hey, maybe this is my superhero origin story. That's basically how the Canadians made Wolverine."

Dr. Bunt raised an eyebrow. I don't think he got the reference.

"So you're not a comic book guy, Doc? He was a mutant, one of the X-Men. The second greatest Canadian ever, behind Wayne Gretzky."

Dr. Bundt cocked his head slightly to the side, ignoring my attempt to change the subject. "Tell me . . . how much do you remember about the program?"

"Almost nothing," I lied. You can block some of it out, but you don't exactly forget months of drug-cocktail fueled torture sessions. "It doesn't matter now anyway."

The doctor wouldn't let it go. "Mr. Valentine, you have been a patient of mine for some time. I need you to be honest with me, and tell me how much you remember. It does matter. It matters a great deal. You're not the only one who has been through such conditioning."

What? "There are others?"

Dr. Bundt nodded. "I can't give you any specifics, for privacy reasons, but no, you are not the only one. However, you have dealt with the aftereffects of that program better than most, I believe it's due to your ability to enter into a serene mental state during extreme stress—"

"I've always called it the *Calm*." To me it wasn't anything special, it just was what it was. When things get really dangerous, I get detached. Not from reality, if anything I was even more rational when I was Calm, but things seemed to slow down, or maybe I processed everything faster, but it was handy in combat.

"Indeed. I have friends in the mental health industry who would love to be able to bottle that and sell it. Regardless, you're the only one who has been through this Indigo program retaining much at all. So please, tell me what you remember."

I took a breath, and looked down at my lap. "It's hard to remember a lot of it. It's like a dream, how it slowly fades after you wake up. I wrote a lot of it down in a journal, like you told me to, last year. I haven't gone back and read it. I get . . . I don't know, I get itchy thinking about it. It makes me uncomfortable."

"It is good not to dwell on such trauma, but I think there is more to it than that. This aversion to recalling the process, to discussing it, I believe that is part of the conditioning. I believe the same of the memory loss. I was concerned such a thing would happen, which is why I asked you to keep that journal after your recovery. You really should go back and read it."

"No. Like I said, it makes me uncomfortable." I squirmed on the exam table a little. I wanted to get up and walk out of the room. I didn't like it when he dug like this, but Dr. Bundt was the man who put the people Exodus rescued back together, both physically and mentally. He wasn't going to let it go, but I didn't like thinking about what would have happened had Exodus hadn't gotten me out of there. What kind of brainwashed, screwed-in-the-head asset for the Majestic organization would I be today?

So the doctor and I had a bit of a stareoff for a while. He folded his arms and looked like a really disapproving Albert Einstein. Sadly, he was such a nice guy that I couldn't just tell him to buzz off.

"Are you done with him yet?" someone asked, startling both Dr. Bundt and I.

Ariel was standing in the examination room doorway. There wasn't much left of the terrified adolescent I'd first met in Mexico. She was a lovely young woman now, with platinum blonde hair and intensely blue eyes. I suspected that if not for being sequestered in the Exodus estate in the middle of nowhere desert of Azerbaijan, she'd have her pick of young men.

"Yes, my dear," the doctor said. "Not to worry, he's quite physically healthy."

"Note, he specified physical. I'm still a mental basket case."

"Okay great, Michael. Will you walk with me? We need to talk."

Relieved at the distraction, I stood up. "I need to go, Doc. Thank you."

Dr. Bundt seemed reluctant, like there was more he wanted to ask me, but he let me go. The Doc was a really important man in Exodus circles, but everybody around here usually gave in to Ariel's wishes. He wasn't the only one. I'd gotten used to all of Exodus' secretive paramilitary badasses deferring to a kid, but that didn't make it any less weird. I'd spoken with her several times, and had even saved her life, but the girl was still a mystery to me.

She led me to the garden. The Exodus manor was built in the restored ruins of a medieval fortress. The modern part of the structure was U-shaped, with a nice garden in the middle. Being out in the desert, the garden was well watered, climate controlled, and protected from the blowing sands by a glass ceiling. It was, essentially, a large, beautiful greenhouse.

Ariel ditched her shoes. "I like to walk barefoot on the grass," she said idly, even though I hadn't asked.

"You're a weird girl."

"I like you the best because you're at least honest to me. Not wearing shoes reminds me of when I was small, when I was home."

"Where are you from anyway?"

She smiled at me but didn't say anything.

I cocked my head to one side. "What is your deal, kiddo? The sworn Exodus people won't say a word. Why all the hocus pocus and mystery? I mean, look, I don't know anything about you. Why are you even here? Why are you so important to Exodus? Why—"

Ariel shushed me. "So many questions."

"Well nobody else is going to answer them for me. They just tell me you're so observant you see patterns other people don't." Even Ling wouldn't tell me the whole deal. It isn't fun to ask your girlfriend questions and get blown off with BS like about recognizing patterns. "Asking why you'd have a little girl planning combat operations seems like a pretty reasonable question to me."

"You're right to ask them. I know so much about you, and you don't know anything about me. It's not fair." She looked sad for a moment. "Okay, I'm from Fresno, California. I haven't been there since I was a toddler, but that's where they say I'm from. I don't talk much about my past, mostly because I don't remember a lot of it."

Ariel was young, but her eyes looked older. Sad. Seasoned. I knew that she was frighteningly intelligent and almost unbelievably observant. She was probably a certified genius, if there was any sort of certification for that. She was weird, too. Like, sometimes you got the vibe she acted the way she did just because she was trying to mimic the people around her, to blend in. I didn't spend a lot of time around teenagers, but remembering how things were back when I was in high school, I could tell she wasn't typical. She almost reminded me of myself at that age, but only after my mom had been murdered, and after I had taken a human life. That was a crappy thing to be compared to, but there it was.

"When I was a little girl I was kidnapped. Like you, I was taken, tested, experimented on. They changed me, just as they changed you."

My heart sank for the poor girl. "Who took you?"

"You know them as Majestic, but that's not really what they're called."

"Oh, I've got plenty of names for them."

"The one I've heard you use the most is *fucking assholes*."

"Language, young lady."

That made her smile. She paused to smell some white flowers. Then she plucked one and stuck it in her hair just over her ear. "You'll laugh at why they took me. It was because I was good at chess, puzzles, math problems, that sort of thing. I don't remember most of those days. It's like there isn't room enough in my brain for things like that anymore. They had problems with me, I know that. When they were done, they put me with a family to be monitored. I guess I needed a *normal environment* to see how I'd turn out. It was under a fake name. I don't even remember my real one."

Now that really was sad. "How did you end up on a Russian arms dealer's boat in Mexico?"

"Federov wasn't just some gunrunner, Michael. He was an asset of Russian foreign intelligence. They watched me for years, and then they grabbed me one day while I was walking home from school."

"What about your foster parents?"

"I don't know if Doug and Linda were working for Majestic or not. Either way, it's better to let them think I'm gone forever. I never even asked to go home. I don't have a home to go back to. None of that was real. It was all a puppet show, a fabrication. It was *fake*." Her tone and her pretty face both darkened. "It's not real and it's not my life."

I took a deep breath. I could certainly sympathize with her situation. "That's a tough break, kiddo."

"Exodus was watching Majestic's program the same way the Russians were, so after they grabbed me, Exodus grabbed me back. I've been with them ever since. It's not so bad, you know. I have a good life here. I don't want for anything."

"This isn't a life. This is a gilded prison." I looked around the lush garden make sure no one was listening, and leaned in closer to her. "Are you being held here against your will?"

She laughed at me and shook her head. "No, Michael. You're such a sweet man, though. You were going to try to rescue me, weren't you?"

I didn't admit to anything, but as a matter of fact, the gears had already been turning in the back of my mind.

"I'm not a princess locked in a tower. I'm here of my own free will. This is where I belong, for now. This is where I can do the most good." There was an uncompromising certainty in her voice that made me understand how grown men could take her advice seriously. She didn't sound like a teenager just then. "But I think that's changing, which is kind of why I had you brought here."

"I thought Exodus invited me here to stay off the radar." Majestic's best operative, Underhill, was hunting me. I'd gone out on a couple operations in the last few months and had had some close calls. Exodus probably didn't want me dragging them into a war they couldn't win against Majestic. "I'm confused."

"I know, but just listen. There are things happening out in the world right now. Big things, and they're not good."

"That's . . . not really helping."

Her intensely blue eyes almost burned holes in me. The shift from out-of-her-depth teenager to commander was a little unnerving. "The time has come for you to find Katarina Montalban. You need to stop this Project Blue, whatever it is, from happening. If you don't do anything, if you just sit here in exile, she will succeed."

"There's like half a dozen people in the world who know what that even is, and none of them are talking to us. How do you know all this?"

"Because I *know*, Michael!" she snapped. "Okay? I can see things other people can't see. I know things other people don't know. That isn't just some line Ling feeds you to get you off her back. It's hard to explain. I see lines of causation, strings, patterns, whatever you want to call it, and I can see where it's all leading. You have to find her and stop her. You will probably, like, have to kill her though, but that alone might not stop her plan. She's very smart, but she's crazy and she's dangerous. The important thing is you stop Blue."

I really wasn't sure what to say. "Um, okay then. Take out the leader of a powerful organized crime family, but first dismantle her wacky scheme that nobody understands first. I'll get right on that."

She shook her head. "I know you think I'm crazy. I'm not. You asked me why Exodus thinks I'm valuable, why the Russians thought I was valuable, and why Majestic thought I was valuable. This is why. I know things and see things and feel things that other people can't, and I'm usually right."

"So . . . you're like a psychic?"

"No! I'm not . . ." She was obviously frustrated. She pointed at a nearby bench. "Sit down." I did, and she plopped down next to me. There was a little fountain gurgling in front of us. The garden even smelled nice. It was a rather pleasant place to talk about the apocalypse.

"I hate when people call me psychic. Making what I do sound like magic is insulting to my intelligence. Look, I don't read tarot cards or palms or whatever. It's about facts and probabilities. Some things fit and others don't, but everything goes somewhere, and when you get enough things together, it is pretty easy for me to see what comes next. No offense, I don't know how to explain this to you in a way that you'll really be able to understand. Regular people just don't get it. You just have to trust me."

"I do trust you. I'm just trying to understand. You know, wrap my feeble mortal mind around it all." I shot her a lopsided grin.

She shook her head, looked up at me, and smiled back. "I said no offense. That means you can't get offended, stupid."

"Yeah, that's not really how it works."

"But listen, okay? I'm totally serious. I read everything that Robert

Lorenzo found out about it and everything from the Majestic info that was dumped. I can read between the lines based upon Majestic's reactions, and now that they've lost control, they fear it more than anything else, ever."

"I figured that when they were torturing me for information I didn't have."

"This is what we *do* know: Majestic thought Blue up as a doomsday scenario. Four operatives were given the mission to prep it, but their superiors were in the dark on the details. Of those four, one was assassinated, the second died in Zubara, you killed the third but only after he'd cut a deal and given Blue to Big Eddie Montalban, and when the last operative, Anders, saw that everyone else was dead, he assumed Majestic was cleaning house, and threw in with Big Eddie's successor."

"Katarina."

"Exactly. Majestic opened Pandora's box, and then promptly handed it to a psychopath, so now they're freaking out. I don't know what they're planning, but I see where it leads. There will be war, chaos, and worse. The world is on the brink of falling apart already. This might be all it takes to push it over the edge."

"Colonel Hunter . . ." That was Ariel's *second operative*, but he had been my commanding officer in Zubara, so I couldn't just give the man such a casual designation. I'd been there when he'd died. Crushed and bleeding, his dying confession was how I'd learned about Blue, and his barely coherent last words had been to command me to find someone named Evangeline to stop it. Majestic had tortured the hell out of me to try and find out who that was, but all I had was her name. "Hunter's journal mentioned a Project Red in China. Millions of people died in the Chinese Civil War, and I think Majestic caused it, just like they used my Dead unit to destabilize Zubara. He said Blue was even bigger."

"So you know I'm right, then," Ariel said levelly as she squished her toes back and forth in the grass.

I sighed. "I'm afraid you might be. That's pretty close."

"This isn't about me or what I see, Michael. We're way beyond that. This isn't even about Exodus, or Majestic, or any of the other factions fighting for scraps. This time the world is at a crossroads, one path leads to an unknown future, but the other takes us to a hell that even I can't wrap my brain around."

"It's not fair, you know."

"What's not fair?"

"You're too young to have this burden on your shoulders. The world's about to blow up, but you think you're the only one who can see it coming. The only people who buy into your theory are a handful of fanatics who think they can make the world a better place if they just shoot enough bad guys."

Ariel smiled. "It's okay. This is how it has to be for right now."

"Why me?"

"Why you what?"

"Why me?" I repeated. "Why do you think I'm the one who can do anything about this?"

She shrugged. "I just know. You always seem to be in the right place at the right time. Trust me."

I'd made my living kicking doors and pulling triggers. Ariel talked about a world on the brink, but it was men like me who'd put it there. I had spent my whole life fighting somebody else's war. *Here I go again.*

"This isn't someone else's war, Michael," Ariel said softly. "If you're going to win, this has to be *your* war."

We sat in the garden for a long time, quiet except for the fountain. I didn't know if she was crazy, or if I was crazy for believing her. "What should I do first?"

VALENTINE
Salzburg, Austria
September 3rd

Lorenzo raised an eyebrow at me. "Just so we're clear, you're here because a teenage girl told you that you need to save the world."

"It sounds bad when you put it like that, but yeah, basically."

He shook his head slowly, looking between me and Ling as if we were inmates in a mental ward.

"There's something else you should know," I said hesitantly. "Hawk is dead."

Lorenzo was quiet for a long moment. "How?"

I took a deep breath and looked down. I couldn't look Lorenzo in the eye anymore. "It's my fault. It happened right after the Battle of the Crossroads."

"Your fault? You were on the other side of the planet."

"The people that held me . . . Majestic, whatever you want to call them. They're looking for me. They couldn't find me, so they went after the one person they could find. They killed him over the phone while I listened."

"Hawk," Lorenzo said, the word coming out as a harsh accusation.

"Yeah, I don't remember it, but I probably said something about him under interrogation. They had me so jacked full of drugs that I didn't even know what was real."

That sounded pathetic. Shameful. I thought Lorenzo would be angry at my excuses. From him, there would be at least harsh words, or maybe even a gun in my face. Instead he just exhaled and said, "It happens. Don't blame yourself. What's done is done."

"That's . . . mighty charitable of you."

"You do what you need to do to survive when you're in captivity. Every man breaks, sooner or later."

From what I knew about Lorenzo, that was a strangely humble thing to say. Whatever he'd gone through had left him changed. Had Sala Jihan broken him?

"I called Hawk after the battle. I hadn't spoken to him since I was captured. I wanted to let him know I was okay. They already had him. The Majestic operatives were waiting for my call. He said his name was Underhill. Older guy, maybe in his sixties. Hawk tried to fight back and they shot him down in cold blood, right on the fucking phone."

"Anders mentioned something about a guy named Underhill, and being worried that was who his old bosses were sending after him. Anders is probably the deadliest man I've ever known, so anyone who worries him is one scary motherfucker. He's probably still after you."

"Underhill didn't strike me as the easily discouraged type."

"Good. That makes it easier for us to find him and kill him, doesn't it?"

"I don't mind being the bait, for Hawk."

"For Hawk," Lorenzo agreed.

"Boys, please," Ling said, interrupting. "Let's put our penises away and focus on the here and now." She looked at Lorenzo. "Have you spoken to Jill?"

"No," Lorenzo admitted. "I wanted to. I thought about it, but the fewer people who know I'm alive the better."

"Mm-hm," Ling said, looking down at her phone. She had been sending text messages while I'd been telling my story.

"If they're not expecting me, I have the advantage. Kat doesn't know I'm coming for her. She won't until it's too late."

"You keep tossing her guys out of windows," I said, "and she'll figure it out."

"Varga jumped, but no. She'll be suspicious, but she won't think it's me. She has a lot of enemies. I intend to become Kat's worst nightmare, and Jill doesn't need to see that."

"You know," I said cautiously, "it wasn't easy for Jill. They came after her." I raised a hand before Lorenzo got too worked up. "It's fine. She's fine. She ran. I guess Kat pulled some strings. The government of the Bahamas seized most of your assets. Tax adjusters went to your house. Nobody was home because Jill had already bugged out, so the police searched the place. She destroyed all your documents, scrubbed everything, but they found your armory. All those guns are illegal in the Bahamas, so . . ." I trailed off.

"I'm glad I never paid taxes, then. Where is she now?"

"I'm not sure. She went back to the States for a while, I think. She's using one of the other identities you guys had set up, and Reaper was watching over her too. I haven't talked to her in a while but she's okay. I promise you, Lorenzo, she's okay."

"Good. She was always tougher than she gave herself credit for."

Ling's phone buzzed. "Hello?" she answered. "Yes. No, I didn't know. Yes, he's here. Okay." She reached past me and held her phone out to Lorenzo. "It's Jill," she said. "She wants to talk to you."

Lorenzo's eyes went wide. "What? How?"

"I texted her and told her. The only one you're fooling with all of that *she's better off without me* prattle is yourself. Being a stoic loner will not help you. Here. Take it."

Jill spoke loudly enough into her phone that we could all hear her, even though it wasn't on speaker. "You son of a bitch, you pick up the phone right fucking now!"

Lorenzo meekly took the phone. I turned back around and slumped into my seat. It was about to get even more awkward in the van.

LORENZO

Ling held out the phone to me. I hesitated before taking it. I was a con man who could smooth talk his way out of anything, but I didn't know what to say to the woman I loved. I was . . . scared? That wasn't the right word. Maybe *ashamed* was more appropriate, not that I'd ever been good at feeling shame like most people. Jill had never seen me at my worst, and that was where I'd descended in order to survive Jihan's prison, and where I'd planned on staying in order to get this job done.

"Damn it, Ling. I can't drag her into this."

"Seriously, Lorenzo? I can totally hear you!" Jill yelled.

"It's for the best, Lorenzo. I can see that prison damaged you. There is an emptiness in you, a wound, here," Ling said, placing one hand over her heart. "The choice is yours how you will fill that hole."

Metaphysical Exodus bullshit. The only thing over my heart was a big-ass burn from a branding iron. Hooking up with Valentine had turned Ling sappy. I snatched the phone from her, put it to my ear, and took a deep breath.

"It's me."

The line was quiet for a really long time, but I could hear Jill breathing. *"You're alive."* It wasn't a question, more of an accusation. I couldn't tell if Jill was shocked or angry or happy or what.

Suddenly, my chest hurt. My face burned. "Yeah." There wasn't a lot of personal space in the back of the van. I looked at Ling and Valentine. "Give me a minute." I didn't want to cry in front of the terrorists.

Ling nodded. "This line should be secure and encrypted, but it would still be best to avoid names."

Valentine gave me one last odd look before turning around, like he actually got it. But fuck him and his pity. Trying to get as much privacy as I could in the van, I slunk down, and spoke quietly. "I got out. Are you okay?"

"I thought you were dead."

"Me too. Are you okay?"

"Am I okay? I grieved for you. They told me you were dead." She

sounded out of breath, like she was walking fast or had just gotten done running. *"I'm too shocked to cry. Where have you been? How did you escape? When?"*

"I was locked up until a couple weeks ago."

That had to be a slap in the face. *"Why didn't—"*

"It wasn't safe to contact you. It still isn't."

"Come back to me. Come home."

This stung. "I can't yet. There's something I've got to do first."

"Then I'm coming to you."

"It's not safe—"

"It never is with you. But a lot has changed since you've been gone. I need to see you."

I missed her so much. She was the one who'd kept me alive and sane in the dark, and she didn't even know it. I wanted to be with her. But then what? I was on a cross-country murder spree. To win, I had to embrace the hate. I couldn't drag someone so good and decent into that. "Please, Jill. Just stay where you are."

"I'm in Paris."

That didn't make any sense. To Kat, Jill was just another loose end to tie up. She was hiding from the Montalbans, why go where they had so many eyes? "What?"

"I'm here to take care of your ex. Our friends know how to reach me. I've got to go."

Jill was trying to assassinate Katarina Montalban.

I could hear sirens in her background. "I love you." But Jill had already hung up.

That hadn't gone the way I'd hoped, and it sure as hell hadn't lived up to my dreams in prison. "Fuck!" I smashed my fist into the side of the van.

Valentine turned back around. "What's the—"

I cut him off. "Damn it, Ling. What the hell were you thinking?"

Ling faced me. "I misled Jill to believe you had died, so she wouldn't throw her life away trying to get you back."

It was blunt, incredibly cruel, and we both knew if Jill had come back for me, the Pale Man would have destroyed her. I was pissed off, but I did manage to mutter, "Thanks for that."

"And now I have stopped you from throwing away the one thing in your life that makes you an actual human being. She loves you very much, and she needs you, almost as much as you need her. Jill balances you, Lorenzo."

"Whatever, Ling."

"Do you truly think you are the first warrior so tempted to do evil, that you'd set aside all the good in your life because it might hold you back? You know what kind of broken people end up in Exodus? Freed slaves, refugees, and former child soldiers who have lost everything. They hunger for revenge more than even you can understand, yet, if we have to destroy everything we stand for to achieve victory, then what's the point?"

"I'm not in the mood for Exodus' cornball philosophy. Here's the deal. I'm going to Paris. Contrary to Valentine's assurances that Jill is okay, you must have missed the part where she's stalking Katarina Montalban."

Valentine was stunned. "She's doing *what?*"

"You didn't know, did you? I gathered that by the stupid look on your face when I said it. You're hunting Kat, it's your business to know. Varga told me Anders shipped Bob to Paris. He's their patsy. If Kat's there now, that's got to be where Project Blue is based out of. After I stop Jill from getting herself killed, I'll see if I can't track down my brother's whereabouts."

"Exodus has contacts in Paris," Ling said. "I will reach out to them for information. If Katarina has moved her operations there, we will find her."

"Good. Because Jihan made it sound like time is running out."

"So did Ariel," Valentine said.

"So your little angel and my devil are on the same page then. Fantastic. Before Varga took a header he talked about Blue killing millions." Valentine and Ling seemed discomfited by that, but not shocked. The description must have matched up the general idea they'd gotten from Exodus' weirdo mystical teenager. And here I'd been hoping Varga had been exaggerating. "Bob talked about it being big, but I don't know if he ever realized it was that big."

They were tight enough now that Ling and Valentine had reached that point where they could share a lot of information just in glances. Valentine gave Ling a questioning look, like *hey, I guess I'm supposed to be the leader, but what do I do now, honey?* And she nodded in the affirmative, as if to say, *go for it.* He swallowed, then turned back to me, looking a little uncomfortable. "We're shorthanded, Lorenzo. We could use all the help we can get. Work with us."

"The last time we partnered up, I collected several exciting new gunshot wounds and ended up rotting in the Pale Man's prison."

"It was your idea to team up with the Montalbans," Ling said pointedly.

She had me there. "Oh, believe me, I'm full of regret for that little partnership. It gave me something to focus on during the beatings."

"Call it an uneasy alliance then, but Blue has got to be stopped," Valentine said. "Are you going to help? Or would you rather keep bouncing around the countryside murdering assholes and ruining months of our work?"

"Yeah, I can't imagine how that feels."

Valentine frowned as he realized he and Dead Six had done the same thing to my carefully laid plans in Zubara. "No wonder you were such a prick when we first met."

"Falah, Adar, Hosani? Because if we're keeping score on ruined plans and general fuckery, you've still got a lead."

"I do, don't I?" he asked smugly.

"Enough. Our goals are the same," Ling said. "Let's not waste any more time getting in each other's way. We will do what we can. If fate is in our favor, perhaps we will learn enough to tip off the authorities, and they will stop Blue for us."

"Fat chance of that. You saw what the FBI did to Bob when he started poking around in Majestic business." Not that I would mind Kat and Anders getting arrested. I could arrange for them to get shivved in a prison way easier than I could pop them on the streets myself. "Fine. Whatever works. But I figure this doesn't end until we put a bullet in them ourselves."

"I don't have a lot of faith in the system either. Does this mean you're in?" Valentine asked suspiciously.

Normally when somebody tried to persuade me to do something, my instinctive reaction was to tell them to go to hell. As much shit as we'd gone through, he'd never like me, and I'd never like him, but I knew he'd shoot straight with me, and that was better than *at* me. Say what you will about him, but Valentine knew how to get a job done when he stopped moping long enough to focus.

"I'm in." My one-man rampage had somehow turned into another messy teamup. I needed some air. "Let me out somewhere I can boost a car. I'll see you in Paris."

VALENTINE
Exodus Compound, Azerbaijan
Several months earlier . . .

I stood off at the edge of the room, not saying anything. The faces of the other twelve appeared on a large screen, in two rows of six, as part of a secure video teleconference. They were electronically distorted so I couldn't make any of them out. Sir Matthew Cartwright, the councilman who owned the Azerbaijan estate, stood off to the side, hands behind his back, while Ariel addressed the bank of screens. Ling was with me, arms folded across her chest, looking unhappy.

Ariel turned out to be an eloquent speaker. Her conviction and confidence was impressive, even if she did still say *like* too much. She had just explained to the council what she had previously explained to me, except in greater detail. Once again, the teenage girl sort of disappeared, and all of a sudden there was this brilliant tactician in her place, making her presence felt.

She was a strange kid.

Despite Ariel's reassurances that this was all for the best, I still felt bad for her. A girl that age should be going to college, hanging out with friends, not making life-or-death decisions and weighing the fate of the world.

"It's unfair, getting robbed of her childhood," I whispered to Ling.

My girlfriend smirked at me. At that age Ling had already been conscripted into the Chinese army to fight in their civil war. She didn't even have to say anything.

"Yeah," I agreed. Compared to Ling I'd had it easy. When I was about Ariel's age, I had been in the Air Force. "Never mind."

Ariel was still making points. Her skills as an orator would have given any politician a run for his money, but it was a tough sell. She was arguing that Exodus should focus all of its present efforts on stopping Katarina Montalban and preventing Project Blue from happening, whatever that entailed. Only Exodus was—by legal definition at least—a terrorist organization. And though they were absolutely committed to stopping evil, righting wrongs, and all that good stuff, they had just gotten their asses kicked at the Crossroads.

She was trying to convince them that Project Blue, if allowed to continue, would set in motion a chain of events that would end with the deaths of millions and possibly trigger a major war. Only she seemed unwilling or unable to get into the specifics of how this was going to come about.

Our host, Sir Matthew, was one of the dissenters. He was one of those distinguished, proper English gentlemen types. I barely knew the guy, but I had a hard time imagining how somebody who looked and sounded like he did had risen through the ranks of a secret vigilante army that spent most of its time blowing up warlords and freeing slaves, unless he'd had some swanky James Bond thing going on in his youth.

"My Lady, we all appreciate your conviction, but you must consider our position. We lost a significant percentage of our strike steams at the Crossroads. Word about the battle has gotten out. There are rumors of it on the Internet, satellite photos showing the damage to the dam and the resulting flooding. We have attracted the unwanted attention of the world's law enforcement and intelligence agencies. It is my belief, and has been the belief of the Council, that our best course is to take some time to collect ourselves and recover from our losses."

Ariel glared at him. "You mean retreat? Go into hiding? Give up on the work because of a setback?"

"No, child, I don't mean retreat." Ariel's eyes narrowed at being addressed as *child*, but Sir Matthew either didn't notice or didn't care. "It's more of a strategic realignment. We are operationally limited right now. We need time to recover, recruit, and train. When we are ready, we shall reenter the fray from a position of strength."

"There is no time! None of you seem to understand this. We are *out of time*. Project Blue is happening *now*. Katarina Montalban isn't going to wait while we sit in the corner and lick our wounds."

"You are being impetuous. Exodus has survived for centuries because we have operated in the shadows. That has become increasingly difficult. Yes, many powerful people have known about us, but have allowed our work to proceed because we were doing the things that they could not, things which their governments lacked the stomach to do. One slipup now, while we are so weak, could mean the end of us."

An Exodus councilwoman, hailing from India from the accent, spoke up from the screen. "We've all read the projections of the Oracle." From the look on Ariel's face, I could tell she thought her designation was absurd. "We know that Project Red, whatever the specifics were, was an American operation to destabilize China."

"We don't know that," another council member protested. He had a slight Canadian accent. "Mr. Valentine provided that information." That was the first time I'd been recognized in this little shindig. "There's no way of proving that the journals of this Colonel Hunter are genuine, and even if they are, there's no way of knowing if he was correct in his assessment. We're making far too many assumptions for my taste."

At least he didn't cast any aspersions on my character. Considering how much blood I'd spilt and shed on their behalf, that was nice.

The Indian woman protested. "The Oracle has made it clear that—"

"The Oracle was the one who said we should go into the Crossroads in the first place! Have we not had enough of her mystical nonsense? Have enough of our people not died because of her?"

The councilwoman from India looked aghast. "James, please. Things didn't go exactly as planned, but—"

"No, it's okay." Ariel raised a hand, and the Indian woman fell silent. "He has a right to speak his mind. Go ahead. Tell us how I screwed up everything."

"As I was saying, on her advice we went into the Crossroads, and how many people did we lose to that butcher? I admit that our so-called Oracle has been right on many occasions, but on this one, she was spectacularly wrong, and we paid for her error in blood."

That was remarkably impolite for a Canadian. I kept waiting for him to say *sorry*.

Another councilman chimed in. His accent was thicker than the others, some kind of Spanish. "I agree with our colleague. Will we continue to place stock in this, this nonsense? She may be brilliant, but she is still human. Her advice to concentrate on the Crossroads led us to disaster."

Ariel looked up at the screens, her face a mask, in silence. She lowered her gaze and looked at me briefly, as if considering what to say next. She nodded to herself, looked up again, and spoke. "The councilman says that I was spectacularly wrong. Was I? Did I say that the operation in the Crossroads would go as planned? Did I say we would not suffer casualties? No. I warned you not to underestimate Sala Jihan, and I had no role in the tactical planning or execution of the operation."

"So you'll lay the blame on Ibrahim?" Sir Matthew snapped.

"Of course not. He did the best he could. I simply told you what most of you already knew, Sala Jihan is a force for evil in this world, thousands die in his mines every year, and that he had to be stopped."

"But we failed," Sir Matthew insisted. "Now we are unable to conduct other missions, missions that could save lives, in other places in the world."

"We did not fail!" Ariel insisted, raising her voice, her hands balled into fists. "Sala Jihan lives, yes, but the Crossroads are gone. His mines are flooded. It will be years before he can regain the power he's lost. It's not the ideal outcome, just as it wasn't the ideal outcome the last time Exodus took him on. We suffered major losses then, too, but Sala Jihan was left impotent and powerless. It took him six decades before he showed his face again."

I had no idea what she was talking about. Sixty years? Lorenzo had met the warlord in person, but he'd not described him as old.

Taking a deep breath, Ariel looked directly at the portion of the screen that displayed the Canadian's image. "Had anyone told me about making an alliance with the Montalban Exchange, I would have advised them to abandon the mission altogether. I could have told you that was going to end badly. And, if you remember, I was the one who said Michael Valentine was important. I was the one who said we needed him. If not for his leadership, the effort at the dam would have also failed, and the whole mission really would have been for nothing."

The council remained silent for a moment. I was awkwardly looking at the floor. I knew Ariel was playing up my role in the battle for the dam to get her point across, but it still made me uncomfortable.

Ariel shifted her intense gaze across all of the faces on the big screen. Her eyes reflected the light of the screen and seemed to burn with a blue fire. "You think I didn't predict the cost? You think I haven't felt every single loss? None of you hurt as badly as I did. None of you."

Ling had told me that Ariel had gone nearly catatonic when the results of the battle came in. They'd even called Dr. Bundt in because they were afraid she would try to kill herself. She had retreated to her room, barely eating, not coming out for over a month.

Today, though, Ariel was resolute. "But that doesn't matter now. The work has to continue, even if we suffer losses, even if we have setbacks, even if we fail. There's too much at stake to stop. You all know this. If we don't do it, no one will. People will suffer without hope. For this operation, we don't need a bunch of soldiers. We can get by with a few volunteers, but from the organization we need logistical and intelligence support. I can't see for certain what will happen if we attempt this, but I do know what will happen if we do nothing. So please, let's not give up now. Too much is at stake. Authorize the mission."

"No." the Canadian said.

"I agree, no!" said the Spanish-speaker. "Young lady, we've had enough of your fortune telling. Am I the only one who sees it? Are we so blinded by her that we don't realize what we're doing? We're letting this American girl have a say in life-or-death decisions while a thousand miles from the action. She's clearly out of her depth, and quite possibly out of her mind."

The Indian woman tried to defend Ariel again. "Marco, the Oracle—"

The Canadian cut her off. "Enough of this talk of oracles! Enough! This has gone on for too long. It's time to put the adults back in charge. She doesn't know anything. She's no gift from God. She's a charlatan who's been fooling us all along!"

Ling looked at me with a worried expression on her face. This was not going well, and it was pissing me off. I started to step forward, but Ling put a hand on my arm. "You won't help here," she said quietly.

I stopped. Ling was right. I was an outsider.

Ling stepped forward, as if to say something, but before she could, Ariel balled her hands into fists and shouted. "I don't know anything, you say?" she asked, looking up at the screens. "James, I know about that torrid little affair you're having with your secretary, and that the only reason your wife hasn't left you is because of your money."

Too bad the image was blurred, because I imagined the look on his face would be priceless.

"Matthew," she said, addressing the Englishman in the room, "I know *you* haven't yet found the courage to come out to your family. Believe me, it's the twenty-first century, nobody cares."

Sir Matthew looked aghast, but didn't say anything.

"The clues are everywhere. It isn't my fault the rest of you are too stupid to put things together. All I have *ever* done," Ariel said, her small voice booming with conviction, "is give you people the best advice that I could. It was you who sought *me* out! It is you who came to *me* with your questions! The half-baked mysticism came from you guys. All this oracle talk is your words, not mine."

Ling looked me in the eye, and stepped forward, until she was in view of the screens. Dressed in fatigue pants, a t-shirt, and combat boots, she looked out of place in the luxurious office. "I think it's a sad day when this exalted council seeks to blame its failures on a mere advisor," she said coldly.

Sir Matthew seemed taken aback. "Ms. Song, I've allowed you to watch these proceedings, but I'm afraid I must ask you to—"

Ariel cut him off. "Let her speak! She's been there for all of this, while you've been reading about it from the safety of your offices afterwards."

Ling gave Ariel a really nasty scowl, and I think the little genius realized that she was being a hypocrite, and shut up. They might have been on the same side of this debate, but Ling was a whole lot more hands-on.

Ling spoke softly. I was pretty sure she did that on purpose, not through any sort of meekness—trust me, not an issue—but rather because it forced everyone to listen carefully. "I was involved in the planning of the Crossroads operation. The decision to meet with the Montalban Exchange was made by the commanders in the field. Ariel had no part in those discussions. We had our reservations, but given the situation, we made the best judgment call that we could."

"Your call cost hundreds of lives!" Marco insisted.

"I was there," Ling said coldly. "We made a gambit and it failed. I accept responsibility for my decisions. Ariel was not wrong about Sala Jihan. Having seen his operation firsthand, I can tell you that it was even worse than you can imagine. His reach was expanding daily, as more innocents died or were enslaved, and—as is our mission—we rushed to stop it. Our greatest failing was, I believe, in moving too soon. I point this out to this council, because the timetable for the operation was your decision, not Ariel's."

The council had no immediate response to that.

Ling continued. "I do not know how this girl knows the things she does. God help me, she's tried to explain it to me, and I'm still unsure. But she is right more often than she is wrong. So here we are, with this esteemed council calling her a false prophet on one hand, yet denouncing her for not foreseeing everything on the other. Is this what defeated Exodus has become? Is this how we honor our fallen, by trying to assign the blame to someone who was not there?"

"The situation is more complicated than you know," Marco said. "Katarina Montalban is a very well-connected woman, above the law, who now has total control of one of the most powerful organized crime groups in the world. She hasn't forgotten about us. Ever since the Crossroads, international authorities have been haunting our steps, breathing down our very necks. We've been subjected to countless cyberattacks and attempts to steal our information. Safe houses have been compromised, and many of our suppliers have gotten nervous and have severed ties. Our connections in national governments advise us to go to ground for a time, stay off the radar, especially in Europe. And in the midst of this, after suffering the biggest defeat in generations, with unprecedented assaults on our operation from every angle, you propose we try to take the Montalban woman head on?"

"That is exactly what I propose," Ling stated. "Was I not clear?"

Ariel butted in. "I'm aware of all of that stuff, Marco. You think I'm naïve, but I understand what's at stake way better than any of you do."

"You are not helping now," Ling muttered under her breath. Then she addressed the council again. "Katarina Montalban is a psychopath, an unstable, amoral, ruthless psychopath, who has been given the keys to Armageddon. Apparently Project Red destroyed my country and caused the death of millions. If we let such evil proceed unchecked again, then everything Exodus stands for will mean nothing."

Ariel spoke up one last time. "If we don't find a way, no one will." Without another word, she turned her back on the council and stormed out of the room.

After some searching I found Ariel in her room.

"Go away!" she demanded when I knocked on the door.

"It's me, kiddo," I said, leaning in close to the heavy wooden door. Music loudly thumped from the other side. She didn't answer, but after a moment the door opened. She didn't say anything after opening the door; she just went back to her bed and sat down. It was obvious she'd been crying.

Cautiously, I sat down next to her, and looked around, trying to think of what to say. Her room was cluttered and messy, but smelled nice. Scented candles were burning on her dresser. A couple strands of Christmas lights were tacked to her ceiling, giving the room soft, moody lighting. Band posters decorated her walls. Of course I didn't recognize any of them. Wrinkled clothes were piled in a heap by the wall. An electric guitar and a small amp sat in one corner, next to a TV and a Playstation.

"The council voted no," I told her.

"There was an eighty-two percent chance that they would, but I got my hopes up anyway. What are you going to do?"

"What I have to." I wasn't going to back down, and Ling was pissed. "Could you turn that down?" I could barely hear myself think over the racket of her music. It sounded like little girls singing heavy metal, but I think it was in Japanese.

"Okay, grandpa," she said, tapping a little remote control. The music volume went down to where I could hear her talk.

"Thank you. I've been around a lot of gunfire. My hearing's not so great."

"What do you want?" she snipped. After a second, her expression softened. "I'm sorry, Michael. I don't mean to be bitchy to you."

"No, it's okay. You have good reason to be upset. A bunch of grown-ass men are blaming a bad op against a bloodthirsty warlord on a teenage girl. It's ridiculous and they should be ashamed of themselves."

She sniffled and wiped her eyes. "They're not wrong, you know. I didn't see everything. I didn't know how badly the Crossroads would go."

"Will you listen to yourself? You told me you're not psychic. How in the hell do they expect you to predict the future, then? Don't listen to them. It's probably been a long time since any of them have gotten their hands dirty, if ever. It's easy for them to second-guess you."

"I know, but . . ."

"No buts. I've made decisions that have gotten people killed. It's the nature of the beast in this business. You can either forgive yourself for not being perfect or you can let it eat at you until you're paralyzed. Either way, it doesn't change the past or bring back the dead. And, honestly? Sometimes, you do everything right, and still lose. Sometimes, even if you win the fight, good people still die. Turn left instead of turn right, die. I don't care how good you are, you're not going to predict that. You guys, you're fighting a war, right? This is war. People die in war, even if you win every battle and execute every operation perfectly. There's no getting around it."

"I know that up here," she said, pointing at her head. She then put her hand on her chest. "It just hurts here."

"Ariel, how old are you?"

"I'm eighteen." She paused for a moment. "I'm pretty sure. My records aren't, you know, complete."

I raised my eyebrows. "Wow, there's a way to get some guy in trouble."

"What?"

"Nothing. Look, what I'm getting at is, you're too young to be doing this stuff. You're making life-or-death decisions for others and you haven't even lived your own self yet."

"I already told you. I'm right where I'm supposed to be. This is where I can do the most good."

"Is it? Seems to me that those guys just scapegoated you, and probably won't be listening to you much from here on out."

"I don't know," she said quietly.

"Yes, you do. Hell, if anybody knows, you do. Just like you knew all that other stuff about them. You know. So you probably know what I'm going to suggest next."

"I can't just leave."

"Why not? You don't owe these people anything."

"They saved my life and gave me a home. They took care of me."

"No, Ling rescued you. I helped, by the way. Besides that, you've more than paid your debt. Has it ever occurred to you that they've just been using you?"

"It's not like that," she said, a little defensively.

I shook my head. "I was a mercenary for years, kid. I know what it means to be an asset. To be honest? Your services are worth a hell of a lot more than room and board. I've heard what you can do. They give you an Internet connection, feed you intel, let you see what's going on and connect the dots and you're a goddamn oracle. How many successful operations have you fed them?"

She sniffed. "Sixty-four."

"They are the ones who owe *you*, Ariel, not the other way around. They saved your life, granted, but that doesn't make you an indentured servant, and it's pretty hypocritical of an organization like Exodus to treat you like one."

"It's not like that!" she insisted, more forcefully. "They asked me, you know, if I wanted to go home. I didn't. I have nowhere to go."

"How's Europe sound?"

"What?"

"You've been cooped up in this mansion for years. Have you been out, even once, since you've been here?"

"Yes," Ariel said softly. "I've actually traveled quite a bit, but it's usually to some safe house or base or whatever place. The last time I got to actually go outside was a few months ago. They took me shopping down in Baku. I even got to go out on a boat on the Caspian. It was so awesome that I wanted to sing. It was like in *Tangled* when Rapunzel got to leave her tower."

I didn't admit to having seen that movie, but in fact we'd watched a bootleg copy of it, with Chinese subtitles, in Mexico. I didn't want to lose points off my man card.

"Why?" she asked. "What are you getting at?"

"Catch up, genius. That's where the heart of the Montalban family business is. I can use you more than Exodus can right now. Come with me."

"They won't like that. That's where Katarina Montalban will be."

"You said I had to make this my war? Then fine. I'm drafting you. Help me figure out Blue. And frankly, I don't trust that these guys are going to let me talk to you once I leave here. I want you to come with us."

Ariel suddenly looked very unsure of herself. Her eyes darted back and forth. "I don't know. It's unexpected. I didn't think of this. It's an unknown, a rogue variable. I don't like rogue variables. I don't know about this. I need to think about this. There are implications that—"

"To hell with the implications. You're overthinking it. Stop trying to see every end, every possibility. You can't. I don't care if you actually are psychic or whatever, you're not omnipotent."

I could almost see her thinking. "You . . . you're right. I do need to go with you. I can't do much from here, not anymore. There isn't a lot of time left, Michael. I think I can see the end of the world from here."

"Then pack your shit." I stood up. "We're going on a road trip."

Sir Matthew Cartwright was, as I expected, not happy.

"Absolutely not!" he insisted, raising his voice. His secretary, Penelope, hurried alongside us, her heels clicking and clacking on a polished wooden floor. "You can't take her!"

I got in front of him and blocked his way. The aristocrat and his secretary were quickly surrounded by Ling, Shen, Antoine, and Skunky. Four badass Exodus operatives, all of whom had been there to rescue Ariel in Mexico, all of whom had been at the Crossroads, and all who were ready to openly revolt, and me, the meddling outsider. It turned out Ling's guys were a lot more loyal to Exodus' mission than to the parties running it. They took this protecting the helpless stuff real serious.

I looked Sir Matthew in the eye, coldly. "Try and stop us, Elton John. Ariel is an adult, and she's going with us of her own free will. We'll be driving her right out the front gate. I suggest you not be in the way."

"Ling," Matthew said angrily, turning toward the woman he'd worked with for years. He should have known better. "When the Council said no, I knew you'd disagree. Yet, I said I'd allow you and your assets to leave without repercussion if you felt you must. Those assets did not include the Oracle."

Ling glared right through him. "Exodus fights against slavers. It is a sad day when we become them."

"You know it isn't like that! We need to keep her here."

"What difference does it make?" Ling asked, pointedly. "You've made that abundantly clear you won't listen to her. What good does she do here, literally locked away in a castle tower, if you're not going to use her talents?"

"Bloody hell, it's not about that!" he insisted, lowering his voice a little. "It's about keeping her safe. She's safe here. She won't be safe out there in the world."

"Kid's gotta grow up sometime, man," Skunky said.

"Not like this! You understand nothing." Desperate, he turned back to Ling. "If you do this, you will be cast out of Exodus. You would throw away everything you've worked for, everything you stood for?"

"I'm standing now," Ling stated.

"I won't allow it! Stop this madness at once or I'll get security down here!"

"Do not do this, Matthew," Ling stated flatly. "Not like this."

I felt for Shen, Antoine, and Skunky. They were true believers. They'd devoted their lives to this outfit. The *security* they were being threatened with were their friends, but they didn't back down. Ling was like a rock. Her principles never wavered. If doing the right thing meant turning her back on Exodus, which had freed her from slavery, which she'd fought and fled for ever since, she would, in a heartbeat. That was one of the reasons I loved her.

"Penelope, get the guards."

"Don't, Penelope," I warned. This poor woman looked like she was going to faint. She looked at me, looked at Matthew, then back at me. She then hurried off down the hall without another word.

A pulse went through my body, a muscle twitch, and my heart rate slowed, ever-so-slightly. I was carrying one of Ariel's bags in my left hand, my *gun hand*. I slowly set it on the floor and stared Sir Matthew down. "If that's how you want to play it, we'll paint the walls red. I promise you this, bullets start flying, you won't make it out alive."

He didn't bend. Sir Matthew may have put on airs of being a foppish rich guy, but right then I could tell from the way he carried himself that he was made of sterner stuff than that. He wasn't going to come out of this confrontation alive, but I doubted I would, either.

"Stop it!" Ariel shouted. I had not heard her approach. "All of you, stop it!" She pushed her way in between Shen and Antoine, and walked up to Sir Matthew. "Please," she said. "Don't do this."

"My Lady," Sir Matthew said, "I can't let them take you. It's too dangerous."

"Matthew, you're such a sweet man," she said, putting a hand on his arm. "But I need to go where the work is, and it's not here, not anymore."

"But, Ariel . . ."

"You've kept me safe for the last few years, but you can't keep me safe from the world forever." She looked at me, then back at Sir Matthew. "Besides, Michael isn't joking. This time the future is perfectly clear: he will kill you. But the five of them would not make it out of here alive. Among these are beloved heroes to the rest of your soldiers, and their death at Exodus' hands will shake the conviction of your remaining soldiers, leading to desertions and betrayal. Exodus would never recover. In the next few seconds you will decide the fate of the entire organization. It's not worth it, not for me."

He clenched his jaw, torn, but believing. *Do the right thing, man.* I really didn't want to get into a gunfight with people I nominally liked.

"So just let me go. Please. I need this."

Sir Matthew looked up at me, bitterly, daggers in his eyes, then back down at Ariel. His expression softened, and I could tell that he really did care for the girl. He wasn't protecting her because she was an asset; he protected her out of love. "Perhaps you're right."

The Exodus operatives all breathed a sigh of relief. That had almost gone sideways.

"I pray you are right. In any case, as you say, you're an adult now, Ariel. You're free to go. Exodus is not in the business of keeping captives."

"Thank you, Matthew." She hugged Sir Matthew, squeezing him tightly.

"Just mind yourself, child. It's an ugly world out there. Worse than even you know." The British councilman then looked at Ling. "Promise me you'll keep her safe. She's more important than you know."

"We are in the wrong line of work for guarantees, Matthew, but I will do my best." Ling began walking away. She was done here. "Come on."

"One last thing, Mr. Valentine. If anything happens to her, I will hold you personally accountable. Please believe me when I say that I have great resources at my disposal."

I picked Ariel's bag back up. "Yeah, well, get in line."

Chapter 5: Rogue Variables

VALENTINE
Wels, Austria
September 4th

Ariel was waiting for me when we arrived at our safe house.

"Oh my God, what happened?" she said, as we made our way through the door. The three-story house on the outskirts of Wels had been our base of operations for several months at this point. Progress had been slow in our efforts to track down Katarina Montalban and her cronies; there had been many days when we had nothing to do, so we just sat around the safe house trying to stave off boredom. This was the most excitement we'd had in a while.

Ariel was freaking out. "You need to tell me everything!"

"Okay, okay, everybody is fine," I said, setting my gear bag down on the floor.

"Something went wrong," she said pointedly.

"Indeed," Ling agreed. "Stefan Varga is dead."

"Well, okay, yeah, Varga's *not* fine. I meant none of us got hurt."

Ariel looked confused, like she sometimes did when things didn't go how she expected them to. "What? How?"

"Lorenzo's alive," I said.

It wasn't often that I left Ariel speechless, even momentarily. "*What*? I didn't . . ." She trailed off, eyes darting back and forth. "He's a variable. Too variable. The probability is . . . I didn't see this. I should have. It makes sense."

"I'm glad this makes sense to you, honey, because I was surprised as hell."

"Ariel," Ling said, "did you suspect Lorenzo was still alive?"

"No . . . I mean, yes. Kind of. I didn't want to say anything because, well, if he was alive, that meant that Sala Jihan was keeping him alive, and that was just too awful. I need everything you have, the video, the pictures, and you need to tell me everything Lorenzo said. Where is he? I have so many questions for him. He's a rogue variable. Don't you see, this totally changes everything?"

"Slow down," Ling said. Ariel tended to talk faster and faster the more excited she got, as her vocal cords struggled to keep up with her mind. "You can debrief us after we get cleaned up, I promise. Here are the SD cards from our cameras."

That seemed to satisfy Ariel. She took the cards from Ling, hugged me, and headed upstairs, to where her personal command center-slash-bedroom was. The house had six bedrooms, enough accommodations for all of us to have a bit of privacy. This was good, since Skunky's hobby was playing the banjo, and Ariel enjoyed listening to Japanese heavy metal.

Like I said, she was a strange kid.

Despite our earlier disagreement with the Exodus Council, occasionally a runner would stop by, bringing either supplies or information that was deemed not safe to transmit. Apparently kidnapping their oracle had forced their hand. Better to help us not get caught than to stay out of it and lose their precious asset. Aside from that little bit of aid, we were more or less on our own.

Ling looked over at me, smiling. "You called her *honey*."

I thought about it for a second. "I did? So?"

"Then she hugged you."

I was confused. "Is that bad?"

Ling sighed, shaking her head. "Michael, you are incredibly dense sometimes. Think about it for a moment. That girl doesn't have any family, just like us. You know what happens. You find yourself a family. She's picked you as a father figure."

"I'm not old enough to be her father." At least, I didn't feel old enough. Still, what Ling was saying made sense. After losing my parents, I'd found myself a family first in the military, then later on with Switchblade 4. Skunky had been like my brother, as had Tailor, whom I hadn't heard from since we left Zubara. I still thought of Hawk almost like he was my father.

Looking smug, Ling watched me as I came to the uncomfortable realization that she was right. "Well, that's intimidating." I had spent a lot of time with Ariel during my stay in Azerbaijan, but I figured she liked hanging out with Ling and me because she didn't have any friends in the sprawling estate, and certainly not any friends her own age. "It's just, you know, she's a grown woman."

"Is she now?" Ling asked, as we made our way upstairs. "Were you all grown up when you were eighteen?"

"I was in BMT at Lackland," I said. "But not really."

"I had already been conscripted into the PLA. This was before Shanghai was destroyed and the ceasefire talks began anew. But I was still very much a child, and I missed my parents dearly." She paused. "I still do."

I put my hand on her shoulder. "I know. Me too."

"If that poor girl needs a stand-in parent, then so be it," Ling said. "She's been through enough hell. I'm glad you brought her with us, Michael. That was a good decision."

"Does that make you Mom then?"

"Oh, of course not. I'm far too young. And . . . hip? Is that what they call it? In any case, I'm more like her big sister."

Ling was actually a couple of years older than I was. "Sure, baby, hip. I'm just glad Sir Matthew didn't have me shot." I stopped at my door. I had my own bedroom, but spent most nights in Ling's. The others in the house were polite enough to pretend they didn't notice. It was the sort of thing that was probably frowned upon in Exodus' bylaws, if they had such a thing, but I didn't really give a damn about such nonsense anymore. I was a fugitive working for a paramilitary organization that had been labeled as terrorists by the UN, the European Union, and Interpol; breaking Exodus' fraternization rules with Ling didn't even register, compared to all that.

"Hey, I'm going to get cleaned up and maybe take a nap. Wanna meet downstairs in a few hours for dinner? We all need to sit down and have a hot wash about what happened, too, make sure everybody's on the same page."

Ling raised an eyebrow. "Hot wash?"

"Air Force jargon. We'll just go over the operation, what went right, what went wrong, stuff like that."

"I see. Right? Lorenzo didn't shoot you. Wrong? The man we needed to question fell to his death. Good call. Yes. I'll see you at dinner." She kissed me on the cheek and continued down the hall.

I usually didn't leave the house if it wasn't necessary. Majestic, and every organ of the United States government that it could influence—which was probably all of them—was still looking for me. If I were spotted, I'd have to run, and the entire effort to stop Katarina Montalban would be compromised. Even though Dr. Silvers had finally believed me when I said I didn't know what Project Blue was, they weren't just going to let me go after escaping from their black site, especially since I was the one who gave Bob Lorenzo the Project Heartbreaker files. Shadow governments weren't big on forgiveness or loose ends.

I thought about exposing them, from time to time, just going public with the whole thing. Calling up some big network news outlet back in the States and saying "My name is Michael Valentine, I was the one who originally acquired the Project Heartbreaker files, and boy, do I have a story for you." I doubted it would accomplish anything, though. One way or another, it'd end badly for me. If Majestic didn't kill me outright, they'd use the legal system against me and I'd end up in prison. I'd broken countless laws back home, killed people, and there were those who thought that whoever released the Project Heartbreaker files was guilty of treason. My only hope of avoiding that would be to try to defect to another country, live in exile, getting worked over by their intelligence organizations. *Fuck that.* I'd spent enough time being interrogated and held captive. Just because my own country had gone to hell it didn't mean I wanted to work for somebody else's.

No, trying to come clean, tell the truth, shine the light on everything, would end up with me discredited, imprisoned, and probably dead. That was the way the world worked. All I really wanted to was to go home and live a quiet life, but I doubted that that would ever be an option for me.

Bob Lorenzo was such an idiot, I thought bitterly. The damned fool thought it was still possible to work within the system, to effectuate positive change. After the incident in Quagmire, Nevada, he'd practically begged me to go with him. He talked about the "legitimate government" and called Majestic a "cancer." What he failed to see is that Majestic wasn't the cancer; Majestic was a symptom of a much, much bigger problem. He acted like his so-called legitimate government wasn't giving materiel support and tacit approval to the operations of Majestic. Even shrouded in layers of secrecy like they were, none of it would be happening if they didn't have approval from on high. One man wouldn't be able to fix that problem. I doubted the problem could be fixed at all.

Hell, I'd given Bob all the info Colonel Hunter had given me on Project Heartbreaker, and he had gone public with it. He exposed Majestic to the cold light of day, and what changed? Nothing. They scattered, laid low for a while, but that was it. It had just been one more scandal out of dozens, whitewashed by the politicians and a compliant media. The whole exercise was for nothing.

Still, I wondered, what would have happened if I had taken him up on his offer. I probably wouldn't have been captured by Majestic and sent to North Gap. Colonel Hunter's last words had been about somebody named Evangeline, who was somehow related to Project Blue, and Silvers had drilled my mind into Swiss cheese trying to figure out who the hell Evangeline was. Maybe if I'd gone with Bob I would've been able to find out. I certainly wouldn't have given him or Hawk up under interrogation. Hawk would still be alive and Bob wouldn't be missing.

There was no sense second-guessing the past, not now, not here, alone in my room. I was exhausted, and needed to take a shower before my housemates used up all the hot water. After that, I badly needed a nap.

It was hours later when I awoke to someone gently knocking on my door.

I opened it to find Ling waiting for me. Her black hair was done up in a messy bun with a pair of sticks shoved through it. She wore a purple spaghetti-strap t-shirt and black yoga pants, and was barefoot.

"Did I wake you?" she asked, stepping inside.

"Yeah, but it's okay. I need to get up anyway. All these stakeouts are hell on a sleep schedule."

"You look like you got some rest," she said. "I thought I'd come check on you."

"We still need to sit down and have that hot wash."

"Dinner, or perhaps it is closer to breakfast, is cooking now. And you are right, following criminals makes setting a reasonable schedule difficult. We will all sit down together and discuss what's happened shortly. Since we are short on time, I have some proposals, but no matter what, I want you to know in front of the group that I will defer to your judgment. This is your operation."

"Is it?"

"This mission is your doing. The group looks to you for leadership. It's good to see. It comes naturally to you."

"I'm glad one of us is confident in my abilities," I said glumly. "Half the time I feel like I don't know what I'm doing, like I'm just winging it and hoping for the best."

"To a large extent, that's exactly what we're doing. But it's all we can do right now. This is unfamiliar territory for all of us."

"I wouldn't be able to do any of this without you," I said. I squeezed her hand. "You keep me sane."

Ling leaned forward and gave me a quick kiss. "I've seen you at your finest, Michael. You have every reason to be more confident."

"I've gotten too many people killed."

Ling shook her head. "That is the nature of this business. People die."

"I told Ariel that same thing before we left. But, I've been thinking, I really should have gone with Bob Lorenzo when I had the chance. None of this would have happened. Not like this."

"You don't know that," Ling said. "Perhaps it would have worked out better, perhaps not. Bob would have been found out eventually, even without you being interrogated. There was no way a lone FBI agent could go up against an organization like Majestic without penalties. It was only a matter of time. In any case, perhaps this is selfish of me, but I'm glad things went the way they did."

"Why is that?"

"Because now I have you." Nobody ever accused Ling of being tender, but with me she tried. "And you have me. Things work out. They always do. The Crossroads ended badly as it was, but it would have gone even worse without you."

I leaned forward and kissed her again, longer this time, more deeply.

After a moment, she moved to get up. "I need to get dressed."

I didn't let go of her hand. "I don't think so."

A playful, mischievous smile appeared on her face. "Oh really?"

I nodded. "As a matter of fact," I said, kissing her on the neck, "I think you're overdressed as it is."

"Is this how it's going to be?" Ling asked, eyes closed as I kissed her neck and shoulder. "You use your authority to take advantage of your subordinate? Shameful."

"Shameful," I agreed.

Ling pulled away, her dark eyes twinkling. She gave me a gentle shove, pushing me back onto the bed, and climbed on top of me.

"Well then," she said, straddling me, hands on my chest. "Let's see who's really in charge."

Sometime later, Ling and I lay together, naked beneath a sheet. She had her head on my shoulder and was listening to me breathe, something she often did after sex. If you didn't know Ling, and only judged her from the public face she wore, you'd think she was an ice queen. She tended to be standoffish and, often, needlessly formal. She'd lived a hard life. I knew full well why she put up the walls that she did, but that didn't make it any less striking when they came down.

For someone normally so distant, when we were alone, she was very touchy. She liked to hold hands and cuddle. She was never one to engage in public displays of affection; a quick peck on the corner of the mouth was the most I would get out of her if there was any chance anyone would see. But behind closed doors, she was a different person: sweet, sensitive, passionate, enthusiastic in the sack. One time, we even watched *Steel Magnolias*, and I held her while she bawled her eyes out.

Other times, we talked about the bad stuff. She had seen as much combat as I had, and the horrors of the Chinese Civil War were well known. Cities burned, mass starvation, fields of bodies. I could talk to her about the bad days, about the things I'd done, about how I desperately tried to cling to my humanity, and she actually understood. I could talk to her about the friends I'd left behind, the people I'd watched die, the things I'd swore to lock away, and she didn't just listen, she *got it*.

When I woke up in the middle of the night, soaked in sweat, reaching for a weapon to fight an enemy that wasn't there, she held me until I calmed down. When she found me drinking myself stupid, crying, regretting the past and feeling sorry for myself, she didn't judge, didn't shame me for cracking, didn't look down on me for not always being able to keep it together. She just wrapped her arms around me and told me it was okay.

Fate had brought us together, time and time again, against all odds. Ariel had insisted that Ling and I were meant to be, and even though I told myself I didn't believe in such things, I was beginning to believe it with her. Ling wasn't just my girlfriend, or my lover. She was my partner, my other half, my warrior, my beautiful angel of death. I couldn't imagine life without her.

I wanted to tell her. I wanted to tell her so badly what she meant to me, how I'd be dead without her, how my heart skipped a beat when she smiled. I wanted to tell her, but I couldn't. I didn't have the words, I didn't know how to say it in a way that wouldn't sound stupid.

"I love you," was all I could manage.

"I love you, too," she said.

Somehow, that was enough.

We sat around the dinner table, scheming. The house in Wels had a large dining room with a round dinner table, big enough for all of us. We six were all the manpower we had, and that included Ariel, whom I wasn't about to take out on a mission. In fact, we'd gone over contingency plans over and over again covering what she was supposed to do if we were compromised in any way.

Our crew was small and our resources were limited. We were down two vehicles now, in the aftermath of the fiasco in Salzburg, limiting our transportation options. We had a small pile of cash, guns, whatever information we could get our hands on, and not much else. Against us was a crime family with limitless resources.

Sometimes it seemed hopeless, but I couldn't let the team think I had my doubts. Ling had been right; this operation was my baby. These people had volunteered to follow me on this fool's errand, and I owed it to them to not let uncertainty get the better of me.

If I was trying to seem upbeat, Antoine was dour. The hulking African always struck an imposing figure, even when casually hanging out at the dinner table. He was actually a very kindhearted, gentle man, but ferocious in his convictions, and not the sort you wanted to piss off. Shen was, as usual, quiet and unassuming. It was as if he wanted people to forget he was there. Skunky was a bit of a smartass, but he was damned smart. Shen and Antoine had worked with Ling for years. Skunky was one of my oldest friends, and we'd been in Switchblade together before he joined Exodus. Despite our challenge, I couldn't ask for a better team.

"The information Lorenzo presented is disturbing. It seems that we have less time than we thought," Antoine said.

Nods and grunts of agreement came from around the table. Even Ariel was quiet. She chewed her food absentmindedly, seemingly zoned out, but I had seen her like this before. Her mind was racing, trying to process everything, account for every possibility.

"Varga says the pieces are in place, but if we just pop Kat, it'll launch. So what do we do about it?" I asked. "How do we stop this when we don't even know where to start?"

Ariel blinked hard a couple of times, swallowed her food, then joined the conversation. "I've been thinking this over. The answer is there; I just can't see it yet. Elusive, you know?"

"No," Skunky said. "Not in the slightest, scary computer brain girl."

"We need more information. I need more if I'm going to be able to put it all together."

"Yeah," Skunky agreed. "I'm on board with you guys until the end. You know that. But I'm not gonna lie, bro, I'm pretty lost."

"Perhaps," Antoine suggested, "it would be helpful to start with what we *do* know. Katarina's operation has moved west, and so must we."

"Varga told Lorenzo that Katarina Montalban is in Paris, so that's where we need to go."

"Agreed," Ling said.

"Yay!" Ariel cheered. "I've always wanted to see Paris. It's the city of love."

"I thought it was more the city of ham sandwiches myself," Skunky said. "Seriously, they've got like a little bakery like every twenty feet there, and they're all awesome."

"I guess it could be both," Ariel said, thoughtfully. "If you love sandwiches, I mean."

Ling was not impressed by love or sandwiches. "Let's stay on topic, yes? Operationally speaking, Paris is solidly Montalban territory. We have been able to operate with relative impunity over the last few months because we have been poking around the outskirts of the Montalban empire. Paris is the heart of it. They will have eyes everywhere and informants in the government and among the police. Any contacts we have with the criminal underworld can be assumed to be compromised."

"Assume that anyone we speak with will immediately inform our enemies," Antoine grumbled. "To find intel among Paris' criminals will be difficult. That is something we could use Lorenzo for."

"True that," Skunky said. "We spent how many months tracking down this one Varga dude without getting caught, and your old buddy from Zubara found him in what, a couple of days after getting out of a torture dungeon?"

"Something like that," I mumbled. Yes, Lorenzo knew the underworld better than anybody, but I suspected the reason he'd found Varga so fast was that he just didn't care about getting caught. I'd seen it in his eyes in the van, he simply didn't give a damn if he lived or died as long as he took his target with him. I recognized the look because I'd seen it in the mirror when I was after Gordon Willis. Maybe Ling had saved his life by putting Jill in his path, maybe not. Time would tell, but in the meantime I had people to take care of. I didn't have that luxury of risking him dragging us down with him. "We'll work with Lorenzo, but I'm not sure we can count on him for anything."

"Because he's traumatized," Antoine said.

"More like kamikaze," I corrected.

"We may be flying blind, but I have received word from Sir Matthew," Ling suggested. This was probably the part she'd warned me about earlier. "He has made contact with another player who may help us, and believes he may be of use."

"Could you be more vague?" Skunky asked.

"Oh, trust me, she can be," I answered.

Ling scowled at me before speaking. "His name is Alastair Romefeller."

"So who is this guy?"

"The chair of Romefeller Fund Management and head of the Romefeller Foundation, his philanthropic apparatus. He's a hedge fund manager worth something like twenty billion U.S. dollars. He is also the sole owner of a think tank and private intelligence gathering firm called Romefeller Military Intelligence."

"He's Illuminati," Ariel said flatly. "One of their power-hungry overlords who imagines himself ruling the world. You can't trust him."

"Whoa, whoa, wait a sec," Skunky said. "*The* Illuminati? That's conspiracy theory bullshit. It's just a bunch of rich bastards who like to do favors and pull strings for each other. The Montalbans belong to that social club and you want to talk to *them?*"

"It is not ideal," Ling said, "but there's a mutual interest here."

"The Illuminati are real, and they have always stood in the way of Exodus and the work!" Ariel protested.

I couldn't let this degenerate, and ultimately, I had to make the call. It may have sounded crazy, but I knew there was something to it. Gordon Willis had me assassinate Rafael Montalban as part of the secret war between Majestic and the Illuminati.

"Bob Lorenzo said that Project Blue was Majestic's way of destroying the Illuminati. We know both sides are assholes, but let's back up. Everything I've heard about the Illuminati comes from pop culture, a bunch of wealthy elites who secretly run the world, and all that. If anybody is actually running the world, they're doing a terrible job since it's falling apart, so I know that's nonsense. What's their actual deal, Ling?"

"We don't know everything," Ling said. "Much of the truth is buried in layers of misinformation. This conspiracy theory bullshit, as Jeff calls it, helps obscure their real objectives. As soon as someone starts talking about the Illuminati, he's immediately dismissed as a nut."

"But the actual conspiracy is real," Antoine said.

"Yes, they're very real," Ariel said. "Once you get past the lies and legends and bullshit, they are basically an alliance of descendants and heirs of European aristocracy. Their leadership all comes from several powerful families. The Romefellers are one of them, as are the Montalbans. The different families' influence goes up and down over the years."

"Well, I checked Google," Skunky said as he placed his phone on the table. "Wikipedia says that the Illuminati were founded in Bavaria in 1776."

Ariel rolled her eyes. "That's not true. They go back way further than that."

"Like I'm going to trust you over Wikipedia."

"Older than Exodus?" I asked.

"Exodus and the Illuminati share common origins, according to the lore," Ling said. "Both were products of the Crusades and, later evolved during Enlightenment. Both were founded with the goal of bringing justice to a base and, at times, unbearable world. Exodus chose the path of direct action, fighting evil wherever it showed itself. The Illuminati chose . . . well, another way. Manipulation through the levers of power. They do not seek to combat injustice so much as they wish to implement order and control."

"With themselves in charge, of course," I said.

"Obviously!" Ariel said. "And that's why you can't trust them! They think that people can be managed. They don't get probability. They freaking started World War One!"

"What? How?"

Ling just shook her head, but Ariel went off.

"Well, not started, but made it spiral out of their control. Their attempts at manipulation, gaming the system, were at an all-time high. They thought they could manage a regional conflict to gain more power, and bring about a tide of internationalism. It backfired. They got their League of Nations, but they didn't predict the rise of communism or fascism. This took away the base of their power for a while, so they watched, and waited. They were key players in the founding of the United Nations and, later, the European Union. They are, I think, more powerful today than they've ever been. They are rivals of Majestic."

I scratched my head. "Why would a secret U.S. government organization want to attack the Illuminati? Jesus, this sounds crazy just talking about it. Majestic was formed, originally, to fight communism. That's what Hunter said."

"The Illuminati long supported communist expansion—that's just another kind of lever to them—but that made them natural enemies of Majestic. After the Second World War, Europe had lost its power base. The United States emerged as the superpower, so the power shifted, but Majestic kept the Illuminati from getting their hooks in. It was a turf war. So the Illuminati did their best to help the Soviet Union along as a hedge against the Americans. Ultimately, they wanted a unipolar world with themselves at the top. In the meantime, they settled for a bipolar world on the brink of nuclear war. When the Soviet Union collapsed, and then China fell apart, the Illuminati saw a chance to reshape the world. The Illuminati never wanted the United States to be the military and economic power it became. They've funded efforts to counter American supremacy for decades."

"It's working," I said sadly. "My country is in decline. It's a mess."

"When your country has a civil war that involves the use of atomic weapons," Ling said, "then you can call it a mess."

"Fair enough," I admitted. "So how is this Romefeller guy going to be able to help?"

"They have a thousand times our reach," Ling replied. "Hopefully the threat of catastrophe will make him listen to us."

"Hmmm . . . They do not want the world destabilized," Ariel mused. "That's not to their benefit. Plus, regardless of what Blue is, it was designed with them as the target, so it can't be good for the Illuminati to have it executed." She obviously didn't like where her current train of thought was taking her.

"Say Romefeller does listen, and he's smart enough to see that Katarina's nuts. What's in it for us? Because they're part of the same *social club* he finds her for us?"

"That's the idea," Ling said.

"Then what?" Skunky asked. "I'm sure this is a dumb question, but is there any reason we can't just shoot her in the face and call it a day?"

I shrugged. "Varga told Lorenzo that that isn't good enough. She dies, Blue goes off. It's insurance. Is that true? I've got no idea."

Ariel gave me a long look, one of those unsettling gazes that reminded you of just how intensely, almost unnaturally, blue her eyes were. "Maybe. She's dangerous. I think you will have to kill her before all of this is over with. I'm sorry, but you probably will have to."

"I'm okay with that," Shen stated. Which I believe was the first thing he'd contributed to the conversation in days.

"But that won't do it, by itself. She's not dumb. She's very, very smart, actually, and more sadistic and vindictive than you know. She's angry, so angry. She would burn the world down if it meant she could be queen of the ashes. She'll have everything planned out so that even if she's gone, Blue will still happen."

I sighed, a little frustrated. The kid was probably right. "What are the odds Romefeller sells us out to Katarina, or otherwise screws us?"

Ariel tilted her head to the side as the whole group watched her.

Strangely enough, this group of trigger pullers actually put that much faith in her opinion.

"Flip a coin."

It was my decision to make. "Romefeller it is, then. Anybody disagree?"

There were a lot of uneasy glances exchanged, but they didn't have any better ideas.

"Just be careful, Michael," Ariel said. "Making deals with devils out of desperation is the main reason the mission at the Crossroads fell apart. Romefeller *cannot* be trusted. Promise me you'll be careful."

"Okay, kiddo, I . . ."

"*Promise me!*"

Yikes. "Okay, okay, I promise. I won't trust the son of a bitch as far as I can throw him. The feeling will probably be mutual, considering I offed one of his golf buddies a couple years ago."

Chapter 6: The All-Seeing Eye

VALENTINE
Zurich, Switzerland
September 10th

"You know," Ling said, looking up at me as she straightened my tie, "you clean up rather nicely. It's nice to see you in something besides cargo pants and combat boots for once."

I looked her up and down as I smoothed some wrinkles out of my suit jacket. It had been a long train ride. "You're not so bad yourself." Ling's gray suit looked like it had been perfectly tailored for her. Her skirt was short enough to be attractive without looking unprofessional. From the way she walked in them, you would have thought she wore heels all the time. Her hair was done up in a tight bun, and she wore a pair of thick-rimmed glasses. She didn't need them, but even a bit of Clark Kent level disguise helped when you were traveling through unfriendly territory.

"You look like a naughty Asian librarian."

I never would have teased her like that in front of her team, but it was just the two of us. She struggled to keep from smiling as she told me to keep quiet and focus on the task at hand.

"Yeah, you shushing me isn't doing anything to diminish the librarian thing." That actually got her to laugh a little before she put her serious face back on. Truth be told, I was cracking jokes because I was nervous. I was unarmed, in an unfamiliar city, and I was a wanted fugitive. So far, the fake identity that Exodus had given me had held up: I was allegedly a Canadian citizen. Probably backpacking across Europe, seeing the sights, I liked to imagine. Ling told me that I had, perhaps, gone overboard in my fake backstory, but it's not my fault the woman has no imagination.

The people we were seeing today knew who I really was, and I wasn't comfortable with that. I scanned the busy streets of Zurich nervously, expecting Underhill and a Majestic black ops team to pop out at any moment. But it had to be this way. This was my mission, and my real identity lent authenticity to my claims. My fake Canadian alter-ego couldn't get a last minute, one-on-one private meeting with a billionaire. Michael Valentine, the soldier of fortune, who had exposed Project Heartbreaker, and was supposed to be dead, could.

We entered the lobby of the gleaming office building and made our way to the reception desk. "Yes?" asked the bored-looking looking receptionist. She had a thick French accent.

"We're here to see Mr. Romefeller," I said quietly.

"He's expecting us," Ling added.

The receptionist looked at one of her computer screens. "Ah, yes, there you are, Monsieur, Mademoiselle." We hadn't even given our names. "He is expecting you. Please, take a seat, and someone will be along shortly to take you to where you need to go."

Ling and I sat in the lobby, next to a fountain, for an agonizing twenty minutes—there weren't even any magazines to read—until a pair of security men came to get us. They were dressed alike, in dark suits, with ID badges hanging from lanyards around their necks, and radio earpieces. The taller of the two, a German man with closely cropped blonde hair, politely asked us to follow him. He led us out of the lobby into a secure area, swiping his badge to get the door to unlock. Inside, we were checked with a metal detector. The German patted me down very thoroughly, while a Swiss woman in a blue security guard uniform did the same to Ling. Once they were satisfied, we were led to another elevator.

The security man once again swiped his badge and punched some numbers onto a keypad, calling the elevator, and indicated for us to step inside once it arrived. "This will take you directly to the correct floor. Someone will be there to meet you. Good day."

"Word," I said, stepping into the elevator. Ling rolled her eyes at me and thanked the man. The secure express elevator took us all the way up to the top floor.

"Tread carefully, Michael. By all accounts he is a charming and reasonable man, but one does not rise to the top of such a conspiracy unless possessing merciless cunning."

The elevator came to a stop with a soft, electronic ding and the doors slid open.

"This is it," I said to Ling. The room we found ourselves in was huge and well-lit, a luxurious foyer. Floor-to-ceiling windows along one wall gave us a spectacular view of Zurich. Ling's heels clicked on a marble floor as we made our way to yet another reception desk. Leather couches and wooden coffee tables, set upon an expensive-looking rug, made for a nice waiting area.

The woman behind this desk was expecting us, but before we reached her, a door off to the side opened, and a trio of men in suits approached. Two of them carried suppressed MP9 submachine guns, and my body tensed up. Ling put a hand on my arm, warning me to chill out.

The man leading the security detachment wasn't openly carrying a weapon. His suit jacket was unbuttoned, and he was a good bit shorter than his compatriots. He wore sunglasses indoors for some reason, but something about him seemed immediately . . . *familiar.*

It hit me like a ton of bricks a split second later when the bastard opened his stupid mouth.

"Well, well, well," Tailor said, taking off the shades. He'd lost some of his Tennessee twang and more of his hair, but there was no mistaking that lumpy, misshapen head. "I can't believe what I'm seeing. Michael Valentine, showing up here? You got a lot of balls, Val, I'll give you that."

"Tailor?" I hadn't seen him since after Exodus had snuck the survivors of Dead Six out of Zubara. We'd been friends for years, but our last parting hadn't been on the best of terms. I eyed the pair of armed goons flanking him, both of whom stood a head taller than him. This would have been awkward even without the hired muscle, but they weren't helping.

"And if it isn't the mysterious Miss Ling," he said, nodding at her. "I don't believe I ever thanked you for getting us out of Zubara."

"You most certainly did not," Ling said coldly. As with me, every muscle in her body was tense, though she tried to hide it.

"What in the hell are you doing here, Tailor?"

"That's it? Seriously? No 'hey, man, good to see you'? No 'I'm glad you're alive, buddy'? Just 'what are you doing here'? I work here, that's what. The question is, what are you doing here? I oughta have my boys here shoot your ass."

I shook my head slowly. "Then fucking do it. Get it over with. Any world where you can get a supervisory position is a world I don't want to live in." I looked at his men. "Trust me. He used to be my boss. Get out while you still can." I looked back at Tailor. "Get on with it."

His face twisted into a smile, and he started laughing. His men looked at each other awkwardly as he cackled. They looked outright confused when he stepped forward and hugged me, slapping me on the back. "Holy shit, Val! I can't believe you're here! Sorry, man, I was just fuckin' with you. Couldn't resist. How the hell are you?"

What an asshole. I looked down at his name badge. "Wilhelm Schneider? Really?"

"Yeah, well, I don't really pass for Swiss."

The whole thing was bewildering. "What . . . what in the hell are you doing here? How did you end up in Switzerland?" I looked at his two men again. "And what's with the mooks? No offense," I told them. "Mooking is honest work. Is it mooking? Mookery? Whatever. You know what I mean. I used to mook myself."

The security men scowled at me, but didn't say anything.

Tailor just shook his head. "You got a reputation around here, you know. You killed Rafael Montalban."

"Motherfucker, you were there, too!" I protested.

Tailor raised a hand to calm me before I got too riled up. "I know, I know. Just relax. Look, it's a long story. Believe me, it took me a long time to work my way to this position. You're going to see the big man in just a minute. He's been waiting for you. Later on, when we get time, I'll catch you up."

The receptionist at the desk looked over at us. "Mister Romefeller will see you now, Mr. Valentine." Her English was perfect. Way better than Tailor's.

I nodded at her, then looked back at Tailor. "I'm glad you made it okay."

"You too. Good luck in there." We shook hands and parted ways.

As we headed for the office door, Ling whispered in my ear, "Don't trust him."

"Of course not."

✣ ✣ ✣

Alastair Romefeller's office was palatial, to say the least, and huge. It took up the corner of the building, with floor-to-ceiling windows on two walls and a waterfall decoration on another. The fourth wall was lined with bookshelves and mementos of military service, including a UN officer's beret and a suit of medieval armor. An ornate wooden desk filled one corner.

Romefeller himself was standing by one of the windows, hands behind his back, looking out over the city. As Ling and I approached, he turned to face us, and we were looking at a very unassuming man. He was older, probably mid-sixties, with hair that had skipped gray and gone right to silver. Romefeller had probably been a very handsome man in his youth. He was thin but appeared fit, and wore a dark blue three-piece suit.

He stepped forward and shook my hand firmly. "Good to see you, Mr. Valentine," he said cordially. He gave Ling a much gentler handshake. "Ms. Song. Thank you both for coming." He had a hint of an accent that I couldn't quite place.

"Thank you for agreeing to meet with us," Ling said.

"It was an unusual enough request that it piqued my curiosity." He indicated the chairs in front of his desk. His attitude was confident, but not smug, like he understood he was important, but wasn't going to be a dick about it. "Please, have a seat. We have much to discuss."

The chairs were big and plush. Ling sat down, crossing her legs primly, and adjusted her fake glasses. I sat down next to her, feeling out of my element. Romefeller's desk looked as if it had been carved by hand. The engraving seemed innocuous from a distance, but upon closer inspection some of the imagery was odd, with things like all-seeing eyes above pyramids. It wasn't exactly subtle. Miniature flags of the United Nations and the European Union were mounted in a wooden holder on his desk.

"Drink?" He offered. Ling and I both politely declined. "I hope you are not offended if I have one." Romefeller produced took a bottle from his desk and poured himself a shot of golden liquor before sitting down in his gigantic leather chair. The floor had to be raised on that side, because even though I was taller than he was standing up, he now appeared to be looking down at us. That had to be some CEO psychological trick. It made his chair seem vaguely thronelike.

"This is unorthodox," he said, almost apologetically. "I don't normally agree to meetings with known members of a terrorist organization. It has, as you might say, poor optics. As such I greatly appreciate your discretion in this matter."

"Discretion is something we also value, Mr. Romefeller," Ling answered. "This is unorthodox for us is well."

I exhaled heavily. "Yes, yes, we're all very mysterious and secretive. Forgive me for being blunt, sir, but we have a serious problem on our hands."

"Oh? Do you now?"

"I said *we* have a problem, as in what's about to go down is going to ruin your day too. That's why we're here."

Ling looked at me like she was trying to kill me with her brain. Romefeller leaned back in his chair. The leather was so soft it didn't even creak. "I appreciate your candor, Mr. Valentine. I'm afraid I don't get enough of it these days. What is it I can do for you?"

"Are you familiar with a program called Project Blue?"

Romefeller's demeanor barely changed, but that had gotten his attention at least. "Vague rumors, that's all. It was some manner of plot against . . . let's call them European interests."

"You know who I used to work for, so let me clarify what I do know for you, Mr. Romefeller. Project Blue was originally concocted to be a master stroke against the Illuminati meant to disrupt their operations and remove their influence form the world. The groundwork was laid, but it was never intended to actually go forward, except in the gravest extreme."

He nodded slowly. Apparently that matched what he'd heard. "As I said. Rumors."

"Do you know what Katarina Montalban has been up to?"

Romefeller was quiet for a moment, processing what I had just asked him. Those two questions in a row were like asking *do you know where the matches went?* Followed with *by the way, how is our local arsonist?*

"Though I've not seen her recently, I know Katarina Montalban. You could call her a family friend."

"I didn't think that psychopaths had friends."

"Ah, so you're acquainted with Kat then." He was playing it cool. "This must be about the recent unpleasantness in Asia. I heard a bit about that, terrible business. I can see why Exodus would want to have a word with Ms. Montalban, but I'm unclear how that relates to me in any way."

"She has Blue."

At first he just shook his head and chuckled, like *silly terrorist, quit pulling my leg*. But then he slowly realized I wasn't lying, and as he thought through the implications of a crazy woman inheriting a shadow government plot to really fuck up his world, the cool demeanor cracked.

"Dear God. It's worse than we feared. Please tell me everything you know."

So I did. Ling and I spent the next twenty minutes or so explaining what little we actually knew. From the genesis of the project, to Hunter spilling the beans, to Gordon selling it to Big Eddie, and culminating with his little sister inheriting it and a whole bunch of baggage.

When I was done, Romefeller sat there in silence, his liquor untouched in front of him.

"Does the name Evangeline have any significance to you?"

"I'm afraid it doesn't mean anything to me," he said. "Why?"

"Evangeline was the last thing Colonel Hunter said to before he died. The name is related to Project Blue somehow. Even the men who authorized Blue didn't know how, and the only living person that helped set it up has defected. So they don't even know, but whoever Evangeline is, she was important enough to torture me for months trying to find out, so I was kind of hoping the name rang a bell."

"It's an extremely common name here. Without knowing details of their foul plot, who knows? Perhaps it was a code name for someone? Katarina Montalban, perhaps? Your former employers were quite fond of their code names and such."

"Evangeline is the key to this whole thing. At least, the people plotting your downfall seemed to think so."

"We know Project Blue could potentially kill millions," Ling said. "Perhaps it's some kind of attack, or a weapon of mass destruction. Everything we've gathered so far indicates it is a mass disruptive event. We need to know more."

"So your sources claim. May I assume, Mr. Valentine, Ms. Song, that this isn't merely some convoluted trick to sow dissent among my . . . business alliances? Or perhaps even an attempt to get me to take care of Exodus' problems for you? My understanding is that you are currently short staffed."

"That's a polite way to say that half of us died recently," Ling stated.

"I'm unfailingly polite. However, if I found out you were lying to me in the hopes that I'd remove Katarina Montalban on your behalf, I would be greatly offended, and the limits of my courtesy would be severely tested."

Romefeller had been a perfect gentleman, but I assumed when he got offended people got murdered. *Hell, why else would somebody hire Tailor?*

"Don't take our word for it. Perhaps a discrete look into Katarina's affairs would be in your best interests," Ling suggested.

"She is . . ." Romefeller tried to find the right word. "Erratic. If you had come to me with this outlandish story about anyone else, I would have dismissed it out of hand. But Katarina, even an allegation like this is plausible. Frighteningly so."

"Don't you have people that can police your own? It seems like you know full well how dangerous Katarina Montalban is. Why would you let her be a member of your secret club when she's a nut job?"

Romefeller scoffed. "Secret club?"

"Is this really the time to be coy?" I leaned forward and tapped one of the all-seeing eyeballs on his desk. "I know about the Illuminati, so does she, so do you. There's nothing to be gained from pretending otherwise."

"I assure you, Mr. Valentine, that you know *nothing*. We are merely a confederation of altruistic individuals dedicated to human progress and enlightenment. If anything, we have stood as a balance against the aggressive, militaristic, meddling of your nation's darker elements."

"You pull strings in secret."

"We organize and guide decision-makers, so that humanity can achieve its potential. Amongst members of my *club* there is an order, and there are rules."

"To hell with your rules. Big Eddie Montalban paid off Gordon Willis to have Dead Six murder his own brother, so he could take over. That sounds pretty dirty to me."

"Each family refrains from interfering in other families internal affairs, unless it threatens the security of all. Though loosely allied, each of us has our areas of interest, whether geographic, or pertaining to certain industries, and we do not meddle in each other's business."

"Turf."

"A crude way to put it. We merely manage events behind the scenes for the greater good of all. Do you really believe that a system so complex could survive without guidance? No. Society requires management, and that role had traditionally been quietly filled by the families. The Montalbans were once a respected family. Sadly, things went rather astray for them after Rafael's untimely death." He looked pointedly at me as he said that. "Perhaps if such a powerful family had remained under sound leadership, we wouldn't be having this predicament now."

My eyes narrowed. Sure, maybe if I'd not shot Rafael with a .44 and tossed him from a moving helicopter into the Persian Gulf with his hands tied, everything would be sunshine and happiness. "If you're fishing for an apology or something, you won't get one. I made the best decision I could with the information I had."

"There is no use dwelling on the past." Romefeller down his drink, and poured himself another. He offered drinks to us as well. I declined again, but Ling accepted this time and had a shot of brandy. After taking a sip, the billionaire was quiet for a few moments, and looked contemplative. "Rafael was a friend of mine, and a colleague of many years. We rarely saw eye-to-eye, and he would argue with me to the very end, but we were friends. I never thought I'd be sitting here sharing a drink with his killer."

"I never thought the Illuminati were real, and that I'd be explaining to them how the sister of a guy I killed is trying to burn the world down with a shadow-government plot." I shrugged. "It's been a weird day for all of us."

"Burn it?" Romefeller shook his head sadly. "Perhaps you do not know Katarina nearly as well as you think you do. Yes, she is destructive, but she is not suicidal, nor is she a nihilist. She was the unloved bastard child of a harsh, manipulative man, who spent her life trying to prove herself worthy of their family name, first to her father, and later to her brothers, the rightful heirs. Rafael humored her, and Eduard tormented her in what was rumored to be vile and despicable ways, yet she never quit. Deprived of her family name, she still rose through their organization using intelligence and cruelty, until now she is the last of the Montalbans. Someone who has risen above so much does not simply throw it all away out of spite. No, Katarina does not want to burn the world, she wants to rule it."

"But if Blue was designed to destroy your organization, that means Kat thinks you're what's in her way."

"A reasonable assumption." Romefeller was quiet for a long time. I could tell there was a lot going on in there, but he showed very little of it. He played the affable businessman really well, but beneath that he was something else entirely. "Mr. Valentine, I don't mean to pry, but I must ask . . . how did Rafael die? How did . . . how did it happen?"

"He didn't suffer, if that's what you're wondering. I pulled the trigger. He looked me in the eye. He didn't beg or plead. It was dignified." I kept it vague, because I didn't know what Tailor had told his new boss.

Romefeller seemed satisfied with that, and nodded. "Good, good. I respected Rafael, but his inability to keep his family under control has brought us nothing but trouble. His brother Eduard used you. He was . . . well, I needn't get into that. To say he was an embarrassment doesn't nearly go far enough."

Embarrassment, to describe Big Eddie? Romefeller was a master of understatement.

"Sir," Ling said, "we come to you with all of this in hopes that you understand our sincerity. Your organization and mine have clashed over the years, but right now we have a larger problem and a common enemy. We would not be coming to you with this if we could take care of it ourselves, or if we thought the normal authorities would stop her, and, to be blunt, she is one of your own."

"I do not jump to conclusions," he cautioned. "However, if you are correct, this has the potential to spiral out of control. Whatever else you may think of my associates, we are a force for order and stability. I will look into this."

"That's it?" I scoffed. "You'll look into it?"

Romefeller's expression grew stern. The cordial businessman was replaced with the kind of hardliner you'd expect to run an international conspiracy. "You've made assumptions about my people, yet not all of what you believe about us is incorrect. I assure you, Mr. Valentine, when the all-seeing eye turns its mighty gaze upon you, the results can be most *unpleasant.*"

Again with the understatement.

VALENTINE
Zurich, Switzerland
SEPTEMBER 10th

Tailor and I had a lot to discuss. I hadn't seen him since our escape from Zubara. I had been wounded and was recovering on a freighter that belonged to Exodus. Tailor and the other survivors of Dead Six decided to disembark in Mumbai, India, and dispersed from there. Tailor had been my best friend, like a brother to me, but we didn't part on good terms. Basically, he had wanted me to go with him and I—if not in so many words—told him to go fuck himself.

In my defense, the woman I loved had just been killed and I had a traumatic brain injury, so I hadn't been in the best state of mind. Years had passed since then, and I never imagined I'd see Tailor again. The survivors of Zubara were liabilities, and Majestic would kill any they found. So I figured he would be dead or in hiding. I certainly never expected to find him working for a European billionaire in Switzerland.

Both of us had been through a lot, it seemed, and I wanted to catch up. Not just because he was an old friend; Tailor was also security for a big shot whose help I needed. That's how I found myself in one of the nicest McDonald's restaurants I'd ever been in sitting across from Tailor.

Ling had gone back to the hotel, and Tailor had told his mooks he was taking a lunch break, so it was just the two of us. I thought about telling him that Skunky was with me—Jeff Long had been our sharpshooter on Switchblade 4—but I thought it better to keep that to myself. Right then I wasn't sure where Tailor's allegiances lay, and we could always have our Switchblade reunion later.

"Are you sure this is where you want to eat, Val?" he asked as we sat down. "You know I actually make good money now, right?"

I opened my box of McNuggets and peeled the lid off of a little tub of barbecue sauce. "I've missed good old American junk food. I don't get to eat out much, and the people who do the shopping where I'm staying like to eat healthy. I'm sick of it. If I have to suffer one more plate of kale and baked fish I'm going to flip the fuck out."

"Where are you staying?" Tailor asked, sipping a Dr. Pepper.

"Don't worry about it," I said, bluntly.

"Eat a bag of dicks. I wasn't gathering intel. I was going to say you could crash at my place while you're in town, asshole."

"What are you doing working for Alastair Romefeller?"

"What are you doing with Exodus?" He shot back.

Fair question.

"Isn't it obvious? They saved my life."

"What happened after we got off that boat?"

I didn't answer his question. "What happened to the others? Hudson and the other survivors, I mean."

"Everybody went their separate ways. We were stranded in India with no documentation and nothing but cash on hand."

"I don't want to say I told you so, but I told you so. I stayed on the boat for a reason."

"You stayed on the boat because you were being a mopey bitch."

I glared at Tailor. He just grinned at me. "What happened to Hudson, at least?" He was one of the original members of our four-man chalk in Zubara. We'd gone through a lot together.

"Last I heard he made it back home to Detroit, legally dead and living under an assumed name. He has cousins there or something, if I remember right."

Like everyone selected for Project Heartbreaker, Hudson had no immediate family. It made us easier to dispose of without anyone noticing. "Good. I'm glad. Detroit is a good place to disappear." Motor City hadn't been doing so well. I hadn't been there in years, but I'd heard half the city was abandoned and crime was sky high. A place like that wasn't a bad choice to hide when there were people looking for you.

I paused for a moment to chew my nuggets. I had to know the truth. "Tailor, level with me, man. How in the hell did you end up working for Alastair Romefeller? Zurich is a long way from India."

Tailor looked out the window and sighed. We were on the ground floor, and the street outside was lined with parked cars and bicycles. Pedestrians went about their business, walking, talking on phones, or going shopping. Zurich was a clean and beautiful city, a model of modern Europe.

"Remember the last time we had lunch like this?" he asked.

"Yeah. Ruth's Chris, Las Vegas."

"Do you remember what I told you about the real world? Look at those people out there, Val. They don't live in the real world. They live in their own little worlds, worried about phone reception and going on holiday or some stupid soccer match or whatever. I study medieval history, you know, as a hobby."

I interrupted. "You? Study? Really?"

"Shut up. Yeah, I study medieval history. Europe went from centuries and centuries of warfare, topped off by the two most destructive conflicts in human history, to decades of peace and prosperity. That didn't happen by accident. World War Two is what happened when the people I work for lost control and got sidelined. They're not some shadowy cabal secretly controlling the world. They're just people with the means, who got together to ensure peace. They make sure the right people, stable, reliable people, get into positions of political power. No more crazies, no Hitlers or Mussolinis. They do what they do so those people," he nodded at the pedestrians, "only have to worry about whatever stupid bullshit they worry about."

"That sounds exactly like a shadowy cabal secretly controlling the world," I pointed out. "Also, a lovely defense of fascism."

"Oh, fuck off." This time Tailor scowled, and I grinned. "It's not even like that, Val. We've both seen what happens when order breaks down, shit, we made a living off it. You think the world has to end up like Mexico? Or Africa? You see how nice this place is? This is what the world can be like if we let it."

I wasn't about to get into a political and economic debate with Tailor, but his last comment did cause me to raise an eyebrow. "Wow. You sound like a true believer. You've changed."

He smiled and shook his head. "I believe in the big-ass paycheck I get, and the nice flat in the city they provide for me."

"Flat? You're calling apartments flats now? Jesus, you've been Europeanized." It sounded all the more hilarious to me with Tailor's southern accent. "But you didn't answer my question; how did you end up working for the Illuminati?"

"That's a stupid fuckin' name for it," but Tailor looked thoughtful as he took a bite of his burger. Chewing gave him time to think of an answer that wouldn't sound like bullshit. "They found us in India.

They'd been keeping an eye on Zubara from the start, but after we killed Rafael Montalban they got real interested. It wasn't too hard for their intelligence guys to locate a bunch of bewildered Americans stranded in India. They offered us jobs, some of us took 'em up on it."

"So that's it? A job? What kind of job?"

"Like you have to ask." Like me, Tailor was good at one thing, and it wasn't the sort of thing you bragged about in a public place.

"So now you're all in, lecturing me about World War Two and world peace? I don't buy it. This isn't like you."

"How do you figure?"

"I told your boss, and I'm assuming he told you, about Katarina Montalban. The woman is a dangerous lunatic, and he's all, 'oh, we need more proof,' and 'hey, let's not jump to conclusions.' The Tailor I knew would tell his boss to let him go put a bullet in the bitch and be done with it."

"There are rules. These people have their own way of doing things. It keeps everything stable."

"See? This is what the hell I'm talking about. Since when does William Jefferson Tailor give a fuck about the rules, or stability?"

"Not so loud," he warned.

"What? Your real name? Oh, like it matters. The sheep around us aren't paying attention and you know it. This isn't like you at all. You know damned well how to solve this problem, and stop this Project Blue from happening. We need to find and kill Katarina Montalban. Problem solved, problem staying solved." I'd been warned that killing her wouldn't stop anything, but I didn't buy it. If we could get close enough to her to put her down, then we could track down the rest of the operation and interrupt it.

"It doesn't work like that!" Tailor snapped. A couple of nearby restaurant patrons looked up at us briefly, before returning to their meals. He exhaled heavily and lowered his voice. "Look, Val. These guys have their rules and their methods. A lot of it doesn't make sense to me, either, but they've been doing this for hundreds of years and they're pretty set in their ways. I'm not in a position to change the way things get done. I'm just the hired help."

"Bullshit. You're a fucking sellout."

"Fuck you. I have a pretty impressive résumé, you know. After

Rafael Montalban bought it, people like Romefeller started to get real worried about their personal security."

"You helped kill him!"

Okay, that had been a little too loud, and since most people around here understood English, several people looked our way.

Exasperated, Tailor put his face in his hands, shook his head, then put his hands flat on the table and tried again. "No shit, Sherlock. Who better to help him plug the holes than a guy who had been involved in that mess? He knew it wasn't personal. Besides, what else was I going to do? I'm sure as fuck not going back to East Knoxville, even if it was safe to return to the States, and we both know it's not. Hudson's living in a shack out of *Mad Max* to stay off the grid. I got a pretty good gig here. More than a gig, man. I've got a life."

I looked at him for a long moment. Tailor was totally sincere. "Holy shit . . . There's a woman, isn't there?"

"What does that have to do with anything?"

"It has everything to do with everything. You met someone and now you're all settled down. Domesticated. Housebroken!"

Tailor got even more defensive. "What's wrong with that? I'm over forty, Val. I've been all over the world and done all kinds of crazy shit, but I'm tired. I'm too old to be out there door-kicking, riding around in helicopters, and all that. Now I go home every night and Sophia makes me dinner. I sleep in a real bed, wear nice suits, and make six figures without having to roll around in the mud. Do you know how long it's been since I've stabbed somebody? Like fucking forever! That's a good life."

"Okay . . . how'd you meet her?"

He was still pissed at me, but you could tell he was proud because Tailor immediately took out his phone and showed me a picture. She was a really attractive blonde woman, younger than him by at least ten years, with her hair done up in a tight braid. "This is her. She works as a bartender in the Widder Bar, a few blocks from here."

"So you went out for a drink and one thing led to another, huh?"

"It helped that I grabbed a drunk asshole tourist who was harassing her and showed him the door. Tossed him out on his face, actually."

"Well, look at you, all civilized, big salary, nice apartment, and a pretty girl."

Tailor put his phone away. "You know, I told her about you, Val."

"What you'd say?"

"That I loved you like my brother, and that you'd saved my life a bunch of times, but I didn't know what happened to you, and I figured you were dead."

"Yeah . . . sorry, man."

"So you want to give me shit for getting respectable, kiss my ass. Like you know anything about respectable. Vanguard? Left us to die. Dead Six? Left us to die. I'm tired of being left to die, Val, and you should be too."

"I am. That's why I'm still with Exodus. I'm not really *with*-with them, but anyway. They came back for me, well, Ling did, at least."

"Sure," Tailor said, obviously not believing me about Exodus.

"No. Really. The assholes we worked for in Zubara, they had me in a secret prison, and Ling got me out."

"How'd you end up in prison?"

"Remember Gordon?" Of course he remembered Gordon. "Yeah, well, I kind of murdered him."

That made him grin. "Serves that fucker right." Now that was the Tailor I remembered. "Ha!"

I spent the next little while catching Tailor up, about my time in North Gap, and what had gone on since, though I kept the recent details fuzzy. I gave him shit about having a girlfriend, he would give me far more if he knew I had one too, not to mention, *oh yeah, I'm doing this because a teenage girl who can predict the future asked me to* would go over great.

Surprisingly enough, he tried to be comforting about what I'd gone through in North Gap. Of course, being Tailor, he sucked at it. "Man, Val, that's bullshit what happened to you, but you got through. That's what matters."

I realized then that I hadn't told him everything.

"Val, are you okay?"

"Hawk's dead, Tailor."

"What? How?"

"I think I gave him up under interrogation. They couldn't find me, so they went and got him instead. I called him to let him know I was okay, and they were waiting. He tried to fight back and they shot him, right there on the fucking phone."

Tailor's face started to turn red. Tailor had been nearly as tight with Hawk as I had been. "Who shot him?"

"Majestic. You know who."

"No, *who*. I want the name of the motherfucker that pulled the trigger."

"Underhill. He was an old guy named Underhill, and he's still after me."

"Oh, fuck . . ." Tailor glanced around, suddenly nervous. He leaned in and whispered, "No shit? Underhill? *The* Underhill?"

"You know him?"

"Of him. He's a fucking legend, Val. I'm talking old school, wild west days, Cold War, Phoenix Program, shit like that. The people I work for now are at odds with the people we worked for in the Zoob, so we keep tabs. I've seen a lot of intel about them since I've been here, and I've heard a lot of stories. Underhill is the unrelenting motherfucker they let off the chain when they absolutely, positively, need somebody caught. They call him the bloodhound, because when he finds your trail, you can't shake him. Everybody I work with thought he was retired. If they pulled him back, Majestic really wants you."

"It doesn't matter."

"Listen to me real careful, Val, I'm saying this as your friend, get out, and go someplace far, far away. Take Ling, she's really rocking that sexy librarian thing, whatever, but get the fuck out of Dodge. Because otherwise Underhill will find you, and you're dead meat."

Tailor really was worried about me. Regardless of his cushy job working for the bad guys, he was still my friend. "I can't do that, man. I've got to stop Blue first."

"Well, look," Tailor said. "I know the boss was pretty skeptical of what you had to say, but I was still told to give you whatever support you need. I've got people. I'm a pretty big deal in this outfit now, and the boss trusts me. We'll find the Montalban woman and end this, I can promise you that."

"And Underhill?"

Tailor had an evil glint in his eye. I'd seen that look before, it meant he was getting fired up. "There's a truce between my boss and Underhill's people. If he's operating in Europe without permission, he's breaking the rules. You can talk shit about the rules all you want, Val, but they're there for a reason. They keep wars from happening. If that Majestic son of a bitch comes here, I'll show him this is *my* house. Now finish your fucking nuggets so I can get back to work."

It was good to have Tailor back.

Chapter 7: La Ville Lumière

LORENZO
Paris, France
September 10th

Things had gotten tough in Paris since the last time I'd been here. There had been several nasty terrorist incidents recently and sporadic rioting. I'd never seen so many armed cops on the streets in a European city before. There were four-man military patrols, complete with rifles and armor, wherever large numbers of people congregated. Some of the immigrant neighborhoods were no-go zones, and the *gendarmes* didn't enter them unless it was in large numbers. If they did arrest somebody inside there was a good chance the incident would turn into a full-blown riot.

Personally, I think the French get a bad rap. I've worked with way too many tough, sensible, pragmatic Frenchmen to disrespect the culture. From my outsider's perspective, their problem was similar to my home country, in that people with a clue how the world worked were outnumbered by easily manipulated wishful thinkers with their heads up their asses. But it was still pretty damn sobering, driving through some immigrant neighborhoods and seeing flags I recognized as belonging to terrorist factions being openly flown. I'd never expected to see that in a place like this.

Being in a hole for a year and a half had put me behind on current events. I'd read a few newspapers on my trip, but as usual the news coverage was naïve garbage written by twenty-something journalism grads who never ventured outside of Manhattan, making stupid assumptions about how the world worked. The way I saw it, the fall of Zubara had been the beginning of a chaos avalanche, and many parts of the Middle East were eating themselves. That led to lots of refugees, who the kindhearted first-worlders naturally wanted to take in. Unfortunately, among those masses were the parasitical scumbags the refugees were running from in the first place. To the psychos, refugees were just a delivery vehicle to hide in so they could start trouble in vulnerable new locations.

So the countries taking in the refugees got fucked, the refugees got double fucked, and the fanatics had a field day. Some countries went soft on them, which just made them look weak. Trust me, I made my career off of conning and robbing terrorist organizations. You can't reason with people who think they're righteous conquerors and Western civilization is a minor stumbling block. On the other hand, when a country goes too harsh, out comes the big brush and they start pushing in the wrong direction, it pisses people off and increases recruiting. Rooting out fanatical assholes requires a fine touch . . . and governments' fine touch is more like Captain Hook, Proctologist.

One street I drove past was covered in trash, debris, and a few stores that were ashen wrecks. It was clear what had gone down here; I'd seen a lot of riots in my day. You can't make a career out of profiting off the collapse of society without being around for some. Rich country, poor country, it didn't matter. Everybody had some disaffected, angry bunch ready to blow up. When you are a professional thief, riots make for a fantastic diversion. In the western world they usually handled things with kid gloves and let the assholes burn things until they tired themselves out, but in the third world, they just machine-gunned the troublemakers and got on with life.

Strangely enough, from looking at the bitter cops, annoyed soldiers, and tired locals, the normally civilized, law-and-order types were getting mighty sick of the state of things. You could almost sense it in the air. They had tried to help by opening their doors to people in need, and got smacked in the face for it. You know things were getting bad when a major European capitol city gives the same bad vibe as Zubara did.

Paris felt *tense*.

The address Jill had given Ling was next to an old industrial park on the west side of the city, in the surrounding department of Hauts-de-Seine. She'd picked an area far from the nice, shiny, business and tourist parts of town. The majority of the factories here were closed down, and judging from the nearly empty parking lots, those that *were* still making things were running at less than capacity. Even then it was nicer than some of the other communes I'd passed through to get here. At least there weren't any burned-out cars abandoned on the sides of the road in this neighborhood.

I parked on the back side of the old tenements, in one of the few spaces that wasn't covered in broken glass. The apartments were old and shabby. The asphalt was cracked and weeds were growing through it. Some young men were sitting on some nearby planters. They were the unemployed, disaffected, bored types. When they glanced my way, seeing if I looked like an easy victim, I gave them my best *don't fuck with me* look and they were smart enough to realize I wouldn't be worth their time.

Inside, the apartment building was even sleazier. There were junkies hanging around and winos sleeping in the corners. Somebody on this floor was playing really loud rap music. The elevator was out of order, so I took the stairs to the fifth floor, found the right room number, and after the briefest hesitation, knocked on the door.

This was awkward. It felt like I should have brought flowers or something. I was really excited, happy, but nervous. It was hard to explain. While I waited, I realized that a very discrete camera had been installed at the end of the hall. The peephole was already dark, so I never saw when she looked through it. From the sound of metal being moved on the other side, the door had been reinforced. Apparently Jill had been paying attention all those times I had lectured her about how to survive in this lifestyle.

The door opened. She'd changed her appearance. Her hair was shorter, and dyed lighter. She'd put on a little stress weight, and looked tired. But it was Jill. *My* Jill.

I could still read her expression like I'd never been away. It was a mixture of joy, disbelief, relief, and a little bit of bitterness.

Without a word, she stepped out of the way so I could come inside. While she closed the door and put down a heavy security bar, I looked around. Unlike the rest of the building, her tiny apartment was clean, orderly, and there was a half-assembled bomb on the table. There was a tablet next to the Semtex, with the screen showing feeds from four different camera angles around the block. I'd only spotted the one.

"I missed you," she whispered.

I stretched out one hand for her, but she moved away, just the tiniest bit. But then she realized what she'd done and froze there. I stayed where I was. She'd thought I was dead. Jill had gotten on with her life. I couldn't imagine what she'd been through, and she had no comprehension of what I'd been through, and I wanted to keep it that way. Tentatively, she reached out and touched my cheek, as if testing that I was real.

"Sorry I didn't call." It was a remarkably lame thing for me to say right then, but then we were pulling each other's clothes off, so words didn't really matter.

Later, the two of us lay in bed, listening to distant sirens through the open window, content to enjoy the human contact. Jill's head was resting on my shoulder. It felt good to be alive. I had told her a little about the prison, but I'd glossed over or left out most of it, especially the parts I wasn't sure had been real.

Jill ran her fingertips across the bandage on my chest. "What happened here?"

"Nothing. It'll be just another scar."

She'd seen the newer puckered bullet holes and fading knife lines, but she sensed this one was different. "You already had a ton of those when we met. What makes this one nothing special?"

"Sala Jihan burned me with a branding iron. Like a parting gift."

"So you'd remember him?"

"More like a warning to never come back."

Jill gently traced the edge of the bandage with her fingertip. "Would you go back?"

Normally I liked to finish what I started, but I was never going back to that place, no matter how much that evil son of a bitch deserved to die. "I'm never leaving you again."

There was a lot of bitterness in Jill's laugh. "Liar."

That was fair. "No, I . . . I mean it. I just want to forget that place ever existed. I just want to be done." I turned my head enough so I could look into her eyes. "I swear to you."

"What about this thing you've got to do?"

She had me there. "Well, there is that."

"That's why you didn't try to contact me." She shifted slightly against me as she said it. It was remarkable how you could be this close to someone, yet distant at the same time.

"Listen, Jill, I had to do some horrible things in that prison." How do you explain what it was like, putting a knife in some other poor unlucky bastard, just so you could maybe live one more day? Fighting for a warlord's amusement, again and again, losing track of the lives you take as the days bleed into months in the perpetually whispering darkness. You can't make someone understand what that's like, and that was my problem.

"I don't care what you had to do."

"The only way I could survive was to go back to being the man I was before I met you. When I got out, it was easier to stay that way."

"What was it Carl called it? Monster mode?"

"Heh . . . Yeah. Carl had a funny way of putting things." Only Carl hadn't been joking. I could never admit it to her, but part of me enjoyed being that way. Offing Diego and Varga's men? I'd enjoyed that. Living with a complete disregard for dying was why I'd been the best. It was a cruel addiction. My foster father had seen that in me, and he'd done his best to steer me away from it, but ultimately failed. Jill had gotten me to live in peace for a time, but that had been nothing but a brief illusion. It turned out the evil was always there, eager to be used. "It isn't the kind of thing you can just turn off and on, Jill. I didn't ever want you to see that side of me."

"I saw how you were in Zubara and Quagmire. Give me some credit. I don't care."

Jill was right, but knowing that and admitting it were two different things. She'd blundered into this world as a poor innocent victim, wrong place at the wrong time, but she'd risen to the occasion. She'd kicked ass, taken names, and was probably as stubborn as I was. But most importantly, she'd seen me at my worst, but still stuck around. We were a team, and I was an idiot to throw that away.

"I know."

"Running from me still hurt, Lorenzo."

I squeezed her tight and kissed her forehead. "I had to do something first, and I wanted to keep you safe."

"Killing Katarina."

"The same reason you're in Paris, apparently." We'd got the fun part of the reunion out of the way, so now we were getting into the messy, emotional, accusatory parts. I'd always sucked at that those. "Stalking the head of an organized crime family? She's a billionaire, and probably one of the most powerful women in Europe now. What the hell are you thinking, Jill?"

She had an endearing smirk. "You weren't around to stop her. Nobody else would. I thought she was responsible for your death. What did you expect me to do?"

"Take the vast sums of money I've squirreled away, go somewhere safe, and have a long and happy life."

"That was my plan. Right after I killed that bitch," Jill muttered. "What? You think you're the only person who ever dreamed about getting revenge on the people who've screwed you? I guess you rubbed off on me, Lorenzo."

"Damn right I did."

"Jackass." She laughed. Most couples, lying there naked, probably weren't contemplating murder, but we were weird like that. It worked for us. "You know what I mean. She had to be stopped. Period. Exodus was toast. The government still wants me dead. Who was I supposed to get to help? Either I had to do it, or nobody would."

I'd never seen this side of her before. Jill had always been tough, but I'd fallen for her because of her tender side. Now she sounded like me. "Really? You were going to take down Kat by yourself."

"Reaper's helping, sort of."

"Well, that's something. How is he?"

"Not good. I think he took your death worse than I did. I don't know if it's PTSD, or what, but he won't talk about it much. Me? I got drunk a bunch and wallowed in self-pity for about a month, but then I decided to focus on getting even."

I stroked her hair. "I've always been a fan of the healing power of murderous revenge."

"But Reaper, he saw something at that missile silo. I don't know what, but it shook him. I kind of dragged him into this last year, to keep tabs on Majestic and Kat's people. I needed his help, but more than that, I knew he needed something to work on."

"Good." It was kind of hard to imagine a purposeless Reaper. He was like this hyperactive ball of fixation. A Reaper without direction was scary.

"I was—I'm still—worried about him. You'll see for yourself. He should be here soon."

"Did you tell him about me yet?"

"Unsecure line," she explained, though she was probably lying. Reaper was too paranoid to talk to anybody over a regular phone call. She probably just wanted me to have to explain to my best friend why I'd not bothered to tell him I was still alive as soon as I could.

"Jill and Reaper versus the world . . ." The least experienced members of my old crew, up against some of the best professional killers I've ever known. It was amazing they were still alive at all. "How far were you willing to go?"

She mulled that over for several seconds. "Far enough . . . Look, I don't want to talk about it right now."

I was too naked and comfortable to want to fight. So I dropped it.

She was silent for a moment, like she was trying to think of how to phrase something difficult. "I was with the Exodus people afterwards, while we were escaping through Mongolia. Ling gave me a number to contact her. I think she was trying to recruit me."

"I kind of thought you might have joined up." They were a bunch of self-righteous busybodies, trying to make the world a better place. Typical, except unlike most idealists, they were actually willing to get dirty. I could see that kind of idealism appealing to her. She had a good streak a mile wide.

"I kept in touch with Ling, but I'd never join Exodus. I blamed them for your death too. The Exodus survivors told me you could have left them behind and made it out by yourself, but you stuck around, taking turns carrying the wounded. Roland, Svetlana, they all said the same thing. They all would have died otherwise. You stayed behind to delay the brothers to save their lives, even though you knew you'd get caught."

"Something like that."

"Ling and Valentine let me think you'd died."

She didn't understand right now, but they'd been doing her a favor. "There wasn't anything anyone could have done for me."

"They said you were a hero, and it wasn't just to make me feel better. They believed it. *Lorenzo died a hero.*" She gave me a sad little laugh. "I bet you never thought you'd hear anybody say that. But I didn't see it that way at first. It just made me mad at you."

"At first?"

Jill snorted. "I thought you were gone, Lorenzo. How was I supposed to feel? I know it sounds selfish, and they were just trying to comfort me, but . . ." she trailed off. "I don't know."

"I understand."

"You always talked a big game about looking out for number one, being the merciless hard-ass thief, get the job done and get out, all that. From the day I met you, that was how you acted, how you saw yourself, so I thought I'd been rescued and given shelter by a selfish, greedy, self-centered asshole."

"Man's got to keep up his rep." I'd gone down some dark paths and done some things I wasn't proud of. Hell, I'd done some unforgivable, horrible things that I could never atone for, but saving someone as good as Jill from someone as evil as Adar al Saud must have made some sort of dent in my karmic debt.

"Past all that swagger, I saw how much you loved Carl and Reaper, and you were there to try and save family you barely even knew. Then in Quagmire, you risked everything for me. That's the man I fell in love with."

"Sucker."

"Don't be an asshole. I'm trying to have an honest sharing relationship moment here. So yeah, I was mad at you for dying in the Crossroads, but then I thought about it. You gave up your life to save people. How could I hate you for doing what I fell in love with you for to begin with?"

As I'd lain in that crashed bomber, incoherent and bleeding out, with soldiers closing in on me, I'd heard the ghost of my foster father, congratulating me for being the good guy for once. All in all, it hadn't been a bad way to die. Any goodness I had, it was only because I was trying for her sake.

An hour later, showered, dressed, and happier to be alive than I had been in a very long time, Jill walked me through what she'd been up to.

I hated to admit it, but other than being stressed out and trying not to show it, Jill had been doing a pretty damned good job without me. She'd shown a real knack for shady business back in Zubara where I'd taught her some rudimentary fieldcraft. Then in the Crossroads, she'd done extremely well, and if we'd been trying to pull a con on anyone other than the Devil himself, it would have worked. Jill had taken to heart everything I'd ever taught her, and then kept on learning while she'd devoted herself to ridding the world of Montalbans.

I was impressed. On her own Jill had gotten ahold of some illegal guns, surveillance equipment, and quality fake IDs. She had clothing and props to pull off several different roles, from bland work clothes, to outfits that screamed tourist, to a slinky party dress that I was afraid to ask about. She'd been gathering intel on Kat's people for months, and was still alive.

"I've planted cameras around the block, and I've got some of the local drug lookouts double dipping. They're watching the block anyway. I slip them some Euros every week, and they call this burner phone if they see anything out of the ordinary. If I see anything that smells like Kat, I've got three escape routes."

"I saw two on the way in."

"I figured so would Kat's men," she answered with just a bit of pride. "But I rolled a rope ladder down the out of service elevator shaft, and I made a copy of the keys to the electrical service tunnels in the basement."

"Nice. Other hideouts?"

"Two. I bounce between them using a couple different vehicles."

"How's your French?"

"*Pas tres bien*," she said. *Not very good.* "The fake IDs Reaper prepped say I'm from Barcelona." That was a good call. Jill was American, with a Mexican father and a Filipina mother, but she was good at tweaking her accent to sound like a Spaniard. "Or I wear a hijab and pretend not to understand French at all. Lots of service workers in Paris are Muslims. Either way I mostly avoid talking to people. Usually I eavesdrop, record them on my phone, and piece it all together later. The rest of us can't do your language tricks."

"If crime didn't pay so well, I could have been one hell of a voice actor. Got anything to eat?" I checked the tiny fridge. There was food, but sadly, it was all bland, packaged garbage. I'd always been the cook in our relationship. There was a little .32 automatic hidden in the egg carton. "Cute. Want something?"

"Sure." Jill sat down at the table. "You need to eat more. You look terrible."

She should have seen me when I had first gotten out. I had been practically stuffing my face over the last few weeks and had started exercising hard again. I hadn't exercised much in prison. You don't have enough calories to spare for training when you were living off of watery gruel. "Well, you look amazing."

"It must be because you've been blind for a year, because I look like crap right now."

Women got hung up on the stupidest things. Sure, hard living wears you down, but she was still gorgeous. I found some white bread, crappy lunch meat, boring American style mustard—French's, ironically—and processed cheese slices wrapped in plastic. "This is barbaric. Who comes to the culinary capitol of the world and buys plastic cheese?" I sat down across from her and started making sandwiches.

"I've been busy." Jill pushed the tablet across from me. It was a map of the city and its surroundings. "Six weeks ago I followed Katarina here from London. The red dots are places she or Anders have shown their faces. I've got dates and times for each one, but no discernible pattern yet. She doesn't even sleep in the same place more than a few nights in a row, and judging by the times she's been seen and the distances between them, either she can get through traffic like a champ, or I've got a suspicion she's hired body doubles."

Kat had the resources, skills, and mindset to be a hard target. She knew how to be a ghost. Sadly, she'd learned from the best. Despite that, there were still quite a few dots on Jill's map. "Did you get these yourself?"

"In person? No way. Don't worry. I'm angry, not suicidal. Mostly, she stays out of sight and runs her business by phone or proxy. When she does go somewhere, it's never without a convoy of armored cars filled with armed mercenaries. Since you talked Anders up like he's got eyes in the back of his head, I've been too worried he'd make me to ever try following him. These are mostly from snitches and Reaper stealing security video. The problem is, by the time we pin her down that way, she's already moved. I started putting together dossiers of her security people and coffee-fetchers. I've got a lot of names, but since she pays really well, they're not super talkative."

I finished making a sad little sandwich and passed her the plate. "What was your next move?"

"Use one of her employees to figure out where Kat is going to be, get there first, and leave this for her." Jill nodded at the bomb she'd been putting together.

She said it so matter of factly that it took me a second to have that sink in. Jill really had changed. "Just like that?"

"As opposed to what else? It seemed easier than getting into a gunfight with a bunch of hired muscle, a former Navy SEAL, and their boss, the professional assassin, by myself." She gave me a look, like she was daring me to continue.

"I think Exodus will back us up now. There aren't many of them, but Valentine brought a few friends."

"I don't know. I'm still pissed at him for lying to me."

That wasn't fair. Valentine had only been trying to protect her from Sala Jihan . . . But I wasn't going to argue with my woman to defend the asshole who'd shot me and wrecked my hearing. I wandered over to study what she'd been working on.

The bomb was pretty straightforward. Two blocks of Semtex with a commercial blasting cap. The cap was wired to a cheap cell phone, and there was a spot for a nine-volt battery. The phone wouldn't have enough juice to set off the cap, that was what the battery was for. The ringing would close the switch, causing electricity to flow from the battery to the cap. Removing the battery would render it safe, and also keep a stray cell call from blowing her up. The Semtex was wrapped in duct tape. A second layer of tape was stuck with hundreds of nails to serve as frag. It wasn't a complicated device, but it was meant to blow up Kat, not befuddle a bomb squad. Reaper must have been tutoring her.

There wasn't much of an explosive payload there, but still, it was dangerous as hell. "And what if the next place she's going to be is next to a daycare or a school?"

"Or a teddy bear hospital? Really, Lorenzo? You're going to try and play the morality card with me? If there were innocents who might get hurt, I'd wait and try again later."

"Don't get defensive. I'm just asking."

"Why? You afraid I'm turning into Kat? You think I'd just wipe out anybody who got in the way?" Jill seemed really agitated on this point.

"Bombs can be sloppy. That's all I'm saying. They're really easy to hurt the wrong people with."

"If there was any chance of that, I'd back off. You know I would."

"I know." Despite having to do some terrible things to survive, and proving way harder than she appeared, Jill had always retained a gentleness in her soul. Relatively speaking, obviously, since we were arguing about her homemade bomb. I couldn't see it just now, but I figured that gentleness was still there. Well, I hoped it was, because Jill wouldn't be Jill anymore without it. "If there's even a chance of collateral damage—"

"Of course," she snapped. "That's how Kat got away in London. I had her. I found out about a meeting, I snuck in early and hid a bomb in a planter. When Kat showed up I was down the street with a cell phone. She sat at a table like ten feet away. All I had to do was make a call, and poof, she was gone . . ." Jill trailed off, staring into space. "I was *so* damned close."

"What happened?"

"Nothing. Other people showed up. I bailed. That's it . . ." She was remarkably stone-faced as she talked about it, acting like the idea of premeditated murder was no big deal. I'd seen that act a lot in this business, *fake it until you make it.* "See? No reason to worry about me."

I'd never seen Jill this haunted before. "How long have you been at this?"

"Almost the whole time you've been gone. I started almost as soon as Exodus got us out of Mongolia. I've tracked her from city to city ever since. It's sucked. She's got a lot of rivals, so she's nervous as hell. She's also got a lot of powerful friends. When they get skittish, and find out somebody has been looking into them, they send people. So I run, and work other leads while I hide, and then come back and try again."

No wonder she was fried. "I can't believe you've been dodging Montalbans for over a year."

Her expression softened. "Why? Were you worried that when I got over crying for you I'd gotten back on the dating scene?"

That made me smile. "There hasn't been a man who has ever been incarcerated in history who hasn't wondered what his woman was doing without him around."

Now Jill grinned. "Don't forget, I was hanging out with Exodus for part of that. Have you seen Zach Roland with his shirt off? That dude is chiseled." I must have scowled, because Jill laughed at me. "Okay, I'll be honest. You got me. In my time of grief I was so vulnerable that I messed around with *Valentine.*"

"Now you're just being cruel."

"Relax, Lorenzo, I'm kidding. No. I've been a little too focused. The closest I've come to getting any action is dressing up like a call girl to spy on a Montalban party."

"How was that?"

"Lots of techno music and the overpowering stench of cologne." Jill tapped the tablet screen and brought up folders of pictures and documents. "I've not accomplished much recently, but that's because they've been extra jumpy for the last week. Apparently somebody has been offing Montalban employees across Europe." She gave me a very pointed look at that. "Between me on the ground and Reaper being Reaper, we've got a ton of information on their operation. I've been limited on what I could do with it though. Now that you're here, and if Exodus is helping, then we've got a lot more options."

I knew it was doubtful. "Any sign of Bob?"

"Nada. I'm sorry, but I gave up on the idea of him still being alive about the same time I gave up on you."

"Never count a Lorenzo out. Anders wants him alive for some reason. Bob's supposed to be the fall guy for Project Blue, whatever that is."

It was obvious that Jill thought Bob surviving was wishful thinking on my part, but she let me keep my comforting delusions. "Blue, huh?" Jill tapped on another folder. It was titled *Crazy Town*. She opened up a Word document. "Reaper's been doing a lot of digging on that, nothing concrete of course, considering it was top secret and most of the planners are dead, but he's come up with some theories. Get ready for some fun reading. I mean like Sea to Shining Sea AM talk radio stuff."

After the things I'd seen over the last few years, it was getting harder and harder to make fun of Reaper's crazy conspiracy theories. "Please tell me he isn't wearing a tinfoil hat and living in a single-wide trailer out in the desert yet?"

"Not quite, but the sad thing is I've started to believe him."

A couple of days ago I'd had a conversation with a man I'd sprung from a secret government black site about the secret war between Majestic and the Illuminati. My life was a conspiracy theory.

"Screw it. Let me catch up on your intel, and we'll go from there."

"About that . . ." Jill trailed off as she studied me.

"Yeah." I pushed the tablet away. As interesting as Reaper's strolls through crazy town could be, there was some stuff we needed to get out in the open first. "Normally now would be the part where you'd urge me to let it go."

"And the part where you'd worry about me too much, and try to shuffle me off to somewhere safe," Jill stated flatly.

"I'm still just a man. I'd be lying if I said I wanted you anywhere near this mess." I thought about what the Pale Man had told me before we'd cut our deal, friend or foe, death followed wherever I went, and I wanted her to be safe.

But I also really didn't want to be alone anymore.

"This isn't the life you chose, Jill."

"But it's the one I wound up with when I decided to stick with you."

The truth hurts. "Which is why I'm saying this now. They know about Saint Carl, so we can't ever go back there, but I've got plenty of money stashed around the world, enough to live long, boring lives away from all these nut jobs and their plots. We let it go. Kat can be Exodus' problem. Valentine can figure out whatever the hell Blue is without us. We can walk away. There's nothing stopping us."

She was quiet for a long time, deep in thought. She flicked the edge of her plastic cheese with one finger. There wasn't much point to a revenge mission, when the man you were trying to avenge turned out to be alive and sitting there with you.

"What about your brother?"

I had no answer for her.

Jill pushed away her uneaten sandwich. She'd already come to the same conclusion I had and lost her appetite. "You said Varga told you that Blue would kill millions. Could you just let that happen, Lorenzo? Sipping margaritas on another private island, knowing we could have stopped it, but didn't?"

I shook my head. "Not really."

That was actually a pretty profound realization for me. Jill really had been a bad influence.

"Then that's settled. We're committed. I don't think either of us is the kind of person who can do anything half way." Jill gave me that sad little smile again. "I know why you avoided me. You were prepared to do some horrible things to see this though. It's hard to let someone you love see you like that. Believe me, I understand that better than you think."

"I can't let Kat win. That means doing *whatever* it takes."

"I know." Jill reached across the table and held my hand. "Then we'll do it together."

She didn't understand that the hard part wasn't going down that road. It was coming back.

Reaper stood there in Jill's apartment, mouth hanging open.

"Hey, Reaper," I said again.

"Dude . . ." He'd already said that a few times, like it was the only word his brain could process. "Dude!"

Jill closed the door behind him. "Surprise."

"I'm back. I got out."

"Dude." Reaper was blinking rapidly. He was looking a little weak in the knees. He'd gone whiter than usual, and that was saying something. It was like he'd seen a ghost. "Lorenzo?" Articulating my name was good progress.

"Yeah, Reaper. It's me."

He cocked his head to the side, studying me carefully. This wasn't just surprise. It was like he didn't believe me, like this was a con. "But are you still you?" What the hell that was supposed to mean?

"I'm alive. I'm here. I'm me."

That must have finally registered, because Reaper came over and gave me a hug. "Lorenzo! Holy shit, man!" Reaper was holding me so tight that I flinched when he hit the burn on my chest. The kid actually started to sob, but then I realized that wasn't fair. He wasn't a kid anymore. He was a man who'd been through some awful shit. "I thought the Pale Man got you."

"He caught me, but he couldn't kill me." I patted his back awkwardly. Reaper was nothing but skin and bones. *Damn.* He was even skinnier than I remembered. He was in worse condition than I was. We broke apart and I led him toward the kitchen table. "Hey, come on, sit down."

Reaper wasn't in good shape. He never had been, but now he was looking downright ragged, and it wasn't from the sudden emotion of seeing me in one piece. He'd never been one to get out much, living off of Red Bull and junk food in front of his wall of computer screens, but his complexion was worse. I was used to Reaper often having dark circles under his eyes, but those had been his weird goth makeup style when he'd gone out. These dark circles now were from insomnia. It was obvious he'd not been eating or sleeping well. When he sat down, he rested his hands on the table in front of him, and there was an unconscious nervous tremor in his fingers.

"Dude, Lorenzo, shit . . . Man. What the fuck?" The poor guy was bewildered. "I tried. I tried to find out what happened to you, but my world, my world is like, you know, *electrons*, and the Pale Man . . . It's like the stone age there. I can't. I couldn't get in. It's like a different time. Different world, man." Reaper leaned toward me, eyes wide. "He's *outside*."

I looked to Jill. She grimaced and nodded. This was what she'd been warning me about. She went over to the little fridge, got out two cans of beer and put them on the table for us. "You boys catch up. I've got to go check with one of my snitches downstairs to make sure nobody new has been poking around the block. I'll be back in a bit."

After Jill left, I got right down to business. I'd known Reaper way too long to mess around. "Damn, man. What happened to you? You look like I do, but I was in a dungeon, so I've got an excuse. Are you on meth?"

"Of course not! You know I don't mess with that shit. No drugs. No pills, man. I knew I was messed up from . . ." He trailed off, not sure what to say. "I tried to get help after the Crossroads. The shrinks all gave me prescriptions, Zoloft, Paxil, Lexapro, but I chucked them in the trash." He tapped the side of his head. "Pills slowed me down. No time for that."

Reaper had a super genius level IQ, and apparently when the wires got crossed in a brain like that it wasn't pretty. I shoved one of the beers toward him and opened the other. "It's just, you look like—"

"I know. I know. I'm frazzled, man. I don't sleep so good anymore."

"How come?"

"Bad dreams." Reaper grinned at me. It was a kind of crazy grin. "But you're back, so it'll be cool. Everything is cool now. You know what I'm saying? You being alive puts it right! But . . . But I just gotta know, when you were in there with those cavemen, did you see anything . . . *weird*?" He looked strangely hopeful.

"What do you mean by weird?"

"I don't know. I can't explain it." Reaper looked really uncomfortable, and his lip began to tremble as badly as his fingers. "I saw some things on the drone camera, from the silo, but there's no record. We lost Little Bird's recordings when we ran. Ever since then, I don't know if I imagined it, or I'm just going crazy, but I still see them in my nightmares. What happened to those Exodus guys around the Pale Man's silo."

I remembered our mad escape across the canyon, pursued by Jihan's soldiers. During that, whatever Reaper had seen on those cameras had truly freaked him out. The Exodus commander Fajkus had been the only other surviving witness from the missile silo. Even though the Czech was an extremely experienced combat veteran, whatever he'd seen there had screwed with his head too.

I thought about how to proceed. It wasn't just that I needed Reaper in one piece, but whatever he thought he saw, it was slowly killing him. "I didn't see anything while I was there."

He appeared absolutely dejected when I said that. "You know, Lorenzo, when I do sleep, which isn't much, it's with the lights on. I can't even go to a strip club because I'm too scared of the dark. That sucks."

Back in Varga's old club, for just a moment, I thought I'd seen the Pale Man watching, and it had been enough to paralyze me with fear. I understood what he was going through, I just dealt with it differently. As much as I'd tried to compartmentalize and forget it, I had to tell him the truth. "I said I didn't see anything. They kept me in the dark. But, I *heard* things."

"Like what?"

"Things that weren't there, couldn't be there."

Reaper was suddenly curious and strangely hopeful. "And?"

"I'm only going to talk about this once, and then I'm never going to say it again. Jill doesn't need to know what I went through. No one else does, because that shit can stay in the Crossroads where it belongs. Yeah, Reaper, I heard things in the walls, in the floor, in my head, things that couldn't be. There were voices, whispers, even when there weren't people there, and maybe things that weren't people. It never stopped. I could feel it, just burning little holes in my sanity. Like fire ants in my head." Surprisingly, it felt good to tell someone about this.

"But you didn't lose!" Reaper exclaimed. "You never lose, Lorenzo."

"Hell no. I knew that place wanted me to go crazy, to give up, to fall apart. I saw what it did to the other prisoners, it strips away who you are and leaves nothing but an animal behind. You remember Precious?"

"Eddie's dog you shot?"

"Yeah. I used to wake up because something in my cell was growling at me. I just knew it was that fucking poodle. I could feel it there, but I wouldn't reach out to touch it, because I was afraid of what I'd actually feel. I knew it wasn't going to be soft and fluffy, you get what I mean?"

Reaper nodded vigorously.

"It was too dark to see most of the time. I guess I was lucky for that. Was it haunted? Something else? Hell if I know, but it wasn't *right*. Whatever you saw come out of that silo, wasn't *right*."

"So I'm not crazy?" Reaper asked with complete sincerity.

I shook my head. "No. You're not. It was a bad op in a bad place, and we messed with something that we shouldn't have. Some of us caught a piece of it. The rest were lucky. Let them stay that way."

"I knew it." He slammed one skinny fist down on the table hard enough to knock over his beer. Reaper's whole body had begun to shake. Relief, exhaustion, beats me. I bet the psychology types would call it *catharsis*. I let him have his moment. This emotional stuff was more Jill's area, but I could tell he needed it.

"You okay?"

"I couldn't tell anybody else, Lorenzo, you know, because they'd think I was nuts. I tried to talk to Fajkus in Mongolia. Only he wouldn't talk about it. He lied and said he couldn't remember what happened at the silo."

"He didn't want to remember. Big difference."

Reaper wiped his eyes with the back of his hand. "Last I heard, Fajkus left Exodus to become some kind of priest."

"You could have tried that. Father Reaper has a ring to it." We both laughed at the absurdity of the idea.

"Dude, I'm a stallion that needs to roam free." Reaper gestured at his skinny, geeky self. "You can't cage this."

"No kidding. Who is going to put all those strippers' kids through college? Look man, whoever, *whatever*, Sala Jihan is, it doesn't matter now, because we're done there. You understand me, Reaper? That's in the past. That world? We never have to go back. I know it and you know, and it dies with us, because nobody else needs that burden. This world?" I gestured around the ratty little French apartment. "This world is real, and we can still make a difference in it."

"Since when do *you* give a shit about the world?"

"Maybe I'm just tired of sharing it with a couple specific assholes. The people we're after are just flesh and blood, like you and me. They're flesh and blood scumbags who *only* want to kill a million people. I need your help to take them out. Can you handle that?"

"That, I can handle." Reaper picked up his knocked over beer, popped the top, and held it out toward me. "The crew is back together. To kicking ass like old times!"

We hit the beer cans together. "To old times." It was a good toast.

"And murdering your ex-girlfriend. You know I never could stand her." Reaper drank a bit, coughed, then read the label. "What's this cheap shit? Who buys American beer imported to *Europe*? Okay, if we're working together again, Jill is not allowed to buy supplies. Period."

There was a little nagging part of me that was angry, like these moral human beings were going to somehow hold me back from my path of righteous vengeance, but right then it mostly felt really good to be back with my people. It felt *normal*. Ling had been right to call Jill. I'd been prepared to lose my soul to get this done, but maybe I didn't have to. "We've both been living in fear for too long. Now it's time to make Kat afraid."

"You're one scary bastard when you're on a mission, Lorenzo, but we both know there's stuff in the dark way worse than you."

I could drink to that.

VALENTINE
Paris
September 15th

The drive from Wels, Austria to Paris was long, more than twelve hours, and it was also lovely. We drove across southern Germany in a two-vehicle convoy, before cutting to the north. Ling, Ariel, and I rode in front in the little Hyundai; Shen, Antoine, and Skunky followed in the van. We drove carefully, adhering to posted speed limits and staying off the main highways, which were full of traffic cameras. We had enough to worry about already without getting pulled over, especially since the van was full of guns, ammunition, and gear, most of it very illegal.

As it was, we'd had to go out of our way to avoid checkpoints, especially as we got closer to the big cities. The security situation in Europe was deteriorating and national governments were responding in kind. We had to sneak across the border into northern France on a narrow two-lane road close to the border of Luxemburg, where there weren't any checkpoints. The major routes, including all the bridges across the Rhine, had police stops on them.

I had crammed myself into the back of the diminutive car so that Ling could drive and Ariel could sit in the passenger's seat. She snapped hundreds of pictures with her phone, and despite the severity of the situation seemed to be having the time of her life. It made me smile to see her so happy, just enjoying something as simple as a road trip without the weight of the world on her shoulders. She even got Ling to sing along with her when some catchy American pop song came on the radio. I'd never seen her like this, just acting like a normal girl without a care in the world.

God only knew how this would end, but I resolved to find a way to make sure Ariel didn't go back to Exodus. Sequestered away in a castle, cut off from the whole world is no way for a girl to grow up.

Exodus had had, at one point, a safe house or two in the seedier parts of Paris, but with the near collapse of that organization, they had been liquidated. Lorenzo thought it was a bad idea for all of us to pile into the same accommodations, and I think he was correct. A safe house is safe by virtue of it not drawing attention. Having a bunch of suspicious foreigners coming and going at all hours is how you draw attention to your safe house.

Tailor had taken care of us, though, and made available to us a place to stay, courtesy of his employers. Following the GPS, we eventually arrived at a nice stucco house with a red slate roof in the Parisian suburbs. The house and its small yard were surrounded by a high fence and a carport big enough for the van. With the car parked in the drive and the gate closed, no one on the street would be the wiser.

It had been nice to see Tailor alive and well, but I hadn't been lying when I told Ling I didn't trust him. With various electronic bug detectors and RF locators in hand, we scoured the house from top to bottom for listening devices. I was honestly surprised when we didn't find any. Still, we remained cautious, just in case there was anything we missed.

As excited as she was, Ariel got right to business once we arrived. She opened up her laptop, pulled out some notebooks, and set up a little command center in the study. Tailor had come through with a bunch of information on Katarina Montalban's operation, and we had been given a lot of leads to chase down. He explained over the phone that his boss kind of liked having us doing the poking around for him. It gave him plausible deniability. The Illuminati bigwigs were insistent on playing their stupid cloak and dagger games. I could tell it frustrated Tailor, too, even if he wouldn't admit to it over the phone. He swore up and down that Romefeller didn't actually know where Katarina was hiding. I didn't trust the old billionaire, but I didn't think he was lying about that. Kat was a hard mark to track, and she was paranoid as hell. Even with the leads, finding her would take a lot of leg work, a lot of luck, and maybe a goddamn miracle.

We had help, though. Romefeller's private intelligence company, RMI, was doing a lot of the digging for us. Tailor was coordinating, and would feed the intel to Ariel. One of the barren walls of the study soon became plastered with pictures, snippets of printed-out documents, and sticky notes. She'd even put lines of colored string up between them, like something out of a cop show. It was fascinating to watch her work, her brilliant mind moving at Mach 2, connecting the dots, finding the patterns in the deluge of information she was being fed. I could see why Exodus considered her such an asset, even if calling her an *oracle* was a little dramatic. It took a few days, but we finally got our first break.

"Who's she?" Tailor asked. We were video chatting over what he insisted was a secure connection while Ariel laid it all out for us. The rest of my team stood around the study, listening without saying much. Since they weren't big on the idea of allying with the Illuminati, most of them stayed away from the camera. Since Ariel was giving the briefing, she didn't have that luxury.

"Don't worry about who she is," I said. Tailor had been there in

Mexico when we rescued her, but he didn't seem to recognize her all grown up. He didn't need to know about Ariel. More importantly, his employers didn't need to know about her. "The girl works for me."

Tailor frowned. "I know that, dumbass, I'm talking about the lady your little friend is showing us right now." Ariel had printed out a picture, taken from afar with a zoom lens, of a woman in a slinky black dress and red high-heeled shoes. She had night-black hair, long legs, olive skin, and a figure most women would kill for. "Who is *she*?"

"I was getting to that," Ariel said impatiently.

"She's how we are going to get close to one of Kat's men without tipping her off," I said.

"She goes by the name Eloise. She's a prostitute. Word is she's very exclusive and costs about a thousand Euros an hour," Ariel explained. "Is that a lot for a prostitute, Michael?"

Ling folded her arms and shot me a half-smile. "Yes, Michael, is that a lot for a prostitute?"

"What makes you think . . . how the hell should I know how much a high-end French hooker costs?"

"He's got a point," Tailor said, over the video chat. "The whores didn't cost that much in the places we used to work."

Ariel frowned. "Gross."

"Indeed," Ling agreed.

"Look, can we stay on topic here? Keep going. Tell everyone why she's important."

Ariel took a deep breath. "She works for a local, uh, courtesan service that usually serves the rich and famous, businessmen, politicians, people like that. She came to our attention . . ." Jill DelToro had taken that picture. Ariel was having to tread carefully here, because Tailor didn't know about Jill and Lorenzo. They were another thing the Illuminati didn't need to know about. "One of the men our source has been following is a *frequent* customer."

"One of Katarina Montalban's men?" Antoine asked.

"She has a lot of hired muscle for a billionaire philanthropist. It makes her harder to get to, but a little easier to track, since she has this big entourage everywhere she goes." She pointed to a different picture, connected to the photo of Eloise a length of red yarn. "RMI has identified him for us. His name is Georges Mertens, a Belgian national who was on the international bodyguard market right up until last year, when he dropped off the radar. His career has been spent working for organized crime, he's been implicated in several murders, but he's never been convicted."

"The types Mertens works for hire good lawyers," I said.

"Our source has seen him as part of Katarina's security detail," Ariel finished.

Tailor's brown wrinkled up in thought. "So, you want to use the hooker, to find the bodyguard, to find the target."

"It is possible he confides in this prostitute," Antoine suggested. "We could bug her."

"Now hang on," Tailor said. "It may not matter what she does or doesn't know. Someone like Katarina Montalban isn't going to hire guys that can't keep their mouths shut. But we can use her to get to him, roll him up and bring him in."

"That's pretty ambitious. Might tip Kat off, too if her men start disappearing." *Not that Lorenzo's reappearance had been particularly helpful in that respect.*

"It might," Tailor agreed, "but our only other option is to follow this asshole around hoping he leads us to our target."

"We may not have that much time," I said. "Who knows what their schedule is like? This guy might just be working in the city, and might not get anywhere near Kat again. I don't think following him around and hoping for a break is a good way to go. I think we need to talk to him."

"You're talking about kidnapping someone off the street and sequestering him away for interrogation. Paris is not Zubara," Ling said. "Coming to the attention of law enforcement here is extremely risky."

"I think I can help with that," Tailor said. He held up an ID badge to the camera on his phone, but it was hard to make out.

"What is that?"

"Interpol credentials." He grinned. "No shit. I am the law! Special Organized Crime Task Force. Gives me a lot of leeway, and the local cops are usually pretty deferential."

"Are you really a police officer, Mr. Tailor?" Ling asked, incredulously.

"Technically, sorta. Enough for this situation, anyway. My boss pulled some strings. Interpol doesn't actually have arrest powers, but most people don't know that. Besides, I'm only gonna flash my creds if I have to. I'd rather just snatch the guy and never have him find out who we are."

"We can use your creds to get the hooker to cooperate, too," I suggested. "She'll probably be less worried about client confidentiality if she thinks she's keeping her own butt out of jail. Maybe if you roll him up on some human trafficking or vice charge, it'll be less suspicious to Kat than him just disappearing?"

Tailor smiled. "I like how you're thinking, Val. I can make up some crimes. I'm flying over first thing tomorrow morning so we can plan this out in detail." He looked at Ariel. "Good job, kid. Call me if anything comes up tonight." The call was ended and Tailor disappeared from my phone.

"Are you sure about this?" Ling asked me.

Antoine was really not liking our current arrangements. "The Illuminati *and* Interpol? This carries a lot of risk."

"Until we have something better to go on, this is worth at least looking into. Get in touch with Lorenzo and let him know what's going on. If we are going to grab Mertens I want to run it so we risk the minimum number of our people. It'll probably just be me and Tailor."

"Stop trying to protect everybody!" Ariel blurted. "You can't do this all by yourself." Ling looked like she agreed, but she was an experienced leader, and knew the last thing you wanted to do was undermine the decision maker's authority in front of everyone.

"You said this is my war, then this is my call. When Tailor gets here we'll hammer everything out, including a backup and a bugout plan. We'll have you guys on standby, in case we need to call the cavalry."

"In other words, Val here doesn't know if he can trust our old buddy Tailor or not," Skunky spoke up for the first time. He'd been standing off camera, but since he'd been on the same Switchblade team, Tailor would have recognized his voice.

"What do you think?"

That was a tough question. I thought of Jeff as a man of principle, which was why he'd wound up with Exodus, sucked into trying to do the right thing. Tailor was a pure mercenary to the core. We'd all been like brothers, but it was hard to guess how strong Tailor's loyalty would be when we were working for different sides.

"You know I love the guy, but Tailor is Tailor. He's a hell of a soldier, a good leader, but we both know he can be a company man. He's the sort of guy who'll take orders for a paycheck, and not think too hard about what those orders are. It's been a long time." Skunky shrugged. "But I do know one thing for sure, I don't need any more evidence that the Illuminati are pure evil."

"Why do you say that?"

"They trusted Tailor with a *badge*."

Chapter 8: Spy Games

VALENTINE

Paris
September 16th

"Jesus, dude, traffic here sucks."

Tailor nodded without looking at me. The two of us were in his rental car, trying to make it across town. "I fucking hate Paris, man. Between the regular congestion and the police everywhere, it's impossible to get around."

"What's the deal with all the checkpoints? It's like the city is under martial law."

"Almost, but not yet," Tailor said. "They've left most of it to the Gendarmerie, but there are French army units on the ground in the city, too. They got 'em mostly over in the poor parts of town, where the Africans and Middle Easterners live."

I should have been doing a better job keeping up on the news. "They been having some kind of ethnic tensions or something?"

"It's getting pretty bad—oh, come on!" he snarled as a little hatchback pulled front of us, causing Tailor to stomp on the brakes. "People in the States bitch about traffic. They have no idea. Anyway, yeah, there's been a rash of attacks recently. Tribal shit, some of it, but also targeting Jews. Things are tense with that G20 summit coming up in London, too."

"Why does anyone care about a summit in another country?"

Tailor shrugged. "French economy is struggling same as everyone else's. The word is, the government will announce some more austerity

139

measures after the summit. There are a lot of people that depend on welfare. They're gonna be pissed. Paris cops are worried there'll be a riot. Another riot, I mean. Maybe a big one this time."

I smiled and shook my head. "Do you know how weird it is to listen to you, of all people, get me up to speed on current events? There was a time when we didn't know or care what was going on back in the regular world. It was just one third-world shithole after another, and that was all we worried about."

"Yeah, well, things change." Tailor looked almost uncomfortable. I couldn't remember ever seeing him like this.

"You've changed," I said.

"So have you, Val. You're different than you were when I left you on that boat."

The car fell into an awkward silence as we crawled through stop and go traffic. The only people getting anywhere were the motorcycle riders creating their own lanes on the dotted lines.

"You were right, you know," Tailor said after a long moment. "Right about me."

"What are you talking about?"

"Last time I saw you, you said I was a war junkie. That really pissed me off, but you were right. I didn't give a damn about anything but our next job. I lived for the thrill, the adrenaline, the . . ." he trailed off. "The killing."

It was weird to have Tailor open up. "Yeah, it's a rush. There's nothing like it." Combat is terrifying, but also a sort of primal thrill. Like Mark Twain said, there's no hunting like the hunting of armed men.

"But after Mexico, then Zubara, you know. Getting left for dead twice in a row is kind of a bad deal," he muttered.

"It is."

"I guess you came to the same conclusion I did. You just beat me to it."

"Yeah, well. Circumstances."

"I don't think I ever said it, Val," Tailor said, glancing over at me, "but I'm sorry about Sarah."

She had been communications and interrogations for Dead Six, and we'd fallen in love. It felt like a lifetime ago, but I could still see her death as clearly as the second it happened. Not a day went by when I didn't think about her. I didn't talk about it with anyone, not even Ling. Especially not Ling.

"It eats at me sometimes," I managed finally.

"It wasn't your fault, Val. You were the one who saw what was coming. You were the one trying to get everyone out."

"I know. But it doesn't change anything."

He was right, though. A few months into Project Heartbreaker, I could see the writing on the wall. Suffering unsustainable casualties, being sent on virtual suicide missions, all as the tiny Emirate of Zubara spiraled into chaos, my goal had become getting me and Sarah out alive. In the end, it hadn't mattered. Majestic pulled the plug. Gordon sold us out. And nearly everyone, including Sarah, died.

I will likely never forgive myself for that.

"For what it's worth," Tailor said, "I wasn't thrilled with how it turned out either. It don't matter now anyway. I know you're being all secretive about your people, and I get it. It's insulting, and kind of hurts my feelings that after everything we've been through you don't trust me, but hey, whatever. I just want you to know I'm done getting sold out."

Of the few people still alive whom I called friend, I'd known Tailor the longest. He'd been like my brother. He was assigned to train me on my first job with Vanguard, in Africa, right after I got out of the Air Force. He'd been there with me through some of the best and many of the worst times in my life. I wanted to tell him everything. I wanted to trust him. I wanted there to not be any kind of ulterior motive. Only, what I wanted didn't really matter. The people Tailor was working for were nothing but ulterior motives, layers and layers of lies, deceit, and manipulation.

"Well, I don't have faith in your bosses like you do."

"Faith? I ain't got faith in *shit*, Val," Tailor said, an edge in his voice. "I got . . . well, don't worry about what all I got. Let's just say I got contingency plans."

That actually made me feel better. It told me Tailor was still being pragmatic, and really hadn't just bought the Illuminati bullshit hook, line, and sinker.

Night had fallen as Tailor and I waited in an upscale hotel room. He had booked both the room and an appointment with the lovely Eloise.

As far as her *escort service* knew, Tailor was an American businessman, with very specific tastes which—if they thought about it too hard—sounded just like he'd been describing her from Jill's photographs. If Eloise was unwilling to help us, we had ways of applying leverage. I was more worried that she'd be un*able* to help us. If Georges Mertens didn't have an appointment with her anytime soon, our lead could go cold before we were able to exploit it.

"She should be here soon." Tailor was sitting on the bed, watching a German cop show that had been dubbed into French, munching on a bag of potato chips from the minibar. *Were they crisps here? Or was that a British thing?*

I was standing, looking through the glass door to the balcony, taking in the sights. I'd never been to Paris before, and it really was beautiful. The Eiffel Tower was all lit up. Boats slowly moved up and down the River Seine, tourist cruises from the look of them, and the entire city seemed to glow gold in the dark.

"Someday," I said wistfully, not looking at Tailor, "I'd like to visit a place and not be on a mission. Just go somewhere as a tourist without anyone trying to kill me."

"Hell, and you called me housebroken," he said, through a mouthful of half-chewed potato snacks.

"No, I get why. I'm just surprised that you settled down. It didn't seem like something you'd want to do."

"People change, Val. Even me."

I didn't respond.

Tailor persisted. "What happened to you, man? You said you got captured by Majestic. What did they do to you? I ain't the only one who's changed. You're different. More mopey than usual."

"I learned a lot of things the hard way, bro," I said, still looking out the glass door. I turned to face him. "When this is over, your employers might ask you to kill me."

"What the hell are you talking about?"

"You know goddamn well what I'm talking about, Tailor. They'll want me dead for the same reason Majestic wants me dead: I know too much. It makes me a threat. Having you do it makes the most sense. You can get close to me without it being suspicious."

"Val, you might have changed, but you're still a big drama queen. I can't believe we're having this fucking conversation right now. If it makes you feel better, I promise I won't betray and kill you. Feel better?"

I laughed. "You're such an asshole."

"Nice to be working with you again too, brother."

"Just don't make promises you can't keep. If you do decide to come after me," I warned, "you better bring your A-game."

"Fucker, your A-game is whiffle ball."

There was a gentle knock at the door. Eloise had arrived. Tailor used the remote to shut off the TV, then he walked over to the door. "Now shut the hell up and let me do the talking." I stepped off to the side as Tailor loosened his tie and opened the door.

"'Ello," Eloise purred in a French accent. She was stunning, like movie-star pretty, which probably explained how she made more per day as a hooker than I had as a mercenary. She sauntered into the room in a short blue dress and high heels, clutching a small handbag. She noticed me, awkwardly standing by the bathroom door, as Tailor closed and locked the door behind her.

She didn't miss a beat. "I see. That's fifteen hundred an hour for the both of you. Eleven hundred if one of you only wants to watch."

"Mademoiselle," Tailor said, pronouncing it *mad-am-mow-zell*, "you got it all wrong." He pulled out his INTERPOL identification. "I'm Special Agent Wilhelm Schneider, and this is my partner."

"Not the kind of partner you were thinking of," I added.

"Shut up," Tailor said to me. "I need to ask you a few questions."

Eloise stepped back, dropped the sex kitten act, and got very defensive. "I have done nothing wrong," she said angrily. "I work freelance. You are the ones guilty of solicitation."

"Actually we're not," Tailor said. "I didn't say I wanted to have sex with you, lady, I just said I wanted to see you."

Eloise folded her arms across her chest and glared at Tailor. "What is it you want, then?"

Tailor raised his phone and showed her a picture of Georges Mertens. "This man is one of your clients, correct?"

Obviously she recognized him. "I do not discuss my clientele. I'm leaving."

We were ready for that reaction. "Eloise, wait." She paused and looked over at me. "We're not trying to bust your customer for hiring you. We're trying to protect you."

"Protect me?" she scoffed. "As if."

"We don't care about prostitution. Our division profiles serial killers. Georges is a very dangerous man. We've been tracking him for weeks. He's covered his tracks very well, but we've tied him to a string of murders of sex workers in five different countries. If he's hiring you, especially if he's a regular, that's his pattern. You are in a lot of danger."

"He . . . he is a murderer? I don't believe it. I just saw him last week."

Tailor, following my lead, thumbed his phone screen a few times. He approached the woman and showed her a gruesome picture of a beautiful young woman who'd been stabbed to death. He'd just picked some from Google earlier. "This was his last victim. Her name was Greta, and she was from Frankfurt."

Eloise cringed at the photo. "A hazard in my profession."

"We need your help, Eloise."

"I want nothing to do with this! I'm leaving!"

"Please, you're the only connection we have to him. If he gets away, he will kill again. He's a predator. More women will die by his hand."

"We won't let anything happen to you," Tailor added. Originally I was going to be good cop, and he was going to be bad cop, but it was obvious from the expression on her face that she was softening. So there was no need for him to get all threatening. "We're not going to put you in harm's way."

"What . . . what is it you need me to do?" she asked with trepidation.

"We just need you to help us catch him. Could you contact him and set up a meeting?"

She nodded. "I can. It is not how I usually do business, but I can. I have a phone number. I think he is still in Paris."

"Can you come up with an excuse to call him, see if he wants to see you?"

"I do not do business that way," she insisted. "My clients come to me."

"Yeah, but he's a regular, right?" Tailor asked. "Tell him you had a cancellation or something, and you wanted to see if your number one client wants to take that time slot instead."

"Time slot? I am not some . . . some *street walker*, Monsieur Schneider. I do not see multiple clients in a day."

"Fine then." Tailor tried to hide the exasperation in his voice. "Tell him you have a date that opened up, whatever. We just need to get this guy off the streets. He's got an EU passport, and he's been staying one step ahead of the police by moving from country to country. If we lose him here, there's no telling where he'll go next. You're our best shot."

"Will you help us?" I asked, gently.

Eloise looked thoughtful for a moment. She shifted uncomfortably on her high heels, her hands tucked tightly under her arms. "I will," she said, looking up at me. "If it will save another girl from this monster, I will."

I felt bad about lying to her, and not just because I'm a sucker for a pretty face. What she was offering was actually very brave, and I found it to be a very noble gesture on her part.

"You must still pay my hourly fee, though," she added. "My time is valuable."

Okay, so it was only a *little* noble.

LORENZO
Paris
September 18th

After getting settled in at one of Jill's hideouts, picking up some more clothes and another motorcycle, I made a trip to the bank.

I hadn't worked in Paris very often. My specialties—blending in to rob tyrants and scumbags—had ensured I'd spent most of my career in poorer countries. Plenty of swaggering targets and second-rate law enforcement kept things simple. But this city was such an important center of international business, the odds were good that I'd find myself here often enough to warrant setting up a stash.

Having once had to escape across war-torn Africa with what I could scrounge on the fly had been an educational experience, so I'd gotten into the habit of hiding rainy-day stashes wherever I went. Without the money and papers I'd left at a storage unit in Russia, I wouldn't have made it here so quickly. This safety deposit box had been one of my first, toward the beginning of my professional thieving career. My Paris stash was almost twenty years out of date, but it still had some useful stuff in it.

Most of the guns Jill had gotten were the type of cheap, unreliable trash you could procure off of low-budget street punks. Reaper knew better quality illegal arms dealers around these parts, but they would know the Montalbans. Exodus had good equipment, but I didn't like relying on others too much, and I knew the stuff I'd left here would run.

After the bank employee left me alone in the privacy room, I opened the safety deposit box with one of the keys from the ring I'd picked up in Russia. Smart crooks made copies of their keys and IDs to leave at other stashes in the same region. The whole point of a stash was using it when you didn't have anything else, and getting a replacement key required prolonged conversations with bank managers who might remember you later.

A strong smell hit my nostrils. *Cosmoline.* I'd packed the guns in the oily sludge to prevent corrosion. I'd probably used way too much for a climate-controlled room, and it would be a pain in the ass to clean, but then again, I'd been pretty new at this business back then and a little overzealous at preventing rust. I'd come prepared now though, and took the latex surgical gloves out of my pocket before I lay the empty suitcase on the table. I didn't want to get grease spots on my new clothes.

The biggest thing in the box was a Steyr TMP submachine gun. They'd quit making these back in the 90s and sold the design to a Swiss company later. Come to think of it, Carl had gotten popped with one of those. But this one had been a reliable piece. If the French cops ran ballistics tests on this one, they'd match up to a bunch of bullets pulled out of a gun runner and his goon squad in Toulon. Carl and I had done a little job for them, and afterwards they'd tried to *aggressively renegotiate.* It hadn't gone well for them.

There were several thirty-round magazines stuck into a canvas chest rig I'd never worn because it was too big and obvious. The TMP had come with a suppressor when I'd bought it, but that can had been a piece of crap anyway and this was a terrible gun to silence. Anytime you shot it on full auto all the extra gas back pressure venting carbon in your face was enough to gag you, so I'd ditched the can. If I needed to shoot somebody without making a lot of noise, that was what the other gun I'd left in the safety deposit box was for.

I'd taken the .45 one off of a hitman sent to kill me once. I'd learned to shoot with Gideon Lorenzo's old GI 1911. I'd always been fond of that style of pistol, so I'd kept this one. It had been a basic Springfield before some mystery gunsmith had done a lot of work to it. The giant C-More red dot sight mounted on it was obsolete—or *retro*, depending on how you looked at it—now, but back then it had been the hotness. Really, it just made it an impractical pain in the ass to conceal because the only holster I had in the box for it was a goofy nylon rig. Of course, when I checked the sight, the battery was long dead. I'd have to pick another up before I needed to shoot anybody. The suppressor for it was an old, original Gemtech. The tube was bulky and heavy by modern standards, but still pretty damned quiet. At least, nobody I'd ever popped with it had complained about the noise afterwards. Can and pistol went in the case too.

There was an envelope stuffed full of money, only it was francs and marks. Those were completely useless now. I didn't even think I could trade them for euros anymore. It was a waste, but Reaper had brought lots of cash. Another envelope held IDs and passports. They were all expired and way out of date. I'd burn those, just to keep the number of pictures of me in circulation to a minimum. There was a little disguise kit, but the makeup was long since dried out, and besides all of those facial prosthetics were amateurish by my current standards.

I'd forgotten about the other manila envelope.

When I looked inside I saw a sealed plastic baggie with a single old Polaroid photograph inside. I shook it out far enough to study it. The picture was a group shot of my foster parents and all their kids, including me. I stuck out as the skinny dark one. Everybody else was bulky and super white. The Lorenzos were good people, the kind of family that kids who grew up like I did thought were a myth. The picture was cracked, yellowed with age, and water stained. This had been the one memento from my too brief, temporary home that I'd taken with me when I'd fled Texas. I'd carried that Polaroid in my kit the entire time I'd been with Switchblade. It wasn't like I'd ever looked at it, but I'd carried it anyway. I couldn't tell you why.

I'd put together this stash when I'd made the final jump from semi-illegitimate mercenary to full-on criminal. I wonder what it said about me that this was the place I'd finally left my old life behind. I studied the picture. Gideon Lorenzo had been a good man. He'd been a judge, but one of the rare ones who actually balanced justice with compassion and didn't go too stupid one way or the other. Despite knowing my juvenile record, he'd taken me in after sentencing my real father to prison. Any understanding I had of mercy, decency, or honor had come from him. He'd hate that it was my avenging his murder that had put me on this path.

One nice thing about a privacy room was that nobody could hear the fool talking to himself. "Be good, Hector, you said. Well, dad, I tried to follow your advice," I told Gideon's image. "Okay. *Eventually.*" It had gotten me shot and imprisoned, but hell, who was I kidding? That didn't mean he would have changed his advice one bit. There had been nothing flexible about Gideon's principles.

I swear, he did look kind of proud of me in that picture though.

Then there was Bob standing next to me. Even though we were both teenagers there, I looked like a midget next to that man-mountain. Of course, I was the only one not smiling for the camera. I'd gone on to be a crook, and he'd become a cop. It was Bob's quest to expose Majestic that had gotten him captured in the Crossroads.

"This is your fault, Bob." Only that was bullshit. It was my involvement with Big Eddie that had introduced Bob to Valentine and the wealth of Majestic secrets he'd gotten from Hunter. Without me dragging him into that, Bob would have gone on as just another oblivious crusader, far beneath Majestic's malicious notice. Bob had pulled the trigger, but I'd given him the ammo. I started to put the photo with the envelope back in the safety deposit box, but then I changed my mind and put it in the suitcase too.

The last thing in the box was a stainless steel knife . . . Man, this was turning into a regular trip down memory lane. It was the old, custom Italian switchblade I'd carried in Africa, not that I'd ever used it much. My working blade had been a surplus US Air Force combat knife. I'd never used this flimsy little decoration for anything more strenuous than opening a package. But because his merc company was named Switchblade, Decker had given his troops these as gifts. He talked a big game about brotherhood and loyalty, but the second he needed to spend our lives to accomplish a mission, he did it, and slept like a baby afterwards.

If Gideon Lorenzo had shown me how to be an actual human being, Adrian Decker had taught me how to be a merciless bastard who got things done.

I picked the knife up, slid the button forward, and the skinny blade popped out. *Click.* It made me smile. This was a toy compared to the folders I usually carried, with a locking mechanism that would probably break if I ever had to really go to town on somebody and hit a bone. I tested it with my thumb. It still held a good edge. What the hell, I was feeling sentimental and would never be coming back here again, so I closed the blade and stuck it in my pocket.

Suitcase full of useful implements of destruction, I left the bank. Valentine had cooked up a scheme, and I was going to tag along and make sure he didn't screw it up.

VALENTINE
Paris
September 20th

It took a couple of days for Eloise to set everything up. I had been afraid that she'd want to back out, or would just bolt, but with reassurances from me and daily cash payments from Tailor, we kept her on board with the plan. She contacted Mertens and gave him some story about how a client had cancelled on her, freeing up her entire weekend. He—quite understandably in my opinion—took her up on her offer. We dealt with the rest.

I was standing in the rain on a busy street beneath an umbrella, waiting for Tailor to pick me up, talking on the phone Reaper had given me to stay in contact with Lorenzo. That was one of the three phones I had to carry now. This spy stuff was complicated. The umbrella wasn't really that necessary, but it kept my face off any security cameras that might be around here.

Unbeknownst to Tailor, I was keeping Lorenzo in the loop. He was desperate to get his hands on any of Katarina Montalban's people, and he was probably better at this sort of information extraction than anyone on my ragtag team, so he could have Mertens. Part of my decision there was that I was still worried that Lorenzo was going to go off half-cocked and expose us all if he got impatient. Sala Jihan had messed him up, and my gut was telling me that Lorenzo was one setback away from going on a rampage. Regardless, there was no way we could get any information out of him and then let him go. He'd tip off Kat, and we'd lose her. It was cold, but having Lorenzo dispose of Mertens was easier. Also, despite what you see in the movies, it is hard to get rid of a body in a major city without getting found out.

Tailor knew I had my people, but he was under the assumption they were all Exodus personnel. The last time he'd encountered Lorenzo was in Zubara, where Lorenzo's partner had whanged Tailor on the head with a shovel. Tailor didn't know about Quagmire, St. Carl, or the Crossroads, and I wasn't ready to explain it all to him. It was just simpler this way.

"You have everything you need?" Lorenzo asked.

"I think so. We're waiting for a message from our girl. She thinks he's in Vaugirard, but didn't have his exact address yet."

"I know it. Nicer residential area, some good bakeries. You need to keep control of the situation. Things go wrong, it's not like it is in the slums. The cops will be there in a hurry, especially if there's gunfire. Don't shoot anybody."

"Fine, Mom, I'll try not to shoot anybody."

"This isn't a game. Don't fuck this up. I've watched you work for a long time. Catching people really isn't something you're good at."

I chuckled. "We caught you that one time."

Lorenzo didn't have an immediate answer to that. He just breathed through his nose a couple of times, angrily. *"You had a small army and I still had to break into you oblivious bastards' fort. Just stick to the plan, Valentine."*

"Are you sure Kat won't get spooked once this asshole disappears?" It didn't help that Lorenzo had already left a bloody trail of dead Montalban toadies across half of Europe. She had to know someone was gunning for her.

"She won't run. I know her. She's too territorial. Push her here and her instinct will be to push back. She's going to be well protected, and she'll be confident that nobody can get to her. She'll already be on alert, but if we get good info from Mertens, something actionable, it might not matter. Either way it's the best shot we've got."

"You're not wrong," I agreed. Tailor pulled up, this time in a different black rental sedan that probably had no connection to his employer's expense accounts. "I gotta go. I'll call you when it's done."

"Do not fuck this up," Lorenzo repeated.

"I love you too," I said as I got into the passenger seat.

"Was that Ling?" Tailor asked. "You guys are pretty serious then, huh?"

"Huh? Yeah, we're pretty serious."

"I just got a confirmation from Eloise. The appointment is on. She's supposed to be at his flat at nine-thirty. I got the address."

"You tell her to split?"

"No, we need her to get us to the door without spooking him. She agreed. She doesn't seem as scared now. This might actually work."

"I sure as hell hope so. Text me the address. I'll relay it to Ling, tell them to start getting ready. We've only got a couple hours."

Darkness fell over the City of Lights as Tailor and I drove down a quiet street in Vaugirard. It was a nice, middle-class area, free from most of the commotion that had rocked the city recently. The streets were tight, with little cars crammed into every space they could possibly be parked in. Apartment buildings lined both sides of the street, built into one another so as to make me feel like we were driving down a narrow canyon.

A few cars ahead of us was a nondescript blue Renault Clio, Eloise's car. I was sure she made enough money to afford something nicer, but that particular model was one of the most popular cars in France. For a professional who valued discretion, using a common car, even if it wasn't fancy, made a lot of sense. In Tailor's Audi we followed from a safe distance, keeping a few cars in between us when we could. I received a text that Shen and Antoine were in our Sprinter van, approaching our destination from a different direction. They would cover the back of the apartment in case our target bolted. Ling and Skunky were in another vehicle ready to fill any gaps or to provide extraction.

"Not too many people out," Tailor said, scanning the sidewalks. The rain had turned to a thunderstorm and it was keeping people indoors. The wipers were keeping a steady beat. He even had to turn on the defroster because we were fogging up the glass. "This is good."

"Once we bag him, I'll have my people bring the van up and we'll toss him in. If any lookie-loos show up just flash your badge and tell them to move along."

"Then we'll take him to meet my people and hand him off." Tailor was still under the impression we were going to drive Georges across town, to meet with some of his own people.

"Right," I lied, not missing a beat. I was hoping he wouldn't be too mad when he found out I had no intention of doing that. He was my friend and my former partner, but I didn't trust his employers, and I wasn't giving Romefeller our sole lead. Giving him to Lorenzo kept Tailor's hands clean, and by extension his employers', which seemed really important to them. Tailor would be pissed at me, but he would just have to deal with it.

I watched the GPS' screen. "We're almost there."

"This brings back memories, huh?" Tailor asked, after a moment.

"What do you mean?"

"Zubara, man. Think about it. We're rolling down a street in a major city, trying not to get noticed, planning on snagging some asshole to drag him back for interrogation."

"Hopefully without getting our asses shot off or bringing the cops down on us. Yeah, this all feels familiar."

"Right? You nervous?"

"A little," I admitted, but that was mostly because I was lying to Tailor about what we were going to do with our target once we grabbed him. "There's a lot that can go wrong."

"Stop being so negative, Val. We'll be fine."

I chuckled. "You sure about that?"

"Always remember, I am never wrong."

We were prepared just in case. We didn't have long guns, but my team in the van did. My big .44 was riding under my right arm in a vertical shoulder holster. I was wearing a concealable soft armor vest under my jacket, which wouldn't stop rifle bullets but would protect me from anything less than that. I was also packing a CZ-75BD 9mm pistol on my left hip, with a couple of spare magazines. The barrel was threaded and I had a sound suppressor for it hidden in my jacket pocket. I didn't ask, but I was sure Tailor was packing too.

"Alright, she's parking," Tailor said. I watched as Eloise found an open space and pulled into it, parallel parking like a pro. Unfortunately, there was nowhere for us to leave our car. "Shit, I can't see another open space."

"Let me out," I said. "We've got comms. I'll keep eyes on her. My team is in position." I opened the door as Tailor came to a stop. "You find a place to park and get your ass back over here."

"Got it," Tailor said, before he drove off and left me there alone. I immediately realized I'd left my umbrella in the car, and the rain was cold.

I scanned the street as I made my way up the sidewalk, walking with my hands in my jacket pockets and my head down, hoping my baseball cap would hide my face from any high-mounted security cameras. There were very few other pedestrians out that I could see, and only the occasional car drove past.

Eloise was waiting for me near the door of the apartment building. She wore a long coat that came down to her knees, undoubtedly over some classy but too-tight dress. "Where is your partner?"

"Parking." I touched the mic on my neck. "Where the hell are you?" Far down the sidewalk, a pair of policemen rounded a corner and turned up the street, headed my way. *Shit.*

He sounded exasperated. *"I'm stuck at a light!"*

"I don't like this waiting out here," Eloise said. "He is expecting me. He will become suspicious."

"Tailor, I can't wait, man," I turned away so Eloise wouldn't hear what I said next. "I'm too exposed out here. There are cops coming."

"What? Why?"

"Routine patrol, I don't know." They might not even give me a second glance, but a foreigner standing around in the rain in a residential area was suspicious, but worse, if the cops stopped to talk to me, it would be obvious to Eloise that I wasn't the law. And I still needed her to get inside. "Look, I can't stay here. I'm going in with the girl."

"Val, just wait, damn it!" Tailor argued. *"Give me a minute."*

I made my decision. "Eloise, how do you get into the building?"

"He is in flat number 3B. But the door is locked. He has to, how do you say, buzz us in."

"Right. Tailor, apartment 3B. The lobby door is glass. Just smash it if it's an emergency. I'm taking her up." I let go of my throat mic and looked at Eloise. "Let him know you're here."

"As you wish," Eloise said, more calmly than before. She pulled out her phone and sent a text message. A few seconds later, the door unlocked with a loud click. I held the door open for her then followed her in.

The lobby of the apartment building was a small room with

mailboxes built into the wall. Eloise made her way up the stairs, her heels clunking loudly on bare wood. I followed, cautiously, heart racing, feeling exposed. There were no cameras that I could see, only the clunk of Eloise's shoes, the scent of her perfume, and the incessant buzzing of fluorescent lights.

On the third floor, we turned down a carpeted hall, so our approach was a lot quieter. The hall was, thankfully, deserted, and apartment 3B was the first one on the right. This was it. I drew the CZ 9mm from my belt and screwed the suppressor onto the muzzle.

"That is not a policeman's gun."

"Interpol standard issue."

My heart rate slowed as I did so, my senses seemingly heightened. I noticed every detail of the hallway; the carpet was a dark blue, a light at the end flickered irregularly. The doors were heavy wood, and there were eight apartments on the third floor. Eloise was suspicious of me now, but kind of stuck. She shifted nervously, but seemed more collected than I expected she'd be. It was odd.

I was ready. I was *calm*.

"Let's do this," I said quietly. I positioned myself to the side, so that I couldn't be seen from the peephole. Tailor spoke into my earpiece, telling me he was on foot from a block away, having finally found a parking space. I clicked the mic to acknowledge, but didn't say anything. I held the pistol in both hands, tucked tightly to my chest, as Eloise softly knocked on the door. Footsteps approached. *Click, clack,* locks were undone. The door swung inward.

"Ello," Eloise said.

Calmly and smoothly, I pushed her aside and went past, raising my weapon as I moved. The man that had opened the door was young, probably in his twenties, with dark skin and short curly hair—*that isn't Georges Mertens*—and he was aiming a gun right at me.

I'd walked right into a goddamn trap.

I just reacted. He'd been ready to shoot me, but I was faster. Somehow, Eloise knew to duck. As the prostitute hit the floor, I pushed the gun out in both hands and shot him three times.

The gunman went stumbling away. Behind him, there was a short entryway that opened into a larger room. Another man was standing there, and he didn't even wait for his friend to fall out of the way before he started shooting. His shotgun blast tore a chunk out of his associate and the frame next to my head. There were more people moving behind him. I thought one of them might be Mertens, but he'd already disappeared around a corner. Bullets zipped past me. I fired a barrage into the apartment, as they took cover amid the cloud of plaster dust and gun smoke.

Reaching down, I grabbed Eloise by the arm and pulled her to her feet. "Come on!" I yanked her away as a hail of gunfire echoed throughout the building, bullets peppering the wall on the other side of the hall. I squeezed my throat mic. "Compromised! Ambush! Get up here now!"

"*I'm at the lobby!*" Tailor said. Glass shattered as he smashed through the door two floors below me. I kept my gun trained on the doorway to the apartment as long as I could, firing off a shot whenever his men tried to poke their heads around the corner, until we were out of view down the stairs. Even then I tried to keep my body between their bullets and Eloise. Footsteps thumped on the wooden stairs as Tailor ran up to meet me.

"Eloise, you need to get the hell out of here. Run!" She went down as Tailor came up past me, suppressed VP9 in his hands. He popped off several muffled shots as one of Mertens' men came blundering into the hall with a short-barreled shotgun. That one was dead before he hit the floor.

The terrified occupant of apartment 3A cracked her door open. I was certain some of the stray rounds had gone through her wall. "*Interpol,*" Tailor shouted with authority, and then a rapid bunch of half-mangled French that was probably *lock your door and stay down.* Whatever he said worked, because the lady fled. "Come on, Val, we gotta get out of here. This has gone to shit."

"I think he's still in there. We can—" A cylindrical object flew out of the doorway, bounced off the opposite wall, and hit the stairs.

The flashbang detonated before I could even warn Tailor.

LORENZO

The first thing that went through my mind when the bullets started flying was that I'd told Valentine not to fuck this up.

I had been tailing him all evening. I'd even been watching Valentine while we had been speaking on the phone, sitting under an awning at a brasserie a hundred yards away enjoying a cappuccino and his lame attempt at blending in. Valentine was one hell of a soldier, but he would have made an awful thief. When the other guy had picked him up in an Audi, I'd followed on a used Ducati I'd bought for cash.

They had never even come close to making the tail. Paris was a motorcycle-friendly city. There were thousands of them here, so I didn't stand out. Bikes made sense, since you could cut through their awful traffic, parking sucked, and for me in particular a helmet kept my face off of the security cameras. Sure, riding was miserable and dangerous in the rain, but many of the locals just used these zipup leg covers to keep the water out of their laps, and called it good.

When the mystery driver had dropped Valentine off, I parked. And unlike them, I could park damn near anywhere. I picked another building down the street with an awning to keep out of the rain, and hung out there. When the cops Valentine had avoided walked by, I simply wished them a pleasant evening in perfect French. I don't normally smoke, but carried a pack and a lighter anyway, so to Paris' Finest I just looked like a regular dude having a smoke break while avoiding the worst of a shower. Once they were past I went back to watching.

Valentine would probably be torqued if he found out I was following him, but unless something went wrong, he'd never even know I was here.

So of course, something went wrong. Valentine is a shit magnet.

A couple minutes after Valentine and the hooker went inside somebody started shooting. My first thought was *I told him not to fuck this up.* Then his friend—I still didn't know who he was—ran up and kicked in the front glass. I checked the other way, the cops had turned the corner and hopefully mistook the noise for thunder. That wouldn't last long. "Damn it, Valentine," I muttered as I tossed the cigarette and reached for the little plastic Steyr subgun stashed in my bag.

But then I realized something was up. The door had opened on one of the apartment buildings across the street and four men had come running out, heading directly after Valentine and his buddy. They had their hands down at their sides or inside their jackets, trying to hide their weapons. They'd been camped this whole time. This had all been a setup. *But how—?*

Before I'd even finished thinking the question, I got my answer. The hooker ran outside, but rather than getting gunned down, the man in the lead shooed her out of the way, and neither of them seemed surprised to see the other. She had tipped off the Montalbans.

The Kat I knew, if warned beforehand, would have just left a claymore in the apartment and blown them all to hell. The fact that she hadn't—and this was a relatively restrained amount of gunfire for her people—suggested that she wanted to take somebody alive, probably because she was curious who had killed Diego and Varga. Was it someone moving in on her business? Was it personal? Or were they poking into Blue? She'd want to know.

So technically, since Valentine hadn't been smoked immediately, by raising those questions in Kat's head, it was like I'd done him a favor. And since I was now walking toward the four armed men who were about to storm the lobby, I was about to do him another.

I ran, crouched, along the parked cars, keeping my gun low so hopefully they wouldn't see it until it was too late. A flashbang went off inside and the window over the second floor stairwell blew out. The four dudes must have been waiting for that as a signal, because three of them rushed through the broken glass. The gunfire had really picked up to an unmistakable level, so those gendarmes that had been here a minute ago were probably calling for backup and hauling ass back. This was about to get really complicated.

They had left one man as lookout. He saw me coming, assumed I was a law-abiding citizen, pointed his subgun my way, and started shouting about how this wasn't any of my business. But I simply lifted my TMP to waist level, and put a burst through the windows of the Peugeot parked between us. Hip firing is stupidly inaccurate, but I still winged him. As he flinched back, I raised the gun, put the front sight on his torso, and the next burst stitched him from nipple to neck.

I ran toward the entrance, but out of the corner of my eye I thought I someone in the shadows off to the side. White skin and black eyes. I spun, ready to fire, but there was nothing there but rivulets of water pouring from a broken gutter. For just a split second I thought the Pale Man had been there.

CRACK.

The bullet passed through the air where I would have been if I'd not stopped. It smacked into the concrete and fragments flew. I dove behind a parked car, cursing myself as I realized that the men hadn't come out of the lobby across the street. They'd been waiting in one of the apartments above it, and they'd left a shooter in the window to cover them. Using something big and semi-auto, he went to town on the car I was using for cover, pounding rifle rounds through the sheet metal as I hugged the gutter. The burn on my chest ached when it landed in the cold water.

I glanced back the way I'd come from. The two cops were running this way. They had drawn their pistols and were heading directly toward the sound of gunfire, balls to the wall. It was brave as hell, but Kat's men would have no compunction at shooting the police. I shouted a warning and tried to wave them back, but the Montalban shooter had already seen them. He turned on the police, and bullets started smacking the walls around them. One cop got hit in the leg and crashed. His partner skidded to a stop, and by some miracle didn't get hit as he dragged the wounded man behind a planter.

It sucked for them, but I used the distraction to scramble up and bolt for the entrance. By the time the rifleman had swung back toward me, I was already through and heading for the stairs.

VALENTINE

That had been one hell of a bang. The stairwell was filled with so much smoke it was hard to breathe. All I could see was flashing purple lights. I could barely hear Tailor shouting over the ringing in my ears. There were men above and below us, and they fired a bunch of rounds through stairs to let us know they were there. We were surrounded and there was no way out. One of the men below was shouting something in French.

"What's he saying?" I asked. "And when the hell did you learn French?"

"Asshole wants us to surrender. I told him I was Interpol. Didn't faze him. Guy's a pro."

There were tears in my eyes as I kept blinking, hoping my vision would clear up in time to shoot somebody. One of the men yelled something else. "What's that?"

For once, Tailor sounded worried. "He said there's two of us, but his boss only needs one alive. They're going to count to ten, and then start shooting."

"I'm not getting taken alive. Not again. Call their bluff, let's see how brave they really are."

Tailor shouted back something in French, then for my benefit said. "I told him his mom gives lousy head. We only got a second here. Up or down?"

The man downstairs started counting.

It was a bad situation to be in, but I was *calm*. Down was the most obvious direction to go in. Down would bring us to the street and give us room to maneuver. Trouble was, we didn't know how many of them were below us. I thought I had seen Mertens above, there couldn't have been too many stuffed into that little apartment, and we'd already killed at least two of those. There would be a fire exit or at least a window at the back. Antoine was covering that side, and if we could get to him, we had our egress route. By the time the count had reached *trois* I had made my call.

"We're going up."

LORENZO

"Quatre!"

I didn't know why the jackass at the base of the stairs was counting, but he was armed and jumpy. The other two were ahead of him, further up the stairs, so all I could see were their legs. They were all focused in the other direction. They must have thought my shots had come from the man they'd left guarding the door, and that he and their rifle guy still had their asses covered. They assumed wrong.

Before he could say *cinq*, all hell broke loose. Val and his friend must have gone for it, because there was a chain of suppressed *pops*, the sound of feet pounding stairs, and somebody above started screaming bloody murder.

"Merde," the man muttered, right before I bashed him upside the

skull. Plastic guns make shitty clubs, but I still hit him hard enough that he spun around and crashed into the mail boxes. Before he could shout a warning, I throat-punched him with the hot muzzle of the Steyr. This thing had a vertical foregrip too, so with both hands I really put some oomph into it. He went down hard enough to bounce his face off the tile floor.

By the time I looked up, the other two were gone, chasing Valentine. I went after them. Taking the stairs two at a time, I caught them just as they were drawing a bead to shoot Valentine in the back as he ran down the hall. Valentine's little friend had been faster, and had already dived over a dead guy and through an open door. I opened up, stitching the rest of my magazine into Kat's men. Valentine heard the shots, spun around, and fired a suppressed pistol at them. One of Kat's men went down spraying blood all over the carpet, and the other flipped over the railing to plummet back into the lobby.

The instant Val's pistol had locked back empty, he'd switched guns, and I had that big stupid shiny revolver aimed at me *again*. The dude was quick, I'll give him that.

"Point that somewhere else or I'll stick it up your ass," I warned as I reloaded.

"Lorenzo?" He lowered the hand cannon. "What're you doing here?"

"Cleaning up your mess."

"Val! Mertens is getting away!" His friend shouted from inside the apartment. "There's stairs down the back!"

Valentine went in. I followed. I would have loved to get back to my bike and get out before half the cops in Paris descended on this place, but I didn't know how dedicated the rifleman across the street was. He might have run at the first sound of sirens, but I didn't want to risk getting my head blown off if he was feeling stubborn.

There were bodies in the hall, and another in the entry. It smelled like blood and smoke. The apartment was small, but there was a back balcony. The glass door was open, the curtains were billowing, and rain was coming inside. There was a circular metal staircase leading down into the alley. Valentine started talking into this radio, it sounded like to Antoine. I pushed past him and hit the stairs. They were shaky, wobbly, and slicker than snot in the rain, but I managed to bound down the steps, two and three at a time, without killing myself. I spotted a shape that had to be our guy, twenty yards ahead, leaping over garden fences like they were nothing. Geroges must have been a track star. Valentine's friend was already at the bottom and had taken off after him.

The rain was really coming down now. Beyond that rumble was the sound of sirens, *lots* of sirens. The neighbors had heard the gunfire and there were a lot of faces pressed against windows, trying to figure out what was going on. Unfortunately for us, this back area was lit, so witnesses were sure to see the four of us having a foot chase, and they'd vector the cops right in on us.

I sprinted after Georges. That son of a bitch was *fast*. He'd already reached the end of the block. Lucky for me, rather than turning right or left and heading down the sidewalk, he crossed the little side street and entered another foot path between apartment buildings. Montalban connections or not, he didn't want to get busted by the cops. Valentine was coming down the stairs behind me, shouting directions into his radio. Valentine's friend reached the street and nearly got creamed by a passing car. They hit the brakes, he wound up in their headlights, briefly, before sliding across their hood like T. J. Hooker. Somehow he stayed on his feet and kept up the chase as the car honked at him.

I scrambled over a metal fence—glad that I was wearing a motorcycle jacket as the spikes stabbed at me—and hit the other side running. I even looked both ways before crossing the street and managed not to get hit by a car. *Way* ahead, Georges was still booking it. My lungs were burning and my legs were on fire. There's not a lot of space to practice your wind sprints in a dungeon. These apartments had their own little yards, and hurdling the little fences was killing me. Dogs were barking. A little schnauzer tried to bite me. I dodged it and hoped it bit Valentine when he caught up. It would serve him right.

We cleared another street. There were flashing red and blue lights zipping through the intersection at the end. *Don't look this way. Don't look this way.* One of their own had just got sniped. They were going to be pissed. I'd almost caught up with Valentine's friend, who was soaked, gasping, and starting to lose steam. Ahead, at the end of the *next* block, Georges was damned near out of sight. He'd already crossed another street, and this block was mostly shops and hotels with living quarters above. It would be really easy for Georges to dart into one of the buildings and disappear. He turned into a skinny alley behind a café. I pushed myself harder to keep him in view.

A van appeared, tires sliding on the wet street, as it took the corner way too fast, and followed him in. I sure hoped it was the Exodus guys and not Montalban reinforcements. It was too close to drive far inside, and I saw brake lights. Luckily, I learned it was Exodus when Shen leapt out of the passenger side while the van was still screeching to a halt.

This was it. This street was clear. I didn't see anybody looking at us. The cops were going in the opposite direction. There would be some confusion before they were pointed our way. We had a few seconds where we could still pull this off.

By the time I reached the back of the van, our quarry was stopped in the headlights. There was a chain link gate behind him, he didn't have time to make it over, and Shen had him at gunpoint. Antoine had the driver's door open and was using it for cover. Georges' chest was heaving from the exertion. The bodyguard slowly turned around.

"Gun," Shen warned.

There was a pistol in his hand.

Antoine barked at him to put it down. The other man who'd been pursuing Georges with me moved up on them, his handgun aimed at Georges too. He was terribly out of breath but he started shouting for Georges to surrender in really bad French.

A strange look came across Mertens' face. It was the expression of a man who knew there was no way out.

I never knew why he went for it. We had him dead to rights. He couldn't know who we were, but maybe he assumed anybody trying to capture one of Kat's men weren't the type to let him live when we were done. Or maybe Kat had told her people that if they let themselves get caught she'd assume they'd flipped on her and she'd kill their families. I wouldn't put it past her. Hell if I know. Whatever his reasoning, he had made a fateful decision. I could see it in his eyes. *Resignation.*

"Don't do it!" I shouted.

He swung his gun toward Shen.

Several bullets punched Mertens' chest.

I couldn't blame them. There was none of that *shoot him in the legs* or *shoot the gun out of his hand* bullshit. When somebody is about to send a bullet your way, you put them down. Period. Anything less just resulted in a wounded man killing you.

Georges Mertens fell backwards, rattling the fence as he slid down, until he came to rest sitting in a puddle.

"Son of a *bitch*!" the man who'd chased him all this way shouted, in English, with a southern American accent . . . that sounded strangely *familiar*. "You fucking asshole!" I don't know if he was yelling at Mertens for basically committing suicide, or at everyone who'd shot him. Which included himself, since his pistol was now at slide lock.

Keeping their guns up, Shen and Antoine approached cautiously. Shen pushed Mertens' pistol away with his shoe. Antoine felt for a pulse. He looked back at me and shook his head.

Everyone who'd just fired was using a suppressed weapon, so hopefully nobody inside the café had heard the noise. We could still get out of here. I looked back. Valentine had almost caught up. He was a lot bigger and heavier than me or the other guy, so not nearly as fast on foot, but his giving directions over the radio had worked. I glanced back at the corpse. *Kind of worked.*

Another setback, and worse, from the ambush, it was clear Kat was hunting us while we were hunting her. Things were about to get a lot more difficult. I walked in front of the headlights, swore, and kicked the bumper.

Antoine was already patting down the body for intel. He found Mertens' cell phone and stuffed it into one pocket. "I am sorry, Lorenzo. He left us no choice."

"Shit happens."

"Lorenzo?" The little angry dude looked over at me. "Who the hell is . . ." He was still breathing hard. He fell silent when he got a look at my face.

I couldn't quite place him. The voice was familiar, an angry Tennessee twang that I'd heard before. It came to me in an instant. A mosque in Zubara. Valentine with his arm around Jill's neck, using her as a shield. And *this* asshole . . . they called him *Xbox* then.

"You!" He didn't even blink, just threw a punch. Lucky his gun was empty or he probably would've shot me. I narrowly blocked his arm, and pointed my subgun—which was very much loaded—at his dick.

"Back off, stumpy."

"Whoa, whoa, whoa!" Valentine came running up. "For fuck's sake, guns down!"

The Southerner was seething, but he wasn't stupid enough to try anything else. I took a step away and lowered my weapon. What the hell was Tailor doing here? Or at least I thought his name was Tailor, as we'd never been formally introduced. We had met during a gunfight ... on opposite sides.

"Val, this is the guy from Zubara, the asshole that hit me with a shovel! What the hell is he doing here? Are you *working* with him?"

"Technically my partner hit you with a shovel."

"Yeah, sorry I'm a little fuzzy on the memory details there, bub, because *I'd just got a concussion from a fucking shovel!*"

Valentine got between us. "Everybody calm down, we're all on the same side here."

The Southerner had been Dead Six. "He's Majestic."

"Mr. Tailor is Illuminati now," Shen corrected helpfully.

"Don't tell him my name!" the Southerner, Tailor, protested.

"You've got to be kidding!" They were the last people I wanted to know I was still alive. "Those are Montalban allies!"

"Gentlemen," Antoine boomed, "the police are coming. We don't have time for this nonsense! Sort it out in the van!"

Chapter 9: Breaking Point

LORENZO

I made it back to one of Jill's—hideouts—one step above a crack house, late that night, exhausted and bitter. I gave her a quick debrief, and then tried to go to sleep, angry at Valentine for being stupid, angry at Kat for being smart, and basically angry at the world for not cooperating.

Yet despite all that anger, with Jill resting next to me, I actually calmed down enough to rest. No matter what, as long as I had her, everything would be okay. She'd been my anchor in prison, and out.

Only I had another terrible dream that night. Nothing elaborate, nothing special, just Sala Jihan standing in shadows of the bedroom, whispering that I was not focused enough, that I had lost my way, and that the *son of murder* had no time for distractions.

I had bolted awake, chest burning, snatched up my .45, and pointed it at the darkened corner . . . to see nothing. Still, I waited, until I was absolutely sure there was no one there, and the whispering had stopped.

"Go away, Pale Man," I muttered. "You can't have her."

"Huh?" Jill asked, mostly asleep. "What's wrong?"

"Nothing." I put my gun away and went back to sleep.

Nothing at all.

Jill was suspicious, but she'd done as I asked. I told her to dress nice, because our stakeout would be in the classy part of town, the rich, touristy part. So when she met me at the riverside, just before sundown, she was wearing a fashionable dress, a nice jacket, and a scarf that was probably really expensive. Jill wasn't big on the hair and makeup, but she'd gone all in tonight. She was gorgeous. I had just gotten this new suit tailored this afternoon. We actually made a really cute couple.

I offered her my arm. "Right this way, my dear."

"What's the deal, Mr. Secretive?" Jill glanced around. There wasn't really anything of much note here. Behind us were some businesses, ahead of us were boats. "You made it sound like a party."

I led her down the stone steps. "Kind of."

"At least warn me if there are going to be metal detectors. I'm wearing a thigh holster under this thing."

"That's actually kinda hot, but don't worry. There's no security. It should be pretty quiet."

We followed the walkway closer to the Seine. Now it was obvious we were heading for the docks. One nice thing about all the rain yesterday was it knocked the city stink down and left the air nice.

"Okay, seriously, Lorenzo, who we spying on? I didn't bring my snorkel. Look at all those cute little boats. You know, I really miss having our yacht." Then Jill saw the boat we were heading for. It was a long rectangle. It had one floor that was enclosed in glass, while the top was flat, open, and had tables with umbrellas. "Ooh, floating restaurant. Fancy."

"This is supposed to be one of the best ones in town. The guy who runs it even won on 'Iron Chef.'"

"American?"

"No way. Old school Japanese."

"*Nice* . . . Let me guess, some Montalban dickweed has reservations for tonight, so we're going to spy on him? Score. I guess that's way nicer than impersonating a maid and cleaning hotel rooms." But then Jill realized that there were no other customers inside. "Are we early . . . No . . . Please don't tell me we're pretending to be wait staff. I'm a terrible waitress. The only reason I got tips at that greasy spoon in Quagmire was because of my legs."

"No, now be cool. And if anybody asks, I'm a rich, eccentric Bollywood film executive producer."

"Okay then." It said a lot about our relationship that Jill took that in stride. "What does an executive producer even do?"

"Produce things? Executively. I don't know."

"As long as I don't have to dance and do a musical number, I'm happy. I can't dance in heels."

There was a hostess waiting for us. She greeted me as Mr. Kumar (the single most common name in India, which made fake IDs a piece of cake) and told us our table was ready. I'd specified that if the weather was nice, I wanted the best spot on the roof.

We were seated at a very nice table, with a great view off the front of the boat. There were even fresh flowers and candles lit. I swear they'd perfumed the air. Nobody did this sort of thing better than the French. I even got her chair for her, very gentlemanly like.

Jill waited until our hostess had left. "Where is everybody else?"

I made a big deal of looking around, like the fifty other empty chairs up here came as a surprise. "How about that? Must be a slow night."

"Lorenzo . . ."

"Go big, or go home. Hang on." They were bringing out the wine. I knew a bit about the subject, enough to fake it in polite society, but I played it safe and had ordered a bottle that cost about the same as a good used car. When the server was gone again I explained, "I took the liberty of ordering drinks, but if you want a Diet Coke or something—"

"Lorenzo!"

"I wanted to give you a nice night on the town, but all the classy places are in public with lots of witnesses and cameras. But not this, so I rented the whole place."

She was cute when she was incredulous. "What did that cost?"

"One of Reaper's suitcases full of Euros, but he knows I'm good for it." There was some noise below as our boatstaurant began moving away from the dock. "We're taking a little cruise and seeing the lights while enjoying a fine gourmet meal. We'll head past Notre Dame, that big wheel thing, and by the time we get to the main course, we should be down by the Eiffel Tower."

"Are you crazy? With everything that's going on, this?"

I reached across the table and took her by the hands. "Tonight, it's just us. No mission. No business. Just us. We've both been through a lot. Tomorrow, we'll go back to work. But tonight . . . Tonight I just want to remember what it is that we're fighting for."

As I said that she had gotten a little choked up. "I don't deserve this."

"You deserve the world." I didn't know where her attitude had come from. She was awesome. I was the crook who would have a rap sheet as long as my arm—if I wasn't so good at not getting caught. The last year had beaten her down, and it was my job to bring her back up. "Let me do this for you, because I love you, and because you saved my life in more ways than you can ever know."

For once, Jill was speechless. She was so surprised, that for a moment I thought I might have broken her brain. "You? You're trying to be romantic?"

"Trying?" I spread my arms wide, with the lights of Paris stretched out behind me. "More like *nailing* it."

"What are you *really* doing, Lorenzo?"

I thought about the whispers in the dark, and the still aching burn on my chest, about revenge and justice, and about how *none* of that mattered without her.

"I'm taking my life back."

She smiled, and for the first time since I'd been free, that was the smile of the Jill I used to know.

LORENZO
Paris
September 23rd

It had been Reaper who had demanded a face-to-face meeting with Valentine. His latest snooping had turned up some really bad news. Valentine also promised that he'd share all their new intel, which was mighty considerate, considering he'd teamed up with the Illuminati without bothering to tell me. It might be just Reaper's paranoia, but he said Majestic had access to some *next level* tech, and didn't trust phones when they were the topic. Since Reaper's fieldcraft and ability to move through a foreign city unnoticed was nonexistent, I got to be the bearer of bad tidings.

We picked a café in Goutte d'Or to meet, specifically because it was in a poorer neighborhood that was mostly North African immigrants.

All the police cameras around the place had been smashed by the residents. I didn't think my face was in Majestic's database, but Valentine's certainly was, so better safe than sorry.

The place wasn't crowded, but I asked for a table in the back where it was quiet. Two minutes after I was seated by the waiter, Valentine joined me, wearing a hoodie, ball cap, and big black Ray-Bans. "You look shady as fuck," I told him. "You'd blend in better if you dressed like a tourist."

"Yeah, well, this secret agent bullshit is still new to me. Are we actually going to eat? I'm starving."

"If you want. I've got plans for tonight, but I'm free until then. Oh wait, that's right. You already know about me scouting the smugglers by the airport because I filled you guys in beforehand."

"I *said* I was sorry. What do you want, flowers? Did you drag me out here to try to guilt-trip me, or do you need help with your thing tonight?"

I shook my head. "It's just a sneak and peak. The less presence nearby the less chance they'll ever know I was there."

"Do me a favor. I want you to keep one of my people in the loop tonight."

"Oh, are we keeping each other in the loop now? Is that what we're doing?"

"Jesus Christ, do we need to go to marriage counseling over this?"

It was so entertaining getting him agitated like that. For someone who was so eerily calm during combat, it sure was easy to push his buttons the rest of the time. "Who's this person of yours? Backup?"

"Not like that. She's not going out there. She's . . . it's hard to explain. She's good at analyzing stuff. Pieces of information that seem random to you might reveal a pattern to her."

"Fine. I thought about inviting an Illuminati hit man too, but I didn't because I'm a team player like that."

"You're not going to let that go, are you?" The waiter came back with our menus. Outside of the trendy, touristy parts of the city, the service was actually a lot better than the stereotypes. Even there, if you weren't a stereotypical douchebag tourist, people still tended to be pretty cool, and you wouldn't end up with a stereotypically snooty waiter.

"*Merci.*" Valentine's French was truly awful. The waiter left. "So what's the bad news you have for me?"

"Next time you're caught on camera, try to smile. Somebody got some cell phone video of an *Interpol agent* the other night after a shootout."

"How bad?"

"It's a little blurry, but it got uploaded to YouTube."

Valentine sighed. "Super."

"Look, Reaper thinks this is really bad. He walked me through how the latest facial recognition software works. Glasses aren't enough to throw off the programs anymore. The good stuff measures your available face, maps your bone structure, builds a 3D model, and extrapolates out anything you cover. If you do have to move in the open somewhere with cameras, best thing to do is keep your head down and watch your feet. Most of them are mounted up high so they don't get vandalized. Reaper says the software still struggles with angles and profiles."

"It's hard to keep your head down when you're chasing a guy and trying not to get lost. If Majestic knows I'm here, that complicates things."

"Being a left-handed shooter with the right height and build probably sealed the deal if they had any doubt."

"This stuff is your wheelhouse or whatever, right? What can I do?"

"Have Antoine's complexion. No, seriously. Darker skin makes it harder for the cameras to measure facial features. Something about contrast and shadow depth. If you were any whiter you'd be translucent."

"Sure, I'll take some time off to hit the beach, get my tan on."

"For future reference, I've got my super genius hacker trying to get into the local police system so that if you show up there, it doesn't get flagged. He can't know about every camera phone upload in the world, though, so you need to be more discreet from now on. We can't afford another fuckup like that."

"Fine. How is Reaper, anyway?"

"Better . . ." *Maybe.* He seemed happy to be working, but I was a little worried I might have validated his fears by telling him about my experiences in prison. "He's working on that police thing, but apparently Paris is a lot harder to crack without getting caught than Zubara. Go figure. But if we need to meet again, this neighborhood is a good one. Rough enough there's not a lot of cops, but not so rough that French intelligence is camped on it looking for terror cells. Just don't go a mile that way. It's Jihadi asshole central."

"How can you tell?"

"Graffiti mostly, and lopsided signposts." Valentine nodded when I said that. He'd been around disintegrating cities enough to know that trick. The local hooligans would shake any pole stuck in the concrete so that it was loose. That way when—not if—a riot broke out, all they had to do was yank the already loose pole out of the ground. They were handy for smashing windows, and the holes broke the surrounding concrete to give them a supply of useful throwing rocks.

"I'll skip that leg of the bus tour then."

"Trust me, you'd need a lot better disguise. You're too tall, too white, and too corn-fed-looking. You look like you just stepped out of a John Deere ad."

"Number one, you're just mad because you're short. Number two, that's racist. Number three, what are you anyway? Like, what ethnicity?"

I could pass for lots of things when I put my mind to it. "Mutt mostly, but my real dad was a gypsy."

Valentine thought I was messing with him. "Right. And for your information I'm not white. I identify as an albino Samoan."

"I'm serious. My birth parents were Roma."

"Whatever. Listen, don't stress too much over Tailor. I didn't tell you because I didn't want the distraction. I haven't told him anything about you, and believe me, he wanted to know how it is I'm working with you. I don't think he'd believe me if I told him the whole story anyway. He works for one of the Illuminati families, but we've got kind of a deal worked out with them right now. They're helping us track down Kat. That's where we got the lead on Georges Mertens from. They also helped steer the investigation of the aftermath so that we don't have to worry about the cops looking for us. Tailor's employers can pull a lot of strings when they want to. Right now we need every advantage we can get, especially if Majestic shows up again."

"You ever wonder about the screwed up life choices we've made to end up where we're talking about Majestic versus the Illuminati and it's not a joke?"

Valentine raised his eyebrows over his sunglasses. "I wonder about my life choices every day. I had to work really hard to get this screwed up. Anyway, Tailor's boss is Alistair Romefeller. Know him?"

"Not really." That name sounded familiar, but when I'd worked for Big Eddie, I'd been in the dark about all this global conspiracy stuff. "Was Tailor your contact with him?"

"Actually, no, if you can believe it. I had no idea he was working for him. It just so happened."

"I'm a professional con man. *Nothing* 'just-so-happens'. Assume any coincidence is probably somebody like me trying to manipulate you. You trust this guy?"

"Tailor? I knew him from Vanguard. We were on Switchblade 4 together, and Dead Six after. He was like a brother to me."

"My brother got me into this mess."

"He got me into some shit, too. Like, Zubara. He recruited me. I want to trust him, but his boss? As long as what we're doing benefits him, we're okay, but once we stop being useful we start being a liability. Tailor doesn't think it's that bad, but he always was the optimist." Valentine chuckled. "You know what's really screwed up? I actually kind of trust you."

"That's not funny. It's sad."

"No, really. I mean, you're probably a sociopath, but you're a consistent sociopath. I understand your motivations. Tailor, the Illuminati, Majestic? That whole mess is so convoluted I doubt they even know what they're fighting for. The truth is buried under layers and layers of secrets and lies. You, you're straightforward. A guy who tries to murder you is, at least, being honest about his feelings toward you."

That was actually a nice compliment. Our waiter came back and I asked for the spiciest thing on the menu. I'd missed flavor almost as much as I'd missed sight. Valentine surprised me by ordering some chicken tagine. I'd kind of figured the big corn-fed Midwesterner would have asked for a hamburger or something.

"What are you going to do if Underhill comes to Paris looking for you?"

An evil smile split Valentine's face. "He'd better hope he doesn't find me. You should know, it's pretty likely he'll turn up if they manage to ID me. He's been haunting my footsteps since we left the Crossroads. It was enough that I had to lay low for a few months, let the trail go cold. He's a persistent bastard."

"Look, I get it. He killed Hawk and you want to kill him back. Awesome. Me too. But know going in that Underhill is a beast. Anders is one of the toughest, sharpest, meanest bastards I've ever had the displeasure to meet, and Underhill *frightened* him. Anders faked his death because he was worried they'd pull Underhill out of retirement to go after him. That old man is the best hunter-killer Majestic has ever had, and let me accentuate, *old man*. You realize how hard it is to live long enough to get old in this business?"

"Like Hawk?" Valentine's demeanor changed subtly. I'd seen him get like this before. It was like flipping a switch. One second he was a normal, almost likable, guy. The next he was a killing machine. There was no emotion when he was like that, no fear, no remorse. Just action and reaction. That switch was what made Valentine so damned dangerous, and I had just managed to move it a little. It was weirdly fascinating to watch. And to think, this nutjob thought *I* was a sociopath!

I leaned back in my chair. "If he comes for you, he'll probably have some sort of official credentials to hide behind and diplomatic immunity. You're a fugitive, a wanted criminal. The French government will be backing him. You've got jack and shit. Local cops are going to be on the lookout. They'll be working their CIs and it wouldn't surprise me to see your face plastered all over the news soon. That's the surface. I'm betting Majestic sends an army with him. They won't risk you being picked up and talking to regular cops. They'll kill you or disappear you into another black site like before."

"I'm sure they'll try."

I had no doubt he'd stack the bodies when they did. "You think that's what Hawk would want? This isn't about just you anymore, Valentine. Exodus doesn't need another bloodbath. They need a leader."

Just like that, I was talking to normal Valentine again. It really was that quick. They'd done some weird shit to his brain in North Gap. Or had they? He was like this before that, too, if not as intense. "I told them everything Hunter told me, but Silvers wouldn't let up. *Who is Evangeline? What is the Alpha Point of Project Blue?* I don't know who Evangeline is or what Project Blue does. I told them, I fucking told them everything. What the hell more do they want from me?"

"Underhill wants you dead, or in a cage."

"He doesn't even care what I know, as long as he's got the thrill of the chase," Valentine muttered.

We didn't know much about Underhill beyond his rep. He'd been some CIA type back in the old days, before Majestic had taken him down the rabbit hole. All the rumors since were that he was a tenacious son of a bitch, and that no matter what rock you were hiding under, he would find you.

"You need to watch your back, Valentine. A man like that searching for you is going to make it tougher to catch Kat."

"I'm not going to run away, if that's what you're suggesting."

"I wasn't suggesting anything. I'm just telling you like it is."

"I'm going to kill that son of a bitch, Lorenzo, or I will die trying. He's going to know it was me, too. My .44? Hawk gave me that gun. Tuned it himself. The muzzle of that revolver will be the last thing Underhill ever sees. But . . ." he trailed off, looking around uncomfortably. "There'll be plenty of time for that. They'll never stop hunting me. In the meantime, what we're doing here has to come first. It's more important than my grudge."

He said it in a way that almost sounded like he wanted my affirmation. Either way, it was a lot more level-headed than I expected from him. "You're not wrong. I think Ling is making you soft."

Valentine was distracted, lost in thought. "If killing Katarina isn't enough, and Blue would launch anyway, we've got to derail the whole damned thing somehow. Maybe we can use Underhill?"

"What're you getting at?"

"All we know about Project Blue for sure is that it was a Majestic scheme to wreck the Illuminati. They never thought they'd actually launch it. Now Majestic is pissing itself over their doomsday plot actually happening. If they have a team looking for me in the same city as Katarina . . ."

He might be onto something. "You want to aim Underhill at Kat."

"If we can get them killing each other, everybody wins." Valentine thought about it for a moment. "I don't know how to make that happen, though. Everything we've learned so far makes it sound like the two sides have a truce. That's why Gordon having me kill Rafael Montalban was such a big deal, because it broke their precious rules. Hmmm. I'll need to think on this."

He had gotten smarter since I'd first met him. Then he'd just been a kid, really good at killing people, sucked into a bad war. The man I'd freed from North Gap had been a suicidal mess. Now he seemed more squared away, like he had a purpose and a clue, or maybe I was wrong. I wasn't that Ling had made him soft. It was that she'd actually given him something to live for.

LORENZO
Paris
Later that night . . .

It took me nearly twenty minutes to break into the truck rental company in Villepinte. Sure, I was out of shape, and I had to dodge security guards and attack dogs, but still . . . *Twenty minutes.* That was embarrassing.

Reaper's digging found that one of Varga's shell companies owned this facility a few miles south of Charles de Gaulle airport. Their call history showed that both Diego and Mertens had both called this business. I'd checked the layout on Google Earth, and then done a drive by. It was the sort of close to everything but secluded spot that was perfect for a smuggling operation.

Dressed in an innocuous dark gray hoodie, I'd come back in the middle of the night to work. This was just a little sneak and peak. I wasn't expecting trouble. I'd packed light. If I was spotted, my plan was to run and hide. That way hopefully they'd think I was some junkie looking for an easy petty theft.

There had been a couple of security guards on duty, but they appeared to be the typical, just-over-minimum-wage, rent-a-cop types, and they were mostly interested in guarding the fenced enclosure that held the trucks, trailers, and heavy equipment. There was a regular boring office building and a modern garage in front. I skipped all that stuff. Customers and normal employees would be through there all the time, and Varga wouldn't conduct his real business in front of potential witnesses. So I avoided the guards and went right to the interesting part.

There was a large workshop at the rear of the property. The satellite images had shown that it was secluded, fenced off from the rest of the facility, and had its own gate leading to a side road. It was only a short ride to the airport, so this was perfect for sorting and storing illicit cargo.

I made my way through the maze of broken-down heavy equipment and rusted out trucks. Weeds were growing through the tracks and over the tires. There wasn't much light back here, but I reached the back fence without banging my head or shins too much. There were places to park around the workshop, but no new cars. The chain link fence was topped in razor wire, and the scent of dog shit warned me what was inside. A couple of big, nasty Rottweilers had smelled me and come over to bark and raise hell. I could have just shot the dogs with a suppressed pistol (which was why they'd nicknamed them *hush puppies* after all) but my goal was to recon the place without Varga's men ever knowing I was here. You can't exactly do that if you go around leaving dead dogs all over the place.

Besides, I'd come prepared for dogs: a Ziploc baggie with some tranquilizer-loaded steaks. I dumped it over the fence, and ten minutes later the slobbery Rottweilers had wandered off, stoned and drowsy. Once I was sure nothing else was going to come out and bite my nuts off, I climbed the fence and went to work. The good thing about there being dogs was that meant there weren't any motion detectors around the garage, because otherwise they'd be setting them off nonstop.

The shop was made out of cinderblocks and rusty sheet metal, but the door was heavy duty and had multiple locks. The windows had bars on them and were probably wired, so I picked the locks with my bump keys. My out-of-practice fingers were clumsy, and it took me far too long, like almost a minute for the first lock. Once I'd gotten all the locks off, I suction-cupped a little octopus-looking device to the door. I didn't understand the science behind it, but Reaper said it screwed with the magnetic fields for door alarms. Once the light on the octopus turned green, I opened the door.

There were a couple of lights on inside the garage, but most of the place was in shadow. For supposedly being for truck maintenance, I didn't see much in the way of tools or machines inside, just lots of shelving for storage. There were a couple of vehicles parked inside by the roll up door, but most of the place was stacked full of boxes and crates. I didn't go right in. There could be motion detectors inside, but probably no cameras. They wouldn't want any recordings of what they moved through this place. I spotted one motion detector mounted high on the wall to the right of the door. The little white box was a familiar brand and about five or six years old, so I pulled out my little IR flashlight and shined it on the motion detector to blind it. Then I closed the door behind me and moved in, looking for other detectors. I didn't spot any. Once I was out of its field of view, I turned the IR light off and checked my watch.

Twenty minutes . . . Shit. Sure, most of that was waiting for the dogs to get sleepy, but prison had still kicked my ass.

I keyed my radio. "Reaper, I'm in."

"*Sweet. I was monitoring the tower. No signal sent. You're good to go.*" If I had screwed up, Reaper had set up a rogue tower—a decoy cell phone relay—to hopefully intercept the alarm call. And trust me, in this business? The alarm company wouldn't be calling the cops.

"*What took you so long?*"

"The dogs were massive. It took forever for them to doze off. You should have used more drugs."

"*Too much Ketamine makes the meat tastes funny.*"

"You know this from experience?"

"*Still better than your girlfriend's cooking.*"

Jill cut in. "*I'm on the same the channel, dumbass. My cooking is fine.*"

The banter made me smile. After so much time alone it felt good to have the company.

Jill was parked a mile down the side access road, at a truck fueling station. Reaper had dropped me off in front and was waiting on the main street. It never hurt to have multiple escape options. While the other two bickered, I went to work. Behind the parked cars—newer and nicer, so probably stolen—there was a desk with a computer on it. It was on and flicking through a screen saver loaded with porn. I stuck the evil-looking thumb drive with the bigass antenna that Reaper had gotten me into the USB port. While his malware or worms or whatever he called them molested the smugglers' privacy rights, I started looking for a good place to hide our bug.

Contrary to what you see in the movies, you can't just stick these anywhere. A listening device needs a power source, and unless you want to sneak back in repeatedly to change the batteries, you want it connected to a steady power supply. This one used both. I found an old phone jack on the closest wall, used my multitool to unscrew the faceplate, clipped the bug in, and then screwed the plate back on. That would provide it with its power normally. It had a battery backup just in case.

"Testing, testing."

"Got it," Reaper confirmed. *"Loud and clear. Hopefully Varga's guys will say something stupid into it soon."*

I doubted the smugglers knew anything, and it was unlikely they were stupid enough to leave any incriminating records on their computer either. As much material and money as the Montalbans moved, they had to keep some records, probably vague and in code, but all large successful criminal enterprises needed good accounting. Would they actually write down anything related to Kat's pet project? Probably not. This whole snooping visit was a crapshoot.

I retrieved the drive and took pictures of every paper on the desk. It was probably useless, but Reaper had surprised me before with the connections he could make from seemingly random bits of data. "Reaper, I'm sending you some pictures."

"Their shitty computer is already giving me everything. I'm sending it all along to our little friend as requested. They call her The Oracle." He snorted. *"What a pretentious call sign."*

"Yeah, that would be like calling you *The Reaper.*"

"That's totally different."

The bottom file drawer was locked, so I picked it. Inside were more file folders. I picked the ones that looked interesting, cargo manifests mostly, and started taking more pictures.

Reaper's scary computer brain read them in less time than it took me to move the papers around. That wasn't a joke. I'd seen him read whole books over breakfast. *"Wow . . . Huh . . . This could be something."*

"What?"

"It's interesting." He sounded distracted. *"These are shopping lists. This is stuff the bosses want their thieves to be on the lookout to steal. But it's weird stuff, not valuable movable merchandise they'd normally be taking. Hang on. I've got to make a call."*

I kept on taking pictures. They'd either burned the really incriminating stuff, or they were lazy and overconfident, because there was a lot of paperwork.

It took a while to get through all of it. It was the middle of the night, the roads were empty, and the dogs were still asleep. I figured I had time. I started searching the rest of the place. The shop was huge and packed, so going through every box would take all night, but I figured anything interesting would stick out. It appeared to be a fairly typical smuggler's stop. There were some stolen prescription drugs, but most of the crates were filled with things like auto parts, electronics, bundles of clothing still wrapped in plastic, cigarettes, basically anything that might *fall off the back of a truck*. Petty criminal stuff, nothing special. If there was anything good staging through here right now, there would have been real live human guards posted.

There were several side rooms. They were mostly full of more stolen junk that they hadn't found a buyer for yet. I kept taking pictures in case any of it turned out to be useful. All of them went right to Reaper and Valentine's brainiac.

Reaper sounded kind of excited. *"Why are the Montalbans collecting tons of mundane stuff they can just buy? I need to check these manifests against insurance company claims from the shippers."*

He was working off of a couple of laptops from inside a rental car. "How do you even do that?"

"By being a badass. I'm cracking and retrieving. Oracle is analyzing. She's actually pretty cool, boss . . ." He was quiet for a second. Reaper was probably working with an earpiece in each ear. *"She says hello. You worry about the breaking and entering and shooting people, chief. We've got this."*

His brain really wasn't right.

I found a curtained doorway hidden behind a rolling shelf. They always kept the human smuggling out of sight, probably so whoever was guarding the door, answering the phone, or doing paperwork wouldn't have to listen to all the sobbing. That sort of thing really grated on all but the most psychotic criminals, and your violent nut jobs—though useful—weren't your best day-to-day operations types.

The next room was divided into a few cells made of chain link, like a dog kennel, only each one held a cot. Each cell had a drain hole in the middle of the floor and a coiled garden hose for "sanitation". I figured this part would currently be unoccupied, because if any sex slaves were being held in here, there would have been real guards. It was a relief to see I was right and nobody was home, because freeing any captives would have tipped off the Montalbans that I'd been here. If this was where they moved Bob through, there was a possibility he had left me another bread crumb. I started searching the cells.

"*There's something to this . . .*" Reaper muttered. I hated when he felt the need to narrate his extremely convoluted thought process to me over the radio. He was hard enough to keep up with him when I was wasn't in the middle of a burglary. "*Most of the stuff they got ordered to steal makes sense, stuff you can move quick for a profit, but . . . no, some of these shipments they took don't make any sense at all. Industrial goods, chemicals, some medical stuff. What? Yeah. No. Yeah, this shit is too specific to unload . . . Whoa. You're right. It's too specific. Right.*"

It turned out it was even worse when Reaper was having two simultaneous conversations.

I got on my hands and knees and started checking under the cots for scratches. It was a lot faster going this time, since I wasn't under water.

"*But why steal this stuff when they could just buy it anywhere? Yeah, Katarina's got billions . . . There has to be something in each of these they needed, something special, and the rest is just junk. What pattern?*" I could hear the furious typing. "*Okay, you look at that.*"

There was nothing in any of the cells except for old blood stains. If Bob had been held here, it hadn't been for long enough for him to do anything. I wondered how much misery this place held. It filled me with disgust.

"*You're right, buying those parts would raise terror alert flags. But stealing bits and pieces mixed in with a bunch of other stolen goods spread out over months, and nobody catches on. But what could you build out of this junk?*"

Reaper was quiet for a long time. Now I was curious.

"*Don't leave us hanging here, Reaper,*" Jill said.

"Yeah, suspense is killing me," I muttered as I left the last cell. Next time the junior think tank could do their brainstorming while I wasn't trying to be sneaky.

"*Dear God . . . No.*" Now that wasn't a very Reaperly exclamation. "*No way. No way. Shit. I think you're right.*"

"Right about what? Spill it, man."

"*Sorry. Oracle thinks Katarina has a nuke.*"

Suddenly very cold, I stood there amid the empty slave cells as a terrible pain developed in my guts. "Hold on. You're telling me Kat built a nuclear fucking bomb out of this junk?"

"*No. She probably already had the bomb, or maybe she's planning to get one soon. I don't know. But mixed in all these tons of stolen cargo, is everything you'd need to deal with an alpha particle emitter."*

"Particle emitter? Like what?"

"Like uranium or plutonium, chief. As in, detection and concealment. Oracle says it's probably not in good shape or even a complete weapon. She thinks a . . . what? Physics package. She says the physics package could have been clandestinely transported or maybe damaged."

"What the hell is a physics package?"

"It's the part of the bomb that actually makes the nuclear reaction. That's what they call it."

"Who is *they*?" Reaper and this Oracle had come up with that insane theory after a few minutes of doing a jigsaw puzzle with cargo manifests. "Bullshit." I almost never doubted Reaper, but I didn't know the girl who was working for Valentine. I hoped that they were wrong. I wanted them to be wrong. I didn't want to think about Kat with a nuclear bomb.

"Lorenzo, there's some traffic down here." Jill warned in my ear, snapping me back to the present. *"You read?"*

"What've you got?"

"Headlights heading your way fast. Hang on. They're turning onto the access road. Definitely headed your way."

I didn't think I'd set off any alarms, but it was possible that this was just regular seedy middle of the night Montalban business. Either way, it was time to go. "Understood. Heading for the front. Reaper, get ready to pick me up."

"Hang on, chief. Two big, black cars just blew past me. They're . . . shit, they're stopping at the front gate!"

I must have tipped them off somehow, but there were a lot of them, and they'd gotten here fast. There was no way three cars were going to simultaneously roll up on a random alarm, so they must have been expecting an intrusion and staged nearby.

"Both of you stay put. I'll evade, and once I'm past I'll call for a pickup." I ran for the front of the garage. It would still take a minute for those cars to get here, and by then I'd be in the wind. There were plenty of places to hide around—

The front door was open. I was sure that I'd closed it.

A cardboard box next to my head exploded.

I hit the floor rolling, and then scrambled forward on my hands and knees between the shelves. A crate went flying, a pattern of holes torn through the wood. A box just above my head violently flew into pieces. *Buckshot.* Motivated by that thought, I ducked even lower, and made it around the corner as a dozen holes appeared in the shelf behind me.

The gunfire had barely made a sound.

The shooter didn't have a bead on me, so I crept along behind the shelves, looking for better cover. Whoever was firing at me was using some sort of suppressed shotgun. He wanted to keep this quiet. I pulled a Hungarian FEG pistol, one Jill had bought from the local hoodlums, out from beneath my hoody. I was about to make this loud.

I heard footsteps on concrete. The first shooter had moved behind one of the parked cars. "Come out," he ordered in rough French. It was a deep, commanding voice. "The place is surrounded." He sounded really familiar.

Son of a bitch. It was Anders.

I gave my radio three rapid taps. The signal for *oh shit everything has gone to hell.* I was pinned down by one of the best killers alive. We fought together in the Crossroads, and I watched him drop dozens of Jihan's men. He was ruthless, calculating, and supremely skilled. I had come a long damned way to find him, but this was *not* how I wanted it to go down.

Mind racing, I looked at the pistol in my hand. It was a clunky knockoff of a Browning Hi-Power, not my first choice for getting into a gunfight against one of the baddest motherfuckers I'd ever met. For Anders? That would have been an RPG or a Carl Gustav. I kicked myself for not bringing something bigger. I'd wanted to be discreet, though, and you aren't very discrete with an antitank weapon strapped to your back.

Anders switched to English. "When Diego bought it, I got nervous. The way he'd been cut, it told me somebody interrogated him. I wondered what that little freak might have said before he died. Then Varga shattered his skull on the sidewalk? No way that was a coincidence. It got me thinking, what could he have given up before taking the plunge? You probably knew about all his places at least."

I risked a peek past the edge of the desk, but I couldn't see Anders. I didn't want to stick my head any further out, because I had no doubt he was ready to blow it off. My best defense was that he probably didn't know exactly where I was. If he did, I'd already have extra holes in my body.

He spoke again, a little to the side from where he'd been a moment before. Anders was searching for an angle, trying to spot me. "Then after that shit-show the other night, I knew whatever you fuckers wanted, you weren't going to let up. You're operating in our hometown. You know who you're coming after. It's ballsy. Stupid, but ballsy. Figured I'd get ahead of you, have a talk face-to-face."

Anders was talking because he knew time was on his side. He had reinforcements on the way, no doubt. He'd said the place was surrounded, but I figured that was a bluff. I needed to get the hell out of here now. Preferably, right after I put a bullet in his brain.

Leaning out, I cranked off a quick shot into the side of the car he was behind, hoping to make him jump, but Anders wasn't the flinching type. The little 9mm was a whole lot louder than his suppressed big gun. He retaliated by quietly blowing a massive hole through the side of the desk next to me. Firing wildly to make him keep his head down, I leapt up and ran behind another set of shelves.

Taking cover in one of the doorways, I waited in the shadows, listening. My good ear was ringing now. My bad ear was *always* ringing, thanks to Valentine, but I couldn't tell where Anders was now. Had I got lucky and hit him? Fat chance.

"You've been a real pain in my ass," Anders called out. He wasn't wounded. Hell, he didn't even sound flustered, just mildly annoyed. There was the roar of an engine outside and tires on gravel. "Those are my associates. You got nowhere to go. I don't want to kill you. I only want to talk." He managed to say that while sounding perfectly calm and rational. Of course, he wanted to know what I knew first, and *then* kill me. "You don't need to stay quiet. I know who you are, Jill DelToro."

Huh?

"I didn't know you'd gotten out of the Crossroads until that bomb in London. You've got to be a pretty careful bomb maker nowadays because it's amazing the forensic evidence they can lift off of an IED, especially one that fails to detonate. Your signal got through, but your detonator was faulty. It was just blind luck you didn't get Kat that day."

That was bullshit. Jill had told me she'd not set that bomb off on purpose. Anders was trying to goad the wrong person. There wasn't time for this. I peeked around the side of a crate. There were shadows moving in the doorway. More shadows went bounding past the closest window. I was cut off.

"If it makes you feel better, it wouldn't have mattered. Even if had killed her, her plans would've kept going. She's more stubborn than you are. How many of my guys have you killed over the last year? Ten? Twelve?"

Jill must have been busier than she'd let on.

"That's dedication. Seriously, young lady, I'm impressed. If I'd known how much potential you had, I wouldn't have tried to kill you in Zubara. I would've told Gordon to hire you. But right now? You're out of your element. I don't know how the fuck you managed to do the things you've done, but no clever tricks are going to save your ass now. Stop being stupid and come out."

One of the men at the door asked Anders something.

"Form the perimeter. I've got this." He raised his voice again. "We're just having a little conversation, right, Jill?"

It was time to put Anders off his game. "Guess again, fucker."

Buckshot slammed into the crate in front of me, but I saw the tiny flicker of suppressed muzzle blast, and opened fire. I put out the passenger side window of a new Mercedes, but Anders had already ducked back down. He was big, but he was fast, too.

Someone darkened the doorway. It was too dark to see the front sight, but I pointed it, yanked the trigger, and was rewarded with a surprised yelp. The shadow disappeared.

"I said stay the fuck out!" Anders roared at his men. They did as they were told. "Well, holy shit. I've never talked to a ghost before. How you been, Lorenzo?"

"Rotting in Sala Jihan's hellhole prison because of you."

"You escaped the Pale Man?" Anders had been a Navy SEAL, HRT sniper, and Majestic hitman, but even then I think mentioning Sala Jihan freaked him out a little. "Bullshit. Nobody escapes from there."

"You're right about that: I didn't escape. He sent me to kill you."

The silence dragged on too long. Anders laughed, but it was forced. "Heh. How's that working out for you, killer?"

Quietly as possible, I reloaded. It was too dark to get a bead on Anders. Sooner or later he was going to get tired of talking, and then a whole bunch of assholes were just going to start shooting in this direction until there was nothing left for me to hide behind. Someone shined a flashlight through the closest window, searching for me. I needed to think of something fast.

"Lorenzo, stay away from the west wall," Jill warned through my ear piece.

I couldn't risk responding to her out loud. I was ten feet away from the westernmost wall of the shop, couldn't risk moving again, and had no idea what she was planning on doing. So I clicked the radio once for *negative.*

"Shit . . . Okay, in sixty seconds I'm going to make a new door in the middle of the west wall. If you're close to that, you're going to want to move."

She didn't specify the definition of *close,* but my options were pretty limited just then. I clicked the radio twice. *Affirmative.* Now I just needed to stay alive for a minute. "Hey, Anders, I know about Project Blue."

"The fuck you do."

I still hoped Reaper was wrong. "I know about the nuke."

The silence was damning.

"You don't want to do this." I had no idea what *this* actually was. "Innocents are going to die. Eddie was nuts. Kat is worse. You spent your life preventing this sort of thing—"

"You don't know shit about my life, Lorenzo." There was a bitterness in Anders' voice. "I've lost count of how many people I've killed for them, and it didn't make a bit of difference. Majestic had me, Gordon, and Hunter prepping to level cities on a *whim.* On a fucking *contingency.* It's one big game to these people."

"We've both worked for some truly evil bastards," I agreed.

This time Anders' laugh was sincere. "Yeah, well, when this is all over, Majestic will be ruined, and the Illuminati will be unopposed on the world stage, under new management. I never could stand those stick up their ass, snooty Eurotrash cocksuckers. I'm done working for anybody but myself."

"You're working for a psychopath right now!"

"Katarina is more of a strategic partnership. She needs me and I need her. She's got clout and vision, but you get one guess who really calls the shots in our organization. She's not exactly the management type. Trust me, Lorenzo. The world will be a lot nicer place with me running it behind the scenes."

"So the mighty Project Blue, the doomsday plan for one shadowy conspiracy to destroy another shadowy conspiracy, has become nothing but a power play?" I shouted back at him. "A coup, and you assholes are willing to kill millions of innocent people to pull it off?"

"You think this is unique? Like some special event in the grand scheme of things? Jesus, Lorenzo, the whole history of the world, the real history, has been like this forever, games within games. Powerful screwing the powerful, while the guys like us bleed. I'm done being a pawn, and I'm done with you."

Anders opened fire. Buckshot slammed into the boxes around me.

A truck crashed through the wall.

The corrugated steel wall barely even slowed the big Renault. Shelves and crates were tossed aside as I was pelted with debris. I got a brief glimpse of Jill in the cab, practically standing on the brakes, but the truck still flew past me, smashing into the Mercedes and sending it spinning across the shop before the truck screeched to a stop.

Anders' man with the flashlight moved in front of the window, probably surprised he'd almost been hit by a truck, but I shot him in the head. Then I leapt up and ran through the swirling dust and the bright yellow headlights. This was my chance to take Anders out. Gears ground as Jill tried to get the stolen truck into reverse. I moved around the back of the crumpled luxury car.

Anders was gone. He must have gotten out of the way. "Shit!"

Men were piling through the doorway, shooting wildly at the truck. I opened fire, trying to drive them back. Windows shattered as other gunmen opened up from outside.

"Lorenzo, come on!" Jill shouted. The big truck made a *beep beep* warning noise as she backed it through the wreckage of the shop. I ran to the passenger side of the truck, hopped onto the lowest step, and held on with one hand, pistol extended in the other. A thug in a suit rushed through the doorway, firing a subgun from the hip, but I clipped him and he went to his knees, rolling beneath the Mercedes.

I got the door open and climbed up into the cab. "Drive!" But the encouragement was unnecessary, because Jill had already put the hammer down. These things were built for torque and had surprisingly quick acceleration. Bullets were striking the truck. Holes appeared in our windshield.

"Hang on," Jill warned as she backed the truck through the improvised door. There was a sudden *clang*. Jill screamed, a combination of pain and surprise.

I looked over. A circle of holes had appeared in the driver's side door. Stuffing had been blown out of the seat and was floating between us. There was blood on her arm. Blood on her chest. "Jill!"

Anders had flanked us and shot her right through the door. But then we were outside. "I'm hit. I'm hit!" She had one hand on the wheel and one pressed against her side. Eyes wide, teeth clenched, she was too focused on trying to drive us backwards through the junkers to think about the pain just then. If she struck something solid enough to stop us, we were dead. "I'm fine."

They shot Jill. "Motherfuckers!" It must have been the adrenalin because I didn't even remember kicking out the window. Then I started shooting at anything that moved. Anders' men were running into the lot after us, firing. I picked out each muzzle flash, aimed, and popped off a couple of rounds at each one. We were lurching and bouncing, so I probably missed a lot. These things were pretty damned fast when they weren't attached to a trailer.

Despite getting hit, Jill kept her head turned, watching her mirror, trying to drive the giant vehicle too fast in reverse without crashing us into some of the abandoned heavy equipment. The light stuff, though, she didn't care about, and our rear end slapped the side of one of the recently parked cars. I barely felt it, but from the horrible metallic rending noise, that car wouldn't be following us.

We were putting distance between us and the shooters. "Are you okay?"

"I'm okay," Jill insisted, but she didn't sound okay. The words came out dripping with pain and focus.

I was shoving in my final magazine as the truck crashed through the outer fence, beeping the whole time, and out onto the access road. She kept us straight for another twenty seconds, giving us a good lead. "Flip around here." Only we kept going, across the road, and into a field. "Stop!" I shouted as we ripped through the bushes, but Jill didn't respond. Her chin had dropped to her chest. I reached for the wheel, *too late,* because then we were tipping backwards, and our rear end slammed hard into the bottom of a ditch.

The impact caused me to bounce my head off the ceiling. The padding there didn't do much. I blinked myself back to reality a second later, staring up at the night, our one unbroken headlight launching a beam at the stars.

"Jill?" All I got in response was a moan. I reached out and found her in the dark. My hand landed in hot, sticky blood. There was blood *everywhere.* She was hit worse than I thought. "Come on, we've got to go." I found my radio. "Reaper! We're on the access road. We need extraction, now!"

"Already on my way."

Jill's door was stuck against a tree. Mine still opened. She was groggy, with the clumsy, drunken movements of somebody with dropping blood pressure. I pulled her tight against me, and fumbled my way out of the steeply angled truck. I don't know how I kept hold of her, but I did. I fell backwards into the weeds, Jill on top of me. She gasped when we hit. "It's going to be okay." I kept repeating it, like a mantra. "It's going to be okay."

I dragged Jill up out of the ditch. "Can you walk?" But she didn't respond at all. She'd passed out, dead weight. Anders and his men would surely be here any second. Desperate, I looked around for Reaper's headlights, but I couldn't see them yet. I couldn't afford to wait. I didn't know where she was hit, or if this was going to make it worse, but I didn't have a choice. I hoisted her over my shoulder and started jogging through the bushes with her body over my shoulder. I could feel her blood pooling in my clothing and running hot down my shoulder. "It's going to be okay."

I could hear Jill's ragged breathing on top of mine. I needed to stop the bleeding, but I had to keep running. To stop, even for a second, was to die.

They'd gotten closer to the truck. Someone spotted us. "There!" A bullet whizzed past my legs. I turned, found that asshole, thirty yards away, and popped off a shot at him. I don't know if I hit, but he put his head down, so I kept running.

Headlights appeared ahead of me. *Please be Reaper.*

Someone else shot at me. It was so close I could feel the vibration of the bullet. It whined off into the darkness. *It's going to be okay.* Another bullet smacked into a tree right behind us.

Reaper's little rental Peugeot was speeding this way. I waved my gun overhead as his headlights engulfed us. He was going so damned fast that he had to slam on the brakes to keep from hitting us. I don't think he intended to skid sideways, putting us right next to the rear door in a cloud of rubber dust, but it worked.

Opening the door, I shoved Jill's limp form inside. "What happened to Jill?" Reaper shrieked when he saw her. I ended up knocking several laptops and tablets onto the floor.

"Drive," I shouted as I got in behind her. To punctuate the severity of the situation, the Peugeot's back window shattered.

Wheels spinning, Reaper got us moving. Terrified, he looked back over the seat at her. "Is she alive?"

"Get us out of here *now!*" The lights from the screens were enough for me to see by. I already had her shirt open. There were a bunch of scratches from the glass fragments, and right there, weeping blood, was a bullet wound on her abdomen. Then I saw another, and another, right next to each other. "Fuck."

"There's a first aid kit under the passenger seat," Reaper said, as he took us around a corner way too fast. "Hang on."

The only thing I was hanging onto was Jill, and she was barely hanging onto life. *Stay cool.* I'd seen lots of gunshot wounds. I got the bandages open and got pressure on the wounds. There were three entrance wounds, low on her left side. I rolled her over a bit. Two exit wounds. The exit wounds were small, and appeared to have gone through the muscle and fat at a pretty shallow angle, thank God. But the innermost round was still in there. If she was hit in the liver or kidney . . . *Shit.* Her breathing didn't seem strong enough. *Shit. Shit. Shit.*

I didn't see headlights behind us yet. She needed a doctor now, but when Anders saw the blood in the truck, every real hospital would be watched by Montalban. But in every major city the criminals always had people they could call on for emergency medical attention. "Get us to Doc Florian's place."

"I can't. He committed suicide last year. I heard about another guy. His place isn't too far."

I kept pressure on the wounds. I could feel her weakening pulse beneath my palms. I'd gotten the bleeding slowed, but I had no idea how much internal damage there was. Projectiles could do crazy things once inside a body, I'd seen it all, on myself and others, but never felt it like this. I've got a reputation for being a focused, no bullshit, get the job done type, but when it is the woman you love bleeding to death right there, under your hands, you start to come apart at the seams. "Faster, Reaper."

"I'm already doing a hundred!"

"Go *faster*." I used one bloody hand to stroke Jill's cheek. "It's going to be okay, Jill. Stay with me. Please."

She was fading in and out. "It hurts," she mumbled. "This is my fault. All my fault."

That didn't make any sense. "You saved my life. We'll get it taken care of, just hang in there."

"I deserve this."

"No. It'll be okay." But she'd already lost consciousness again.

Then I heard Anders' voice. For a second I thought it was in my mind, taunting me, but then I realized it was coming from the floor of the car. Careful to keep pressure on Jill's wound, I picked up a tablet. It *was* Anders' voice. I turned up the volume, leaving bloody streaks on the glass.

"*We got a problem.*"

"That's from my bug!" Reaper exclaimed.

"*What now?*" It was Katarina. Anders must have had her on his phone's speaker. I could barely hear her, but that smoky voice just filled me with revulsion and hate.

"*Lorenzo is still alive.*"

The line was quiet as Kat digested that revelation. "*That's impossible.*"

"*I was camped at Varga's place. Lorenzo's alive and he's here. He said Sala Jihan sent him. He got away, him and that Del Toro bitch, but there's blood all over so I plugged at least one of them. Don't worry. We'll catch him.*"

"*You don't know Lorenzo like I do. He's harder to kill than a cockroach. He'll find a way to ruin everything.*"

"*He knows about the package.*" Anders stated flatly. "*I was fishing and got the impression he doesn't know the target or the timetable though.*"

"Unacceptable! We can't afford an interruption now! Find him and kill him!" She hung up.

"Bet your ass I will," Anders muttered to himself. Then it was quieter, as he walked away from the bug. *"Let's go."*

"Lorenzo!" Reaper exclaimed. "My rogue tower is still up for intercepting their alarms. Anders' phone was using *my* tower."

"So?"

"Jill and I could never crack the Montalban's encrypted communications, but with this, I can tell you approximately where Kat is, or at least which cell tower she's closest to." Even though we were going extremely fast, Reaper reached down and began reading the screen of a tablet he had resting on the center console. I probably should have told him to keep his eyes on the road, but I wanted Kat *dead.* "She's way over on the other side of town. But I know that area! There's a fancy hotel there that the Illuminati have used for meetings. That's got to be where she's at."

We had to get Jill medical attention ASAP. There was no way I could get over there before Kat was gone.

But Valentine could.

Chapter 10: Poor Life Choices

VALENTINE

Paris
September 24th

The quiet moments in my life always turned out to be like a lull between storms. It made it that much harder to enjoy them, knowing that it was only a matter of time before everything went to hell again, but I tried my best.

Unable to sleep, I lay there in bed, staring up at the darkened ceiling, and wondering what would happen next. Ling was asleep next to me. She denied it, but she snored. I thought it was adorable.

Sleeping was the one time she looked at peace. Like me—like so many other people I knew—Ling had just seen too much. I rarely slept for more than five or six hours at a time. Ghosts haunted my dreams, and I saw dead faces almost every night. People I'd watched die, people I'd killed, people I couldn't save, all blurred together, until they were hard to tell apart. I'd lost track of how many people I'd killed. There'd been so many, from the Skinner Brothers back in high school to the Battle of the Crossroads, everywhere I went I left a pile of corpses in my wake.

Some deserved it, others were just fighting for the other side, and some were just in the wrong place at the wrong time. I'd never been religious, but as I stared at that darkened ceiling I wondered if hell was a real place, and if I was truly damned.

Ling stirred and brushed the hair out of her eyes. "Can't sleep?"

"Sorry, I didn't mean to wake you."

She snuggled up close to me, resting her head on my shoulder. "You didn't. You're not the only one who has a hard time sleeping. Just try to relax."

Without any new leads, we had entered one of those dreaded lulls. There was nothing for us to do until we got something new, leaving the team with little to do but wait. Lorenzo was off grasping at straws, but Ariel was monitoring it. She insisted that there might be something worthwhile there, so we just let her do her thing and hoped for a break. Tailor was on standby in case I needed him, but until we had something solid to go on there wasn't anything he could do, either.

"I've just got a bad feeling."

"Are you actually worried about Lorenzo's operation?" Ling asked.

"Maybe a little. I'm more worried about what happens if we fail."

"We won't."

I yawned. Having Ling with me was terribly comforting, and not just because I was curled up with a beautiful, naked woman. She understood what was going through my mind. It was rare enough that I met someone who understood me at all, much less someone I could really relate to. I was damned lucky to have her and I knew it.

"Are you going to fall asleep on me?" Ling asked.

"I might actually get back to sleep, yeah." I yawned again.

"I don't think so," she said. Before I could say anything else she climbed on top of me and kissed me. A moment later she pulled away from our embrace. She looked down into my eyes, her hair hanging in my face, and smiled. "I love you."

It always sounded strange to hear her say that. "I love you, too." I meant it. I loved this woman with all of my heart, and I would do anything for her.

Ling leaned in closer to me, eyes twinkling in the darkness. "You know what I think we should do?"

"Well, that's pretty obvious."

BRRRRRRT.

She sighed. "I think you should answer your phone. It's probably important."

BRRRRRT.

"Goddamn it," I growled. Ling laughed and moved off of me so I could reach whichever of my three phones was vibrating on the nightstand. *BRRRRRRT.* This time it was the one Reaper had given me.

"It's Lorenzo. He must have found something." I tapped the screen and put the phone to my ear. "Go ahead."

"*Valentine!*" Lorenzo was out of breath. Something was wrong. "*We've got a problem!*"

"What's going on?"

"*Jill's been shot.*"

"What?" Ling looked a question at me as I sat up. "Jill has been shot." I spoke into the phone. "What happened? Is she okay?"

"*No, she's not fucking okay!*" Lorenzo snapped. "*She's losing a lot of blood.*"

I put him on speaker phone so Ling could hear. "Where are you? What happened?"

"*Reaper is driving us to a doctor. We can't go to a hospital.*" He said something I couldn't make out, talking to somebody else. "*I fucked up, Valentine, I fucked up. This is all my fault.*"

I'd never heard him like this. It was bizarre, hearing Lorenzo on the edge of panic. "Calm down."

"*Don't tell me to fucking calm down. Anders shot her.*"

"Listen—"

"*No. You listen. Reaper knows where Kat is right now. She's at the Hotel Gueguen, or at least really close to there.*"

"Okay, what do you want me to do?"

"*Valentine, she has a nuke.*"

I felt my heart drop into my stomach, and hoped I'd misunderstood him. "I'm sorry, what?"

"*She. Has. A. Nuclear. Weapon!*"

"At the hotel?"

"*No! Fuck, I don't know. I don't know where it is, but she has one. That's what Blue is. They're going to nuke a city!*"

"What city?"

"*I don't know!*" Lorenzo roared. "*Get over there and kill her!*"

Ling had gone to work and had already pulled up the hotel on her phone. She showed me the display. It was a five-star establishment not too far to the northeast of Place de la Concorde. It was a short walk to the Louvre or the Grand Palace from there. The area would be covered in cops.

"Just like that? Just waltz into a hotel and have a shootout in the middle of fucking Paris?"

"Like you haven't done it before!"

"What does he expect you to do?" Ling asked, concern in her voice.

"Alright, alright. Lorenzo, take care of Jill. I'll handle the rest."

"Handle it how? You have to take Kat out."

"Just trust me. Take care of Jill. As soon as he can, have Reaper send me whatever he has on that place. I'll talk to you later." I cut the call before he could say anything else.

"What is it you plan on doing? We can't just rush in there. There are only five of us." Ling didn't count Ariel on a combat op for obvious reasons. "Katarina will have twice that." Ling was right. We didn't know anything about the situation. Going in blind, guns blazing, was a sure to get some of us killed, or all of us caught. "Her security detail was extensive *before* she knew someone was hunting her. Now she expects trouble."

I set down the phone Reaper had given me and picked up the one Tailor had given me. "Yeah, but they won't be expecting *this*."

LORENZO

Reaper had called ahead and woken up his contact, who had agreed to meet us. Before hanging up, Reaper had offered him a whole lot of money to keep his mouth shut. It wasn't like off-the-books doctors were super honest types to begin with. The address he'd been given wasn't a hospital, but a clinic in an immigrant neighborhood, and it had been closed down for the night. Most of the lights were off, but there was a fat, sweaty man, smoking a cigarette by the open back door. When he saw Reaper tear into the parking lot, he wheeled out a gurney.

"What you got?" he asked, with a thick Serbian accent as I got out of the back seat.

"Three gunshot wounds to the abdomen. She's unconscious and lost a lot of blood."

He *tsked* disapprovingly. "Why you bring girl to gunfight? Get her on cart." Reaper ran around to help me, and the two of us, as quickly—but gently—as possible, lifted Jill out. With the cigarette still dangling from his lip, the Serbian wheeled her inside. "Shoot with what? Big bullets? Little bullets?"

I remembered the sudden pattern of holes. "Buckshot." *Fucking Anders.* "From maybe ten yards away, but they punched through a truck door first."

"Is good. Pellets not fragment, but maybe bounce around a little. No problem." He pushed the gurney down the darkened hall and into a small operating room. A man and a woman were already waiting inside, wearing scrubs and masks. The woman's eyes were bleary and red from drinking. The male was probably still a teenager. They took the gurney, lifted the bandages to inspect the damage, and then waited, not doing a damn thing.

Why weren't they working? "Save her."

"Cash first," the fat doctor said. "Then we start."

Before I could say anything, Reaper stepped in. "This is what I've got on me." He held up a thick wad of euros. Reaper slammed the wad down on a stainless steel table. "You know who I am, so you know I'm good for the rest."

The fat face broke into a scowl. "Yah, I know you, Mr. The Reaper, which is why I know who shot this girl probably. The Montalbans already put out call for extra doctors for the men you shot tonight. They have more money than sense, but they will wonder why I did not answer. Which is why you pay extra up front."

I got in his face. So close I could taste the cheap cigarette smoke, and glared into his greedy pig eyes. "If you know who he is, then you can guess who *I am*." I put as much menace as I could in the words, and right then, pissed off and covered in Jill's blood, I had menace to spare.

"You are him?" He looked me over suspiciously, but he wasn't the easily intimidated sort. "I heard infamous Lorenzo was dead."

"You heard wrong. That's my girl. So get your ass to work. Save her and I'll make you rich." It wasn't unusual for off-the-books doctors to double dip, as in get paid to take the bullet out, and then rat out their patient to the people who put the bullet into them in the first place. "Cross me, and they'll be picking pieces of you out of that drain."

Apparently, he believed me. The Serbian nodded toward the other two, and said something in his native language. Despite their shifty appearance, they immediately flew into action, and even appeared to know what they were doing. The fat surgeon went to the sink, spit his cigarette out, and began washing his hands. "For you, Mr. Lorenzo, special price of only double my usual fee for bullet holes. This is good?"

"This is good."

"Then go to waiting room. Drink coffee. Have a smoke. Read magazines. Clean off the blood first. You look like shit. Do not get blood on the couches or I must explain it in morning. I'll save your woman."

"You better." I turned without another word. In a daze, I walked out of the operating room. Reaper asked me where I was going, but I was having a hard time hearing him. I said something about ditching the car. We couldn't have a car with broken windows and bullet holes sitting out in the open parking lot. He tossed me the keys. Then I went and sat in the car, stared at the blood, and punched the steering wheel until my hands hurt, worrying that Jill was going to die, and cursing myself for being powerless to stop it.

I prayed for a chance to murder everyone who'd wronged me. I shouted, and cursed, and slammed my fists against the dash, so incredibly furious and filled with hate that I couldn't even contain it. I'd never wanted to kill anyone that badly before. Until the ringing in my ears got so bad that for just a moment, the briefest of moments, I thought I heard the familiar whispers of Sala Jihan's dungeons.

I stopped. Put my face in my aching hands, and wept.

VALENTINE

The Hotel Gueguen had once been a Directorial-style manor house. According to the info Reaper had just sent me, this small luxury hotel only had five suites, but all of them were currently being rented on the same credit card, which more than likely belonged to a Montalban shell corporation.

The streets were nearly deserted as the dawn began to overtake Paris. It was a cool but lovely morning. Next to the street-level entrance was a small coffee shop, where a few early risers sat drinking the local brew and eating croissants, conversing, or staring at their phones. There were a few tough guys, trying to look inconspicuous. Security men, undoubtedly Kat's. With a ball cap on, I looked like just another tourist. In any case I'd never met Kat. They would be looking for Lorenzo, not for me. I was six inches taller than him, so there was no mistaking us for one another.

This is insane. You are out of your goddamn mind, I told myself. I'd made Ling drop me off a couple blocks away before falling back a safe distance. She was adamantly opposed to my plan, but for once I got her to listen and do as I asked. She had been really angry with me, though. If I somehow lived through this I was going to catch hell from her later.

Actually, all of my Exodus comrades had been angry at me. Once we roused the team, they all thought my plan was stupid. Skunky called it "suicidal," which I thought was melodramatic. In any case, Katarina Montalban apparently had a nuclear weapon. There was no more time to screw around, and it was better to risk just my life. They had decided that I was in charge of this show, so it was my call to make.

The only person who *hadn't* disagreed, surprisingly, was Ariel. But that was mostly because when we'd found her, she'd been staring at a computer screen going through shipping manifests, mumbling about Kat having a nuclear weapon. So it wasn't so much that she was opposed to my plan, but that she was too distracted by potential Armageddon to notice.

When I asked her if she was sure Katarina had a nuke, Ariel swore that she was certain. That was enough for me. This was worth the risk. If I went down, it would be by myself, and Exodus would still have another shot.

My phone buzzed in my pocket, a text message from Tailor. He called my plan stupid, but he still backed my play. He had called in his reinforcements. Now his team was in position and standing by. *Good.* Now there was only one thing left to do.

I bought myself a hot chocolate from the little coffee shop, sat down at one of the tables on the sidewalk, and pulled out a different phone, a prepaid flip phone I'd paid cash for. I paused for a moment, heart racing, and dialed Hawk's old number. It rang, and rang, and rang, and I just let it go. After about twenty rings with no answer, I hung up, and waited. *I hope this works,* I thought to myself. Part of me hoped it didn't.

After about five minutes, the phone buzzed in my hand, a call from a hidden number. My heart was pounding in my chest now. I didn't want to answer it. Taking a deep breath, I flipped it open, and brought it to my ear.

Underhill didn't waste time on pleasantries. *"You evaded me for a year and a half, and now you want to talk?"* He sounded like he was in a moving vehicle, but I couldn't be sure.

"I'm assuming you've triangulated my location and are en route as we speak."

"What's your game, Valentine?" His voice was gravelly and cold. He sounded weary, and he should be, since they'd pulled him out of retirement for me. *"Just go quiet. You try anything stupid and more innocent people will get hurt."*

"I'll save you time trying to zero in on my exact location, old man," I growled. "I'm at a little coffee shop next to the Hotel Gueguen." I didn't bother trying to pronounce the French name correctly. "Staying in that hotel is Katarina Montalban."

"I don't care about some Illuminati harpy. What is it you think you're doing?"

"I know what Project Blue is. You remember, the thing you guys tortured me for months for? I didn't know then, but I know now."

"We can talk about it when I get there."

I gave him a sardonic laugh. "Hard to talk with a bag on my head. Listen to me. There's something bigger going on here than you assholes wanting me dead. Katarina Montalban has a nuclear weapon. I don't know how, I don't know where, and I don't know when she plans to use it, but that woman has a nuke. If you want to stop Project Blue, if you're really so goddamn worried about it, come get me. How far out do you think you are?"

"Just stay where you are and nobody else has to die."

"Right, threatening bluster. Where are you? Will I be waiting long? Should I have another hot chocolate?"

I could tell that Underhill wasn't used to being talked to like that. I knew I was pissing him off, but he kept his cool. *"You just sit tight."*

"Whatever. Look, I'll be waiting for you, with the Montalban woman. Valentine out." I ended the call and snapped the phone in half, dropping it in a trash can as I made my way toward the hotel lobby. I sent Tailor a text: *He's coming.*

Tailor's only response was, *Rgr.*

An Illuminati strike team couldn't do anything to Underhill, and vice versa. For the same reason, Romefeller wouldn't let Tailor and his team simply grab Katarina Montalban. I had kind of assumed that shadowy organizations operating above the law wouldn't have so much bureaucratic red tape to deal with, but that's what you get for making assumptions. These people took their gentlemen's agreements seriously. In any case, Underhill might not care about Katarina Montalban, but her guys would probably start shooting the moment Underhill showed up, especially since they were paranoid that Lorenzo was gunning for them. If this worked, I'd take out both of them in one move, and I might even get out alive.

If it didn't? Well, I told Ling I loved her and said goodbye. It was about all I could do. I even left my custom .44 Magnum with her. My lucky charm had seen me through countless bad days, but not today. If the worst happened, I didn't want Underhill taking it as a damned trophy.

I was unarmed. There was no way they'd let me get close to Kat with a gun on me, and having a gun wouldn't matter when I was this badly outnumbered. The chances of this working were slim. Ling was right: it was stupid, but somebody had to do something. Better me alone than everyone. I thought about how anguished Lorenzo had sounded with Jill bleeding in his arms. I'd done that once with Sarah. I'd be damned if I was going to do it with Ling.

The small reception area of the hotel was ornately furnished, including a sitting area with plush furniture. Two guys, also trying to look nondescript, watched me over their newspapers as I walked in the front door. The newspapers weren't for reading, they were for hiding the guns on their laps. I smiled at them but didn't say anything as I made my way to the reception desk.

"Good morning, Monsieur," the woman behind the desk said. She was a pretty thing, wearing a tight dress, her hair done up in a bun. I must look American, because she spoke English to me. "I am so sorry, but we are completely booked at the moment. I can direct you to other hotels in the area if you are looking for a place to stay."

"Thank you, darlin', but I'm not looking for a room. I probably couldn't afford it anyway. I'm here to speak to one of your guests."

That certainly got the security guys' attention. The receptionist didn't seem to notice the change in the wind, and was oblivious to the fact that a gunfight could break out any second. "I see, but, I cannot disclose who is staying here. We value our guests' privacy."

"Could you send Katarina Montalban a message for me? Tell her that I know where Lorenzo is."

"Monsieur?" The receptionist seemed confused. The two security men both stood up, and the woman behind the desk got very nervous.

"It'll be okay, I promise," I said reassuringly. I stopped her before she could pick up the phone. "I think you should deliver the message in person." If they were going to just blast me, she really didn't need to see that. I could see them in the mirror. Both were staring me down, and one was on his phone, but neither approached.

She nodded at me slowly, then stepped back from her desk. "*Oui.* I will go knock on her door. Please, ah, wait a moment." Her shoes clicked on the floor as she hurried out of the room.

One of the goons, a muscular man with blonde hair cropped into a flat top, walked over to the main entrance and locked the door. The other, a short, skinny fellow with long hair, remained staring. Neither one was bothering to hide the pistols in their hands.

My heart rate slowed, and the anxiety receded. I felt the muscles in my face relax as *The Calm* washed over me. I didn't want to die, but I was prepared to.

"Nice morning, huh?"

They looked at each other and blinked. The long-haired man stepped toward me.

"Relax." I raised my hands to show they were empty. "I'm here to talk to your boss about the guy trying to kill her. She'll be mighty pissed if you do something stupid and she doesn't get that information."

"Indeed I would be."

I heard multiple people coming down the marble stairs behind me, including the distinctive sound of a woman in high heeled shoes. I turned around. A woman in a white dress stood on the stairs. With her were four armed men, guns all drawn.

"I do not like people interrupting my breakfast; however, I am *very* interested in where Lorenzo is." Katarina Montalban was blond and could've been a supermodel ten years ago. She had a little bit of a Swiss accent, and a smoky voice that put sex line operators to shame. "If you are wasting my time, I will be most upset."

"Right. I'm just here to talk. I'm unarmed. I'm not trying to start anything."

She nodded and the two lobby guards grabbed me and roughly patted me down, not being shy about getting all up in my nooks and crannies. Katarina Montalban slinked down the stairs. Once they were done with the search, they still held onto my arms.

"Now, that's better," she purred, stepping close to me. "Who are you?"

"Michael Valentine."

She tilted her head, a little taken back. "It must be the real you. Only a fool would come here claiming the name of the man who murdered my older brother. How did you find me, Michael Valentine?"

"It's a long story."

"Do not worry, you will tell it. Because I need to know which of my men needs to have his tongue cut off for talking too much." Her guards shared nervous glances. Apparently that wasn't a bluff. She sensually ran a fingernail down the side of my face. I could smell her perfume, and her sleeveless dress was both tight and low cut. Who the hell dressed like that before six in the morning?

Lorenzo had warned me about his ex-girlfriend. She was frighteningly intelligent, but loved when men just assumed she was some dumb sex bomb. Everything about her was a weapon, including her looks and her charm. She could go from flirting to murder in seconds. He swore that she'd had good qualities once, but I didn't particularly believe him.

"But first, tell me, how do you know Lorenzo, and where is he hiding? I miss him. I want to see him again."

I glanced at a clock on the wall behind her, then looked Kat in her cold blue eyes. Her features were lovely, her lips were full and pouty, her makeup was perfect, but her eyes were dead. She had the eyes of a killer. "It's . . . complicated. But I can tell you what you want to know."

She ran a hand down my chest, to my pants, and rested it on my crotch. Even though *the Calm*, I winced a little as she grabbed my junk and squeezed. "I should hope so, or I will cut your cock off and fuck you with it." She let go, smiling again. "Now, you may talk as I finish my breakfast."

My survival depended on my ability to bullshit a manipulative psychopath for a while, until another psychopath showed up to arrest me. Not for the first time, I found myself questioning my life choices.

"And that's how it happened," I explained. "Lorenzo took off on his own and left us to die. He's a fucking coward, and I hope you skin him alive." I was sitting in a very plush chair in Katarina Montalban's hotel room, which was probably the nicest hotel room I had ever seen. She sat on her giant bed, her long legs crossed, daintily picking at a bowl of fruit. There were four armed men in the room with us, and none of them looked happy I was there.

"Mm," she said. "That does sound like my Lorenzo. He was never one for commitment."

Yeah, I simply couldn't *imagine* why Lorenzo hadn't put a ring on that finger.

"But, Michael, I find myself curious . . . why would an Exodus operative come to me, all things considered?"

"I'm not an Exodus operative." That much was true. I had never officially joined. "I'm an independent contractor. I go where the money is, and they offered a lot of money for my expertise. I had worked with them before, in Mexico."

"Anders told me of your involvement in Zubara as well. He also told me should I ever have the opportunity, to just kill you. He said you are most troublesome."

"You can tell Anders to go fuck himself. I still owe him a bullet to the face." That was also true. Lying is easier when you're sincere about it. "I'm not here because I want to be your friend, lady. I'm here because Lorenzo took off and left my team to die in the snow. I'm the only one who made it back. I've wanted payback ever since."

"I don't recall seeing you at Sala Jihan's fortress," she said coolly, leaning in a little.

Truth be told I had never been inside Sala Jihan's fortress. I was on the other side of the valley, at the dam, during the battle, but I had been briefed on what happened well enough to lie about it, convincingly. "I remember you," I said, ice in my voice. "I remember you taking off in that big fucking helicopter and leaving us to die."

She smiled a hateful little smile, like abandoning a bunch of brave men and women to die at the hands of a bunch of fanatics was amusing. "Indeed. So tell me why you're so concerned with Lorenzo, and not concerned with me? After all, you would not have been stranded on that mountain except for me. I would hate for you to harbor such vengeful feelings toward me." She popped a grape into her mouth. "Perhaps I should just have my men shoot you now?"

"You want to know the truth? I can't do anything to you. I never trusted you. I advised them to leave you out of the operation. You did exactly what I thought you were going to do. I *trusted* Lorenzo. I trusted him and six men died because of it. So no, he doesn't get to escape Sala Jihan's mines and live his life while my friends are still buried there. He doesn't get that." I took a deep breath. "Besides, I figure that when you try to kill him, there's about a fifty-fifty chance he'll kill you in the process. Either way, I win."

Had I not still been under the influence of *The Calm,* Katarina's glare may have been intimidating. Even still it was unsettling. After a moment, the mask went back on, and she looked much more pleasant. "I see. I must say, Michael, I appreciate your candor. I'm . . . unused to people being so casually blunt with me. I daresay it's refreshing."

"I don't deny that I'm the one who shot Rafael, either."

She barely reacted to that, like I'd just said I was the one who ate the last donut. "So Anders said. I never thought much of that stuffy fool."

It was the death of Rafael at my hand, and Eduard at Lorenzo's, which had put Katarina into her current position of power. Ultimately, whatever she did, it was on our heads.

"So you screwed me over at the Crossroads, sure, but I screwed you over first. The way I see it, we're even. And I'll give you Lorenzo in exchange for a small fee. He's in Paris, and I know where he's been staying. I don't know what happened to him in Jihan's mines, but he's sloppy now. He's not as good as he thinks he is. I was able to track him down."

Katarina cocked her head slightly to one side. "Why not just go after him yourself, if you're so certain?"

"Because I'm one guy with a couple of friends who do intelligence stuff. He's still dangerous, and I'm pretty sure he has a crew with him. Besides, I can risk getting killed doing it myself, or I can bring it to you and have it done for me, and maybe make a little bit of money in the process."

One of her guards stepped out and took a phone call, but the Montalban woman ignored him and continued to focus on me. "How much is *a little bit of money*?"

"Two million Euros sound good to you?"

Katarina sat back a little bit, looking perplexed. "Is that all?"

"Lady, I'm pushing my luck enough just coming here, and I'm under no illusions that this Cruella de Vil bit is just an act. You have a reputation. It'd be stupid to get greedy. I figure you're a billionaire, so this won't be a big deal for you. It's plenty for me to go retire someplace. I can't go back to the States. Your buddy Anders' old crew is still looking for me."

"You know I could just *make you* tell me."

"I know. But torturing people takes time. We both know Lorenzo won't stay in one place for long. You hand me the cash, I give you his location, and nobody has to get their hands dirty or waste any time." *Underhill, where the hell are you?* "In any case, if I don't walk out of this hotel, alive, and with all my bits and pieces right where they're supposed to be, my friends will tip off Lorenzo and you'll never catch him. I may be crazy, but I'm not stupid."

That actually made her smile. On some level, I think my brashness impressed her. "You have placed me in such a predicament, Michael! Honestly, at first I was just going to kill you. I could not stand Rafael, as he was always daddy's favorite, and standing in my way, but it would be awful for me to let such an insult to my family name pass unchallenged. But giving me Lorenzo inclines me to like you."

"Thanks?"

"The money means nothing to me. That's done. Now . . ." The security man who'd taken the phone call approached. He whispered something in her ear about a problem outside. Underhill's forces must have arrived. "I see." She looked back at me with a glare that could freeze boiling water.

"What's going on?"

"Just what do you think you're doing?"

The Calm pushed that all to the background. I had to fake looking scared. "I don't know what you're talking about."

"I'm talking about the Majestic strike team that is currently surrounding this hotel." She got off the bed, kicked off her heels, opened the closet door, and went inside. "Inform the Americans that

I'm inside, and that if they do not want an incident, they should pull back. The council will not stand for overt action."

"Ma'am," the guard said as he went to the window and peeked through the blinds, "we should get you to the garage—"

"In a moment." She came out of the closet holding a really big knife with a wickedly curved blade, and she looked really comfortable with it. "Now where were we, Michael? Oh yes, you were about to tell me where Lorenzo is, and I was deciding how painful your death is going to be."

"I thought we had a deal."

"That was before you brought Majestic to my doors."

Underhill was here, and Katarina was done screwing around, but so was I. "I know about Blue. What do you think you're going to accomplish?"

"World domination." She answered without exaggeration. "But that answers my question. Painful then."

"Ma'am," the man with the phone said. "They say they only want Valentine."

"Did they specify if he needs to be in one piece? Because that is looking exceedingly unlikely right now. You know what, never mind. The Americans can go to hell. They can have him when I'm done. Where is Lor—"

Before she could finish, a window shattered, and a metal can spewing smoke landed on the floor. My eyes immediately began burning. *Tear gas.* I had guessed right about the Bloodhound. He wasn't big on diplomacy.

The Calm helped me focus through the water in my eyes and fire in my lungs. It was a frustrating state, where I could think and process everything so much faster than my body could react, but everyone else seemed so much slower. They were coughing and partially blinded. Kat was too far, so I lunged at the closest security man. He wasn't ready for it. I was on top of him in a flash, and I was bigger than he was. We both went down, rolling across the floor. He had a death grip on his pistol. So I bit down hard on his hand. The hot, coppery taste of blood filled my mouth as he thrashed. He shouted a warning as I got control of his pistol, stuck it under his chin, and pulled the trigger.

BLAM!

Blood and brains stained the carpet. I rolled off the dead man, and stuck the gun—a Steyr M9—out in both hands and shot the nearest of Kat's guards four times before he could get a shot off. The other two bodyguards were dragging Katarina Montalban from the room. I turned and opened fire just as they shoved her through the door. I cut one of them down and wounded the other, but Katarina was gone.

She won't get far. Gunfire erupted from the lobby. The Montalban guards were in a firefight with Underhill's men. It was only a matter of time before somebody won, and whoever won would kill me. I didn't have a lot of time. I ran after Katarina.

The wounded bodyguard was waiting for me. I came out of the smoke shooting, and dropped him. But where had Kat—

She crashed into me, trying to stab me in the chest. Rather than fleeing, she had moved to the side to ambush me. I narrowly avoided the blade as I twisted my gun toward her body. Her blade struck the pistol and traveled toward my hand. I lost my weapon but managed to keep my fingers. Though partially blinded, Kat swung hard for my throat. I dodged it by an inch and she embedded the knife deep into the door frame.

I tripped over the dead man in the doorway and fell to the floor. She was on me in an instant, enraged, seemingly oblivious to the gun battle going on downstairs and the room full of tear gas. She kicked me on the side of the head. The impact of her bare heel almost made me black out. She went to kick me again, but I grabbed her ankle. She fell on top of me, fighting like a wild animal. Her nails tore down my cheeks, then she jammed her thumbs into my throat, trying to crush my windpipe.

"You can't stop me! It's mine! It's all supposed to be mine!"

Katarina was vicious, but I was a whole lot bigger than she was. She was losing her mind with rage, and I was *Calm.* She was frothing, snot leaking from her nose, spittle shooting from between clenched teeth as she tried to choke the life out of me. I slugged her.

She let go, dazed. I hurled her off me so hard she bounced off the wall. I didn't give her any time to recover. This time, my hands clamped around *her* pretty throat, and I squeezed. She thrashed, and kicked, and tried to scratch my eyes out, but I squeezed and squeezed. She turned red. Her eyes looked like they were about to pop out of her head. Everything started to go dark around me as I focused on choking the life out of this horrible woman. I saw Dr. Silvers' face for a moment, but this time I didn't let up. I shook off the image and squeezed. Katarina Montalban was going to die.

Then someone kicked me off of her, pulled a bag over my head, and dragged me away.

When they pulled the bag off of my head, I wondered if it was because my captors wanted to gloat, but Underhill didn't even look smug. This was just another day at work for him. We sat facing each other in the back of a big panel van, speeding along, just the two of us. His face was unreadable. He was an unassuming man in his sixties. His hair had thinned out, and his face had the hard lines of someone who drank too much. He had a thick neck and muscular features, staying in shape despite his age. His wide chin and cold eyes made him look like a TV show's idea of a mafia hit man, except he was dressed in a blue windbreaker and slacks. He could have been somebody's grandpa.

There were empty bench seats along each side of the back. I was handcuffed, my wrists were chained to my ankles, and my ankles were chained to the floor. I certainly wasn't going anywhere.

"Took you long enough."

Underhill was silent.

I was undeterred. "Did you kill Katarina Montalban?"

He just stared at me.

"Damn it." My plan had failed. I was a fool. "I was hoping you'd kill her. Either that or that she'd kill you. If you'd have waited one more goddamn minute, I'd have choked the life out of that psychotic bitch and saved us all a lot of trouble."

He finally spoke, in that same rough voice I remembered from our phone conversations. "I couldn't let you do that once I was involved. It's against the rules."

The Calm was gone, and my temper flared. "Man, *fuck your rules!* Do you know what that woman is going to do? She's going to use a *nuclear weapon!* She's the one who is going to execute Project Blue, the thing you assholes have been so worried about for the past two years, and you *let her get away!* Do you have any idea how royally, how totally, you screwed this up? Jesus Christ, Anders is working for her! I know damned well you're looking for him, too!"

Underhill raised an eyebrow at the mention of Anders' name. "I'll be sure to pass that on. The rest of it is not my problem. My orders are to bring you in, not start a war. The rhyme and reason aren't for me to decide."

"You stupid asshole! Project Blue *is* the reason! It's the reason you people tortured me for months! It's the reason you're looking for me!"

"Not the only reason. You made some bad choices. Now you got to answer for them."

"Will you spare me your folksy homespun wisdom bullshit? I know who you are, and I know what you do. You shot an unarmed man down in cold blood."

"Your pal, Hawk. Sure, I did. I'd do it again, if I had to. You'd have done the same thing in my place. You have. I read your file. You're a killer, just like me. If you hadn't been stupid, you'd be me in thirty years. None of us are clean, kid. It's just a matter of who we work for."

I jerked at the chains binding my wrists to my ankles. "Yeah, well, we all have to answer for our choices, don't we? And believe me, you're going to answer for yours, too."

"No shit." He shook his head slightly. "You think you got it all figured out, don't you? Boy, you don't know a goddamn thing about me. Your old friend Hunter? I was fighting communists with him before you were born, you jumped-up little shit. We protected our country so regular folks could live their pointless, mundane lives without worrying when the Soviet missiles were coming. The enemy changed, but we stuck around. We did the dirty work that kept most of the world clean."

I stared back at him as the van rolled through the streets of Paris. "I'm sure that's what they told you, old timer. You ever think that maybe they were lying to you? All they do is lie. They'll tell you whatever they want you to hear to get you to do what they want. You were protecting America from Communists; well, guess what? The Berlin Wall came down and you assholes had nothing to do with it. The only thing you fought for was to keep your bosses in power."

To my shock, Underhill actually laughed. A brief, sardonic chuckle, but before that I didn't think the man could smile lest he crack his face. "Everything you know about the fall of Communism is the story we wanted you all to hear. People would accept that rah-rah-America bullshit, that optimism or patriotism, or economics, or whatever brought the Soviets down. You know what really brought them down?

Us. Guys like me and Hunter. Years, decades of planning, of covert action, of infiltration, assassination, and sabotage. You know how many men we lost over the years? How many people we killed?"

"You're taking credit for the CIA's work now?"

"The CIA is a joke." Underhill scowled. "After the sixties they lost their nerve, so we stopped working with them. Our leadership had no balls, but some of us kept on doing what we needed to do. Not every politician is a pussy. Those backed us in secret. We put together our own outfit behind the scenes, black budgets, all the best intel, no babysitters, and it grew from there. Since you didn't grow up speaking Russian you should thank God every day we did what we had to do. Presidents come and go, administrations change, people are stupid, and voters are fickle, but we're there behind the scenes no matter what, making sure the shit that needs to get done, gets done."

"Thanks for the Majestic history lesson."

"Majestic?" He snorted. "Whatever you want to call us, the world is fucked up, but we're there to keep it on track. When we do our job right, nobody even knows we exist, and people go on living."

Underhill sounded just like Romefeller. They were opposite sides of the same megalomaniacal coin. "Funny, I heard damn near the same exact thing from the guys Blue was designed to destroy. What's your point?"

"The point is, kid, that nuclear war that all the expert analysts, all the supercomputers, all the data said was almost inevitable? Never happened. Red China, rising to be the next superpower after the fall of the Soviet Union? Never happened. Communism is dead. It's preached in college campuses, but only four countries in the entire world claim to be communist. You think you know about us, about how we do business, about what we fight for? You don't know a goddamn thing. You had your chance to be on this team and you threw it away. Now you're going in a hole so deep you'll never see the sun again."

I laughed at him. "You tried that already."

He shrugged, then leaned back in his seat. "Silvers was sloppy. Nobody's going to make you a science project this time. Nobody will know what happened to you. Your survival now depends entirely on your cooperation."

My chains jerked taut as anger pulsed through my body. *"Cooperation?* Motherfucker, I *handed you* the woman executing

Project Blue, with the help of Anders, and you *let her go!* What the fuck else do you want from me?"

"Not for me to decide. Your statements regarding Project Blue, the Montalban woman, Anders, all of it, will be vetted and if they're determined to be genuine, followed up on. You might be lying, or you might just be wrong. Ever consider that, that maybe you don't have it all figured out, smart guy? Of course you didn't. You're a damned fool."

"When a nuke goes off in some city somewhere, it'll be on you. Your bosses will be looking for a scapegoat to hang, so I expect I'll see you in the cell next door in whatever hole you're sending me to."

Underhill shrugged again. "We'll see."

I was at a loss for words. I slumped back in my seat, jingling my chains. "I have to piss."

"Go ahead. I'm not the one who has to clean this thing."

The driver of the van looked at me in the rearview mirror, but didn't say anything. He turned his attention back to the road. I glared at Underhill, trying to read his face, but he was unflappable. He stared at me blankly. I hated him for killing Hawk. I wanted to wrap my chains around his neck and throttle him until his eyes popped out, but I could tell it really hadn't been anything personal. It was like being mad at an attack dog for biting when commanded. He was a professional, and he was just doing what he was trained to do. He clearly felt no remorse, but I doubt he took any pleasure in it either. To a man like him, killing was just work to be done.

To men like us.

Was I really so different? Did I really have the right to hate someone for taking a life, at this point, or was I just a self-righteous hypocrite?

CRASH!

There was a spine-jarring impact. Metal crumpled and glass shattered. Underhill wasn't wearing a seatbelt. He seemed to float in space for a moment, looking slightly surprised, but that was it, and then the van was rolling over. We landed on our side, grinding to a halt.

I must have gone out for a moment. When I opened my eyes, the van was still and filled with dust. Hanging there from my chains, I was listening to the sound of metal twisting and squealing in protest. The back doors were being pried open.

Underhill was lying there, blinking, just out of my reach. He grimaced in pain as he sat up, and drew a government model .45 from under his windbreaker. He aimed it at my head and waited. Daylight flooded the sideways interior of the van as they broke the doors open. Men in tactical gear and masks stormed in, hunched over, weapons ready. Three laser dots appeared on Underhill's chest, but he stayed where he was, his face as unreadable as before.

One of the masked men spoke. It was Tailor. "By order of the Council of the Thirteen Families, Michael Valentine is under our protection. He's coming with us. Any interference on your part will be considered a hostile act and a violation of our organizations' agreement."

"You're not taking him," Underhill said calmly.

"Tailor, shoot him!" I screamed, still dangling, chained to the bench seat, Underhill's .45 pointed at my face. "Shoot this asshole! He killed Hawk! Shoot him!"

"Shut up, Val," Tailor said angrily. "Let me handle this."

"This man is my prisoner," Underhill stated plainly. "You can't take him."

"You're in our territory now, buddy. You being here at all is a violation of the rules and you damned well know it. Now pack up your shit and get the hell out of Europe. You have no business here."

Underhill's finger was on the trigger and I was staring down the barrel of a .45. "Valentine is my business, and you Illuminati fucks aren't taking him. Shoot me and there will be hell to pay."

"Tailor, just fucking shoot him!" I screamed again.

"Val, shut your damned mouth!" he snapped back. Sirens wailed in the background. "Time's running out, Underhill. My team? We've got proper Interpol Special Enforcement Operations IDs and the best lawyers in the country. My boss says one word and the French government says thank you very much. You guys are a bunch of trigger-happy Americans on temporary visas, with CIA creds, who just shot up a hotel in the capital of France. You wanna try me? Walk away right now, or rot in a French prison for the next thirty years. I guarantee your superiors will just disavow your ass, and have you shivved if you cut a deal. You know how they work better than I do."

Underhill mulled that over for a moment. He was stuck. It was surrender or shoot me. Underhill wasn't suicidal. He was a professional. The old killer took a deep breath, safetied his pistol, and put it down. "Fine. We'll do it your way for now." One of the Frenchmen grabbed Underhill by the sleeve and dragged him out. He gave me that same blank stare as he went past. It told me that he wasn't done with me.

"That man killed Hawk!"

"I know, Val, I know. I'm sorry, buddy. I don't have a choice." Another operative, fully kitted up with a slung shotgun, handed Tailor a pair of bolt cutters. The sirens were right on top of us. Tailor spoke to one of his teammates. "Claude! Talk to the police, keep them off our backs. Don't worry, Val. I'll get you someplace safe and explain everything."

I hung there, head throbbing, as Tailor cut me free.

Chapter 11: A Force for Good

VALENTINE

Ancient secret societies sure know how to keep a guy waiting. It had been hours since Tailor and his team had rescued me from Underhill. I was dragged out of one van and stuffed into another, rushed off as Tailor's men worked it out with local authorities. It turned out that Tailor's credentials had a lot more official backing than he'd originally let on, or Romefeller had a lot of officials under his thumb.

From the back of a windowless van, I had no way of knowing where they'd taken me. When we stopped, I got out in a high-security, underground parking garage. I was whisked inside and brought to what looked like the building's security office. I wasn't a prisoner, exactly, but the security guards kept telling me to sit down and wait in broken English. I was looked at by a medic or a doctor—I'm not sure, he didn't speak English—had bandages applied to my surprisingly minor injuries, took a bunch of Tylenol, and was left to wait.

So wait I did, for what seemed like forever. I sat in an uncomfortable plastic chair, sipping water from a paper cup, wondering what in the hell was taking Tailor so long. I was getting frustrated. Katarina Montalban had a nuclear weapon, and God only knew what she planned to do with it. I hadn't been able to contact Ling and let her know I was okay, and she was probably going crazy by now. This was no time to be screwing around. I got up and started to pace around, much to the annoyance of the security guards watching over me, but to hell with them.

I looked up when an elevator chimed. Tailor and two of his men

215

stepped into the security office. One of Tailor's men spoke with one of the guards briefly, in French, before I was waved over.

"Sorry that took so long, Val." Tailor had removed his armor; his black combat shirt was still damp with sweat. "There is so much bureaucratic bullshit in this organization that I don't know how they get anything done. Come on, you're going to talk to the boss man again."

I followed Tailor into the elevator, noting quietly that his two men were still wearing armor and still carrying submachine guns. "Are they here to make sure I don't make a run for it?"

"Dude, shut up. I've had enough of your self-righteous bullshit," Tailor spat. He hit the button, and the door closed, leaving his men behind. We started going up.

"None of this would be happening if we'd just shot the psycho and been done with it!"

"Goddamn it, Val, it doesn't work like that!"

I wasn't in any mood for his excuses. "That guy that had me? That was Underhill. He killed Hawk in cold blood, and you just let him go."

Frustrated, Tailor reached over and hit the hold button. We were going to have this out in private. "You think I don't know that? I can't just go around killing whoever I want, Val!"

"When Katarina Montalban blows up a city, I hope it's Paris, so you, and Romefeller, and all of you Illuminati assholes can die thinking 'man, I'm so glad I stuck to those rules!' *She's* not following your rules."

"No, but Underhill is. And that's the only reason you're still alive. You're welcome, by the way. This whole thing was stupid. I told you it was stupid, and you just wouldn't listen."

"What would you have me do, Tailor? Pass up a chance to put a stop to this? If that woman goes through with Project Blue, a lot of people are going to die!"

"Would you listen to yourself, Val? Christ, you sound like one of your Exodus buddies. You can't save the world if you're fucking dead, alright? That wasn't just stupid, it was suicidal."

"Some things are worth dying for, Tailor."

He laughed at me. "Holy shit, Ling has done a number on you. She's got you wrapped right around her little finger, doesn't she?"

"No." That was crap, and it made me want to punch him in his mouth.

"All this hero bullshit is going to do is get you killed. It's not going to change anything, and it's not going to save anybody."

"Hero thing? And what, your way is better? You traded in the dirt and the blood for some civilization, you cleaned up and got a suit, but you're still doing the same damned thing, pulling triggers for money. I'm not a hero, but I'm not just going to sit by and let a psychopath blow up a city."

"Neither am I!" Tailor shouted. "For fuck's sake, Val, I'm on your side here! I'm trying to help you!"

"You had the chance to help and you walked away, because you're more worried about your cushy job and your stupid rules than you are about doing the right thing. I thought you changed, but you haven't. As long as you've got yours, you'll watch the world burn down."

To my surprise, Tailor wheeled around, grabbed me by my shirt, and slammed me against the wall, hard enough to shake the whole elevator. "You don't know a fucking thing!" I don't think I'd ever seen him that angry. "I've been risking my ass for you, for this pet project of yours. I risked my life, and the lives of my men, saving you back there. Not only could you have gotten yourself killed, but you could have gotten me killed too, but I went along with it anyway because I *am trying to help you.* What the hell did you *think* was going to happen?"

"Let go and back off," I ordered.

Reluctantly, he did, but he stuck an angry finger in my face. "I told you this wouldn't work, but you were so ready to be the hero that you just wouldn't listen. Tell me straight, man, no bullshit. Did Ling put you up to this? This is the kind of shit Exodus would do."

Anger pulsed through me, but I kept it in check. "No. She thought it was stupid and would get me killed too."

"Well, you're just a brain genius then, ain't you?"

"I never claimed to be smart, man. I'm just trying to do the right thing. I'm sick and tired of everybody sitting around, wringing their hands, saying there's nothing they can do. Well, I'm doing something."

People say violence never solves anything, but that's a lie they tell school kids to try to stop them from fighting. Violence solves everything, if applied correctly. Whatever the problem, if you shoot enough people, it will go away. It's just a question of logistics, time, and maintaining the resolve to keep bringing the violence to bear for as long as necessary.

"Look," Tailor said, more quietly this time, "I told you, it frustrates me too. I need you to trust me here, okay? Believe me, I was hoping this scheme of yours would work. If it had, if Underhill had gone in and actually killed Katarina, then I could've put him in the dirt for violating détente. We could have killed two birds with one stone. Those are the limitations we have to abide by, whether we like them or not."

"*You* have to abide by," I corrected.

"Listen, don't cop this attitude with Romefeller, okay? Can you be cool?"

"Yeah. I'm cool."

Tailor collected himself, nodded, then pushed the button. The elevator started moving again.

"Did you tell your boss about Katarina's plans?"

"I told him what you told me. I didn't tell him that I knew you were going in there as bait. I have to cover my ass. So don't volunteer that shit, please." The elevator chimed again as we reached our destination level. "Take a deep breath and explain what happened, calmly. He doesn't respond well to people getting all huffy. You stomping around like a teenage drama queen isn't going to get this done any sooner. Okay?"

"Fine," I said, as the elevator doors opened. "But we are running out of time."

I found Romefeller waiting for me in an office that was just as ornate, if rather smaller, than his one in Zurich. We were on the twelfth floor, and his office afforded a good view of the city. He was leaning on the glass, gazing out across Paris. The Eiffel Tower cut its iconic image in Paris' skyline. It was a beautiful day, the sun was shining, and a secret society was mad at me.

"That was a bold, brazen, but foolhardy act, young man," Alistair Romefeller said as he turned around. Today he was wearing a charcoal gray suit with a red vest, and he did not look happy. He saw Tailor, and dismissed him with a nod, like he was a butler or something. Tailor left without a word. "If I had known that your plan was to go in there and murder her, I would never have sanctioned it."

"The plan was to let Majestic do it for me. It didn't work out."

"You've made the situation worse. Now you've tipped your hand, and she'll be that much more careful in future. Do you realize what you've done?"

I wasn't sure if he was actually mad that I'd made the situation worse, or if it was just sour grapes because I had the gall to violate their precious rules. "I improvised."

Romefeller groaned, and ran his fingers through his silver hair. "And now Underhill is here, confined to his embassy. He is a relic from another era, when both Majestic and my associates were more willing to engage in, how would you say, direct action. If they dug up that Cold War dinosaur for your sake, you must have really, really gotten on someone's bad side."

"It was a string of unfortunate coincidences." I shrugged. "Most of the time I was simply along for the ride. That doesn't matter now though. I know what Blue is."

"I heard from Mr. Tailor. How confident are you in your assessment that the Montalbans have such a weapon?"

He was being mighty goddamned nonchalant about it. "The assessment that psychopath has an atomic bomb? Pretty good. What part of that doesn't scare the crap out of you?"

"How did you come by this information, exactly?" he asked, skeptically. "That's a serious charge."

Is he for real right now? "What difference does it make? Hell, even if I'm wrong, don't you think it's at least worth looking into? Why in the hell do you think I would go in there, risking my life, trying to kill that woman? If there's even a chance—"

Romefeller raised a hand, silencing me. "Mr. Valentine, listen to me. I don't doubt that you believe that what you say is true, but I can't very well level such a charge at one of my peers going on just your word. You keep talking about how she is crazy and dangerous, but think of how this looks from the outside. You're the one who tried to murder her."

My eyes narrowed, but I didn't say anything.

"I suspect I know where you got that information. I would urge you not to trust Mr. Lorenzo so much. He may be playing the role of your ally now, but his reputation is well known. I assure you it is only an act. The only thing motivating him is a personal vendetta against the Montalban family, and it looks to me like he tried to use you to carry out his revenge fantasy for him."

"How did you know?"

"About Lorenzo? I have my sources. After an event last night at a truck depot, Mr. Anders is not only convinced that Lorenzo is alive, but has put out a bounty on him. Minutes later, you were sent on a this fool's errand."

"Doesn't it bother you that a guy who was once the sworn enemy of your organization is now advising one of your members? Anders doesn't raise any red flags up in your little clubhouse or whatever?"

Romefeller actually chuckled at me, as if I were a child who had just said something adorably naïve. "We operate in a complex world of shifting shadows and temporary alliances. Allegiances change. People aren't chess pieces. They can change sides, move around as it benefits them. Men such as Mr. Tailor. You can't see the big picture, from where you sit, but you should be grateful for our liberal attitude concerning the matter. Otherwise, we would have placed a price on your head for having killed one of our members, much like the substantial one that is being offered for Lorenzo."

I raised an eyebrow. "How substantial?" *Just out of curiosity.*

"Ten million U.S. dollars, and another ten million for you."

"What?"

"You can't be surprised. Considering what just transpired between you and Katarina it should not come as a shock that she just put out the same offer for your head. You went in there, announced who you are, and then tried to strangle her. That's rather insulting. The optics are bad, as they say."

"I got the same price as a Lorenzo, huh?" *That'll piss him off.* I smiled.

"You needn't worry about it, though. You're still under my protection, as I believe you're still useful to me." In other words, Romefeller was suggesting that our *friendship* was the only thing keeping me alive. "It would be ironic if you are in this situation because Lorenzo lied to you."

Lorenzo may be wrong, but I trusted Ariel. "I got an independent confirmation of the data."

"Interesting. My sources suggest that Exodus has an exceedingly brilliant intelligence analyst. The mind boggles at what someone with my resources could accomplish with such a mind in my employ. She wouldn't happen to be involved in this confirmation, would she?"

I didn't like that somebody like Romefeller knew that Ariel existed, let alone that his sources were good enough that he knew she was female. I could tell he was fishing for information, but I wasn't going to give him anything. I used a different tactic instead. "You know how I know she's got a nuke, how I really know?"

Romefeller didn't answer.

"Because I helped her *get it.*"

That got his attention. "I'm sorry?" he said. "Did I hear you correctly?"

"I didn't have any reason to think about it until last night. One of our missions during Project Heartbreaker, we left Zubara and landed in Yemen, where we intercepted a stolen Russian ICBM warhead that was being delivered to General Al Saba's forces. Anders led the mission, and after letting one of my teammates bleed to death, took charge of the warhead and took it Christ-only-knows where. Do the math. You think Anders' involvement in all of this is just a coincidence?"

I could see the realization in Romefeller's eyes, but he kept his composure. "I . . . see," he managed.

"No kidding. Now you guys need to quit dancing around and commit."

"It doesn't work like that, I'm afraid."

"Are you serious right now? You people keep telling me it doesn't work like this, or it doesn't work like that. You dither and let innocent people die, because you're too polite to violate Robert's Rules of Order? You put on this big show about how you're trying to guide the world, but you act like a pompous model UN club. Tailor gave me a big spiel about how you all are working so hard to maintain peace and order, but when it gets down to it, you're too chickenshit to do anything without voting on it first!"

"Enough!" Romefeller roared. It was strange, hearing a man like him raise his voice. I could tell he was normally too dignified for that sort of thing. "Overt action would lead to family on family violence. If you're so concerned with innocent lives, tell me, how many people will die in the crossfire when my men have a gun battle with hers in the streets of every city in Europe?"

"A lot less than if that bomb goes off."

"Perhaps, but then what? Do you know for sure that taking her into custody will stop this from happening? Do you know where this hypothetical bomb is?"

I didn't.

"I thought as much," Romefeller said, smugly. He moved in closer. "I understand your position, and I'm not dismissing you. I can only imagine what it must be like for you, having helped recover that weapon, only to find out that it may be used for some terrible purpose. I can see how weary you are. I understand the impulse to make things right."

I rather doubted he understood any of my impulses. "Alert the authorities and tell them there's a rogue warhead on French soil. That will get their attention. They'll listen to someone like you."

"Perhaps, perhaps not. She has as many politicians on her payroll as I do on mine. It all comes back to your word and Mr. Lorenzo's, with no evidence to speak of. Do you know how many false threats of a weapon of mass destruction attack the authorities get every year? I can tell them that the Montalbans have such a weapon. They may even go arrest her. Then what? What evidence do we have? All it would do is strengthen her position in the council and weaken my own. It would amount to nothing, and may serve only to buy her more time."

"Then convince them."

"I will. I have called for a face-to-face meeting of all the families to discuss matters. We share lofty goals, but we can be a fractious and argumentative lot. You must understand that a grand council is a rare and momentous occasion, reserved only for times of dire crisis. Katarina will have the opportunity to defend her actions there. In the meantime I need you to continue your mission, only tread softly. Investigation, but no overt action. Do not make it easy for Katarina to play the victim. If we can provide them with evidence the other families will have no choice but take her into custody."

"And then what?"

Romefeller nodded toward one of the weapons hung on the wall. "That is an executioner's ax. It is not just a decoration. My organization takes our traditions very seriously. You will continue to have Mr. Tailor and any of my assets you need at your disposal, but please, before you do anything rash, keep me in the loop. Mr. Lorenzo is welcome to show himself, too, if he cares to. I assure you I won't turn him over to the Montalbans. I own paintings worth more than the price on his head."

Well, la-de-freakin'-da, Richie Rich. "I'm sure. I'll pass that on."

Romefeller came over and put a comforting hand on my shoulder. "I am on your side, Valentine. I took a solemn oath to use my resources to better the world. I've spent my life and my fortune trying to give humanity a better future. I will not allow Katarina to undo all of the good the families have accomplished. You have my word that I will get to the bottom of this."

I nodded. "Understood. I should get going. My friends don't know where I am."

"I would not dream of standing in your way. Mr. Tailor will take you wherever it is you wish to go."

"Thank you for your help. I'll be in touch."

"Godspeed, Mr. Valentine."

LORENZO
Paris
September 28th

As soon as it was safe to move Jill—and even that was questionable— we'd taken her back to one of her hideouts. We picked the flat in the boring working-class neighborhood because it was the least likely to get noticed. The doctor had said it wasn't safe to transport her, she was better off staying, and that nobody at his clinic would talk, but I didn't trust him or his people to not get greedy. So I'd stolen a work van, rolled the gurney right into the back, and left as soon as we could. I also had Reaper take any medical equipment and supplies he thought might be useful, but to make up for it I paid the doctor a *lot* more than the doctor's agreed-upon fee. He'd saved Jill's life. He could consider it a tip.

She had lost a massive amount of blood and was lucky to be alive. Deprived of actual medical care, she could still die here. The next twenty-four hours passed in a haze, with me sitting next to Jill's bed, sleeping occasionally, and waking up from nightmares to check on her. It gave me a lot of time to fret and to think.

There was a two-sided conflict going on inside my head. Part of me wanted to lash out, pure violence, vengeance. If couldn't get to Anders, I'd find someone, I didn't care who, but I'd dismantle Kat's organization brick by brick, man by man. I didn't need a plan. I'd leave a pile of mutilated corpses across this city, and eventually I'd get the right one. On the other side of my internal debate was the mature, rational, sane part, which knew that was stupid. Sure, I could start popping more Montalbans, but I'd eventually get killed or caught before I stopped them all. We needed to continue with the plan, looking for opportunities to ruin Blue. That side of me was right, but useless.

So I spent a day being useless. Antoine came by to drop off some supplies, check on Jill, and gave me a quick rundown of what had happened with Valentine and Katarina, and the resulting clusterfuck with Underhill.

I sat next to Jill's bed, she was still unconscious and I was in a daze, while Antoine stood in the doorway to the tiny bedroom. "So Kat is still out there, plotting, only now she knows exactly who's gunning for her."

"She will be hunting us," Antoine said. "Worse, Majestic will do nothing to stop her. They will not risk starting a war. The Illuminati are fickle allies at best. It is up to us."

"It always was. Damn it. I wish Valentine would have gotten her. Regardless, tell him thanks for trying. I mean that."

Antoine seemed a little surprised.

"What?"

"You do not strike me as the gratitude type, Lorenzo." I'd grown to like Antoine during our rescue mission at North Gap, and I'd saved his life in the Crossroads. He and Shen were good dudes, honorable men, and I didn't have many friends like that. I actually kind of gave a damn what he thought about me. "I know Valentine has caused you quite a bit of trouble over the years."

I could understand his confusion. Normally when I was in this bad of a mood, I'd be tempted to rip apart any convenient target, but I was just too damned worn out. Today, I was the only convenient target. "Valentine has been a huge pain in my ass. But that was a crazy stunt, and he's lucky to be alive. Walking right in there like that took guts. I can respect that."

"Valentine has changed much since we first met. I saw great potential in him, to be not just a fighter, but a leader. The importance of this mission has brought together the noble. Together, we are a force for good."

"Not counting me, obviously."

"Ha! Of course not! Such a terrible man, sacrificing himself to save the wounded after taking turns carrying them on his back across a mountain all night."

"Don't let that get out. You'll ruin my image." Like the Pale Man said, death followed me, and there had been a lot of death on that mountain. I didn't even know who else had made it out. This was the first time Antoine and I had gotten to really talk since I'd gotten out. "Since you mentioned it . . ."

"The rest of us made it because of you. Svetlana had to retire due to her injuries. She'll be glad to hear you're alive. You did good there."

"Yeah? Well, I blew it here."

Antoine looked at poor Jill, drained and sleeping. "Jill is a strong woman. She will pull through."

"I know she will."

"Call if you need anything else." Antoine turned to leave. "We will continue the search."

"Hey," I called after him. The big Exodus operative paused. "I know what I look like right now. I know I look all fucked up, but don't worry. I'm still in. No matter what, I'm still going to finish this."

"I know. I can see it burning in you. You want to strike out. But for now, we have this. Even if she can't speak, savor this time with her, Lorenzo."

"That's easy for you to say. I need to do *something*, man."

"I have been there." When Antoine folded his thick arms, he was truly an imposing man. "When I was young, rebel militia raided my village. While my wife lay dying, I had to abandon her. I could not be there with her at the end."

"Why?"

"Because they'd stolen my daughters. I had to leave my dying wife to chase after them."

Other than knowing he was from West Africa, I'd never heard him talk about his life before Exodus. "Did you get them back?"

He shook his head.

"I'm sorry." It was a trite thing to say, but that's all I had. That certainly explained why he'd become a warrior for Exodus.

"Keep your loved ones close while you can. The killing time will come soon enough. I can feel it . . . And whether you like it or not, you are on the side of the angels now, Lorenzo. Goodbye."

After he left, I'd cleaned some guns, changed some bandages, and continued being angry.

Reaper had gone back to shaking the trees to see what would fall out, but even he had limited success. Kat wasn't stupid. If she knew I was involved, that meant Reaper was involved too. She would hunker down and send her legions of minions to search for us. She had always hated my *little sidekick,* as she'd derisively called him, but she knew what he was capable of. She also had enough money to hire the best nerds possible to counter him. The idea of, hell, I don't know what to call them . . . *anti-Reapers* scouring the digital world for traces of us was frankly terrifying. I don't know what Reaper took as the bigger insult, them shooting Jill, or Kat thinking some other hackers could beat him on his own turf. I didn't know what Reaper had been up to in the other room for the last day, and he didn't have time to slow down and explain it to me. He was acting like he was waging his own private war. Whatever, at least when he was working, he wasn't being all weird and traumatized about the Crossroads.

Meanwhile, I played nurse or watched Jill sleep, knowing that she'd almost died because of me. Damn Ling for contacting her. It was better for everyone when she'd thought I was dead. I was a fool for not doing this on my own. But that damned rational part of me knew that was bogus. I hadn't dragged her into this. She'd been hunting Montalbans the whole time I'd been imprisoned. It was a miracle she'd survived as long as she had.

The irrational part of me suspected that this was all the Pale Man's doing, and that he'd tried to take her from me, because love was a distraction. It made no logical sense, Anders had pulled that trigger, and Sala Jihan was a continent away, but I still knew it was true. My brand ached as I thought about it, but if Jill died, then I was going to go back to the Crossroads and make the devil pay.

She woke up the next morning.

"Lorenzo?"

Jill's voice was barely a whisper, but I woke right up. I'd been sleeping right next to the bed, dreaming about Kat finding us somehow and Anders kicking the door in to finish what he'd started.

"You're awake."

"Hey," she croaked. Her normally olive skin was far too gray, and her eyes seemed sunken into her face. Her black hair was spread across the pillow, and the contrast only made her look too pale and small. "I'm thirsty."

"I've got you." Of course, an IV would keep you hydrated but it just wasn't the same. I should have thought of that ahead of time. I ran to the kitchen and came back with a cup of water. I held it to her lips. "Easy." I sucked at this sort of thing and ended up spilling most of it down her chin. I was going to have to find a straw.

It took Jill a few seconds to collect herself. That was normal when you'd nearly bled to death and been unconscious for days. There were huge dark circles under her eyes. I'd never seen her looking this frail before. I was scared to touch her. I thought she might break.

"What happened?" At least with the water her voice sounded a little better.

"You got shot." I didn't know how much she would remember. She was still on a lot of painkillers, and would be for quite a while. They'd had to cut her wide open to stop all the internal bleeding. I didn't know how many stitches and staples were holding her side together, but I'd seen them when I'd changed the bandages, and it was a mess.

Jill blinked a few times. "I remember driving backwards. Then this pain, like a lightning bolt. It hurt a lot, and that's it. Is everyone else okay?" Now she was looking at me, panicked. She was more coherent than I expected. "Did you get hurt? Where's Reaper?"

"Try not to move too much." I put a gentle hand on her shoulder to keep her from trying to sit up. Of course, Jill would be worried about the others before she even thought about herself. That was just the kind of person she was, and one of the reasons I fell in love with her to begin with. "They're fine. Everyone else is safe."

"Did Anders get away?" Suddenly, it was the new, focused, scarier Jill talking, and I was still getting used to her. "Please tell me you got that son of a bitch."

I shook my head *no*.

"Damn it . . ." Jill winced and started to move one hand to her side.

"Seriously, don't move. If you start bleeding again, we're screwed."

"How bad is it?" From the look on her face, even with the drugs she was still in a lot of pain. "I feel terrible."

"Anders shot you with a shotgun."

Jill blinked slowly. "I should be dead."

No kidding. At close range a 12 gauge hit like a meat hammer. If you got nailed in the torso up close with one, it was game over. A dozen pellets—each one with as much energy as a .380—hitting you in one instantaneous clump made a real mess. Like you could put your hand in the hole and have room to wiggle your fingers kind of mess, but get a little distance and the pellets spread out and bled energy fast. "You're lucky. He was far enough away that the door slowed them down, and the seat caught most of them. There was still a lot of internal bleeding. It was really close."

"How close?"

She'd damned near bled to death while that fat bastard doctor had taken his sweet time, but right now she needed to remain upbeat. "You just need to rest. You'll recover just fine, but it is going to take a while. That was pretty badass though. I didn't even know you knew how to drive a big truck."

Jill gave me a very tired smile. "I drove a dump truck one summer. My dad got me a job at his friend's construction company so I could pay tuition. That truck I stole handled like a sports car in comparison."

"You're one tough chick."

She started to laugh, then grimaced. "Ouch. Don't be funny."

"I rarely am. You just think I'm funny now because you're high."

"I feel like shit."

"The doctor said that's expected."

"Doctor?"

"Some Serbian war criminal Reaper knew."

Jill sighed. "You called, needing a way out. I couldn't figure out what to do. But this poor trucker had just pulled in to get diesel. I just reacted. I stuck my pistol in his face and stole it. I think I scared the hell out of him. I feel awful about that."

"You saved my life." I lowered my head and gently kissed the back of her hand. "Thank you."

Jill didn't say anything in return, she'd gone back to staring at the ceiling. Beyond the pain and the weakness, there was something else there. Jill was really troubled.

I tried to cheer her up. "Carjacking? That's some straight-up hoodlum level stuff. I'm impressed. When we met you were a law-abiding citizen. I've been a terrible influence on you."

Her eyes looked shiny, like she wanted to cry, but was trying hard not to. Her lip began to quiver. "I've done some bad things, Lorenzo. I'm not a good person anymore. You were dead. I lost myself. I didn't know what else to do. But I still had to stop them, you know?"

"I know." I'd been thinking about what Anders had said, both about the Montalban body count and the attempted bombing in London. I'd been hoping he'd just been trying to mess with me, but that damned rational part had been worried he had been telling the truth. Barely conscious, life passing in front of her yes, Jill had declared that she deserved this. "Believe me, I know."

"I lied to you. I lied to you about what I've done."

"I don't care."

"I thought I had Kat in London. I'd put so much work into it. I damn near died finding out where she was going to be. There was this crew she was trying to arrange a meeting with. They caught me snooping, but since they just thought I was one of the working girls trying to steal some credit cards, they only beat the shit out of me and left me in a pile of garbage."

"Who?" I immediately felt the need to find and kill them.

"Some British mercs. They took turns kicking me, but I didn't fight back, because I'd heard what I needed, so I took that beating. It was awful, but there wasn't anything I wouldn't do to stop her."

"Whatever you did, whatever you had to do, it's in the past."

But this was her confession. I'd spent my life around criminals. I'd seen it before, when the weight someone was carrying simply became too much, and they needed to dump it on someone else. Jill pushed on. "They'd arranged to meet in a little outdoor restaurant on the Thames. It was like a nice little garden inside a wrought iron fence. Great view of the Tower Bridge. I limped straight there, climbed the fence before they opened, and hid my bomb in a planter. That evil killer bitch thought she could kill you and then do her business right out in the open because it was a pretty day.

"I was watching from the bridge, lots of foot traffic so I could stay hidden. Anders and his guys got there twenty minutes early and swept the place, but they missed my bomb. The British merc she was meeting with showed up right on time. Last time I'd seen him was when he was kicking me and calling me a whore, and he sat down not ten feet from that planter. I was really tempted to just blow him up as payback right then, but I waited for her. It was risky, out there in public, but I wasn't just avenging you, I was stopping Kat from doing something horrible, right?"

"Yeah . . ." I held her hand. *Saving the world,* according to Valentine's mystical teenager. "You don't need to tell me this. I'll always love you, no matter what." I didn't know if I'd tried to stop her for her own good, or because I really didn't want to know.

"There were people around, but they were far enough away I was positive they wouldn't get hurt. Sure, I felt bad about blowing her to pieces in front of all those witnesses, but she *deserved* it." Tears began to roll out of her eyes and down her cheeks. "She was supposed to have the whole place to herself. That's how she operates. But then this young couple showed up with sack lunches. They walked past the restaurant, but then they stopped on the railing on the other side of the fence and watched the river, eating sandwiches. I kept praying that Anders would chase them away, but he didn't."

"Oh, Jill . . ."

"Kat showed up ten minutes late—longest ten minutes of my life—sat down, and started talking to the British merc. And I was screaming inside, telling that couple to move, to get up, go to the bathroom, get a drink, go for a walk, something. But they sat there, stupid and laughing. Maybe they were on their honeymoon. I don't know. They looked so happy, like we were on Saint Carl, but I just needed them to fucking *move* and they wouldn't! Kat finished her meeting, all that and she didn't even bother to eat. It was too short. She got up and started to walk away, and I knew I was going to lose her. I had the phone in my hand. All I had to do was push a button."

It sucked. It hurt. I knew exactly what had gone through her head in those fateful few seconds. "You did the math."

"Months, Lorenzo. That's all I'd thought about, all I'd lived for, was stopping Kat. I was standing there, with a concussion. My face covered with a scarf, not to hide from Anders, but so the pedestrians and tourists wouldn't see I was still bleeding, one eye was swollen shut, and I was wheezing from the broken rib I'd gotten a few hours before. Were those innocent people far enough away to not get killed? It wasn't a very big bomb. Probably. But I didn't know for sure. But right then I convinced myself they were out of the blast radius. They'd *probably* be okay." She turned her head to look directly at me, stricken with guilt. "And I pushed the button."

"But it didn't detonate."

"How'd you know?"

"Anders told me."

She began to sob. "It doesn't matter. I'm a monster. I risked innocent lives to get what I want. I had no right. There's no way to justify what I've done."

This was killing me. "That's not true. Jill, listen to me. You know I worked for Big Eddie. Kat and I did his dirty work. You know I've hurt people, good people, on accident, and sometimes on purpose. But you still had faith in me. You pulled me out of that hole. You gave me something to live for beyond looking for the next challenge, the next thrill. I only survived the Pale Man because someone *good* loved me."

She went back to staring at the ceiling. "I lost that at the Crossroads."

"No. You became what I used to be, because you had to."

"I chose it."

"Yeah? So what? Bad things happen in war, and don't kid yourself, this is a war. I got drafted when Bob tried to make a difference, but you had guts, saw something that needed to be done, and volunteered. All that stuff you've said over the years about believing in me, it applies to you now too."

"I made a mistake."

"You think you're the first?" I was heartbroken and angry at the same time. I remembered waking up injured in a hotel room in Las Vegas to the sound of Jill singing in the shower. Even after surviving Quagmire she'd been a ray of sunshine. Valentine had warned me then to get out of this life and stay away, not for my own sake, but for hers, so that she wouldn't end up screwed up like us. Valentine had been prophetic. "I don't know. Maybe you did, maybe you didn't. Hell, maybe God dropped that call. Shit happens. When you're tangling with the evil assholes, sometimes law abiding citizens get in the way . . . I can't complain about that too much, since it's how we met."

Jill looked back and gave me a sad smile. The kind, loving woman

I'd fallen for was still in there, only she'd been stained and hurt by the cruel world I'd introduced her to.

"No matter what, I'm with you, Jill. We're in this together."

Then she squeezed my hand.

I hoped she'd be okay.

VALENTINE

Paris
September 28th

Focus. I took a deep breath, and squared myself off with the mirror. *Go.*

I drew my gun and dry fired at my reflection. *Too slow.* I reholstered and tried again.

Go. My left hand found the grip of my .44. I rocked the gun back, out of its holster, and then pushed it forward. My hands came together as my arms extended, and everything was blurry except the glowing tritium front sight. My arms reached full extension, the sights aligned on my own reflection in the mirror, and I smoothly worked the trigger: *CLICK.*

It took less than a second. *Too slow.* I sighed in frustration. *Too damned slow.* If I'd been just a bit faster, just a bit more accurate, when I'd had my shot at Katarina, I could have shot her and solved half my problems right then and there. I habitually opened my revolver's cylinder, verifying that it was still loaded with dummy cartridges, and reholstered it. I'd ditched the shoulder rig I'd been using for my .44 and went back to a leather hip holster. It wasn't as comfortable when sitting down, but it was a speedier draw.

Go! I drew again. The hammer spur snagged on my shirt, screwing up my draw stroke. "Damn it," I said aloud, returning the gun to its holster. *Again.* Better this time, a little smoother. Smooth is fast. Trying to rush ends up costing you time, every time. *Again.*

Repetitive practice was a good way to lose yourself in thought. As I repeatedly sighted on him, I barely recognized the man looking back at me from the full-length mirror. I had picked up so many scars that it often surprised me when I saw my own reflection.

I was far from being a chiseled pretty boy, but I was more muscular than I'd been in a long time. I was no longer the gaunt shell of a man I was when they'd pulled me out of North Gap. Regardless of what Dr. Bundt thought, I'd gotten back to a healthy weight, and a modest exercise regimen had paid off for me. Actually, considering just how modest it was, I was far better shape than I should have been. I suspected that had something to do with Dr. Silver's science experiment.

Dr. Bundt had called the project XK Indigo. I had no idea what they'd been doing to me in there, but I vaguely remembered Dr. Silvers telling me something about my fulfilling my potential. They had put me in a thing called "the Tank" countless times, and I still didn't know what that machine did other than make nightmares. There was conspiracy theory stuff on the internet about XK Indigo, but it was all stupid rumor and wild conjecture. Popular—if you can call a few dozen kooks commenting on a web forum that— belief held that it had its origins in Nazi Germany, some kind of desperate, late-war program. It would have been nice to have answers rather than comic book bullshit, but I wasn't going to get that online.

It occurred to me then that Reaper might be of help. Lorenzo's buddy was a huge conspiracy theory nut, but he was actually smart. I resolved to ask him about it next time I saw him. I'd have to do it delicately, though. I didn't know what the hell had happened to him at the Battle of the Crossroads, but the kid just wasn't the same after that. He hadn't even participated in the fight, as far as I knew. He'd just been flying Lorenzo's little UAV, but he probably saw a lot of people getting killed. I knew a thing or two about PTSD, and Reaper displayed a lot of the obvious symptoms. Maybe it would help if I sat down and talked to him about it.

Enough thinking about things that didn't matter. It was time to get back to practicing.

Sooner or later, I was going to have to face Underhill again. He was old, but he got to be old in his business by being fast and lethal. I swore to God, or to whoever might be listening, that when I met him again I'd be ready. *Give me the strength, Lord,* I thought to myself, *and the swiftness, to shoot that bastard in the face and send him straight to hell.*

I paused when someone quietly knocked on, then opened, my door. "Is everything alright?" Ling asked. She stepped into my room and closed the door behind her. "What are you doing?"

I was standing in front of a mirror with a gun in my hand. A few hundred repetitions and I had sweat rings on my shirt. "It's, uh, not what it looks like."

She folded her arms across her chest. "You were practicing quick drawing your gun, I take it?"

"I guess it's exactly what it looks like, then."

"You know, you might be faster if you carried a more practical pistol."

I smiled at her, unloading the dummy cartridges from my gun as I did so. "The lady with the engraved Browning 9mm is going to lecture me about practicality, now?"

"It was a gift from my team."

"And this," I said, loading real rounds into my .44's cylinder, "is my good luck charm. If I'd have brought this when I went after the Montalban woman I might have succeeded."

"You never struck me as the superstitious sort."

"I've had this gun with me everywhere and I've always come home alive. Can't argue with success. But it isn't superstition. I just shoot this better."

"We need to talk." *Uh oh.* Ling was giving me that look that told me that this was serious. "What you did at the hotel was stupid, Michael."

"I had to improvise."

"You were improvising *stupidly*."

"The plan could have worked, and Tailor was ready in case I got captured."

"And that would not have mattered if the Montalbans had shot you immediately, or if Underhill had executed you on the spot."

"Damn it, let it go, Ling! I saw an opportunity and I took a chance! You know what could happen if we fail. It's worth the risk."

"You would risk one, but not six." Ling put her hand on my arm. "Listen to me. Risks are necessary, especially when so much is at stake. I understand that, but we can't afford to lose you. We need you."

There was something else going on. Sure, she was mad at me, but it felt like she wasn't telling me everything that was on her mind. "What's wrong, Ling?"

"*I* need you. That's all. Don't tempt fate unnecessarily. We may die, but let's make sure our deaths mean something, yes? Don't throw your life away on a long-shot gambit." She gently touched the side of my face. "Promise me."

I looked into Ling's dark eyes. She was right, of course. I wasn't much for arguing, especially when I knew she was right. I had known, going into it, that my idea was desperate and risky, and it had really managed to do was drive Katarina underground.

"I promise," I said after a moment. "I'll only die if it's for a good reason."

"Good," she said, giving me a quick kiss. "Now stop sulking and come downstairs. It's almost dinnertime. Antoine made a lovely fish and vegetable soup. You need to eat."

Ugh. I needed to introduce these people to junk food or something. I forced a smile onto my face. "Sounds great!"

"You are such a terrible liar. I am amazed Katarina did not cut your throat as soon as you opened your mouth." Shaking her head, Ling turned for the door. "Oh, and fetch Ariel."

"Is something wrong?"

"She's been acting strangely, holed up in her room, buried in her work. She's barely eaten and barely slept."

"Okay, I'll go talk to her. I knew this was too much pressure for her. I'll see you downstairs."

The Oracle was in her room, listening to music through headphones. I had to bang on the door several times before she heard me.

"What?" Ariel sounded annoyed when she opened the door. She really looked frazzled. "I'm busy!"

"Dinner."

"I'm *busy.*" She tried to close the door in my face, but I blocked it with my foot. "Michael!"

"First off," I reached out and picked one of the ear buds off her shoulder. I could hear the music clearly from an arm's distance. "This is too loud. You're going to damage your hearing, and worse, if we have an emergency and have to bail, we're not going to have time to keep uselessly shouting your name, so turn it *down.*"

"Fine, *Dad.*"

"Second, come eat something. You look like hell, kiddo."

She looked down at herself self-consciously. Her hair was a mess, and it was obvious that whatever sleep she did get, she got in the clothes she was wearing. "I'm *working*. Reaper's been sending me packets of information. He's a gold mine. He can reach anything, I mean nothing is safe from that guy, but he can't put the pieces together like I can. The Montalbans are up to something. I'm the only one who can figure it out."

"You can figure it out after you get some food in you."

"No time. I've got to make the pieces fit, Michael. This keeps getting bigger. They've hired a bunch of hackers, really good ones. They're moving money, paying bribes. There's pieces within pieces, but they're all secrets covered in lies. Until I make it work in my head, you guys are going to be in danger. I have to make the pieces *fit*. Garbage in, garbage out. If you guys don't know what's going on, you can't make good decisions. That's my fault."

Suddenly it made sense. She was working herself to exhaustion because I'd nearly gotten myself killed. "Hey, come here." I took her by the shoulders and pulled her out of her room. "Look at me. None of this is your fault."

Ariel's expression softened to the point where I thought she was going to start crying. "You almost died."

"But I didn't. Ling just made me promise not to unless I had a good reason." I gave her a hug. She squeezed me tight, and I could tell she was scared. "It's all right," I said, trying to sound comforting.

"I know." She broke away, and rubbed the moisture from her eerie blue eyes. "We can make it better."

"Now come on. You can fix the world after you have some of Antoine's nutrient-rich fish gruel."

Ariel wipe her eyes, then grimaced. "I'll eat, but can we order a pizza?"

Chapter 12: Beauty and the Beast

LORENZO

Paris
September 29th

"Lorenzo, get in here!" Reaper shouted.

I entered the flat's other room with a gun in my hand. My first worry was that he'd seen something threatening out the window. "What?"

Reaper was sitting in front of a little table that had several computers running on it. He'd probably be using even more if the Internet here was faster. "You've got to see this." He was pointing at something on one of several screens. I was afraid that it was the feed for one of the security cameras Jill had hidden around the block, probably showing Anders and a team of murderous scumbags bearing down on us, but those were all clear.

"What am I looking at?"

"Kat!" Reaper pointed at the screen like it was obvious. There was a black box flashing the word *pending*. "She wants to talk to you."

"Hold on. Katarina is calling us?" She was crazy, but not that kind of crazy. If she was reaching out there had to be a reason, like keeping us in one place while we were being surrounded. "Does she know where we are?"

"No way. Her guys are good, but they're not that good." He started talking about drop something cache packet cryptofuckery, but Reaper trailed off as he remembered everything he did was voodoo to me. "Basically I've made it look like we're somewhere else." Reaper was jittery and excited, but replacing sleep with Red Bull had that effect on him. "They know I'm all up in their shit, and they're having a hard time keeping me out. But look, she pinged me, asking for you, wanting to video chat."

It had to be a trap. "Can she trace the call?"

"Trace the call . . . Man, you are old. No! It doesn't work like that, but sort of, not really, but I won't let her."

"Could you trace it back to where she is?"

"Unless her dude screws up, I probably won't be able to. It's worth a shot though."

I liked how Reaper thought it was possible Kat's equivalent to him could slip, but Reaper making a mistake was impossible. "You sure about that?"

Reaper snorted. "Obviously."

"Hang on. Where's the camera?" He pointed, and I made sure there was nothing on the wall behind me that could give her a clue to our location. The curtains were closed. The room was dark. But to be safe I picked up one of Reaper's empty snack wrappers and put it on top of the camera anyway. This flat was in a quiet neighborhood. I couldn't think of any sounds that would give us away. We weren't even close enough to hear any public transportation that she could match up against a bus or train schedule.

Once I was certain she'd get no clues as to our whereabouts, I pulled up the other chair. "Go." It wasn't even a question of whether to answer or not. When she was rational, Kat was damned smart, but when she was furious, she made mistakes. And I'd always had a gift for making her furious.

"You sure you want to talk to your psycho ex right now?" Reaper asked hesitantly.

"I might be able to get her to slip up and give something away. Record this. Maybe she'll say something we can pass on to Underhill or Romefeller to push them over the edge. Kat's manipulative and sharp when she's being rational, but get her riled up and she's got serious rage issues."

"And you don't?"

"Not like that," I snapped. Though to be fair to Reaper, with Jill getting shot, I hadn't been in the brightest of moods over the last few days. "Answer the call."

Reaper hit the button. Katarina Montalban appeared on one of the screens.

She hadn't covered her camera. Kat had always been gorgeous, and she'd aged well. Maybe she was prideful enough to think she could still charm me like the old days. There were some recent bruises on her face, mostly covered with makeup, and she was wearing a scarf, probably to hide the marks Valentine must have left on her throat. Behind her was a plain white wall, so I'd be getting no hints about her location that way. She tilted her head to the side when she saw nothing but black.

"Lorenzo? Is that you?"

"Hello, Kat."

She had this kind of white, blonde, too smooth Nordic look, and her attitude was either fire or ice, no in between. Since she was a superb actor—anyone who didn't know her found her remarkably charismatic. Those of us who got to know her—without getting killed in the process—knew she swung between charming and terrifying. Even when we'd been lovers, I'd always suspected I was one mood swing away from getting shot. She flashed me her big, fake smile, with her perfect, capped, bleached white teeth. Her eyes twinkled. This was fun for her. Say what you will, psychotic or not, Kat really loved her work.

"You can't imagine my surprise when I found out you were still alive."

"Despite your best efforts."

"Indeed. Why don't you show me your face? I've missed seeing you."

"I don't feel like giving your boyfriend a current snapshot of me to pass around."

"Ah, yes. It is unfortunate how easily you change your face." Kat's accent—when she didn't bother to hide it—was Swiss, and she often turn the S into a Z. "I thought perhaps Sala Jihan had put his brand on it and you were too ashamed to show me."

Just saying that name made my chest hurt. "I'm still plain and boring as ever."

"Better to sneak up on me then."

"I promise. You'll never see me coming."

Kat laughed. It seemed genuine, but most things with her did. "Oh, Lorenzo. Never change. Lucky for you, I didn't fall for you because of your looks."

Or my charm. "How's your neck?"

"You know I don't mind getting a little rough. Mr. Valentine has strong hands." She ran her fingers down the red silk scarf suggestively. Despite the act, I could tell she was still sore. She flipped the subject to something personal to try and throw me. "How is Jill?"

"She's fine."

"Really? I'd love to speak to her again."

"Jill can't come to the phone right now."

"Because Anders shot her?" Kat had a malicious, evil grin. "Did she live? Die? Did you have to bury her in a shallow grave? Or are you too pragmatic, and she didn't even rate that? I bet you put rocks in her pockets and shoved her corpse in the river. I wonder, Lorenzo, can you even truly love someone?"

I didn't say anything. I wasn't going to let her get off on my pain.

"But I think you can. You certainly loved me once. We had some good times, you and I." Kat leaned toward the camera and winked. "Remember our vacation in Northern China?"

"No." I lied. "But I remember dumping your crazy ass in Malaysia."

"I truly wish you hadn't done that. Just think what might have been."

"What do you want, Kat?"

"To make you an offer."

"Let me guess. I step out of your way until you're done with Project Blue?"

She wasn't going to waste time playing innocent, but she wasn't going to admit to owning Blue when I might be recording the conversation. "I simply need you to leave Europe and stay out of my affairs for a time. An extended vacation would be splendid."

"And what would I get for that?"

"Twenty million dollars." That was a little higher than expected, but Kat controlled the Montalbans' fortunes now, so she was easily good for it.

"That's double what you're offering to have me killed for."

"I could have you killed for far less, but then I'd have to go through all the trouble of waiting. I like to expedite things. Take this offer, Lorenzo. In addition, I will let you and all your people live. All of our prior business will be water under the bridge. Your crimes against my family will be forgiven and forgotten."

Fat chance of that. "What about my brother?"

"What of him?" Kat asked innocently.

"I know Bob Lorenzo is still alive." It was more of an educated guess than knowledge. Because Bob had the skillsets, had been missing for two years, and had that whole dishonored federal employee background that Gordon Willis likely would have recruited, Bob made a viable, believable fourth operative. Anders could easily pin Project Blue on Bob. He was the perfect patsy.

Kat just smiled. She wasn't going to say anything that would be passed on to Majestic or the other Illuminati families later. "I've not seen him since the Crossroads. I wish you the best of luck in your continuing search, as long as you do it somewhere far away from here."

Reaper passed over a Post-It he'd scribbled a quick note on. *They tried to pin us. I sent them on a goose chase.* Reaper seemed really smug about it too.

Kat looked down, probably at her phone. Her lip curled back in a snarl before she turned back to the camera. "I am fairly certain you are not hiding at Euro Disney. You are not tall enough to ride all the rides. Well done. My compliments to Skyler."

"His name is *Reaper*." My sidekick was so pleased at that, he stuck out one fist. I obliged his fist bump. Reaper wiggled his fingers and mouthed the word *boom*. "Now, I've got a counteroffer. Do you still have Mr. Perkins?"

"I don't leave home without him." Mr. Perkins was a cut down M79 40mm grenade launcher. It was Kat's personal favorite weapon. It fit under an overcoat, but I'd seen her drop grenades through the open window of a moving car at 300 yards. She was an artist with it.

It was time to start provoking her. "Then stick Mr. Perkins up your ass, and give yourself a beehive round enema."

"So that is a no?"

"I'm not leaving Europe until I take your scalp."

Kat began to unconsciously drum her fingers on the table in front of her. Despite the cool act, she was still a bundle of nerves. "You're not in a position to make threats."

"You know me, Kat. I don't make threats. I'm just describing a series of events that are going to occur as a result of your pissing me off. You can't pay me off. It's never been about the money."

"No. All the things you stole, the impossible places you broke into, it was about doing what others said couldn't be done. You were always such a narcissist."

"I know what I am. And I know exactly what you are too. Which is why I can't let you go through with this. Blue could kill millions of people."

"Since when do you care about *people?* Spare me the sanctimony, Lorenzo. If our circumstances were reversed, you would do the same exact thing I am."

"Bullshit."

"I suppose we will never know." She was starting to flare up, but we weren't quite there yet. "Because I'm the one fate put into this position. I was the illegitimate daughter, unwanted, unwelcomed, and forgotten. They saw me as nothing more than a curiosity, a plaything for when Eduard got into one of his moods. Yet where Rafael lacked the courage, and Eduard was taken too soon, I will succeed where the inferior Montalban heirs failed."

"You're nuts."

Kat still didn't take the bait. "I am a visionary."

"Your brothers died stupidly. Valentine capped one and I shot the other out of the sky. You've already proven them wrong. You took over. You saved Big Eddie's crumbling empire, and from what I've seen, it's stronger than ever before. What more do you want?"

"My birthright!" Kat hissed. "My destiny! I was meant to rule my family, and my family was meant to rule the world. For centuries the Montalbans have been denied their place at the head of the table. Thirteen families have secretly steered the course of the entire world, yet my family was always the weakest, the runt of the litter, making do with the illicit scraps. No more!"

"The other families aren't going to step aside for the likes of you." If I could get her to cop to conspiring against the Illuminati, I could at least give this conversation to Romefeller. Maybe that would get the Illuminati off their ass at their big meeting. "You need professional help."

"Don't be so bitter, Lorenzo!" She wasn't stupid enough to give me what I wanted. "I couldn't have done this without you. I took up with you, my brothers' best unwitting hireling, in order to earn their respect. My ambition, my strength, the total commitment, the willingness to die in order to achieve your goals, I learned all those things from you."

I refused to believe that. "Incest and child abuse made you who you are, Kat, not me."

"That was merely the beginning of my journey." Even talking about her messed-up childhood was failing to provoke her. She remained remarkably grounded. Plotting world domination had done wonders for her. "Who I am, what I am today, I owe that all to the example you set for me."

We had been through some terrible things together, pulling off job after job on behalf of Big Eddie, I'd sunk lower than whale shit, but there were still some lines I'd never crossed. "You're willing to kill all those innocents to reach your goals. I'd never do something like that."

"Only because you lack the spine! I have progressed beyond you. Despite your fearsome reputation, the unstoppable assassin, I saw the real you beneath. There is a frailty to you, Lorenzo. Deprived of morals, you made up your own code, and it binds you far tighter than any law."

If I couldn't anger her, maybe I could appeal to whatever was left of the young woman I'd once known. "You were frail once too, Kat, but I kept you alive."

"That was your mistake. I stamped out that remaining weakness a long time ago."

"This is insanity. You've got to stop," I pleaded. "You want to gain power, take over your old money conspiracy, fine, but give up that nuke. If you set off that bomb, the whole world will hunt you down."

Suddenly, Kat smiled. It was far too devious an expression. That smile was genuine, which meant I'd screwed up somehow. "Why, Lorenzo, you are not as well informed as you think you are."

Shit. What did that mean? This wasn't going very well at all. I needed to switch tactics. *Maybe paranoia?* "Anders is planning on taking over your crime family. He's using you."

"Is that supposed to surprise me? Plant seeds of doubt? Are you hoping I have him killed? Anders is a man of appetites, certainly. He's taken enough orders and now he wants to give them. I respect and understand that. Soon, the Montalban Exchange criminal enterprises simply won't matter to me anymore. He can have Big Eddie's empire, because I will have the whole world to play with." Kat turned the other direction. "Isn't that right, my love?"

"Sounds good to me," Anders said as he leaned in and his stupid Viking face blocked half the screen. "What's up, Lorenzo? It was good running into you again the other night."

Right then I about lost it. Jill had nearly died because of this son of a bitch. I must have looked really pissed off, because Reaper reached over and grabbed my arm. He shoved another Post-It over. *They're getting closer.* Oh, *now* Reaper was wide-eyed and frightened. So much for his earlier confidence.

"That was pretty funny with your buddy, Valentine, trying to sic Underhill on us. I worked with Valentine in Zubrara. He's a fucking mope. Neither of you assholes get the big picture. What did Valentine think was going to happen, going after Kat half-cocked? A Majestic operative like Underhill can't just pop an Illuminati family head. You've got to know the game if you want to play with the big boys."

"I'll pass that on," I muttered.

"They aren't going to listen to you Exodus pussies. Both sides have been wrapped up in this turf war since before we were born. There's traditions and protocols and shit. I can understand you guys being mad though, since I'd just shot your girlfriend. That sure was a lot of blood all over that truck. I bet she's all fucked up. Is she dead? Or just crippled? Where did I hit her? It would suck if she's in a wheelchair. Or did I mess up her pretty face?"

I was quiet. Reaper was shaking his head *no.* I'd gone into this, hoping to goad Kat into giving me something to work with, and instead it was Anders who had me close to bubbling over with rage. Kat had planned this perfectly. She'd saved Anders to taunt me, probably even coached him on what to say to get under my skin.

Reaper added more to his last note. *Can't hold them.*

Anders kept pushing me, while Kat sat there, enjoying my misfortune. "Come on, Lorenzo. I'm looking forward to finishing this. For someone who is supposed to be such a badass, you've been a real letdown in person. If you're going to get us like you promised, you'd better hurry up. I've got some of the best mercenaries in the business descending on this city like a plague. It's going to be biblical. There won't be a rock left for you to hide under . . . You still there, Lorenzo?"

Reaper hit *end*.

That was good. I hadn't known what to say anyway.

VALENTINE
Paris
September 30th

A depressed Lorenzo was a dangerous Lorenzo, so I volunteered to check in on his crew. We'd barely heard from them for the past couple of days, and I knew that he had taken Jill getting hurt very hard. Ling didn't want to go with me. Since she had been the one to tell Jill that Lorenzo was still alive, I suspected Ling was feeling guilty about how things had panned out. She wasn't ready to face her, so I didn't push the issue.

Shen and Antoine were doing surveillance somewhere in the city. Ariel had wanted to come. She'd been cooped up in the safe house since we arrived in Paris, and I actually thought that her getting away from her computer for a while would do her some good. I couldn't risk it, though, especially not going out by myself. Romefeller's words had chilled me to the bone. He knew about her. She was valuable to people like him. For the time being, Ariel was safest at the house with Skunky and Ling. I ended up making the drive across town alone.

Lorenzo met me at the door. He had bags under his bloodshot eyes, and a look of worry on his face that I'd never seen on him before. Antoine had warned me that he was beating himself up over Jill getting hurt, and he sure looked it. "Come in."

"How's Jill?"

"Not great, but okay. She's on a lot of painkillers but she's awake more often. See for yourself." He led me toward the back of the apartment. We passed another room where Reaper was working on his computer, oblivious to the rest of the world. The other bedroom had enough equipment in it that it looked more like a hospital room.

"Valentine is here to see you," Lorenzo told her.

I hadn't seen her since the Crossroads. Jill looked like hell. She was lying in bed, bandaged up, and pretty obviously high on painkillers.

She was pretty lucid, all things considered, and perked up a bit when I approached.

"Val? Come here," Jill whispered.

I went to the side of the bed. "How are you feeling?"

"How do you think? I got shot." Her words were slurred. "Lean in closer."

I did so, and Jill slapped me across the face as hard as she could. I recoiled back, rubbing my stinging cheek.

"Whoa! Easy," Lorenzo cautioned. "Don't strain yourself."

"That was for lying and telling me Lorenzo died at the Crossroads, you son of a bitch."

"He probably saved your life," Lorenzo said, quietly.

My face still stung. "No, it's okay. I had that coming."

"You deserve more than that. You're lucky I can't get out of bed or I'd break a chair over your head. Now beat it," she mumbled. "I just took my meds and I'm going back to sleep."

I walked back to Lorenzo, rubbing my cheek. The douchebag had found that funny, and smirked at me. "Don't take it personally. Jill's Filipina. She says all the women in her family have a temper. If she was actually mad she would have stabbed you."

"Val?" Jill called after me. "I still love you, Val." The drugs were kicking in. "You're my spirit guide and I love you!"

"I, uh, love you too, Jill." I shook my head. "Get some rest." Once we were out of her drug addled throwing range, I asked Lorenzo if she was going to recover.

"Yeah," he said, still looking tired. "The doc got her cleaned up and patched up pretty well, all things considered. Hey, give me a minute, will you? I've got to change her bandages and it's easier when she's asleep."

That was okay. There was something else nagging at me anyway. I went back to Reaper's room and knocked on the door frame. "Hey, can I talk to you?"

Reaper didn't hear me. He was wearing a set of headphones as he sat at his computer. The workspace he had set up in Lorenzo's hideout seemed, at first glance, to be a cluttered mess, but if you looked at it more closely you saw a method to the madness. He had a full tower PC, hooked up to no less than three monitors, and a couple of laptops open. Each screen had something different going on. Reaper bobbed his head in tune with whatever he was listening too, quietly clicking away on his mouse. His dark hair was shorter than I remembered, and he looked older. Empty Red Bull cans filled a small garbage pail.

I entered the room and tapped him on the shoulder. "Reaper?"

"Augh!" he blurted, startled. He turned around wide-eyed, suddenly breathing hard, not so much looking at me as through me. His right hand had moved under his desk, to the butt of a Glock pistol. It was in a plastic holster mounted to the underside.

I raised my hands and showed him my open palms, slowly taking a step back. "Whoa, hey, relax. It's just me. Sorry to scare you."

He took off his headphones. "You didn't scare me. I was just surprised."

"So surprised you were ready to shoot me?"

"Like that's so weird around here lately? What do you want, Valentine?"

"You got a minute? I need to ask you about some stuff."

"I'm pretty busy here."

I leaned forward to look at his screens. "What are you doing?"

"I'm trying to track down Isla, She-bitch of the SS . . ." I must have looked at him funny. "I mean Kat. She's got people trying to track us down, people like me, but they're not as good as I am. It's a challenging game of cat-and-also-cat. She's hiding since you almost popped her, but she can't go completely dark, not with an evil empire to run, so sooner or later I'll find her. Why?"

"That's not what I came to ask you about." I took a deep breath. Even after all that time had passed, it was still hard for me to talk about my experience in captivity. There was a folding chair leaning against the wall. I opened it up and sat down next to him. "Lorenzo told me you took most of the files recovered from North Gap."

A look of understanding appeared on Reaper's pale face. "Oh. Ohhh. Believe it or not, I never really got too far into them. After we, you know, rescued you, I was busy with mission prep and everything. Then the Crossroads happened. Then . . ." He trailed off. "You know."

"That was a bad op."

"You can't possibly imagine how right you are about that."

"A screaming teenage fanatic with the Pale Man's brand on his face tried to bayonet me with a Mosin Nagant. I've fought in a lot of wars, and the battle at the dam was the most vicious close combat I've ever seen. It was . . . it was medieval." I tapped the side of my head. "One more helping of nightmare fuel to lock away in the vault."

Reaper gave me a really sad, burned-out look, and it really sank in how much he'd changed. "Is that how you cope? You just lock it away?"

"I used to. Not so much anymore." I could tell Reaper was messed up. I'd seen it before, but maybe I could help him out. I was no stranger to trauma. "It works for a time, but sooner or later it catches up with you. You have to confront your demons eventually, or they eat you up from the inside."

"Demons?" Reaper asked, slowly. He stared awkwardly at me for a bit, then he shook his head. "Oh, not literal. You mean like *figurative* demons."

"Um, yes. I have not, as far as I know, confronted an actual demon." Sometimes, late I night, I wondered about that, too. "It's like this: I had a long talk with God when I was in that hole in North Gap." I remembered my weird nightmares from the Tank, of me murdering people. *God can't find you here. It's just you and me.*

"You don't seem like the religious type, Valentine. No offense."

"Never been to church in my life. I mean owning up to the things that I've done and the mistakes that I've made, forgiving myself for things that weren't my fault, like Sarah's death. And last of all it means finding something worth fighting for, something to get me out of bed in the morning, when it would've been easier to lie down and die."

"Lorenzo said you think you're trying to save the world."

"The world is going to hell one way or another. I can't do anything about that. It's not about saving the world, it's about picking my battles. It's not very often that you find yourself in a position to stop something horrible, when shit like this happens, you know? My whole life, I've been governed by forces beyond my control. Not anymore. This time, I'm fighting on my own terms. I took ownership of this. That's how I cope. That, and having people I can talk to on bad days."

He brushed a few strands of his long hair out of his eyes. "I didn't have anybody. Lorenzo was gone, Jill wasn't the same, and I don't have many friends. I avoided people. I thought I was going crazy. I couldn't prove I saw anything."

"What is it you saw there?"

Reaper didn't say anything for a long moment, looking at me askance. "You know . . . the battle." He wasn't telling me everything, and then he tried to change the subject. "After everything that happened, you'd think it would leak out somehow, but nada. Some bullshit on Russian TV about separatists and militias and that's it. It didn't even make *Sea to Shining Sea AM.*"

"That's the world we live in, man, secret battles in places the world doesn't care about. I swear, someday I'm going to publish my memoirs."

"Heh . . . Cool, man. I'll buy a copy if you autograph it." Reaper seemed a bit happier. "Thanks for talking, Val. What did you want?"

Now it was my turn to be weird and traumatized. "Have you ever heard of a program called XK Indigo?"

Reaper tilted his head to the side, giving me a puzzled look. "Whoa . . . Dude. Holy shit. Why didn't I see it?"

"See what?"

Reaper ignored my question and turned back to his computer. A few mouse clicks pulled up a folder labeled *Valentine Stuff*.

"You have a file on me?"

"Of course I do. I have a file on everybody. Lorenzo asked me to put it together before we sprung you from North Gap."

Of course. "So what do you know?"

"Lots. You're not very good about information management."

"Yeah, well, I've been busy."

"That book you want to write? I could probably save you a bunch of time." he said, scrolling through his files. "You're like the most interesting man in the world. But XK Indigo? No wonder Majestic wants you dead. That's some weirdass voodoo tech right there."

"So, you've heard of it?"

"Of course I have. Everybody tuned in has. I just didn't think it was real. It's supposed to be about making perfect assassins for the government. I can't tell you what's real because most of the hard drives Lorenzo recovered from North Gap were encrypted enough that I couldn't do anything with them."

"You can't, I don't know, *hack* into the encrypted drives?"

Reaper sighed. "No, I can't hack into it." He made finger quotes when he said the word "hack". "It doesn't even work like that. I wish guys like you and Lorenzo would take a computer class or something. Cracking is math, not sorcery. Without a key there isn't a whole lot I can do. But not everything was encrypted. That Silvers lady was sloppy at times. All I've got is stuff like this. Here, you might find this interesting." He opened a video and set it to playing.

The camera was focused on me, strapped into a chair. My head was shaved and I was extremely pale and thin. Numerous wires connected my body to different monitoring devices. An overlay in the margins of the screen displayed my vital info, like heart rate and other physiological conditions. They were sticking me with needles and probes.

"I don't remember this."

"There are dozens of videos like this. Most of them are uninteresting. This one is flagged, though. Watch."

My vital signs started spiking and falling, fluctuating rapidly. From the convulsions, I think they were shocking me.

"Turn it up."

"There's no sound."

"What the hell were they doing to me?"

"It's labeled *negative stimuli*. I think they were running a current through different parts of your brain. Mostly it looks like they were trying to piss you off."

"It worked," I said, noting how I began to thrash around in the chair.

"Is this uncomfortable for you?"

"Yes? A little. It's weird."

"Okay, good. Keep watching. This is where it gets interesting." With my thrashing and convulsing, I managed to get my hand free of the restraints. A black-clad security man moved in to resecure my arm.

"That's Smoot. I remember that son of a bitch. Hey, what . . ." I trailed off as most of the visible readouts flatlined. I had stopped thrashing. My vitals all leveled off, abruptly. I recognized the *Calm.* As Smoot approached, I reached out, trying to grab him. He hit me with his baton, but I managed to get my one free hand on a pen in his shirt pocket. As Smoot leaned forward to push me back into the chair, I plunged it into his leg just above the kneecap. Smoot howled soundlessly, grasping his knee and falling backward. Another guard, Reilly I think, shot me with his Taser and zapped me while Smoot crawled away. Remarkably, the Taser seemed to do nothing, and I quickly freed my other hand.

With shocking speed, I went after the guards. It was obvious I was going to kill them.

But then Dr. Silvers said something. Without the sound there was no way to tell what it was. And just like that, I stopped, went back to the table, and sat down, meek as could be.

The video ended.

"I don't . . . I don't remember this. I remember, vaguely, stabbing Smoot with the pen, but this?" A sense of dread crept into me. Seeing a video of you doing something you don't remember is unsettling.

"Dr. Silvers had the file flagged as a *success*, that the *conditioning* was working. Now this is conjecture, okay, most of it is probably bullshit, so take this for what it's worth. The XK Indigo conditioning is like brainwashing. It's supposedly meant to heighten someone's abilities while making them easier to control. The idea is that your loyalty is ensured through a series of psychological controls and triggers."

"My God. This is . . . it's almost sick."

"Yeah. Your former employers are some real, evil bastards."

"What did they put in my head, Reaper?"

"Beats me, man. I don't know if you were conditioned to take orders from just that one doctor, or if there was more. There's no clue in here. I can send you everything I've got so you can check it out when you've got time."

"I think that would be best," someone said. Reaper and I both turned around to see Lorenzo standing in the doorway. I didn't know how long he'd been watching, or if he'd seen the video of me rendered into a murderous zombie. "And you're welcome for my rescuing your ass from that place."

I stood up. "What did you do with Smoot, anyway?"

"I doubt they ever found his body."

I smiled, just a little.

LORENZO
October 2nd

Jill was sitting up in bed. Even that much exertion freaked me out a little bit. The two of us had the place to ourselves. Valentine had gone back to work and Reaper had finally crashed. I'd seen him work in streaks before, not sleeping for days at a time when he got all spun up, but never like this. Since Jill had gotten shot he'd been bordering on mania, attacking the Montalbans' networks and finances.

"Try not to move around so much."

"Quit being a big baby," Jill muttered as she flipped through the photo album on Reaper's tablet.

"I just don't want you to hurt anything."

"Says mister I got third-degree burns all over my back, but I'm going to walk it off while I shoot down an airplane," she responded, not looking up from the pictures.

"When you pop some of those staples out and start leaking blood all over, don't come crying to me. I don't know if Reaper's war criminal doctor network makes house calls."

"I'll be fine. Except I'm probably never going to wear a two-piece bathing suit again."

I almost said *they're only scars* but I didn't think that was what a woman was going to want to hear. I sat next to her on the bed. My complaints to the contrary, she was looking a lot stronger, and she was motivated to get back to work, which was good. I changed the subject. "Reaper said Ling stopped by this morning."

"Yeah." Jill pointed at the fresh flowers on the desk. "She actually bought me a get well card."

"Ling is the sweetest paramilitary vigilante I know."

"She felt guilty for getting me involved and came by to give this big, formal, honor-bound apology. It was adorable. I forgave her. We talked."

"What about?"

"You know, girl stuff. She's the only chick over there, and I guess I'm the closes thing she has to a girlfriend. She's pretty freaked out about . . ." Jill went back to scrolling through the surveillance photos. "Never mind."

"Whoa. Hang on. You can't just say something like that and leave me hanging."

"It's a secret, Lorenzo. OpSec, you know?"

"Jill . . ."

She sighed. "Okay, don't tell her I told you. She'd never forgive me. Ling just found out she's pregnant."

"From Valentine?"

Jill looked at me like I was stupid. "Yes, from Valentine. But he doesn't know yet. He's focused on the mission right now and she doesn't want to mess him up with it. I told her that was stupid, but you know how intense the Exodus people are. Swear you won't say a word."

"I promise." The idea of Valentine and Ling having babies was amusing, and kind of frightening. I hurried and changed the subject in case Jill was thinking about talking about our future. I pointed out some of the faces in the picture she was looking at. "Shen took those. He was tailing these guys based on the intel you gave Exodus. That's in front of a bar downtown."

"I know that one for sure," Jill picked the middle one, an ugly, stout young man with a squished nose. "The rest, no idea. As far as I know though, he's just one of the rank and file Montalban goons. Nothing special, usually he's a driver. I called him Pig Face. He's got a brother, or at least a guy who looks a lot like him. I call him Pork Chop."

"Fitting." All of the Montalban crew she had followed that Jill didn't have names for, she'd just assigned nicknames. None of them were flattering, Dickhead, Big Ears, Stinky, and so on.

For the last few days Jill had been bored out of her mind, and demanding to help. That was good, because nothing helped you heal like the motivation to get on with life, but I'd told her she still needed her rest. She called me a *pendejo*, and told me to get her something to do or she was going to walk out of here.

Like I said, Jill was one tough chick.

"Shen tailed Pig Face to a chop shop. He thinks the Montalbans own it."

"Stolen cars? Really? Is there any criminal enterprise Eddie wasn't involved with? Drugs, piracy, counterfeiting, you name it," Jill complained. "It's like he was trying to be a comic book supervillain."

"Eddie was a big proponent of diversifying his assets. A lot of this was, I don't know, like a hobby for him. A game. He was living out a crime boss fantasy by being an actual crime boss, even though he was so rich he didn't actually benefit, financially, from all the crime." Most of his power base had been in Asia, with its heart in the Crossroads, but he'd had a little piece of everything in Europe too. While his family's legit businesses had been out in the open, Eddie had worked in secret. Unlike Kat, he had kept his identity on the down low, and for most of the time I'd worked for him, I hadn't even been sure *Big Eddie* was one person.

"It wasn't just a game. There was a reason for it. I've learned a lot about how the Montalbans work. Now Rafael, he was mostly a legit businessman. He owned stock in everything and ran a bunch of companies. But on the side, he used his little brother for everything shady. Rafael's construction company built most of the high-speed train lines and stations over the last decade. He even bankrolled that new three-hundred-mile-an-hour super train. But on the side, the freight companies still had to pay protection money to Eddie to make sure the trains run on time, and their shipments don't get stolen. They were in everything, Rafael in the open, Eddie in the dark. That's why Rafael indulged Eddie's crime boss fantasy, because it was useful for him. Now, Kat? If anything she's even more ambitious than her brothers. She wears both hats, CEO and mobster. She's expanded a lot in just the last year."

"Regardless, this is a score. This could be the place Kat parks her big armored convoy when she's not using it. I'll ask Reaper to see if he can steal some traffic camera footage or something to confirm it."

"That's useful. If that's home base, do you think you could ninja in there and put a tracking device on one of her cars?"

"Maybe." I liked the way she thought, though I'd been tending more toward a car bomb myself. I didn't say that though, because she still might be a little sensitive about the topic, and I didn't want to sound like a hypocrite. "Exodus couldn't have found this place if you'd not done all that leg work."

"You're just trying to make me feel better," Jill said as she went back to flipping through the pictures. "It's not working. I'm useless stuck here. And since you refuse to leave me alone, I'm making you useless."

"There's nothing for me to do," I lied. There was no shortage of people I could be murdering. "Underhill's superiors have to know about the nuke by now, so they'll have no choice but get off their asses and take her out. Gentleman's agreement be damned, they can't be that stupid. If that doesn't work, Romefeller told Valentine they've arranged a big secret meeting with all the families, scheduled soon. Once he tells them about Kat having a nuke, they'll lose their minds, and put out a hit on her."

"You actually expect the Illuminati or Majestic to come through for us?"

"Sure," I said, while simultaneously thinking *not really*. But Jill was recuperating and I wanted to keep her spirits up. "They'll be motivated."

"Don't blow smoke up my ass, Lorenzo. You read what Bob thought of those people. If they accomplish something good it's by accident. All they care about is themselves."

"Well, having a nuclear bomb go off in Europe has to be bad for business. Majestic has been exposed. Getting blamed for it could destroy them permanently."

"I like you better when you're honestly seeing the worst in everyone," she stated, completely aware that I was full of it. Jill went back to flipping through the pics the Exodus operatives had taken, but she was distracted. "You know, when I was young and naïve I used to dream about taking a romantic trip to Paris someday."

"Why?"

"Because that's the kind of thing teenage girls think about. It's the city of love. The Eifel Tower, and the museums, and the cafes, and . . . I don't know . . . Mimes. But not me. Oh no. When I get here for real, I spend my time skulking around seedy bars and drug dens spying on terrorists, and then get shot stealing a truck. I'm just lucky I guess."

"Fire your travel agent."

Jill sighed. "On the bright side, Paris will always be where I found out you were still alive. That's what matters."

"Our fancy boat dinner date was nice."

"Yes, you did good with the boat ride." She grinned. "As for the rest? Sometimes a woman just needs to vent."

That was the regular old Jill I knew and loved, even with bullet holes in her side she was in a better mood than I was. I couldn't even make a crack about this being a honeymoon. It was kind of hard to describe a relationship when you didn't legally exist. Our fake identities in the Bahamas had been legally married, so I guess you could say our status was *complicated*. "Once this is over, I'll take you on a real romantic getaway."

"Knowing you, that's what, robbing a bank?"

"Don't laugh. I've looted a diamond exchange. You should see the size rock I could get you for a ring."

"Why, Lorenzo, is that an official proposal?"

I shrugged.

"Man, that's some emotionally stunted bullshit. You suck at this. Next time you . . . hang on." Jill looked like she'd seen a ghost. She showed me the picture. "Where'd Shen take this one?"

It was a man walking along a sidewalk, wearing a gray suit and black shirt. He was tall, athletic, mid-forties, prematurely white hair, and a scar that split his chin. He was in the process of taking a fat envelope from Pig Face or Pork Chop.

"Outside Le Bon Marche." I remembered that because it was across the street from the best gourmet grocery store in Paris. "Shen said the white-haired guy was smooth. Good field craft. No words. The exchange was a drop pass, and they both kept walking. Since Shen didn't know who he was, he peeled off and tailed him for a while, but lost him when he got to his car. Exodus couldn't ID him."

"I can. I'll never forget that face." Jill had gotten a lot more serious. There was no flippant nickname here. I could tell Jill was shaken.

"What's special about him?"

Jill was staring at the photo so hard it was like she was trying to burn a hole through the screen with her eyes. "This is the man Katarina was meeting in London."

"The one that had you beaten?"

She nodded slowly.

My anger was building. Even if he wasn't working with the Montalbans, I'd kill this particular fucker on principle. "What do you know about him?"

Chapter 13: The Limey

LORENZO
Paris
October 3rd

"The target's name is Aaron Stokes, mercenary, British national, and all around scumbag." I told the Exodus operatives as they passed around the photo Shen had taken. There were seven of us in the smoky little back room of the underground gambling establishment. It was the kind of place where shifty people could gather and count on not being noticed. We'd reserved the room for a *private game*. Private game, planning a hostage rescue, it was all good. "I want to hit his place ASAP."

"It is not your way to rush into things, Lorenzo," Ling said. "You were uncomfortable moving on North Gap on short notice. Why strike so quickly this time?"

That was fair. Ling thought my stay with Sala Jihan had put me off my game. My blitz attack in Salzburg hadn't been particularly well thought out. I could say something about her being unreliable for emotional reasons too, but then Jill would kill me for blabbing their secret.

"I think Stokes has Bob."

That got their attention. Ling, Shen, and Antoine exchanged glances. Her old team knew my brother from his search for Anders in the Crossroads, and there had been some mutual respect there. It had been Bob who'd coerced Ling into roping me into this mess to begin with. Valentine met my gaze and nodded. He knew Bob better than anyone here but me. He got it. I didn't know the American nicknamed Skunky at all, but I figured if I could convince Valentine, the rest would follow his lead. The weird little blonde girl . . . with her, I had no idea.

"What makes you think he's holding your brother?" the girl asked.

"From what Reaper has been able to dig up last night, Stokes was British Army before he got a dishonorable discharge for doing some things of questionable legality in Afghanistan. His background got him a job doing freelance work for some shady parties."

"Valentine knows about that kind of thing," Skunky said.

"I got an honorable discharge. I just wasn't allowed to reenlist. Huge difference," Valentine said. "I'm guessing Stokes' particular set of skills are what set you off?"

Exodus didn't need to know that it was his breaking Jill's ribs back in London that had caused me to sic Reaper on him. The clues Reaper had found were legit, so I didn't want Exodus thinking I was flying off half-cocked because of a personal vendetta.

"His official training was in interrogation and prisoner handling, but now that he's in the private sector Mr. Stokes specializes in kidnapping people for corporate espionage purposes and then holding them for ransom. Basically, freelance rendition on behalf of people who are probably on your buddy Romefeller's Christmas card list."

"Snatch a target and send him somewhere the authorities don't know about while you torture the hell out of them." Valentine sounded a little bitter, but he'd been on both sides of that equation. "Majestic has places like North Gap. I suppose it makes sense the other side has similar resources."

"So this Stokes is the perfect sort to keep a dangerous prisoner in one piece," Antoine mused, "until it is time to use him as their scapegoat."

I held up one hand and began to tick off my reasons for thinking he was our connection. "The Montalbans are paying him for something. Paris isn't Stokes' normal AO. Jill saw him meeting with Kat in London a few weeks before Varga moved Bob to Paris. One day after that meeting, a shell corporation controlled by Stokes purchased a big, isolated property north of the city. He's got to be our guy, and *this*," I held up a printout of the old real estate listing, "has got to be our location."

Valentine took the picture. "Is that a castle?"

"Technically, it's a chateau. Think of it as a mini-castle, without all those bothersome tourists taking pictures, and no neighbors to hear your prisoner get uppity."

"It sounds plausible," Ling stated. "Assuming your brother is still alive."

"Did Bob strike you as a quitter, Ling?"

"No. He did not."

Shen spoke up. "I saw Stokes had a bodyguard. Do we know how many other men he has?"

"This ain't Mexico," Skunky responded. "Down there you could flash your guard force patrolling the grounds, sporting machine guns and wearing armor. This here is a civilized country, so they won't show us their hand easily. Their protection will be hidden, and hard to scout out."

"If this is basically an Illuminati black site, there will be many guards and an excellent security system," Antoine said.

"That's pessimistic," Skunky said.

"Realistic. You have not met Lorenzo's brother. He was an American Green Beret, and he is my size. Would you go into a cell with someone like that without help?"

"As big as you are, Antoine, I'd bring my whole family and extra batteries for the Tasers." Skunky laughed as he pulled over the map Reaper had printed of area around the chateau. I'd marked the boundaries with a highlighter. "Plus, I bet the Montalbans beefed up security after Val choked their boss. This is a nice area, but it's not too far from other known Montalban turf. They'll call for help as soon as we hit it. How fast can we get out? Assuming we can get in there before they kill the hostage, what shape do you think he'll be in?"

"Bad," Valentine and I answered at the same time. He gave me a knowing look. We both understood how rotten being locked up could be. I'd gone old school, basically medieval, and Valentine had been subjected to one continuous drug-addled sci-fi mind-fuck. I'm guessing either of us would laugh at a stint in a normal prison system, not that there was much danger of that, because if we got caught we'd get disappeared long before any trial.

"Perhaps not," Ling said. "If they've kept him around in order to kill him at the scene and frame him as the rogue Majestic operative, it will raise too many questions if he has been tortured or if there are traces of suspicious drugs in his system. His captivity may have been far easier than yours was."

I gave her a grim smile. I could tell Ling was just saying that for my benefit.

"Assuming they don't simply set him on fire or something like that, so the police can only identify him by his dental records." Antoine stopped speaking when he saw me frowning at him. "Or what Ling said. That's more likely."

"It's fine." By my standards these Exodus types were all optimists. Thinking you could actually make the world a better place had that effect on people. "Bob might be messed up, but he'll still be alive. Anders is smart. He was the last surviving Majestic operative that put Project Blue together. They were all so compartmentalized that his superiors don't know that, though. He needs someone with Bob's résumé, and he needs it to be unquestionable that Bob was the one recruited by Willis to do this mission. They're going to use a nuke, so you know it isn't going to be a half-assed investigation afterward. Bob's death and frame-up will have to be really convincing."

"Look, I'm not trying to be an ass here," Skunky said, "but they could have killed him a while ago and got rid of the body, still pin it on him, and then say he escaped just as easily. He's still on the news, only now he's the subject of a worldwide manhunt instead of suspect dead at the scene."

"They don't need to convince the press or the public, that's easy. But the Majestic leadership is tough. Kat wants to take over the Illuminati. She's not going to want a war with Majestic. She's going to want them thinking one of their own went rogue for the last couple of years and got killed in the act. Bob's still alive. I know it."

Skunky sighed and looked to Valentine and Ling. I was right. Ling was the official decision maker, but everybody here trusted Valentine's opinion. "That's a lot of risk without much preparation or intel based on a hunch."

"The longer we hold off, the more likely we are to get compromised. Twenty million dollars in reward money between me and Valentine, and Paris is crawling with thugs now."

"We need enough time to scope this place out, observe it, see who comes and goes, try to get a handle on what's in there first." Skunky was growing exasperated.

"Normally, I'd agree. I love planning. Planning's great. But it's out by itself away from the city. Look at that map. Where are we going to watch it from?" It was surrounded by grassy fields and hills, but there wasn't a whole lot of cover. The nearest neighbors were farms. "What if we get made between now and then? What if they launch Blue while we're still dicking around? I'm sneaking in there soon, by myself if I have to."

"So jeopardize the whole mission, because you're grasping at straws?"

"Who the fuck are you, again?" I was getting a little tired of Skunky's devil's advocate act. "I made my living getting into places nobody was supposed to be able to get into. What's your background?"

"High-end camera sales and *not throwing my life away* on futile noble gestures on dumb suicide missions! You got a problem with that?"

"Oh my God, both of you, chill the fuck out," Valentine said. "Skunky was on Switchblade Six with me and Tailor. Ramirez and Hawk trained him. Skunky, Lorenzo is old school Switchblade, from back in the Africa days. Decker trained him. We're all family here, and this dick measuring contest isn't helping."

Switchblade? Okay. I had to give him some props for that. He was young enough that he must have been in during their Vanguard era, when Decker had gone all corporate and legitimate businessman, but even then, the Switchblade teams had maintained their reputation of being tough as nails mercenaries who took the shittiest jobs and came back for more. And ironically, for the first time in years, I even had the stupid little knife Decker had given me. I pulled it out of my pocket and pushed the button. The pointy little blade popped out. I held it up in front of my face and wagged it back and forth. "Knife check." That had been Decker's stupid running joke.

Skunky gave me a respectful nod. Young Switchblade must have heard a lot of stories about old Switchblade. I returned the nod. I could still think he was wrong, but it wasn't because he was a wimp. I closed the knife and put it back in my pocket.

"We'll all hug later. Right now, can we figure this out?" Valentine sounded weary.

"Fine." Maybe they were right. I was pushing it. I was angry, frustrated, out of practice, and all that combined was making me sloppy. "Tonight's pushing it. I'll admit that. Look how willing I am to compromise. But it's either soon or never, and you all know it."

All seven of us were quiet for a bit as the maps were passed around. The house itself was twelve thousand square feet with a couple of outbuildings and a big garage. They could have an army inside and we wouldn't know until it was too late. There was four acres of lawn inside the fence. It was hard to tell from Google Earth, but there were some trees and bushes I could use for cover if I got inside the perimeter, even some statuary around the pool area, but there were also balconies on the second floor that would probably have guards posted.

"There is only one lane in." Shen warned us.

"It is entirely fenced in. I wonder if the gate is light enough we can ram through or if we'll have to use explosives?" Antoine asked. "It is possible Stokes installed hydraulic bomb blocks too."

"There is no way to see from the road." Shen ran his finger down the map. The lane was a windy quarter mile that would make it hard to build speed. "It would be suspicious to get close enough to look."

"Two of us they wouldn't recognize could take a rental car, pose as tourists, drive up this lane looking lost, then turn back," Antoine mused. "One visitor is not so suspicious. A minute of looking around is better than nothing at all."

"Good call," I told him. "The real estate listing says the fence is iron bars, but no height given. I wish I could tell if we're talking topped in razor wire or what . . ."

"I bet decorative fleur-de-lis. Only a fat fool would get stuck climbing over." Shen said. I could tell he was thinking what I was thinking. When we'd worked together before, I'd learned that he was *really* good at not being seen. Maybe even as good as I was.

"Shen and I could get in there, pave the way and take out the exterior guards and any dogs."

"I'm betting the Dobermans have poodle haircuts," Valentine said. "Look at this rich bitch neighborhood. My hometown didn't cost this much."

"Spare me, American. I grew up in a hut." Antoine ran one hand across his shaved head to wipe away beads of perspiration. That was one problem with crappy meeting places. You couldn't exactly complain about the inadequate air conditioning to the management, who in this case was an old blind Vietnamese lady. "Despite the price,

I can see why Stokes chose this property. There is no way to insert quickly short of a helicopter. Could your Mr. Reaper get us some more current photographs?"

"I've got him working on it now." Sadly, since Reaper had been semi-retired and gone all weirdo hermit since I'd been gone, he hadn't replaced Little Bird after he'd crashed it in the Crossroads. I was missing our drone already. "He's also checking for any possible angle of getting in there. Lawn care, pool cleaner, food delivery, I don't care. Anything Stokes' assholes have brought in from the outside gives us a potential in. Reaper is all up in his business. If Stokes spent money on anything recently, he'll find it."

"There's nowhere we can get close enough to use a parabolic microphone on the windows." Skunky was checking the elevation on one nearby hill. "If the grass is tall enough here still and they've not run a bush hog over it, I can put on my ghillie suit and crawl in from the main road. I can provide overwatch and cover to three quarters of the property from there."

I checked the scale. "That's five hundred yards away. Are you good for that distance?"

Skunky just grinned. "Heck yeah, man."

"Jeff is very talented with two things, Lorenzo," Ling assured me. "A precision rifle that he babies as if it were his child—"

"It's got a lot of carbon fiber on it," Valentine interjected. "He thinks it makes it go faster, like a sports car."

"What's the other thing?"

"A banjo." Ling waited for that to sink in. "I am not joking. He plays the banjo."

Shen just shook his head sadly.

"Hey, country is cool, Ling. Don't judge," Skunky protested. "I know Shen's all Mr. Tradition but my folks ditched Taiwan when you guys' civil war started getting ugly. I'm all-American."

I'd heard Ling was from Northern China, before she'd been conscripted by the commies. I glanced at Shen. "Hong Kong," he said nonchalantly, which was by far the most information he'd ever shared about his past. So half the Exodus team was of Chinese descent, representing both North, South, and American . . . So of course the American played the banjo. Skunky probably owned an orange Dodge Charger with a Confederate flag on the roof, too.

"We need to figure out their numbers and their security system. You and Shen can't sneak through that field if they've got FLIR cameras up. That means we'd have to kill their power supply, but do they have a backup generator? How long will it take for their reinforcements to arrive?" Valentine was really thinking through all the ramifications, and all of these experienced operators were actually looking to him for guidance. *I'll be damned. At some point he'd really turned into an actual leader.*

Then I got a big surprise, when all of those supposedly experienced badasses looked to the teenage girl. "What do you think, Ariel?"

She was deep in thought, twirling her hair. "It fits. Bob is an important piece of the puzzle. Everything I can see points to Katarina using Blue for its original purpose to weaken the Illuminati, so she can take it over. Placing the blame for a Majestic operation on a rogue Majestic operative prevents their retaliation against her, and furthers her overall goal. So I think Lorenzo's hypothesis is correct—"

"Thank you."

"But we still need more information," she finished. They all nodded like she was brilliant.

"Why the hell does her opinion count? Are you even old enough to drive?"

Shen tried to placate me. "Ariel is very smart."

"Fantastic. I've got a smart person too, and Reaper agrees with me."

"She is like a girl Reaper—"

"Greaper?" Skunky asked.

"But smarter," Shen finished.

"I'm just saying we're going to need more time to figure things out." Ariel rolled her eyes. "Lorenzo changes things. I never thought he'd come back from the dead or be involved now. He's special. He's a unique variable."

I froze. Sala Jihan had said the same thing. I snapped, "What the fuck did you just call me?"

Ariel was taken aback. "Huh?"

My manner had changed so abruptly that I think I startled Exodus. The room got really quiet. "Easy, Lorenzo," Valentine said. His left hand had dropped under the table. I had no doubt it was resting on the butt of that big, stupid sixgun he liked to carry. "She's just trying to help. She didn't mean to, like, offend you or whatever. What the hell is your problem, anyway?"

I was staring at her, really looking at her for the first time. Ariel looked frightened, but was she really? There was something off about this little girl, and it wasn't just because she was too clever, or had a gift for seeing patterns, or whatever that bullshit was. I was really good at observing people, you had to be in order to copy their mannerisms or mimic their voices. I was a master at pretending to be someone I was not. This wasn't a young woman. This was something else pretending to be a young woman. And just for an instant I heard the whispers, pushing against the edge of my sanity.

"So I guess what your Oracle is saying is that *fate hasn't determined a path* for me yet?"

The others didn't notice, but Ariel was suddenly very nervous when I used Sala Jihan's words back on her. Now she was as suspicious of me as I was of her. None of the Exodus people saw what was going on, but somehow . . . I knew this little girl did.

"It's fine." She gave me a nervous smile. "My methods are probably a little weird for him. Mr. Lorenzo and we can talk about it later."

"Yeah . . . sure we will."

Valentine had no clue what had just gone down, and looked bewildered. "Alrighty then . . . so it's settled. Stokes is our next target, but we're going to take our time and do this right. We can't afford any more screw-ups."

"I'm sorry, Lorenzo." Ling put one hand on my shoulder. It was a remarkable display of gentleness and familiarity by her publicly reserved standards. "I understand your frustration, but if Bob has survived this long, he will survive a few more days."

That meant I'd have to wait a bit before I could start killing assholes and get my brother back, but I put on my happy face, because at least I didn't have to try and tackle it on my own. "I'm the spirit of compromise."

After we'd brainstormed and gotten our assignments, the meeting had broken up. Ariel was supposed to ride back to their hideout with Antoine. The street in front of the building was kept dark on purpose. Antoine went to get their car. I waited until she was alone before I approached her. For a while, I thought Valentine would never stop hovering over her like a mother hen.

She saw me coming and looked apologetic. "I didn't mean to upset you, Mr. Lorenzo. I know I sound weird sometimes—"

I cut her off. "Drop the act. What are you?"

Ariel was quiet for a moment. I could still see her blue eyes in the dark. "What do you mean?"

"The whole super-genius thing is a con. Yeah, you can see things, but not the way they think you do. They can't see it, but I do. You actually can see the future."

She didn't say anything. She just looked at me like I was a ranting madman.

"I've seen the other side. You're like *him*."

"I'm not like him!" she snapped. "I don't know of anyone like him."

"You know what? I believe that. He's unique."

"He's evil."

"Trust me, girl, that's really hard to miss." My chest was burning. "He's a force of nature. But you're just this innocent little thing, with a mind that the most powerful secret organizations in the world would kill to possess."

"Something like that," she said. "You wouldn't understand."

"Sala Jihan is evil, you're good. Flip sides of the coin, yin and yang, that's the deal?"

"You sound delusional, you know that?"

"Maybe I am. Or maybe whatever Kat intends to do would mess things up so bad that both the angels and the devils agree it needs to be stopped. If you can see the future, then tell me what's going to happen."

"Don't you get it yet?" She was exasperated. "Nobody can predict your future. That's why you're here! That's why the Pale Man let you go. It's the same reason I talked Michael into taking on this fight. Nothing is predictable once *either* of you get involved! On its current path, things fall apart. *Everything* falls apart! The world is crumbling, it's just a question of how fast. But with you two, we have a chance to change the course." She looked frustrated. "I just wish you could see."

Antoine pulled up with their car.

"Good night, Ariel."

"You know, Mr. Lorenzo, if I were you I would keep your crazy ramblings to yourself. You've been through a lot. The others will lose confidence in you if they think you've cracked." Ariel opened the passenger side door and got inside. "You don't need to be an oracle to see that."

They drove away, leaving me alone in the dark.

LORENZO
Outskirts of Paris
October 5th

I'd learned that it really didn't matter what country or culture you were in, you could always spot the ex-cons, and Samuel had hard time written all over him. If the shoddy prison tats on his forearms and neck hadn't given him away, the bad attitude would have.

Samuel looked me over long enough to know that I wasn't a cop, or whatever they had equivalent to parole officers in this country, then went back to working on the car engine. Shen and I had just wandered into his place of employment and interrupted him at work. The garage was busy, and he had stuff to do. At least he didn't waste my time by pretending he couldn't speak English. "Go to hell, man. I don't know no Samuel."

"You sure?" I looked to Shen, who as usual, just shrugged. "Because you look a lot like the picture of the guy we're looking for. Doesn't he?"

"Yes. The spitting image." Shen wandered over to a workbench and picked up a big wrench. I shook my head in the negative, and looking a little disappointed, Shen put the wrench down.

I knew this was our guy, though the nametag on his coveralls said his name was *Francoise*, that was all fake. Nobody else who worked here would know who this jackass really was. Reaper's digging said this garage was legit, and not even affiliated with any Montalban businesses. A few other mechanics looked our way, but nobody seemed inclined to question what we were doing here. When a place hired low rent scumbags like Samuel, this sort of visit was just another Human Resources issue.

I knew Shen was perfectly happy to beat the information we needed out of this douchebag, but I was trying to keep it diplomatic. "Then there must be another Algerian guy who works here who looks exactly like you, then. Help me find him." I laid a stack of Euros on top of the car battery next to him.

Samuel glanced over at the cash, then went back to work. "Man, I don't know nothing. You're wasting your time."

"This Samuel guy—not that I'm saying you're him, just making conversation—I hear he's really mechanically inclined. The right kind of people can hire him for all sorts of odd jobs involving things like cameras, security systems, and safes."

"Installing them, or getting through them?" Shen asked rhetorically.

"From what I've heard, both. Which is why our guy Samuel needs to have a fake identity at a boring day job so all the many angry Frenchmen he's robbed don't come and cap his ass."

Samuel kept turning a bolt with a ratchet, but he was sweating. "I don't do that anymore."

"I? Look at that, Shen. I think we've had a communications breakthrough." I put more money down on the stack. "You did a freelance install job a few months ago. It was the sort of thing you used to do for Big Eddie all the time."

Now Samuel was really scared. The ratchet was turning faster. Big Eddie wasn't a name you tossed around casually. "The whole time I was in prison, I never said nothing about who I was working for when I got arrested."

"It's cool, Samuel. Big Eddie's dead."

"I don't know nothing about that."

"I do." I was tired of messing around. I got right next to him, leaning over the engine as if I was trying to see what he was up to. "Because I'm the one who killed him."

The ratchet stopped cold. "Oh shit, man . . . You're that guy?"

"Yeah, I'm that guy. Hi, Samuel. I'm Lorenzo." The other mechanics were far enough away and there was enough tool and engine noise they couldn't hear me. This might not be a Montalban affiliated joint, but that didn't mean they weren't clued in enough to know about Anders' bounty on me. Every criminal and dirtbag in France had probably heard about that by now. "Nice to meet you. Now quit wasting my time. Big Eddie's in hell. I'm here. Which one do you think you should be more worried about?"

"But his sister is still around and she's just as nuts." And then he realized that he'd said way too much. Knowing about Kat's takeover meant he was still up on current events.

"I thought you said you were out. Are you working for her?" That was a loaded question, since I knew the rumors flying around Europe right now were about how I was murdering the hell out of Montalban employees, so if he was, and answered truthfully, I'd probably kill him, and if he wasn't, and answered truthfully, and I didn't believe him, I'd still probably kill him. Sucks, but that's what he deserved for being an asshole.

"No way!" he exclaimed. "I don't do anything with them anymore. The Montalbans left me to rot. When I got out, they'd forgotten about me. But my name's still out there, man. I just freelance once in a while, but never for the people you've got a beef with. I avoid Big Eddie's old people like the plague."

"Then let me clarify the nature of my visit, Samuel. A few months ago you were paid a bunch of money by a British mercenary named Aaron Stokes to beef up the security on a chateau in the countryside."

"How'd you know that?" That was supposed to be a secret. Now he'd moved into terrified. *Good.*

"I know everything." That was a complete lie.

Skunky had played lost tourist and taken a detour down Stokes' private road. He had to turn around before the Brits got suspicious, but when Exodus checked the hidden cameras they'd placed on Skunky's car, Ariel noticed that new cameras had been installed along the fence. She identified the brand and model by comparing images on the Internet. Somebody must have put those in recently, so Reaper had checked everyplace that sold expensive security cameras in the region. A large cash purchase in the right time frame had led us back to this clown. A little more poking and a few bribes and we knew Samuel's criminal record, his rep, and the fact that he'd paid off all of his considerable debts and stuck a bunch of money in the bank, all in the right time frame, told me this was probably our guy.

I tell you, criminals make the best detectives.

"Considering what Stokes paid you, either you overcharged him, or you did a whole lot of work to that old place."

"Part of that was him paying me to not talk about it. I haven't talked to them or said a word about them since the job was done. You can't mess with those Brits! His boys are killers, man."

Shen snorted.

"I need to get into that chateau, and you're going to help me."

"You want to die, man?"

"The only thing I'm in danger of dying from right now is boredom. You're boring me, Samuel." Before he could react, I cupped the back of his head and shoved his face against the engine block. From his wailing it turned out that it was still hot. Then I caught the car hood and pulled it down on his body. He squealed when it hit, but let's be honest, it really wasn't a good angle to really hurt him. So I wacked him with it a few times, squishing him. The money was sent flying by the wind gusts. I smashed him as far into the engine compartment as I could, and then leaned my weight on the hood. His legs were kicking and he was letting out some muffled screams, but he wasn't going anywhere. "Check it out, Shen. I'm not bored anymore."

"You need a hobby."

Two other mechanics had seen my *negotiation strategy* and were coming our way. They probably didn't know who Samuel really was, but there was a certain international blue collar code of honor that declared you needed to step in when some outsider started kicking the shit out of one of your coworkers. Both were big, burly, tough guys with nearly as many prison tats as Samuel had. One of them had a jack handle. The other carried a ball-peen hammer.

Shen stepped right in front of them, hands on his hips. All he said was "No," and smiled. The two big guys stopped, looked at Shen, who was half the size of either of them—or one quarter of their combined mass—yet seemed completely confident anyway, and realized this probably wasn't the dude to mess with. They walked away, muttering. Apparently Samuel wasn't popular enough to risk an ass-beating over.

I opened the hood, pulled Samuel out by the ear, and then dragged him out the back door so we could have some privacy while Shen stuck around to make sure none of the others suddenly felt like using the phone. Once we were in the back parking lot, and satisfied there weren't any other witnesses, I let go of his ear.

"Okay, okay!" There was blood trickling from his nose and bruises spreading on his cheek. It turned out I'd gotten more leverage on that hood than I'd thought. "I swear I don't work for the Montalbans anymore! Back when nobody knew who Big Eddie really was, there were rules, you know? You obey the rules, you don't get clipped. But the new boss is all up in everyone's shit. She'll have you killed if she imagines you did something wrong. The money's good, but I'm avoiding that outfit. I swear. If Stokes is in with them, I didn't know it. He told me he's a free agent."

"I believe you, Samuel, which is why I'm offering you two options. Weigh them carefully. I pay you more than what Stokes paid you to begin with to walk me through every aspect of their system, and then you can forget this conversation ever happened. Or I beat it out of you for free. The only part of this which is completely non-negotiable is the part where you tell me everything you know."

"Stokes will kill me," he protested.

"He might later, but I'll for sure kill you sooner. So, bribe and run, or severe beating and probable death? I've not got all day."

I must have been really persuasive, because his decision didn't take too long. "I'll talk, it's good! I didn't like those pricks anyway."

"Fantastic." That was easy. I whistled for Shen that it was time to go. Then I pulled out my key fob, and pushed the trunk button. "Climb in."

Samuel got a really sick look on his face when he saw the Audi's trunk pop open. "Don't make me get in the boot. Come on, man, I said I'll tell you everything."

"Oh, you will. And then you'll hang out with us until the job is over. If we get caught, you get caught too. That should guarantee you don't forget any pertinent details. Plus, I'd hate to be all merciful and let you go, only for you to have second thoughts and warn them we're coming."

"I wouldn't do that!" he protested as Shen joined us.

"Yeah, because you've been a rock so far." I probably didn't need to make him ride in the trunk, but I'd just stolen this car, it was clean, and he had grease all over his coveralls.

Shen wasn't as patient as I was. He just snap kicked Samuel in the stomach, and while he was bent over, gasping, Shen hurled him head first into the trunk.

"At least it's roomy in there," I said as Shen slammed the lid.

As we were driving away, I called Reaper and told him we were on our way back.

Did you get the package? Reaper asked, having watched too many spy movies.

"It's in the trunk."

Oh . . . Did you make sure there wasn't one of those emergency exit pull tab thingies? They mandated those for like when kids play hide and seek in the trunk and get trapped."

"Yes, Dad." I hung up on him. "Sheesh, you'd think I'd never kidnapped anybody before."

As usual, Shen sat quietly, watching out the window as the outskirts of Paris scrolled by.

In the few times we'd worked together, I'd found that Shen wasn't exactly a man of many words. Which meant he was probably the safest person I could say the following to: "Between what we've heard about Stokes' crew, and Samuel's rep for doing quality work, I hate to admit it, but Valentine made the right call. If we'd gone when I wanted we probably would have gotten spotted and chewed up . . . Probably would have gotten Bob executed in the process."

"Yes."

I drove in silence for a moment. This was eating at me, and I kind of wanted to talk about it with somebody. I hadn't wanted to bring it up with Jill since she was injured and had enough on her mind, and Reaper was still dealing with his weird personal demons. But what the hell, Shen seemed like a good listener.

"Ever since I got out, I've been off. I've been making too many mistakes. I've gotten sloppy. That place screwed me up, Shen. If I'd taken my time at the smuggler's shop maybe I would have seen Anders staking it out. Jill wouldn't have gotten shot. This is all on me. I know better, but it's like ever since I got out of that dungeon, I've been seeing red. Like I can't think straight until I end these people. The Pale Man got in my head. I can't explain it."

"Desire for vengeance clouds your vision."

"Is that like the Zen Buddhist way of saying I'm too bloodthirsty?"

"Because I'm Chinese, you assume I'm profoundly philosophical?" Shen looked over at me and grinned. "That is racist."

"Motherfucker, I've seen you fight. You're like a kung-fu master, snatch the pebble from my hand grasshopper, badass. If anybody on Exodus is going to get all philosophical *Art of War* on me, it should be you."

"I checked that out from a library once. It is actually a very good book."

"And here I was thinking you'd spent years meditating under a freezing waterfall and punching rocks before you joined Exodus."

Shen shook his head. "I was a killer for the Triads."

I glanced over at the unassuming little man. In my business that was one hell of a resume item. "No shit?"

"No shit." Shen sighed when he realized I was still staring at him, waiting for him to continue. "Pay attention to the road, please."

"I did. Traffic wasn't bad here, but I didn't want to do anything that would attract police attention while I had a kidnap victim in the trunk. I'd stolen money from Chinese organized crime a few times over the years. They were an unforgiving, merciless bunch." I know the Triads. They're not known for their retirement packages."

"My past is not something I am proud of. When I was a boy, I was a typical Hong Kong thug, but I was clever and had ambition. I worked my way through the ranks and developed my skills. By the time I was twenty, I was a trusted associate."

"That's a big career jump from Triad assassin to Exodus do-gooder. What happened?"

"One day my employers asked me to kill someone. I decided not to."

"I'm guessing that's the abridged version."

Shen was quiet as a police car went speeding by. We both watched it in the mirrors for a moment to see if it flipped around. Samuel's ex-con coworkers didn't seem like the types to call the cops, but you never knew. Once he was certain we were clear, Shen continued. "Being ordered to kill a man who has broken our agreed-upon rules is one thing. Killing his wife and children to set an example is another. The assignment forced me to examine my life choices."

I laughed at that. Shen was like the master of understatement. "And?"

"I hesitated. The Triad does not tolerate disobedience. They decreed I would die along with my assigned targets. I returned to Hong Kong and killed my employers instead." He said that like it was no big deal.

"You're telling me you went to war with a Hong Kong Triad."

He shrugged. "Only with enough of them to settle the matter."

"See? I knew you were a badass. Damn, Shen. Did you wear a white suit? Did doves fly by in slow motion while you used a Beretta in each hand?"

Shen didn't seem to think that was funny. "Nothing so dramatic.

When it was over, I agreed to never return to Hong Kong. I had no purpose and nothing to live for. There had been conflict between the Triads and Exodus. I knew they fought for what they believed to be good. To atone for the evil acts I had committed, I offered Exodus my services. It took years before they trusted me. Some still do not. The ones with us here are my family now . . . Very well, Lorenzo, you wish to know what I think?"

"Go for it."

"Like me, you are experienced in these matters. You understand that only death can satisfy some debts. Regardless of what you have suffered, you must . . ." Shen paused, trying to think of the correct way to phrase it, "Keep your shit together."

"You don't need to worry about that. On my worst day I'm still more than a match for these dickheads." But that was just talk. I was worried. I knew it, and Shen knew it.

"You want to lash out. I have been there. But too much is riding on this mission. We can feel the pressure. The time is close. As you Americans say, it breathes down our neck. You have made mistakes, recognized them, and made fewer. You were still recovering from Jihan's prison. My friends have no such excuse. I respect Ling. I love her as if she was my own sister. She was one of the first to accept me in Exodus. Only her heart follows a flawed man. Valentine is dedicated, but too passionate. He rushed, trying to pit Underhill against Katarina, and nearly paid with his life. It was foolish."

"Harsh."

"Yet true." Shen trailed off as we stopped at an intersection.

When it was a little quieter we both realized Samuel was yelling for help from the trunk. The carbon monoxide was probably making him stupid. "Keep it down in there," I shouted toward the back seat.

"I accepted death long ago, but when it comes I pray it serves a purpose. We can't afford to die without results, Lorenzo. I truly believe the world depends on what we do here."

"The world, huh?" I tapped my fingers on the steering wheel as I waited for a light to change. "You talking about Ariel's predictions?"

"I am."

"While we're on the topic of mystical bullshit philosophies . . ." Under the cold light of day I wasn't going to tell him my crackpot theories. "Never mind."

"I think she sees patterns others do not. I leave it at that. All that matters is that she is usually right."

The light changed. "Damn, Shen, that was remarkably unhelpful."

"Now you understand why I do not make small talk."

Chapter 14: The Rescue

VALENTINE
North of Paris
October 8th

The plan was simple enough: Lorenzo and Shen would sneak up in the dark and try to get the gate open, while Skunky would provide overwatch with his rifle. Reaper—and his unwilling passenger, Samuel the security installer—was parked a ways off with our secondary getaway vehicle. Ling, Antoine, and I were in our van, hidden off the main road, ready to roll in when the infiltrators got the gate open. We had nothing to do until then, and it was maddening.

I sat in the back, with Antoine, dressed out in full combat gear. I had on body armor, with plates, and a load-bearing vest on top of that. Beneath all of that we were wearing normal clothing, so we could ditch the heavy stuff and not look like weirdos if we needed to. Antoine and I both carried old German G3 rifles, with Aimpoint red dot sights mounted. Antoine's had a 40mm grenade launcher mounted under the barrel, though we were really hoping not to use grenades since this was supposed to be a hostage rescue. Regardless, we were ready to provide heavy fire support when the time came.

Ling was in the driver's seat, she was fully kitted out too. Of course, we had left Ariel behind. Despite her enthusiasm, she had zero training, and quite simply wasn't cut out for this kind of work. I had suggested that she stay with Jill to keep an eye on her. Jill was still recovering, and wasn't in good enough shape to get around, only Ariel had begged off, saying she was too busy. For whatever reason, I had the feeling Ariel wanted to avoid Lorenzo's people. She was still at our safehouse.

We were really shorthanded, especially since we had no idea how many men Stokes had. It was too risky to keep the place under surveillance directly, but a little cautious poking around with the farmers in the local villages told us there had been several people staying at the chateau, but the number of cars coming and going had jumped dramatically right after I'd tried to strangle Katarina. That probably meant she had called in reinforcements.

I wished Tailor could help. We'd have a lot better luck getting Bob Lorenzo out alive with a properly equipped tactical team on our side, and from what I had seen Tailors' guys seemed to really know their shit. However, there was the slight problem that I hadn't told Romefeller we were doing this. He thought we were still investigating and searching for the bomb. The big Illuminati meeting was in the morning, so I was afraid he'd declare any direct raid against Katarina Montalban's employees to be *unsanctioned,* and then we would be out of luck. I wasn't just worried that he'd tell us not to, but after the mess at the hotel, Romefeller might actively send Tailor to stop us from going in. But if we could retrieve Bob, Kat would lose her patsy and Blue would be delayed. Romefeller might not like doing it my way, but tough shit.

Antoine must've read my face, even in the darkened van. "You look pensive, Mr. Valentine."

"Pensive," I repeated, keeping one ear on the radio. Skunky was slowly crawling into position. Lorenzo and Shen were doing the same. Since they were going low and slow, the wait was downright nerve-wracking. "That's one way of describing it, I guess."

"It is understandable." It must've been difficult to find body armor that would fit somebody as large as Antoine. He had to be six-foot-five, with at least a fifty-inch chest. The G3 rifle he carried, especially with a grenade launcher attached, is not a compact or especially handy weapon. It looked almost like a toy in his hands. His voice was deep and accented, but despite his imposing figure, he always spoke like a schoolteacher. "There is much that could go wrong. Do you still think this is the right thing to do?"

I exhaled, wiping sweat from my brow. We didn't have the engine running and it was getting warm in the back of the van, wearing all this gear. "I think this is crazy," I said, bluntly. "But it needs to be done. We can't let them frame Bob for mass murder."

Antoine simply nodded.

"Besides," I continued, leaning back in my seat, "Exodus roped Lorenzo into this mess on the promise that you'd help him get his brother back. He went through God-knows-what because of that. It would be incredibly screwed up to not uphold your end of the deal."

"Exodus keeps its promises," Antoine agreed, "no matter how long it takes. But I was not speaking of us, I was asking about you."

"You guys and Lorenzo came and rescued me when I was being held. You risked your lives for me. Bob's in the predicament he's in because of me. Getting him out is the least I can do. It's the right thing to do."

We got the signal over the radio. They were almost there.

Good luck, asshole.

LORENZO
The Chateau

"Do you have the shot?"

"I have the shot."

"Take it," I whispered.

The sound suppressor hid the gunshot, but the impact of the bullet came as a wet *thwack* as Skunky blew the guard's brains out. There was a *clack* as his rifle dropped from nerveless fingers. A shadow passed in front of the light as the man fell flat on the balcony. A red mist hung in front of the lamp for an instant before dissipating in the wind.

"The guard is down." Skunky's voice came through my earpiece. He was excitable in person, but on the job it turned out he was all business.

We had been crawling for hours. Now that Skunky had shot a guard, it was a race against the clock before they realized we were here. No alarm sounded. The compound remained quiet. That wouldn't last forever.

That had been a damned good shot. There was a strong breeze tonight, and it was even harder to judge wind through a night vision scope. My own night vision device was stowed in a pouch on my belt, because it sucked to wear while crawling through the dirt, caught on branches, and after a while the weight killed my neck and gave me a headache.

"Keep holding position. The camera is turning left."

All the cameras tracked slowly back and forth. We were so close that I imagined I could hear the little servo motors, but that was wishful thinking from my hearing damaged, half deaf self.

I waited, hoping that nobody inside had heard the guard fall, but the yard around the big house remained clear. Shen and I had spent three miserable, filthy hours low crawling through the weeds and brush, moving when the camera was pointed away, and taking cover when Skunky warned us it was close. It had to be nearly as exhausting for him, watching it through the scope and repeating the countdown a few hundred times now.

"Four, three, two, one. And clear. Go."

Shen and I leapt out of the weeds and sprinted for the fence.

Samuel had given us the stats, and since he was a mile away, tied up in Reaper's car with the promise that if I got caught, Reaper was just going to leave him there, I was certain he'd been completely forthcoming. There were no motion or contact sensors on the fence. He'd talked Stokes out of it because there were too many deer in the area, and they would always be setting it off. The fence was fifty years old, ten feet tall, and made of thick iron bars, spaced four inches apart, with—Shen had guessed right—decorative pokeys on top, that was it. So it would be a piece of cake for guys like us to get over. My biggest concern was that it would rattle and make a bunch of noise as we climbed it.

We had thirty seconds before the camera on the roof came back around. We reached the fence with fifteen seconds to spare. Shen bent next to it, so I could step ladder my way onto his knee, his shoulder, and as he stood up with my weight on him, I grabbed the top bar. The fence shook a bit, but the metallic noise was less than the sound of the wind. I rolled on top, balancing, letting the fleur-de-lis poke into my soft Kevlar body armor vest as I swung one hand down to Shen. Gloves hit my exposed forearm as Shen pulled. He was pretty damned acrobatic, and made it over the top in a flash, dropping smoothly and silently onto the grass on the other side.

I rolled off and dropped next to him, hitting with a grunt. I'd been pushing my body hard since I'd gotten out of Jihan's dungeon, training as hard as I could while limited to an apartment with no exercise equipment, so I wasn't even close to being in prime shape. Shen was crouched and listening, one hand on his slung weapon. There hadn't been any dogs when Samuel had done his install work, but that might have changed since. There wasn't any barking and no big angry German Shepherds descended on us, so that was good.

I pointed toward the nearest patch of bushes. Shen and I moved out in a fast crouch. The grass was thick, hadn't been mowed for a while, and had gone to seed. Secret prisons were lax on their lawn care. The wind was blowing the leaves and shaking the branches. That was a huge benefit for us, as the noise and movement would help hide us from the patrols.

"Camera coming back in five, four, three—"

By the time Skunky got done, we were already on our bellies in the dirt and roots. This would be the last countdown. After this, we'd be beneath the exterior camera's field of view, and we could push for the front gate. Skunky's earlier lost tourist scout drive-by had confirmed the gate was too solid to ram. Blowing it up would be messy and time-consuming. Short of a tank we didn't have, the terrain was too rough to crash the fence at any other angle. So if we wanted help to roll in, we needed to open that gate.

However, there was now a dead man leaking the contents of his skull all over the rear second-floor balcony. Any second somebody was going to miss him or trip over him, and then we were screwed. So time was of the essence.

On my knees and elbows I crawled through the bushes. I could tell they'd been well trimmed once, probably styled into animal topiary, but now they were lumps of wonderful concealment. The wind helped hide any inadvertent shaking I caused. I reached the edge of the leaves and surveyed the back of the house. There were a lot of lights around the chateau, so I'd made the right call leaving off my NVGs. In fact, there were too many interior rooms lit up for comfort. Hopefully that just meant they liked to sleep with the lights on, and not that there were a bunch of them still awake, but probably not.

Seen up close, this was a really nice estate, but a little too snooty, Euro artsy for my tastes. Everything between the buildings was landscaped into gentle curves and cobbled paths. There were terraces, columns, and even imitation Greek statues. The pool was full, but judging from all the leaves and bugs floating on the water, it hadn't been used for a while. Lights hitting the rippling water cast odd reflections on the walls and statues.

I checked my watch. It was after 4 AM. We were behind schedule. I'd wanted to hit while people tended to be at their natural deepest sleep rhythm, but that weed crawl in had been agonizingly slow and put us behind schedule.

"*This is Skunky. Ghost and Slick are in the compound,*" he reported to the assault element.

Exodus had made up the call signs. I looked toward Shen, like *fuck you, I should be Ghost.* In the dark, with his artificially blackened face, all I could see was his teeth smiling back, like *up yours, I'm Mr. Exodus Cool Guy. You have to be Slick.*

"*This is Nightcrawler. We are ready to move at your signal.*" That had been Valentine's Dead Six call sign, and what I'd first known him as. So in that case, I was lucky my call sign hadn't ended up as *Asshole.*

I had the 9mm TMP subgun hanging from a single point sling at my side. While crawling through ditches all night, the compact weapon had been handy. Now that I was in a compound with an unknown number of heavily armed mercenaries, I wished I had carried something chambered in an actual grown up sized rifle cartridge. Shen had one of those Czech EVO subguns, with some short, fat European suppressor I didn't recognize. I pulled out my 1911 with the old suppressor screwed onto the end of its threaded muzzle. We would keep this quiet as long as possible.

This was my element. There was something addictive about sneaking around in the dark. If we needed to bail, I was ready to disappear in plain sight too. Though I was dirty and sweaty and had my face painted, beneath my soft vest, I was wearing regular clothes. I could ditch the guns and vest, and a quick scrub later I could disappear back into society, not that there was any society within a couple of miles, but you never know. But until we had to run, I owned these scumbags. I felt alive.

Shortly, we'd be clear to move. Then we'd either succeed and get Bob back alive, or we'd fail, and probably all get shot in the process. At this point there was no use dwelling on it. We'd made the best plan we could. This crew was motivated, experienced, and extremely skilled. If something went wrong, we'd adapt, and we'd win.

While we lay there in the shadows, Shen unslung the EVO and quietly opened the folding stock. Skunky began our final countdown. *"Camera is past in three, two, one. Go."*

I was out and moving quickly toward the edge of the pool shack. Shen and I had talked it over beforehand, and he veered toward the right, staying with the bushes. We had the same target. Two different paths let us watch more angles for threats, plus—let's be honest—this whole alpha predator in the dark thing is mostly instinct, so having somebody up close on you is awkward. I kept to the darkest spots, moving from shadow to shadow. I caught one brief glimpse of Shen as he rolled beneath another bush, but then he was gone. The dude was really good.

We knew there were patrols around the interior. For the last few hours Skunky had told us about each one he'd spotted and the path they had taken, but they'd been sporadic enough that there didn't seem to follow a scheduled route. It was just two dudes with guns walking around periodically.

I began to slide around the edge of the pool house, then realized there was gravel here, and gravel is too loud to walk on, so I backtracked and took the other side.

"Slick, this is Skunky. When you go around that corner, I won't be able to cover you."

I tapped my transmit button twice in the affirmative, then I went that way anyway. Like I said, you had to go with your instinct. I made it twenty feet closer to the gatehouse before Skunky transmitted again.

"I've got more movement on the rear balcony. Another guard. He's a few seconds from seeing that body I left."

The angle was such that I couldn't see the balcony anymore. I kept pushing on. I was just going to have to count on our sniper.

Skunky must not have realized he was still transmitting. *"Come on. Turn around. Don't open that door . . . Don't . . ."* There was a long pause. I was far enough away that I didn't hear the sound of the supersonic bullet travelling through the air or the impact against flesh. *"There's another guard down on the rear balcony."*

That was probably the first guard's relief. When he didn't go back inside, the rest would realize something was wrong. They'd sound the alarm, wake everybody else up, and then all hell would break loose. The clock was ticking down fast now. It was tempting to rush, but that would get me spotted, so I just kept on slinking along from shadow to shadow.

Slowly, very slowly, I peeked around the corner. Quick jerky movements were what got you spotted in the dark. The gatehouse was in view, but unfortunately, so was one of the random patrols. Two men were strolling my way, with maybe ten feet separating them. They weren't smoking or joking. They were relaxed, but alert. Heads up, glancing around, these weren't just goons. Their attitude and appearance said they were pros. The ones Skunky had seen during the daylight drive by had been wearing contractor chic, khakis and photographer's vests to hide their pistols, so they looked like security, but not so militant as to make witnesses nervous. Apparently that went out the window after dark, because now they were wearing tac vests and carrying shorty AR carbines.

Skunky couldn't see us. They were going to be on top of me in a few seconds, and I didn't have time to back up out of their way. I'd need to pop both of these guys before they saw me, and I had to do it clean and fast enough that they couldn't shout or yank a trigger. I had been working out, but there hadn't exactly been ample opportunities to hit the shooting range. This was going to be tough.

Then Shen surprised me by appearing behind the man in the rear, wrapping one hand over his mouth and simultaneously running a black knife across his throat. That guard made enough of a noise to catch the other's attention. He saw Shen, opened his mouth to shout something, but then my bullet caught him in the back of his skull. He dropped in a heap.

We'd put them down in the light. If anybody had been looking out a window, we were fucked. I rushed over next to Shen, who was already dragging his body into the shadows behind a stone bench behind the pool house. I grabbed mine by the drag straps of his armor and pulled. Between the armor and mags, the dude weighed a ton. His carbine dragged along through the grass behind him by the sling. It left a red trail. Looking down, I realized the .45 hollow point had gone through his brain and exited through his mouth. Then the fucker blinked at me and I nearly dropped him. It was like he was really confused and trying to ask me something. He was probably my age, had a big mustache, and I'd seen that same look on the faces of many of the other prisoners I'd had to kill for Sala Jihan's amusement. Thankfully, he was dead by the time I caught up to Shen.

"How'd you know I was going to be there?" I whispered.

Shen was wiping his knife off on his guard's pant leg. "I just did."

Nothing else needed to be said. I noted our position. If we had to fall back, we now had a convenient stash of extra guns and ammo. We moved out.

"This is Skunky. I've got visual on Ghost and Slick again, approaching the gatehouse. There is one guard in the gatehouse. I have a shot, but he's behind glass at an angle. Do you want me to take it?"

"Slick. Negative, Skunky. We got this." Rifle bullets could deflect in weird ways hitting heavy glass. A hole would be one thing, but if the whole window shattered, it would make a lot of noise. Besides, I could see the guard now. He was sitting down inside the little building. The interior light was on. Outside was dark. He wouldn't be able to see very far. This guard was younger, buzzed head, military look, pistol on his belt, but street clothes and no armor. Probably in the unlikely event some local farmer rolled up asking questions about the place and they didn't want the neighbors talking about paramilitary looking dudes living here.

Samuel said there was a keypad at both sides of the gate for a driver to put in the code, and a button in the shack. He didn't know what the code was, so that meant button.

I scooted right up on the door and rested one hand on the knob. Shen went down, crawled past me, and got under the window. I'd try the knob. If it was open, I'd sweep in and drop him. If it was locked, the guard would probably hear the knob move, and then Shen would come up and pop him flat through the glass with the EVO.

I put one gloved hand on the knob, pistol in the other. Shen nodded when he was ready.

And then a phone rang. We both froze.

It rang twice more before the man inside answered it. He must have been zoning out. I could barely hear the guard through the door. "Yeah, mate . . . Stokes is coming back?" There was a long pause. "What? We're done! The fuck you say." Another pause. "About bloody time that fucker Anders told the guv what to do with the prisoner."

There was an electric hum, and then a metallic rumble as the heavy gate began to move. The guard had pushed the button for us. We had incoming.

"*This is Skunky. The gate is opening. I repeat, gate is opening.*"

"*Nightcrawler. Rolling.*"

They must have thought we'd done that. Shen hurried and tapped one for negative. They were opening it for somebody else. That meant Exodus would cross paths with them on the road. Sure enough, Valentine came right back. "*We have a single vehicle moving toward the gate at a high rate of speed.*"

The guard started laughing. "We're done! So let's deliver that big bald fucker so we can get paid and go home."

They're moving Bob.

I heard another noise inside, like a chair being shoved back. "I'm on my way."

The door opened. The guard was beaming as he dropped his phone back into his pocket, probably thinking about how he was going to spend all that money he was getting paid for holding my brother prisoner all these months. He was so excited he damned near walked into me, crouched in the doorway. I jammed the Gemtech under his chin and painted the ceiling with blood. He crashed back, hit the wall, and began to slide down. I shot him again before he hit the floor, just to be sure. A .45 shell casing bounced across the sidewalk.

I glanced back toward the house. More lights were coming on. They hadn't sounded the alarm yet, but they were going to move Bob. They were now five men short, and things were going sideways as soon as they realized that. But even worse, the guard had been acting like their job was done. That could only mean one very bad thing.

I came to a very terrifying realization. There was only one reason to move Bob.

Blue!

I keyed my radio. "Nightcrawler, can you intercept that car?"

"*We can try.*"

"Our secondary target is in the car." That was Stokes. "Take him alive. Anders just called him. The target knows the Alpha Point."

"*Damn it.*" I could hear the squeal of tires over the radio. "*We're on it.*"

"Project Blue has launched. I repeat, Project Blue has launched."

VALENTINE
The Highway

Blue was in motion? *What the hell?* Lorenzo said Stokes knew the Alpha Point, the very thing Majestic had spent months torturing me for. But there was no time to think through the repercussions now.

"Got them," Ling stated with the utmost calm. Our lights were off and she was driving with NVGs. There was a pair of taillights moving along the dark and windy road ahead of us. Our man Stokes was in there, and if they arrived while Lorenzo and Shen were still on the ground, our infiltrators would be caught in the open. Ling mashed the accelerator and we began closing on the sedan.

"Get us closer," I said. Hopefully running dark we could close the gap before they realized we were on them.

I pulled open the sliding door on the passenger's side. Wind rushed in as trees whizzed by at a hundred and thirty kilometers per hour. As *The Calm* settled over me and my heart rate slowed, I took a deep breath. "Antoine, slide over and grab onto my vest so I don't fall out. Ling, come up on them and match speed."

"Affirmative."

I leaned outward, bracing myself on the door frame, hoping to hell Ling didn't swerve and send me flying. Antoine had hands like a vise, and he had remained buckled in, but I really didn't want to test his grip strength if I didn't have to. The sedan was just ahead of us and we were closing fast. They hadn't yet realized what was happening yet. I aligned the red dot with the rear of the car as best I could while hanging clumsily out the door of a speeding vehicle, and rocked the trigger.

The G3 bucked against my shoulder as I fired over and over again, as rapidly as I could without losing the target. I didn't know where Stokes was sitting, so I concentrated on the rear tires. They began skewing wildly side to side. Brake lights flared as a tire burst.

I had went through twenty rounds in just a few seconds. "Reloading!" I shouted as I dropped my mag, but Antoine was already handing me another.

Ling used that lull and put the hammer down. She put the edge of our front bumper on the wounded car ahead of us. A couple of muzzle flashes blinked at us from the back seat, as the surprised occupants desperately tried to return fire, but we had the initiative. Ling cranked the wheel into their back end, forcing them into a hard turn. The sedan flew off the road, spun through the grass, and crashed through a fence, disappearing in a cloud of dust.

Ling stomped on the brakes and we slid to a stop on the gravel. Through the swirling dust I could see the car's headlights. They had smashed into some trees. A car door was already open.

"They bailed out!" I leapt out of the van. Antoine was right behind me. Ling jumped out too. "We need Stokes alive!"

That was going to be difficult, because shots rang out from the darkened woodline. The moon was out, but it was hard to see through the trees. From the muzzle flashes, it looked like someone was firing wildly while moving away from us. The three of us crouched, as we moved up, keeping the crashed Mercedes between us and the shooter.

When we got to the car, the driver was still buckled in. His air bag had deployed, and from the way he was clumsily trying to get out, he had been dazed by the impact. From the his size and hair color, I could tell it wasn't our target. When he saw us moving up he went for a pistol on his hip. Ling and I simultaneously shot him through the glass.

"Nice." The back seat was clear. Stokes was our runner.

"Contact," Antoine shouted as he spotted our target moving through the trees. Tall guy, white hair, that had to be him. He must have gotten hurt in the crash, because he wasn't able to run too fast through the brush. Antoine fired a couple of rounds into the trees ahead of him, blasting through branches and bark. He didn't want to kill him, but Stokes didn't know that, and he dove for cover.

"Ling, go around to the left. Antoine, stay with me." Guns up, Antoine and I pushed forward, jogging toward the trees while trying to stay low. Ling moved to our flank, but remained in sight. We were close and he was cornered, but a stupid mistake could still get us killed.

"Come out, Stokes," I shouted.

"Piss off!" Stokes responded, as he hung a handgun over the top of a log and fired off several wild shots. "Do you have any idea who you're fucking with?"

"Screw this," I muttered. I took aim and smashed several rounds into the log next to him.

Odds were that he got pelted with fragments and splinters. That must have put the fear of God into him because he cried out, "Alright! Enough!" His breathing was labored and he sounded like he was in pain. He tossed his gun into the dirt, then slowly stepped into the open. "I'm coming out! Don't fucking shoot!"

Ling turned on her weapon mounted light, blinding him. There was a bunch of blood on his face, but sure enough, he was our target. "Aaron Stokes," I said, more as a statement than a question. "You're lucky we didn't kill you."

"Who the fuck are you people?" he sneered. "Do you have any idea who I am? Who I work for? You're in a world of shit, mate, a world of shit."

I walked up and hit him in the chest with the buttstock of the G3. Not hard enough to break anything—I needed him to talk—but hard enough to let him know I wasn't playing. He landed on his butt, coughing. I realized that he had something in his hand.

"Give me the phone, asshole." I snatched it from him, stepped back, and looked at the screen. He was in a call with somebody, trying to give them information about us. I ended the call. "Nice try, bro, but I saw that movie too."

"Get on your knees," Ling ordered. She had pulled out some zip ties.

"Fuck you, cunt," Stokes snarled. "I'd like to see you make me."

"Oh?" Antoine really didn't like anyone talking to Ling that way.

"We need him alive," I warned Antoine, as I scrolled through Stokes' phone.

"Indeed," Antoine said, right before he slugged Stokes in the face. He crumpled to the ground, knocked silly.

"Jesus," I said, looking up. "I said we need him *alive*."

"He'll live," Antoine said, sounding a little defensive, as Ling hurried and zip-tied Stokes' hands behind his back.

"You could have put him in a coma."

"Being in a coma is still alive."

"Haul him back to the van. We need to go. Lorenzo and Shen need our help." I let my rifle hang on its sling and keyed my microphone as Antoine hoisted Stokes up and dragged him back toward the road. "Slick, this is Nightcrawler, we got him."

"*Say again?*" Lorenzo replied, with lots of static. Down here in the trees our reception was garbage.

"Reaper, Nightcrawler, come back."

Reaper responded much more clearly. He was in a vehicle with a more powerful radio. "*Send it.*"

"Relay to the others, we have our boy, I say again, we have our boy. How copy?"

"*Understood, Nightcrawler. Is he alive?*"

"Affirmative." I glared at Antoine. "Probably. I'm going through his phone now."

"*Awesome!*" Reaper said. "*Probably useful intel on there.*"

"And lots of porn. I mean, wow, lots of porn." Lorenzo had said that Anders had just called and given Stokes the Alpha Point. I scrolled through his recent calls. The contacts were listed with really innocuous nicknames, but there was a call from Draco less than fifteen minutes ago. That had to be Anders. Then Stokes had placed a few calls immediately after. One number appeared twice, probably to tell his men to get ready, and then another to call for help when we attacked. But there was one other number he'd dialed immediately after speaking to Anders. I tried that one.

It didn't even ring. It went straight a recorded message being spoken in French. Something, something, *Gare d'Evangeline.*

Evangeline?

I must have twitched or something, because Ling asked me what was wrong.

I couldn't answer. I was lost in a memory. Colonel Curtis Hunter, buried in the rubble of a collapsed roof, trying to tell me something about Evangeline. He died before he could explain what he meant. *It couldn't be a coincidence.*

Then there was something I understood. "*For English, press two.*" I quickly lowered the phone, brought up the keypad, and tapped 2. Raising the phone back to my ear, I listened. "*Welcome to the automated directory for the Evangeline Station. For train schedules, press one. For ticketing, press two. For customer service, press . . .*" I hung up.

"Evangeline . . ." Images of Dr. Silvers asking me who she was over and over again filled my head. "My God. It's not a person, it's a place."

"What are you talking about?" Ling asked.

I got on my radio. "Reaper, listen to me very carefully. Evangeline isn't a person, it's a train station. That's has to be where the Alpha Point is! Evangeline is where Hunter hid his fucking bomb! Tell Lorenzo they're moving it by train!" I let go of my radio. "Quick, get back to the van."

"What about Stokes?"

"Leave him." Before I'd even finished saying that, Antoine tossed the stunned man into the dirt. "Reaper, we're on the way to Evangeline to stop that bomb."

"What about the mission?"

Shen and Lorenzo were in a compound filled with mercenaries, and since their boss had called them, they knew they were under attack. I looked toward the lights of the chateau. It was *so* close . . . But if Anders was moving that bomb . . .

"I'm sorry, man, this *is* the mission. Tell Slick he's on his own. We don't have time."

"But Lorenzo . . . shit, I mean, Slick and Ghost, they're counting on you!"

"I know!" I didn't mean to yell at the kid, but the hour had just turned out to be a whole hell of a lot later than we thought. "We have to go. Do you copy?"

There was a long pause before Reaper said anything. *"Understood."*

I looked to Ling and Antoine. Skunky and Shen were like family. Lorenzo had saved Antoine's life on the mountain. But from their grim faces, they understood what was at stake. "Slick, Ghost, if you guys are receiving this, I'm sorry. Nightcrawler out." I let go of my mic. "Let's go."

LORENZO
The Chateau

Stokes' men had come pouring out of the chateau when Exodus ambushed their boss. Judging by the sound, there were a lot more of them than we'd hoped. Shen and I were still hiding behind the gatehouse. They'd not spotted us yet, or realized we'd killed some of them, but they would soon.

With Valentine ditching us to go after that bomb, there went most of our firepower and our ride out of here. We could abort, and then Shen and I would have to make a break for it on foot, link up with Skunky, and have Reaper pick us up. Or badly outnumbered and on enemy turf, we could try to grab Bob, and fight our way out. Either way, we were fucked.

The sad thing was Valentine was still making the right call. I would have done the same thing in his shoes.

I gave Shen a look. He was thinking what I was thinking. Run or fight? Shen gave me a determined nod. *Let's do this.*

There was a lot of movement around the front of the house. The garage door was open. Engines were turning over. This outfit was loyal enough to go after their boss. There hadn't been enough time for them to get Bob ready, so he still had to be inside. I whispered to Shen, "We let those assholes drive out of here, then we hit the house."

"Divide and conquer," Shen stated.

"There you go, all Sun Tzu again."

"That's far older than Sun Tzu," he whispered back.

I keyed my radio. There were only four of us left, so this was about to get really informal. "Skunky, hold your fire until their rescue car is down the lane. When I give you the signal, shoot everybody who isn't us."

"Got it."

"Reaper." Deprived of his usual bag of technical tricks, he was our secondary ride out, Samuel's babysitter, but sadly, not super useful in a gunfight.

"I'm ready, chief."

"Boot your hostage and tell him to start walking." Samuel had been honest, and leaving him in the countryside hadn't been part of the deal, but it beat being hogtied inside a car that was probably about to get shot at. "Then be ready to drive in here and save our asses."

"You want me to come in guns blazing?"

Hell no. Reaper was a terrible shot and had the tactical awareness of a potted plant. "Skunky has eyes on the place. He'll tell you when it's safe to move up." What went unsaid was that if me and Shen got shot to death in the next few minutes, then Skunky would also have a good view of when it was time for him and Reaper to run like hell.

A Land Rover gunned its engine and flew out of the garage. Shen and I stayed low as headlights lit up the guardhouse. It drove past us, through the gate, and down the lane. The glass was tinted, but there had to be at least a driver, somebody riding shotgun, and probably another in back to drag their wounded inside. So that was a few bad guys out of our hair for a minute. Sadly, I didn't know what we'd started with, but X minus three was better than X.

Shen tapped me on the shoulder, then pointed back the way we'd come in. We'd hit the house from poolside. *Good call.* It had been glass double doors there, and most eyes would be on the front toward where Stokes had been hit. Shen moved first while I covered him.

There was a bunch of angry shouting from the back of the property.

"This is Skunky. They just found the bodies on the balcony."

The SUV was far enough out that they'd be committed to their rescue now. They'd push on to the ambush site rather than try to turn around in the field and rush back to help their buddies. This was as good as it was going to get. "Open fire."

While I ran, I shoved the pistol back into the old nylon holster on my vest, and brought up the TMP. The little subgun didn't have a butt stock, but between the vertical foregrip and keeping tension pushed out against the sling it made for a decently solid shooting platform.

I didn't hear the shot. *"Winged him. Bad guy is still up,"* Skunky exclaimed. *"He's retreated back inside."* Oh well, nobody was perfect.

Shen had barely reached the poolside before he was spotted. *Too soon!* There was a flash of movement through a window above, the sudden opening of a curtain, and then a pane of glass was shattered as a muzzle punched it out. The man in the window just opened up, hosing down the area on full auto. Shen dove over a railing and crashed behind a stone bench as bullets zipped past him.

I crouched behind the base of a statue. They'd not seen me yet, so I extended the TMP and ripped a burst through the window. The little 9mm roared. More glass panes broke. I couldn't tell if I hit him, but the shooter pulled back inside.

"Are you okay?" I shouted toward Shen as I covered the window, but that indestructible little bastard had already popped up and was running to the next available piece of cover. The curtain moved, maybe the gunman, maybe just the wind, I didn't know, but I put another burst through the window anyway.

"*Hostiles moving up on you from the front and rear of the house,*" Skunky warned. "*Some are holding back. They probably think you two are just a distraction.*"

Sadly, we were the whole damned assault element now.

Shadows appeared around the front corner of the house. I turned and fired. At nine hundred rounds per minute, it didn't take long to burn through the rest of the magazine. I ducked back behind the statue as I dropped the mag and pulled another stick from my vest. There was a *thwack* and a yelp from the rear of the house as Skunky popped somebody coming around that side. We had to count on Skunky to hold that flank, and he was five hundred yards away shooting through wind.

Someone moved on the other side of the glass doors. Shen fired at them, the suppressed EVO sounding like a series of rapid *pops*. I couldn't tell if he hit them through the glass or not, but whoever was in there was smart enough to kill the interior lights so Shen couldn't see them.

There was a muzzle flash ahead of me and bullets hit the statue. Bits of hot stone hit me in the forehead, but I was too busy aiming to flinch. He stumbled back and fell on his ass as I put a short controlled burst into him, but he stayed upright, and shot at me again. That round hit the statue so close to my face I had no choice but to drop.

I must have hit him in the armor, and 9mm wouldn't do shit to it. More guys were coming up behind the man I'd hit while he kept shooting. I kept the pedestal between us and sprinted back toward the poolhouse. Of course, that's when the asshole in the upstairs window decided to pop up again. I pushed the TMP upwards and stitched bullets across the top of the house as I ran. We were catching fire from all over. There were too many of them.

Then a flashbang went off right at my feet.

Sound punched my ears and light kicked me in the eyeballs. I crashed into the wall, tripped, and landed face first on the gravel. The movement in the upstairs window hadn't been him popping up to shoot. He'd been tossing a bang out the window.

At least it hadn't been a frag.

Half my vision was swimming purple blobs. When I pointed the TMP at the approaching gunmen and pulled the trigger, I couldn't hear the gunfire. At first I thought my gun had jammed, but then I realized it was still bouncing around and a stream of hot brass was flying out the ejection port. I was just deaf again. The man I'd shot had rolled over and was trying to crawl back around the front corner. *Fuck that guy.* I didn't have a shot at his head, couldn't see my front sight, but I stuck the muzzle in the general direction of his legs and fired the rest of the magazine at him. He jerked and kicked as bullets ripped into his legs and pelvis. I pulled back to reload again. His buddies were shooting my way, putting a lot of lead in the air, and, I realized too late, a whole lot of holes in the walls around me. So half blind, all deaf, I crawled across the gravel until I hit sidewalk, popped up, found the door—*locked*—and kicked it in.

I couldn't tell you what the inside of the poolhouse looked like, purple blobs and flashing stars mostly. It sounded like ringing. I took cover behind what I think was a couch, blinking and rubbing my eyes.

My hearing was starting to clear up enough to realize that Skunky was yelling in my ears. *Something. Reloading. Incoming. Something.*

I crawled across carpet, bumped into a wall, found the window, and looked up in time to see somebody trying to peek inside, looking for me. We saw each other at the same time. Through the tears and stinging he appeared to be a tall black man wearing body armor, so I was pretty sure it wasn't Shen, and I shot him. The window between us shattered and he flinched back. I guessed at his direction and speed, and kept firing through the wall, chasing him down with bullets as he stumbled toward the pool.

"—*Land Rover returning. I'm engaging.*" I could hear Skunky better now. Stokes' rescuers were coming back.

I could see a little better now too. At this rate, I might even be able to aim again. Adrenalin is one hell of a chemical. There was another door on the other side of the pool house. It would put me closer to the main building and where I'd last seen Shen. I ran toward it.

That doorway was clear. The lights in the narrow path between the pool house and the mansion had been knocked out. I saw Shen—or at least I hoped it was Shen—fifteen feet away, apparently pinned down next to the fountain. There was a chain of splashes as the dude on the second floor hung his gun out the window and rattled off wild shots downward. The TMP's front sight was really blurry right now, but I stuck it up there anyway, and was rewarded with a bloody red flash as

I put a 9mm hollow point through the man's elbow. He jerked back inside, but lost his gun in the process. The M-4 slid down the shingles before falling on the concrete.

I rushed over toward Shen. He was busy shooting at the men who'd come from the front. He didn't see the one coming from inside, but I did. He was moving through the darkened living room. This one hadn't had time to get dressed in anything but a pair of sweatpants, but in one hand he had a pistol and in the other he had a *motherfucking hand grenade.*

His arm was moving forward, almost in slow motion, as he went to underhand toss the grenade at my friend. I opened fire. Red holes puckered across his bare chest. He lurched to the side, hit the wall, and slid down in a red smear. But the grenade had still popped out of his hand and was rolling, lopsided, across the hardwood. "Shen!"

I grabbed Shen by the drag handle on the back of his armor, yanked him away from the doors, and shoved him toward the pool. Shen trusted me enough to throw himself face first into the shallow end. I dove in after him.

I hit the water, then the concrete bottom of the pool just as the grenade went off above us. Even submerged I could feel the blast as it vibrated the pool. *That was close.*

Underwater, holding my breath, I thumped into a body. A hand touched my face, and just from how it touched me, limp and floating, I knew it belonged to a dead man. I rolled over, thinking it was Shen, and that he'd caught a round while we'd been diving for cover, but it was the man I'd shot through the poolhouse window. His eyes were wide and staring at nothing. There was a gaping hole in his neck that was turning the water around us red. He must have fallen in after I'd shot him and the weight of his armor and ammo had taken him right to the bottom.

I popped my head out of the water and gasped for breath as bits and pieces of debris rained from the sky. The grenade had blown a smoking black hole in the side of the chateau. Shen had already waded to the side, hung his EVO over the edge, and was shooting at the men toward the front, turning the shallow end of the pool into an improvised foxhole. I lifted the TMP, angling it forward for a moment so the water would pour out the barrel, then joined Shen, trying to drive them back.

The bad guys must have realized the two of us weren't just a distraction, because there were more of them heading our way. I fired, clipping a runner, who went down behind a railing. Shen was chewing up a statue that someone else had taken cover behind. He saw I was back in it, and shouted, "Moving!"

Which was smart. If we were in the same spot too long, we'd get flanked and murdered. "Covering." I shot the railing and the statue as Shen rolled out of the pool and ran to the side, but my 9mm didn't penetrate for shit. Between their armor and use of the terrain, I was having a hell of a time stopping these guys. I kept firing until my bolt locked back on an empty mag. I needed something bigger, and I needed it before somebody wised up and tossed a grenade into the pool.

While bullets snapped by, I kept my head down and waded back to the corpse. Somebody got brave enough to stand up enough to get an angle, and bullets smacked into the water around me, sending up geysers of water just as I reached the body. The dead man had landed on his rifle. I kicked him over, and saw that he had a bullpup of some kind. Splashing around, I wrestled him over until I got the sling over his head and pulled it free, only to realize that this fucker had brought a grenade launcher. It was an Israeli Tavor, but even better, there was an M203 mounted. I cracked the launcher open and confirmed it was loaded. There were more giant 40mm shells on his vest.

Party time.

The Tavor had a Meprolight reflext sight on top. The glowing dot reticle was super convenient when the light sucked and your eyeballs were fucked up from a flashbang. I popped up, aimed at the top of the statue Shen had a man pinned behind, and pulled the forward trigger. The grenade launcher thumped my shoulder. The 40mm shell flew across the yard to strike the statue. It exploded in a rapidly expanding cloud of white dust and shrapnel, but I didn't stick around to study my handiwork. I'd already sunk back into the water to fish out more grenades.

I shoved another big round in, pulled it closed, then rose from the water already pointing toward the rail. That grenade smacked it solid, throwing hot bits of metal and stone in every direction. The men ducking behind it never had a chance. By the time I loaded the third grenade, gray smoke was obscuring most of the front, but I put a grenade into the corner of the chateau just because it looked like a good place for somebody to hide behind.

It was a good thing they hadn't just lobbed one of these through the poolhouse window when I'd been hiding inside, but these guys were living here. The thought of blowing up their own place probably hadn't even crossed their mind. Me? I loved blowing shit up.

I came up with the last grenade ready, but I didn't have any more targets. Over the ringing in my ears, I could hear screaming and coughing. I'd managed to wound a bunch of them. Nobody had come around the rear to kill us yet, so apparently Skunky had locked that side down.

Now was our chance. I began wading up the steps. "Shen! I'm going for Bob. Cover me."

Shen stayed in position, searching for targets as I got out of the pool, soaked and dripping. Glass crunched beneath my sodden, now heavy shoes as I moved to the blackened hole in the side of the chateau. My nostrils were filled with the stink of carbon and chlorine. This had been a living room of some kind, but now it was just a blasted mess. The half-naked guy I'd shot had blown himself into hamburger with his own grenade. Once I had a good position, I signaled for Shen to run around the pool and come over.

"Skunky. Can you hear me?" I thumped my radio a few times, hoping that the Exodus gear was decently waterproof. We'd only gone hot a couple of minutes ago, but the SUV sent to retrieve Stokes was probably on its way back, and I wanted to know if they'd be waiting for us. "Skunky?" But I got nothing. Shen slid in next to me. He jerked his head toward the hallway and where we thought the kitchen was. I nodded. The chateau was so old there were no blueprints or floor plans on file anywhere. Samuel hadn't spent too much time inside, so his descriptions were crap. But he'd alarm wired the door of the one windowless storage room that was this place's entire basement, so that was the most likely place they'd be holding Bob. The stairs down were just off the kitchen.

We started down the hall, moving fast, with me on point and Shen watching our tail.

The interior of the chateau was as fancy as the outside. Stokes had bought the place fully furnished, so it felt more like a rich grandma's house than a staging area for mercenaries. I glanced down and saw

Shen was leaving bloody footprints on the thick white carpet. I realized there was blood all over his leg. "No time. It's just a scratch. Go."

We'd killed over half a dozen of them for sure and wounded I don't know how many more, but we didn't know what they'd started with, so there were an unknown number of threats remaining. We didn't know their plans for a rescue attempt either. They might have already executed Bob. Or, they might think they were losing, and were saving him to use as a hostage or bargaining chip. Lacking time and manpower, we didn't slow to clear each room. They could be lurking around any corner, or they could be forming up somewhere out of sight getting ready to converge on us.

"Come on! Up the stairs. We've got to move." Someone with a British accent was shouting ahead of us. "If you try anything I'll blow your fucking head off."

I took a knee behind a bookshelf. I didn't have a target, but he hadn't been yelling at me. The voice was coming from the direction Samuel had told us the kitchen was.

"Easy . . . I'm cooperating." The man who responded to the agitated Brit had a deep voice and was playing it cool. I recognized that voice.

Bob.

"To the garage, we're getting out of here! Now, you fuckin—"

There was a crash, followed by a gunshot, then another and another. A man began to scream, but it turned into a horrible, gurgling, choking noise, which was suddenly cut off by another violent impact and the sound of plates breaking. There was a burst from a submachine gun and the sound of bullets tearing through wood.

I rushed through the dining room and swept into the kitchen, stolen Tavor at my shoulder. Suddenly, the door to the kitchen flew open as a man with long blond hair was hurled through it. He crashed hard against the table, a pistol in one hand. Snarling, not losing a beat, he struggled to get up, pointing his piece back toward the kitchen. "Fucking Yank cocksucker!"

Shen and I both shot him repeatedly, practically riddling him with bullets, before he went down.

The kitchen was wrecked. Everything was broken. There were bullet holes in the walls. One of Stokes' men was on the floor, twitching, his neck snapped, probably from the impact that had left an obvious dent in the side of his head.

And standing in the middle of the kitchen, panting and breathing hard, barefoot, wearing sweats and a t-shirt, and holding a frying pan with some blood and hair stuck to it, was the man I'd come all this way to find, my brother . . . Bob Lorenzo.

Bob looked up as we swept in, snarling, obviously ready to fight us to the death with a frying pan. Bob was a huge, scary dude when he was just being his friendly, optimistic self. I'd never seen him in berserker mode before. Considering what he'd just done when provided with a distraction demonstrated why Kat had hired a squad of professionals to keep him contained until she needed him.

"Bob, it's me!" I shouted before he tried to remove my head. I raised the Tavor so the muzzle was pointing straight up. "We're here to rescue you."

He made it a couple of steps then stopped. I'd blackened my face, and that was probably a running mess from the pool water, so I would've been hard to recognize even without the red haze of rage. He tilted his head and asked incredulously, "Hector?"

There weren't many people who used my real name. "It's me. Come on, bro. We've got to get you out of here."

It was like he couldn't believe it. He'd been a prisoner for too long to grasp the idea of being able to just walk away. I understood the feeling. "It's really you. You found me."

"We're not clear yet. There's more of them."

"Fourteen total, as far as I could tell." Bob said quickly. *Good.* That accounted for most of them. "Stokes called and told his men to get me out of the cellar and ready for transport. Then the shooting started." Emotional moment or not, once a professional, always a professional. "We've got to get out of here. You got a ride? Otherwise the one I tossed through the door had car keys."

He was in better shape than I'd hoped. Ling had been right. They'd needed to keep him fed and healthy so there would be no suspicion that he wasn't the fourth operative. We'd be able to make a run for it . . . Only Bob got a puzzled look on his face, stumbled, and had to put one big hand on the counter to steady himself.

"You've been hit." Shen stated.

"Yeah." Bob turned until I could see his left side. There was a black hole right through his bicep and his white shirt was covered in blood. "But did you stop Blue?" Despite the shock of beating a man to death, getting shot, and being rescued, Bob didn't mess around. It was that crazy focus that had made him into Majestic's mortal enemy to begin with.

"Valentine's on his way to the train station now." I picked up a kitchen towel from the counter and stuck it against the wound to slow the bleeding. The bullet had gone clean through, but the exit wound was nasty.

Bob winced at the pain. "Valentine's here, and you know about Evangeline. Thank Goodness." But then Bob got a stricken look on his face. Whatever he'd just thought of was much worse than the gunshot wound. "Hang on. If Anders is pulling me out now, that must mean some of the nukes are already in transit."

"What do you mean *some* of the nukes?"

Chapter 15: Project Blue

VALENTINE
North of Paris

Ling was driving again, flying down French highways as fast as she could without getting us arrested. Even going way too fast, Evangeline was still at least twenty minutes north of the chateau. Thankfully, at this time of night, the highways were fairly deserted, but we did blow through more than one traffic camera. Had our van's plates been legitimate, we would be getting some huge fines later on.

I was in the passenger seat, talking to Tailor on the phone. I had interrupted his beauty sleep. I stopped to read a text message from Reaper. Lorenzo was too busy to communicate but there had been a lot of gunfire and explosions. *The Calm* was wavering and I was tired. *Focus.*

"*Val?*" Tailor asked. "*Did I lose you?*"

"No, I'm still here." I put him on speaker phone.

"*You did what?*"

"Raided one of Kat's holdings in the country."

"*You weren't supposed to make any moves without us! Son of a—*"

"Shut up and listen, I know where the bomb is."

"*No shit? Where?*"

"A train station near Amiens called Evangeline. We should have known."

"*There's like fifty thousand things in this country with that name. Hang on. I'm pulling it up . . . It's just a little place, but it's a hub. A bunch of lines converge there.*"

303

"That's where Hunter stored the nuke, and I bet they're going to deliver it to its target by train."

"And immediately after detonation, Bob would have been conveniently shot to death at the launch point by helpful local police," Antoine said from the back.

"Evangeline isn't close to anything vital. What's the target?"

"That I don't know."

"Wait, there's a G20 summit in London right now!" Tailor said, the realization creeping into his voice. *"They just put in a new line that is a direct shot to the Chunnel, for that new super train, Paris to London. Holy shit, Val."*

Holy shit was right. Leaders from all over the world were going to be there. London was clogged with functionaries, visitors, security, and protestors. The President of the United States, the British prime minister, and French president, and God-only-knew who else was going to be there.

"That is the most reasonable target," Ling stated flatly.

"Look, Tailor, I don't care what you need to do. I don't care if you have to go around your boss on this, okay? He's been really hesitant to break your stupid rules, but I have no idea if we'll get there in time. You need to alert the French government and tell them you have a credible threat of a weapon of mass destruction on one of those trains."

New Tailor would probably want evidence before causing an incident, but old Tailor had always been ready to shoot someone in the face. *"I'll alert the authorities on the way. My boss will cut through the red tape, trust me, he'll call up GIGN."* That was France's premier counterterrorism force. *"Hell, he'll get the Foreign fucking Legion if we have to, but don't wait up for me! Go kill those assholes!"* Luckily, I got old Tailor.

"Will do. I'll keep you posted." My phone beeped. It was Lorenzo. I switched over to him.

"Valentine, I've got Bob. Shen and Skunky are okay. We're on our way out."

Ling smiled at the news. "Ha! Excellent!" Antoine shouted.

"Don't celebrate. We've got a huge problem."

"I know, the bomb could be moving already, Reaper told me."

"No, damn it, listen to me. There are four bombs!"

Ling's eyes went wide. "What did he say?"

"There. Are. Four. Bombs!" Lorenzo repeated, each word a forceful statement.

My heart dropped into my stomach. I felt like I was going to throw up.

"Valentine! Are you still there?"

"Yeah, yeah, I'm here," I stammered. "I copy, four bombs."

"Bob says Blue doesn't have one target, there's four. The Alpha Point was just the staging ground. He doesn't know what the targets are, but Blue was designed to decapitate the Illuminati in one move. Four simultaneous detonations to wipe out their power base forever, blame it on terrorists, and Majestic has one less competitor."

"Where else do trains from Evangeline go?" Ling asked.

"Christ, all over Europe!"

Antoine had pulled up the information on his phone. "The north-south line goes through the Chunnel to London, and down all the way to Rome. The east-west line goes through Frankfurt, all the way to Prague. The line's not done yet, eventually it's supposed to go all the way to Moscow."

"So basically anywhere could be a target." If we knew where they were going, Tailor could get the authorities to intercept them. But there was no way we could figure it out in time. "Antoine, call Ariel. Fill her in. It's up to her to guess where the targets are."

"Give your angel her puzzle pieces but don't count on her," Lorenzo muttered. *"Stop those bombs, Valentine. We'll catch up."*

LORENZO

After telling Reaper and Skunky to extract, and updating Valentine, I'd gotten us out of the chateau. If any more of Stokes' men were still in the fight, they were keeping their heads down. Not that that was a comforting thought. They could be waiting to ambush us, but we had no choice except going out the front. Bob had lost a lot of blood, and Shen's *just a scratch* had turned into a bad limp. We weren't going to be running across any fields.

Luckily, nobody took any potshots at us when Reaper drove through the open gate. He'd picked up Skunky on the way. As soon as the rest of us piled into the back of the sedan I smacked Reaper's seat and shouted "Drive! Drive!"

With all of us pointing guns out the windows, Reaper flipped the car around in a spray of gravel, and got us the hell away from the smoking ruins of the chateau. I kept waiting for a bullet to shatter the back window for a tense few seconds, but we were clear. It was a tight fit, especially since Bob was huge and squished between me and Shen. Skunky was in the passenger seat, still wearing a ghillie suit made out of layers of tattered burlap and covered in local weeds so it looked like Reaper was sitting next to a bush. Inside the Audi it was hot, and smelled like blood, sweat, and gunpowder.

"This remind you of anything?" Bob asked.

"I'm having a flashback to Quagmire."

"Only that time it was your little buddy who got shot in the arm, not me. By the way, good to see you again, kid."

"You too." Reaper was way too focused on the country road to look back at my brother. He was doing the best he could, but as soon as I was sure we were clear, I was going to make him pull over so I could drive. No offense to Reaper, but his video-game driving skills didn't translate over to real life worth a damn, we needed to get our asses to Evangeline fast, and he would be way more useful on a computer figuring out how to stop those trains.

There were headlights just off the side of the road ahead of us. It was the Land Rover that had peeled off to pick up Stokes. It had crashed into a ditch on the way back. "I went by that on the way in," Reaper said. "I didn't see anybody alive."

"We haven't cleared it." Skunky warned. "I put a magazine through the windows as they were coming back." Skunky's rifle was too long to maneuver in the confines of the car, so he'd drawn his Beretta. As we got closer, I could see the mess of bullet holes in the SUV's windshield. That was some damned good shooting. "Movement." Skunky said as he angled his pistol out the window.

The back door of the SUV had opened, and a man had spilled out onto the grass. Before Skunky could open fire, Bob shouted. "Stop the car!" Bob wasn't the one giving the orders around here, but with a command voice like that, Reaper automatically hit the brakes. We slid across the gravel, raising a great cloud of dust. "Let me out."

I had no idea what he was doing, though I could tell now that the injured man who'd gotten out of the SUV matched our pictures of Aaron Stokes. Bob was a pro. Maybe this asshole knew something else important about Blue. "Make it quick," I told Bob as I opened the door and got out of his way.

Bob grimaced as he got out, one arm dangling, slick with blood. Skunky took the opportunity to shrug out of his burlap-covered jacket, and went to check on Shen's leg. I followed Bob over to the wreck. The engine was still running. The inside of the glass was painted red. The mercs who'd rescued their boss were either dead, or really convincing at pretending. Stokes was covered in blood, but I couldn't tell how much of that was his, and how much was from the men Skunky had ventilated. As he slowly tried to crawl away, Bob followed after him.

Stokes was messed up, moving with that dizzy, disoriented, seasick-looking motion of somebody who'd just gotten a severe head injury. I didn't know how much information my brother was going to be able to get out of him in this shape. "Hurry up."

"This won't take long." Bob put his foot on him and kicked Stokes over onto his back. Even in his bewildered state, Stokes seemed really surprised to see Bob looming over him.

From the utterly terrified look on Stokes' face, and the merciless, righteously angry way Bob was glaring at him, I realized this wasn't an interrogation. This was an execution.

"Hey, come on, Lorenzo. I was just doing my job. I'm begging you, mate. You'd have done the same, if our situations were reversed."

"No. I wouldn't." Then Bob lifted a stolen pistol and shot Stokes in the chest. Not just once or twice, but Bob just kept on pulling the trigger, over and over as Stokes jerked and twitched. He kept shooting until the gun was empty, and then I watched the pistol's muzzle wiggle as Bob pulled the trigger uselessly a few more times.

"You done?"

He looked down at the smoking pistol. If he'd not been at slide lock, he would have kept going. For the first time since we'd found him, Bob actually seemed a little out of it. He was a professional, but even professionals can get personal. He took one last look at the perforated corpse then started toward the car. "I'll be done when those bombs are stopped."

We went back to the car. "Move over Reaper, I'm driving."

VALENTINE
Gare du Evangeline

Gare du Evangeline consisted of a concrete and glass enclosure over a whole bunch of tracks. On the other side of that was a depot with several large buildings for maintenance and storage. The train station was quiet this time of night, but the doors were still open. Beneath the street lights, a couple of police officers were patrolling, as could be expected for any mass transportation hub these days. The problem was, there should have been a lot more. With a credible threat of a weapon of mass destruction this place should have been covered in cops.

"I thought your friend Tailor said he was going to involve the authorities," Ling said. We were in our van, parked in the nearly empty lot on the north side of the station.

"They should be here." I checked my phone, but I had no signal. That was odd. We weren't exactly in the wilderness. It had been fine when we had spoken to Ariel a few minutes ago, and Reaper had been sending me information about the station up until about that same time. "Anybody else having a problem with their phone?"

Antoine tried. "I am getting a prerecorded message that the system is out of service."

"Even our GPS says it cannot find a satellite." Ling was scowling hard at the train station. "It must be a signal jammer."

Even if the Montalbans were using a device like that, it wouldn't stop communications outside of the jammer's zone, where our help should have been coming from. "Tailor said help would get here, it'll get here." But even as I said that, I was worried that something had gone horribly wrong. "If Ariel can figure out the other targets, she knows how to reach him."

"That is a lot of ground to search with only three of us," Ling said.

"Ariel said that this is a working station, but there's another section that's not open to the public yet. It's for this new maglev that's supposed to do Paris to London in record times, like the world's fastest train. It's still in testing, but she thinks that part is where the bombs would have been stored."

"How come?" Antoine asked.

"The construction company that built it was owned by Rafael Montalban, and it went up around the time Hunter got killed. Kat owns the whole thing now. We've got to walk through the regular station, and head for the back." Going in like a SWAT team would only end with us in a firefight with French police. "Ditch the tactical gear and long guns, go low profile. The longer we can look around without being spotted the more likely we are to find those bombs."

I stripped off my load bearing gear and pulled a hoodie on over my armor. It was a little bulky, but from a distance nobody would notice. I had my .44 in a pancake holster concealed under my sweater, and had filled my pockets with spare speed loaders. The Taurus .357 snubby I'd had since the Crossroads was stuffed in my front pocket.

"This is it. Once inside, play it by ear."

Antoine slid open the side door and got out. Before I could, Ling reached over and grabbed my sleeve. Normally at a time like this, Ling would be stone-faced, but right now her concern was obvious.

"What is it, Ling?"

"It's . . . nothing. Let's go."

LORENZO

I was tempted to try and call Valentine again to get an update, but since I was driving as fast as I could, passing the other cars like they were standing still, it was probably better for me to concentrate on the road. Thankfully it was still early enough in the morning that the traffic hadn't gotten thick. If we picked up a cop, they could just chase us to the train station.

"What else do you know, Bob?" I glanced in the rear view mirror. "Anything you can think of that might help?"

"Maybe." Bob was gritting his teeth as Skunky tended the nasty hole in his arm. "Gordon's plan was aimed at the Illuminati leadership."

"Killing thousands to get to a handful of old men," Skunky muttered as he kept wrapping gauze. He'd been busy back there. "Assholes."

"The problem was the Illuminati leadership stays spread out on purpose. It's hard to get more than a handful of the family heads in the same place at the same time. Every now and then, when they've got something really important to discuss, one of them can demand a big mandatory meeting and the whole council has to gather. It's tradition, but it can only be called by a family head. That's why Gordon originally approached Eduard Montalban. Majestic intel said he was the loose cannon and the most likely to sell out the others."

"That's why Dead Six killed Rafael Montalban, to put Big Eddie in charge," I muttered.

"Only Eduard and Gordon Willis cut themselves a side deal instead. Gordon was paid to switch sides. Eduard would get a meeting called, Blue would blow it up, and the Montalbans would be the last family standing to inherit the whole damned thing."

Eddie was a psychopath, and his little sister had taken his dream and made it her own.

"Oh, shit. Exodus cut a deal with an Illuminati boss named Romefeller. He called one of those big meetings."

"Because of us hunting Katarina," Shen said as he came to the same conclusion I just had. He was gray and sweating badly. Skunky had gotten the bleeding stopped from the gash on his leg, but Shen wasn't looking good. "The actions of Exodus caused Blue."

"If it wasn't you, it would've been called for something else eventually," Bob said. "That council is what they've been waiting for this whole time."

"Wherever that secret meeting is being held is one of the targets."

"I don't know. They never said anything in front of me about that. All of this is working off of what I've overheard, my investigation from before, and a whole lot of time with nothing better to do than think about it."

"Reaper, relay that to Valentine's buddy. Tailor will know where that meeting is. He can at least get an evacuation started." Not that I gave a shit about the Illuminati, but I felt bad for whatever city their little party was in.

Reaper was in the passenger seat, staring at a tablet screen and typing fast. I didn't know what the hell he was trying to do, but it was important enough I was hesitant to interrupt him. He didn't look up. "Something's wrong, Lorenzo. Everything is falling apart."

"What's happening?"

"The systems are going down. All the systems." He was either frightened, or in awe. It was hard to tell. "Every system in western Europe is under attack. I'm trying to warn the authorities, but they're all swamped. They're making it impossible for me to even call in fake bomb threats to force evacuations. They're hitting police, military, phone networks, utilities, banking, the works, but I think that's just a smokescreen to hide what they're really doing. All the transit hub systems are down, no GPS tracking, nothing. I can't tell where anything is or where it's going. Nobody can."

"Who is doing what now?"

"It's a coordinated cyber-attack," Bob explained. "Nobody in charge has a clue what's real and what's not. It's the ultimate diversion."

"No shit! That's what I just said!" Reaper was freaking out. "Remember when I said Kat had hired some people like me? More like a hundred of me. They must have been working on this for months. Each one targeting different systems. They probably never even knew they were part of a team effort, just hey, here's a million dollars if you break this when I tell you to. I think she just turned them all loose at once. Nobody has ever done this wide of an attack before. It's kind of amazing, actually."

"Can you fix it?"

Reaper laughed at me.

"I'm not fucking around, Reaper."

"Sorry, chief. It's like she just drove a truck loaded with dynamite into a dam and you asked me to plug the hole with my finger."

I punched the steering wheel. There wasn't a damned thing I could do about cyber-attacks, and we were still several minutes away from being able to shoot anyone. "Okay, so the Illuminati meeting is one target, but what about the other three?"

"Some of the second-tier Illuminati leadership will be held back from the main meeting. These people have been in the treachery business for a thousand years. The bombs will be wherever her biggest potential rivals are congregated. This way Katarina pops a bunch of other surviving potential competitors too, and it looks more like acts of terrorism to the rest of the world rather than just a directed assassination against one group."

"There's a summit in London this week, lots of world leaders there." Skunky said.

"Even if the Illuminati aren't present, she might blow them up just so everyone thinks they were the real target." Bob was just making educated guesses now, but my gut told me he was right.

"Where the hell did she get four nuclear bombs from?"

"One was seized by Dead Six. The others were stolen from a Russian demil site and sold by Sala Jihan."

"Son of a bitch." *Should have seen that coming.* No wonder the Pale Man had let me free. He didn't want this to come back to bite him. I knew Kat better than anybody else here, so I tried to think like her. *What would I do if I was Kat?* "She'll probably time the bombs to explode at the same time. That maximizes her chances of getting as many important targets as possible."

"Anders is running the details. This whole thing was his and Hunter's op," Bob said. "I know Anders well. He's one efficient son of a bitch. He likes to run his ops like clockwork. He had Stokes lock me up near for a reason. He wants me to get killed at the launch site as close to the time of detonation as possible."

"He must really not like you."

"I got him fired from the FBI. Majestic never would have recruited him if I'd not ruined his career. But that's just a side benefit. I've got the right résumé. Anders needs to frame me as Gordon's recruit so he can get away with it. No, the bad part is that timeline means that the bombs headed for the furthest targets must already be on their way."

I looked to Reaper. "Any ideas?"

He sure didn't seem happy. "I'm on a tablet with a shitty connection in a speeding car but I'm trying to go around all these cut-rate Chinese hackers Kat hired, break into NATO's command net to warn them they're about to get nuked. So quit bugging me!"

I was too busy trying not to crash into early commuters at two hundred and twenty kilometers an hour to think through all the implications of that. If Bob was right, some of the bombs were already on their way. But the ones intended for closer targets might not have left yet. "Can you stop the trains or not?"

"I've never seen anything like this. I don't know," Reaper said, and that honesty was a little scary.

The rest of Exodus had to be at Evangeline by now. "Then it's up to Valentine."

VALENTINE

The interior of the station was clean and orderly. There were several food stands but they were closed for the night. There weren't very many passengers present in the station, and most of those were dozing on benches, but the cleaning crew was out in force, scrubbing floors and emptying garbage cans. There were elevated screens showing arrival and departure times. I went to the closest and checked. It was sparse until commute time. The next arrival was in twenty minutes, departing in thirty to Paris.

"We must check that one." Antoine said.

"Yeah, but nothing toward London for hours though."

Ling shook her head. "But the experimental line is not open yet. It would not appear on this schedule. Magnetic levitation trains do not run on normal tracks." There was an interactive map on a nearby touch screen kiosk. Ling found the portion of the train station blacked out as still under construction. "They are building a new section for those. The experimental train should be there."

"Assuming it hasn't left yet."

"We can pray," Ling said. "This way."

There were no trains parked under the enclosure yet. Pigeons were nesting in the rafters above. Ling led us to a section blocked off with caution tape and signs warning us to keep out. None of the custodial staff had paid us any mind. I didn't see the cops. None of the weary travelers looked like hired mercenaries keeping watch, but that could be deceptive. So we went down an empty corridor marked with a bunch of signs that I assumed said *keep out* in French. The next area was lined with scaffolding and lit only with work lights. At the end of the corridor, we ducked under some hanging plastic sheets and entered the new, half-built section of the train station. It wasn't very well lit, and it was very quiet. We didn't see anyone.

I looked back at my Exodus compatriots. "Fan out a little, keep your eyes open. There may be night crews. ID your targets before you shoot. I've had a shitty enough day without accidentally murdering a janitor or something."

"No flashlights," Antoine suggested. "Let us keep the element of surprise."

It took us a few minutes to navigate the labyrinthine construction site. The large, open central area was divided up with scaffolding, construction barriers, and more plastic curtains. We moved as quickly as we could without making noise, in case the Montalbans had patrols, but we didn't encounter anyone. I noticed a vantage point that would allow us to observe most of the station, a platform where a large window would eventually be installed. Now it was just a skeleton of metal beams. While Ling and I found a ladder up, Antoine stayed at floor level to keep watch.

A cool night breeze drifted across my face as we observed the yard from our elevated position. Numerous sets of tracks split off the main line, allowing trains to park or get out of each other's way. At least, that's what I thought they were for; I'm not really familiar with the ins and outs of railroading. The maglev track was taller, much wider, and being shiny and new definitely stood out from the others.

Ling pointed. "Those are the service hangars." All four of them were lit up, though there was no movement. The experimental super train was on the other side of those buildings. It was silver, had a bunch of sleek cars behind it, but the important thing was that it wasn't currently moving.

"There's not a lot of cover out there." If there was anyone inside, it was going to be really hard to get close enough to check without being spotted.

"Perhaps they won't shoot first and ask questions later," Ling said. "They are trying to be low key about this, yes? They're also in what is supposed to be a secured area. If we're lucky, they're not being as vigilant as they might be."

"I hope so, but we can't count on it." I checked my watch. That train to Paris would be here soon.

"Listen," Ling warned. At first I thought the sound might be a distant train, but then I realized the noise was from a helicopter. It was running dark, no lights, and the only reason I spotted it was that it moved in front of some of the city lights. It was coming in low and fast from the south. "We have company."

"Hopefully Tailor got ahold of someone."

"If that is French special forces, they are just as likely to shoot us as the Montalbans. Wait. I don't think . . . that isn't a military helicopter."

She was right. It was a little civilian helicopter, and it descended to land near where we had parked our van. The authorities didn't need to *sneak* in. It could have been Tailor, but somehow I knew it wasn't. I just had a gut feeling who it was. Tailor must have gotten the word out about the nukes, but Majestic had been listening. Majestic was *always* listening.

"It's Underhill. He knows I'm here."

"You can't know that," Ling insisted.

I shook my head. "No, it's him."

"Either way, we must hurry." Ling went to the ladder and effortlessly slid to the ground. I followed, not nearly as gracefully. We set out for the nearest hangar.

The cement ended with the construction zone and the ground turned to gravel. We were out in the open now, so stealth was out. "Spread out." If there was a guard posted, it would be harder to shoot us if we weren't clumped together. Then we simply ran for it.

Breathing hard, I reached the edge of the hangar. Nobody had shouted an alarm or started shooting. When I peeked through the nearest window I discovered why.

"They've already left."

Antoine tried the closest door. It was unlocked. Pistol raised, he swept inside. I drew my .44 and followed. Ling was right behind me.

There was a concrete enclosure inside the hangar. It was covered in signs that I assumed meant *danger, high voltage*. It had an extremely heavy-duty metal door, but it was hanging open. Inside the room there were some shelves and four big metal cradles. They were stenciled *War, Pestilence, Famine,* and *Death*. All of the cradles were empty.

"Shit." I glanced around. On the shelves were some plastic jugs, and I recognized the labels as being from the shipments Ariel had keyed off on. There was a Geiger counter and a bunch of tools I did not recognize. The work area looked suspiciously clean, like the Montalbans had probably scrubbed the place so that the only forensic evidence the authorities would find later would belong to Bob Lorenzo. "Where'd they go?"

"Not far," Antoine said. He had gone back into the empty hangar. "Look over here."

I came out to see that he was pointing at a small puddle on the concrete. One of the pipes in the wall had been leaking. There were lines of water, like someone had driven a big cart through the puddle, and it had been recently enough that it hadn't had time to evaporate. There were also a few footprints, big ones, boots, from the treads. They went a few feet before drying into oblivion. They were headed down a walkway, back toward the station.

"The last bomb is going to Paris!" Heedless of danger, I sprinted down the walkway. Ling and Antoine ran after me. That cart couldn't be too far ahead.

Sure enough, a few seconds later, I turned the corner and spotted several men driving a motorized cart up a ramp. There was a big metal box on that cart, about the size of a coffin. There were six of them in total, two ahead, one on each side of their precious cargo, and two bringing up the rear. And those two saw me as soon as I saw them.

I was *Calm.*

I took in everything in that second. They were dressed casually, but had that contractor vibe, not Montalban regulars. Of course, Katarina wouldn't use anybody who could be tracked back to her for this assignment. Short haircuts, a few operator beards, none of them old, all of them fit. If they hadn't been wearing drab jackets to hide their weapons, I bet I would have seen tats from their old units. Deniable, expendable, they were probably doing it for the money, and a few years ago I had been exactly like them.

But that didn't matter now, because they were reaching for their guns, and I needed to stop a nuclear holocaust.

Still running forward, my .44 was already in both hands, punching outward. The rear guards were twenty yards away. I shot one, then the other, before either could clear leather. The sudden roar of gunfire caused the others to reflexively jump and turn. The two by the bomb were even further and I was still moving. I hit the one on the right. My gun jumped, and came smoothly back down as I stroked the trigger. The one the left fell off the ramp.

Then Antoine and Ling were behind me, blazing away.

Of the men at the top of the ramp, only one had managed to move to cover before they nailed him. Antoine began hammering the pillar he dove behind. Everyone else was dead or wounded, and Ling methodically put 9mm rounds into all of the fallen to be sure. I reached the motorized cart as it slowly plodded up the ramp with a methodical hum. It seemed simple enough. There was a green button for go and a red button for stop. The last man risked a quick peek around his cover and I reflexively shot him through the forehead. I punched the red button.

The cart stopped.

It was quiet. There were dead bodies everywhere. We had just saved Paris from destruction.

One down, three to go.

LORENZO

It had been one hell of a quick ride. The car was pretty sporty, and I kept it as fast as I could without flying off the road. There wasn't much traffic, trucks mostly, and I blasted past those. The street lights along the highway were out, and all of the houses along the highway were dark. There were blackouts everywhere. The town was still lit, but the traffic lights on the way to the station had been blinking. The police bands were a mess, with hundreds of fake emergency calls flooding in, right before it all crashed. Our chateau shooting was probably in there too, lost among the sea of bullshit.

The phones were still out, but as we got closer Skunky tried to get hold of his comrades on the radio. So far he hadn't had any luck. It could have just been a matter of range and material between us, or they could already be dead. There was no way to tell.

None of us had never been here, and the GPS was down, but Reaper had downloaded a map of the region before he lost the Internet, and since this was newly-built Europe, instead of old cobblestone streets designed for horses Europe, the streets were actually laid out in a way that made sense. We were getting close.

"How are you guys doing?" That was aimed at Bob and Shen, since they'd both been wounded.

But Reaper answered. "Frustrated. I can't accomplish dick from here."

"Reaper, when we get inside there's got to be some sort of control center for the station. See if you can do something from there."

"Yeah. They've got to have an emergency radio to call the

conductors. I'll force them to park those trains someplace that isn't too populated in case the bombs are on timers. I'll take the whole place hostage if I have to!"

"That's the spirit. Shen? Bob? You up to fight?"

Shen snorted, like that question was offensive.

"I can shoot one-handed," Bob sounded weary, but pissed off. Probably because we were taking him to the very place he was supposed to get framed and murdered. This was really going to suck if we failed, and still managed to deliver Kat her patsy.

"I was talking about the blood loss, Bob."

"It's not squirting."

"You sound like Dad when you say that."

"Thanks."

"We get in there, split up and spread out. If those bombs are here, do not let them leave."

Gare du Evangeline looked like a pretty normal train station. There weren't crowds of panicked citizens fleeing the place so the shooting probably hadn't started. I didn't see any cops yet, so I pulled up right in front of the main doors. All of us bailed out and left the car in the passenger unloading only zone. They could just tack that parking violation onto the other hundred felonies I had committed already tonight.

VALENTINE

I stood next to the nuclear weapon and reloaded my revolver. As I reholstered, there was panicked shouting from inside the terminal. The passengers had heard our gunfire, but it had happened quickly and was over. They were probably still trying to figure out what was going on, but they'd start running sooner or later. If there were any more of Kat's hired goons around, they'd have heard the noise, too. We'd stopped one of the nukes, but we had no way to secure it with just the three of us.

"I've reached someone on the radio," Antoine said. "It is Mr. Long. They have arrived." He keyed his microphone. "We have recovered one device. The others are status unknown."

I looked over my shoulder. The maglev train was still parked, but now its lights were on. That was strange, I thought, as I stared at the high-tech locomotive.

"What is it?" Ling asked.

I didn't answer.

"Michael?"

"There's a bomb on that train."

"What? How do you know?"

"I just know! Holy shit, there's a bomb on that train! There has to be! Antoine, tell the others that we're heading back toward the hangar." I started down the ramp. Antoine and Ling were closer. "Get to that train!"

A voice came over the PA system. It was Underhill.

"I assume you can hear me, Valentine. We intercepted some coms earlier. Seems you've been busy."

"Oh, come *on!*" I snarled. I didn't have time for these assholes now.

"Don't worry. Help is on the way. This will all be over soon. I can't let you get away again. You were one hell of a fighter, son, but you can rest now."

Then he said something I didn't understand. It was in foreign language, Latin maybe? Pain, blinding pain, exploded behind my eyes, like I was suddenly beset with the worst migraine of my life. My legs went limp and I tumbled down the ramp. Ling shouted at me. I thought it was my name from the shape of her mouth, but I couldn't hear her over the buzzing in my ears. She skidded to a halt, turned, and started back toward me.

"Keep going!" I shouted, the struggling to force the words out of my mouth. "Don't stop!" *Please don't stop.* An image of Sarah flashed through my mind, cut down by gunfire as she came back for me.

Ling did as I asked. She hesitated for only a moment, then turned and continued on, leaving me alone. *Thank you.*

Struggling, head still pounding with pain, I grabbed the handrail and pulled myself up. Holding on for dear life, I struggled to get down the ramp without falling again. I was dizzy, I was nauseated, I could barely hear anything. I didn't know what was happening, and it terrified me.

Underhill kept talking over the PA. *"That's right. Just relax. Your time is done."* He said the gibberish word again, and the pain hit me with full force. It was like getting boxed in the ears. My knees buckled, and I fell down again. The pain in my head was unbearable. I thought I was having a stroke. I lay there, face down on the concrete, muscles twitching, in so much pain that I just wanted to die so it would stop.

"That is the idea." I could still hear a voice, only now it was the ghost of Dr. Silvers in my head. *"The control phrase activates the emergency kill switch I have placed in your mind. If there is any hope that the project can be contained or salvaged, the phrase should not be used, for once it is utilized, there is no turning back. The subject is programmed to experience an immediate disintegration of his nervous system, so painful that he will willingly die to make it stop."*

"No," I hissed through gritted teeth. Silvers was gone, but she'd left something inside me. I couldn't tell if her words were a memory or a hallucination.

"Why aren't you dead, Michael? I did this to you as a favor. You were always my most obstinate subject. I could have used this when you tried to escape, but I felt you were still salvageable. You are special, this unique bundle of psychological trauma, brain injury, and life experiences that left you perfectly suited for my program. The sad thing here is that when you give up, my life's work will have been wasted."

I was blinking in and out of consciousness. My heart was beating so fast it was going to tear itself apart. I saw Sarah, and Hawk, and Hunter. Wheeler, Ramirez, then my mom, and everything Silvers had twisted up in my head was telling me to give up and join them. The pain got worse and worse, and more images flashed through my mind. Violence, suffering, death. So many dead faces, staring at me, judging me, damning me, screaming at me. I put my hands over my ears to make it stop, but I could still hear them.

Then there was another voice, a clarion call amongst the chaos in my mind. This time I think it was an angel. She sounded just like Ariel. *"You are stronger than they are, Michael. Calm yourself and fight."*

I gasped for breath. My heart rate began to slow. The voices and the screaming faded. *The Calm* began to push back the pain. Reaching out with one shaking hand, I grasped the railing, held tight, and pulled myself upright. I was in control again.

"The brief said that was supposed to have killed you dead, given you a stroke or something." It was Underhill, and he was no ghost. My vision was still blurry, but I could make him out at the top of the ramp.

"Hocus-pocus science project bullshit I told them. You can't make better soldiers in a lab, but they wouldn't listen. Guys like me and you, we're forged in a crucible."

My eyes cleared up enough to see that he had a pistol pointed at me. It was a 1911 with a threaded barrel.

"I beat her," I told him. "I won."

"Good for you, kid. You gave me a hell of a chase too. I'm almost sorry this is over."

Now I could see with perfect clarity. I was so *Calm* that I saw his grip tighten as he lined up the sights and swiped off the safety.

"This is your last chance," he said. "Get down on your knees and put your hands behind your head. I'm supposed to bring you back alive, but I'm not going to risk your getting away again."

My body moved slowly, so infuriatingly slowly, as my hand moved to my .44. I didn't have time to aim. The instant the muzzle of my revolver cleared leather, I rocked it upwards, tucked my elbow against my body, and fired. The gun bucked in my hand.

Underhill's eyes widened as my bullet hit him in the stomach. The .45 barked and flashed as he lurched.

His bullet smacked hard against my vest as I pushed the big Smith & Wesson outward. I brought my hands together. Underhill fired again. A hot burning pain slashed across the side of my neck, but I acquired a flash sight picture, focusing on the glowing green front sight as I aligned it higher on Underhill's body.

My .44 roared again, earsplittingly loud on the loading dock.

I watched Underhill fall to the ground, slowly, gracefully, losing his grip on his gun. He landed unceremoniously on his back, and the pistol clattered off the ramp to the concrete below.

I stood there for what seemed like a long moment, revolver extended in both hands, pointed up at Underhill. One deep breath and time seemed to return to its normal speed.

The pain was gone. I could feel hot blood trickling down my neck, but I didn't take my hands off of my gun. Muffled gunfire erupted from inside the building, punctuated by people shouting. I ignored it, kept my gun trained on Underhill, and approached slowly.

The old man was still breathing. His breaths were short and ragged, punctuated by a gurgling sound. A dark red blot stained his button-down shirt. I'd shot him right through the upper sternum, just over the top of his vest. Some distant part of my brain thought, *Hawk would be proud.*

I stood over Underhill for a few moments. He didn't say anything. His eyes were focused on me, but his face looked eerily serene. He died doing what he'd been born to do. "I told you this would happen."

Underhill didn't answer. He didn't even try to move. He probably couldn't. That bullet had probably shattered his spine.

"Are you the best they've got? Is this it? How many of you sons of bitches do I have to kill before they leave me alone?"

Underhill still didn't answer. His ragged breathing slowed. The pool of blood under him expanded. I got closer until I was standing in the puddle, big, stainless steel revolver pointed at his face. He didn't look scared. He looked perfectly calm.

"That was for Hawk," I said defiantly.

Underhill didn't respond. His breathing slowed a little more, then stopped. Just like that, he was gone. Then there was nothing. No satisfaction, no remorse, no adrenaline rush, no adrenaline dump. Just an old man dead on a loading dock of a train station in France.

I lowered my gun. I realized then that I had blood trickling from my nose.

LORENZO

It was the quickest draw I'd ever seen.

The old man had him dead to rights. Only Valentine had been faster. *Way* faster.

Back on Saint Carl I'd talked some trash about being as fast with a pistol as Valentine was . . . *Damn.* Not even close. Valentine said something to the man I assumed was Underhill, and then left him there to die alone. Hawk would have been proud.

"Valentine!" And since he looked really jumpy, I immediately added. "Hold your fire, it's me." He was standing near a big metal box on a cart. "Is that what I think it is?"

He looked a little out of it, and had blood trickling from his right nostril. "Yeah."

Well, that was intimidating.

"Where's everybody else?" he asked.

"Converging on those hangars like you said."

Before I had finished speaking, Valentine was running in that direction.

I took one last look at the bomb. It seemed wrong to just leave it sitting there, like I should hang a warning sign on it, *do not touch*, or something. Since all the law-abiding citizens in the station were fleeing for their lives now, I pulled my .45 before I went after him. Across the yard was the sleekest train I'd ever seen. In fact, it looked more like a spaceship than a piece of mass transit. Valentine hopped off the concrete platform and ran across tracks and gravel directly toward it. I went to the other side of the elevated tracks and jumped down too. At least there were a lot of shadows here.

Antoine came over the radio. *"They are loading the train. I am in position."*

"Almost there," Valentine said. "Wait for us."

Far ahead, I spotted a group of men standing on the platform by one of the futuristic cars.

"Down," I hissed at Valentine as I took cover behind a concrete barrier.

They were dressed in contractor garb, cargo pants, vests, and ball caps. From the way they had their guns out and were nervously scanning, they had heard Valentine's gunfire. One of them spoke into a radio, and a few seconds later a man came off the train, driving an empty cart. Behind him was a tall, blonde woman. She had her back turned, but the way she was supervising, that had to be Kat. Of course she needed to see her crowning achievement launched in person. One more person got off the train. Towering over Kat was the gigantic, unmistakable form of Anders. As Anders scanned for threats, I pulled back further behind the barrier.

"I can no longer wait," Antoine whispered over the radio.

There were several security men visible, an unknown number out of view, and probably more still on the train, because Kat was the kind of awful person who would hire somebody to guard a cargo and not tell them it was going to explode. Not to forget Anders, who I'd seen in action in the Crossroads, where he'd been like the fucking Terminator, and Kat was still deadly as hell. I was no hero, but in a few seconds that train was going to leave, and if I let Kat blow up a city Jill would never let me hear the end of it. I'd already been lucky to survive one lopsided gunfight tonight, and unlike the men we'd surprised earlier, these were alert and ready for trouble. They were out of effective pistol range, so we'd have to get closer. I took a deep breath and crept around the barricade.

Apparently Valentine had to do less soul searching, because he was already way ahead of me. I was close enough now to hear Kat shouting orders. The job was done. They were leaving.

Antoine must have made a move. Only with a reaction time that rivaled Valentine, Anders spotted them, lifted a stubby black weapon from beneath this jacket, and fired. From the lack of noise, it was that same suppressed shotgun he'd used to shoot Jill.

"Take them!" Valentine shouted as he took off running. I lost sight of him around the front of the engine.

I was still a hundred yards away, which was too damned far to be shooting a .45, but I opened up on them anyway. I put the red dot on top of the closest man's head, hoping that was sufficient holdover, and popped off a shot. There was either enough drop or wobble in my aim that I only hit him in the chest. The 230-grain hollow point made an audible *slap* against his concealed body armor. Most of the security guys weren't well trained enough that they'd turned to see who Anders was shooting at, but of course the asshole covering my sector was a professional. He saw me, shouldered a subgun, and stated shooting.

Bullets smacked into the concrete in front of me as I took a knee, leaned out, and cranked off a few more quiet shots. The shooters were breaking off and moving to cover. Anders was still shooting down the hall. In the middle of it all, Kat was standing there, actually *grinning*, like this was incredibly exciting, and she was having the time of her life. But then they started taking fire from the far side of the train, and Kat had to duck as bullets went whizzing past. I caught a glimpse of Skunky and Shen coming up the platform at the opposite end of the train. The man standing closest to Kat spun around as they nailed him.

The security men opened up on them as Skunky took cover behind some construction equipment. Only they weren't fast enough. I couldn't tell where Skunky had gotten hit, but he just collapsed in a heap. Shen grabbed him by one arm and dragged him behind cover as bullets struck all around them.

By the time I leaned out to shoot again, we'd broken them. Several of Kat's men were out of the fight, and they were taking fire from three sides. They had nowhere to go except inside the train. The security men dragged their wounded into the train after her. Anders calmly walked backwards toward the door, still firing down the hall. I shot at him, but some stupid bastard stepped right in front of him and I clipped the guard instead. His head snapped back, flinging blood and brains all over my real target.

Anders saw me. We locked eyes, and he knew I'd almost gotten him. But then that bastard was inside the train and out of my line of sight.

The sudden lack of gunfire made it feel far too quiet. Then the radio chatter started.

"Skunky is down," Shen reported.

"I'm hit," Antoine gasped.

The train started to move.

It was shocking how fast it took off, and even worse, how remarkably fast it was building up speed. It was coming my way, but all I had was a pistol, which wasn't anywhere near enough to stop a friggin' train. Not wanting to get run over, I hurried and clambered up onto the platform. I took cover behind a pillar and watched helplessly as the engine floated by, then the first car, but then the second was filled with scumbags who blew out the windows trying to murder me, and I was too busy trying to become one with the floor as they hammered the concrete pillar between us into dust to pay attention to much else.

The gunfire let off, and I leapt to my feet, cranking off a few futile rounds after that second car as it rapidly accelerated away. There was no time to think. I shoved the 1911 into the holster. I was going to need both hands for this next bit of reckless stupidity. It was already moving way faster than I could sprint, but I started running alongside it anyway. I'd hopped plenty of trains before, and I searched for something to grab onto, but this thing was sleek, round, and aerodynamic. There was nothing to grab hold of. It was a hobo's nightmare.

There had to be *something*. I kept running as it kept passing me by, faster and faster. My chest hurt. My legs burned. Tonight had already kicked my ass. Then I was next to the final car. Thankfully, there was a rear door with a safety rail, and a bumper sufficient to stand on. I reached out, and the train was already going so damned fast that the rubberized metal bar hit my palm like a bat. I latched on, and it damned near took my arm out of the socket as it yanked me off the platform.

My boots hit the bumper. I was hanging on for dear life, but I'd made it.

Apparently on the other side of the train, Valentine had come up with the same bright idea, only he wasn't nearly as acrobatic as I was. He caught the rail on that side, and was jerked around and swung hard into the metal door. His shoulder hit way too hard, and he probably would have bounced off and eaten track if I'd not grabbed onto his arm. I pulled him back onto the bumper.

"This is insane!" Valentine shouted.

"No shit." There were handholds leading to the roof, but this thing was supposed to go three hundred miles an hour, which meant going that way would be suicidal. "See if you can get the door open."

Valentine tried the handle. "Locked."

We needed to get inside before Kat's men came back here and just machine-gunned us through the wall. The train station was flying past us. I leaned back to the left to see if maybe I could reach around to smash out the side window and climb through, but I had to pull my head back to keep from ripping it off as another pillar flashed by.

I stuck my head out again. Ling was on the platform ahead, frustrated, and glaring at the escaping train, when she saw me hanging there. Without hesitation, she keyed her radio. *"Grab my hand, Lorenzo."*

We were going much faster than when Valentine and I had made it across. This was going to be tight. As the distance closed, I could see that Ling was focused on me like a laser beam. She'd either make it across or die trying. If anybody could do it, it would be Ling. She stuck her arm out.

But then I thought of what Jill had told me about her.

It wasn't even a conscious decision. I hesitated for just an instant, it was too late, and then we were past, leaving Ling alone on the platform. She watched me, furious at the missed opportunity.

"What are you doing?" Ling demanded.

"Why didn't you help her?" Valentine asked a split second later when he saw his girlfriend hadn't caught our ride.

"You'll thank me later," I snapped at him. "Get that fucking door open." I keyed my radio. "Ling, you've got to find those other two bombs. Use Reaper. He's going for the command center. We've got this one."

"*Roger*," Ling said, tersely, obviously pissed that I hadn't snagged her.

"Try to get Tailor. That one we caught might be armed," Valentine said into his radio.

I hadn't even thought of that. Maybe I hadn't done Ling any favors after all.

He went back to kicking the door. "We could have used her help."

"We're probably going to die if you don't hurry up."

There was a little Plexiglas window. Valentine tried to break it a couple of times with his elbow, but when that failed he pulled his .44 Magnum. *Man, I hated that stupid gun.* "What do you mean I'll thank you later?" He asked as he used the butt of the revolver to bash the little window in.

"You're going to be a dad."

Valentine froze, arm shoved through the door, searched for the handle. He looked like I'd nut-punched him. "*What?*"

"Congratulations, Pops."

Chapter 16: As Above, So Below

VALENTINE

"What do you mean?" The train was speeding up rapidly as I, hand through a broken window, fumbled for the emergency door release.

Lorenzo, his long hair whipping in the wind, looked at me like I was stupid. Judging by how fast we'd left the station, we had to be going over a hundred miles an hour already. "Biology 101! You knocked her up! Now open the fucking door!"

I found the handle and cranked it. An alarm sounded inside the train car. They probably knew we were here now.

Lorenzo readied his pistol as the door slid open. Nobody had shot my arm off, so maybe they weren't watching the back door yet. As soon as it was open, Lorenzo was in, and I was right behind him.

We found ourselves in a tiny room about as big as a walk-in closet. The walls were made of rubber. The connectors between cars must have been like flexible airlocks. There was another door just ahead of us and stairs that went up to the second level.

"Wait, how did *you* find out Ling was pregnant?"

He exhaled sharply. "We don't have time for this, okay? She told Jill, Jill told me, she was going to tell you, but didn't because, I don't know, she loves soap opera bullshit like this. Will you focus? Can't you do that creepy calm-face thing you do? We need to go kill a bunch of assholes."

He was right, but I wasn't going to give him the satisfaction of admitting it. "We're on a train with who-knows-how-many dudes with guns, Kat, Anders, and the bomb. They can't be planning to detonate it if they're stuck on the train with it, right?"

"You sure about that?" Lorenzo asked.

"Uh . . . hell." I wasn't. Not really. The mercenaries probably didn't know they even had a bomb. Anders? No way. But Kat? If she couldn't get off in time, she might set it off, just out of spite.

Lorenzo glanced through the door, then pointed skyward. "Okay, this looks like other bullet trains I've been on. Two levels, stairs at the beginning of every car. We go up. Top level is how you get from car to car. Bottom will dead end."

"What if someone hides below us, let us go over, then comes up behind us?"

"Then we get shot."

We went up the stairs. I risked a quick peek through the window on the door. Armed men were moving this way, guns shouldered. I pulled back and held up two fingers. "The second we go through this door we're toast."

"Not necessarily." Lorenzo removed something from his jacket pocket.

"Is that a grenade?" I asked, hopefully.

"No," Lorenzo whispered, shattering my hopes. "I wish, but I wasn't planning on using grenades when I was going to rescue my brother. Ended up using a bunch anyways, long story. It's a stun grenade, a Canadian nine-banger. After that, it's gonna get ugly. We've got to push straight through. Don't let up. You ready?"

Even though Lorenzo was a real bastard, I couldn't think of anybody I'd rather be doing this with. I checked the cylinder of my revolver. "As ready as I'm going to get. Do it."

Lorenzo nodded and slid the interior door open just a little, his suppressed 1911 at the ready. He tossed the flashbang grenade in and slammed the door shut.

BANG BANG BANG BANG BANG BANG BANG BANG BANG! True to its name, the nine-banger rapidly blasted off nine head-splitting concussions. As soon as the last pop had sounded, Lorenzo shoved the sliding door open and moved in. He didn't give the two stunned men in the room any time to react. *CHUFF CHUFF CHUFF!* Three shots on the closest guy, then *CHUFF CHUFF CHUFF CHUFF,* four shots on the next. Both went down with bullet holes in their heads and necks. Lorenzo ejected the magazine from his .45 and was slamming a replacement in as the empty hit the floor.

The train car, surprisingly quiet now, was filled with smoke.

"Cover the door," I said, crouching down by the nearest dead man. He was dressed in black and had been carrying a compact assault rifle. It was a 5.56mm SCAR with a ten-inch barrel and a holographic sight. He had a couple of spare magazines in his pockets, which I took, before standing up.

I leveled my carbine at the door. "Hurry up, check the—" I didn't get to finish that thought. Bullets tore through the thin door between cars. Lorenzo ducked back down the stairs while I tried to use the economy-class seats for cover. Leaning out, I flipped the selector to full auto and dumped the whole magazine in return fire. The noise of the short-barreled weapon in the confines of the train car was head-splitting, but I ignored it as best I could. "Reloading!"

Lorenzo pointed his gun toward the door and ran up, stepping over the other dead man without stopping to grab his weapon. "They're running." He fired after them. "Move up!"

Nodding, I quickly ran up the aisle, weapon at the ready. I had shredded most of the couchlike seats in this car, and fabric was floating in the air. Lorenzo and I found ourselves on opposite sides of the door that led to the next car. "Got any more tricks?"

"You're not going to like it," he said. "Go prone on the floor in the aisle. Get ready. When I pull the door open, you shoot low, and I'll shoot high."

"Why am I the one that has to lie in the line of fire?" I asked, dropping to the floor of the train car.

"Quit being a bitch. You're *below* the line of fire. You ready?"

"No," I said, looking through the holographic sight. "Do it anyway."

Lorenzo was right. I was below the line of fire. You should've seen the look on the man's face when the door opened and he fired, his rounds passing above me. I stitched him up, firing a long burst into his guts, going under his hard plate. He fell.

Another guy rolled out and tried to blast me with a short shotgun. But I was *Calm*, and he was painfully slow. I rolled to my left, out of the way, with a faction of a second to spare before his buckshot obliterated the carpet I'd been lying on. Before he could pump another round into the chamber, Lorenzo came around the corner and started shooting. He was out and moving before I could even get up. His pistol, that custom 1911 with the can and the old electronic sight, was firing so fast it sounded like an MP40. The shotgunner was hit repeatedly and crumpled.

Lorenzo looked over the top of each seat until he reached the flexible connection. "Clear!"

"If this is the best she's got," I said, pulling magazines out of the pouches on a dead man's armor vest, "we'll be home by dinner."

"Don't get cocky," Lorenzo warned.

Kat's men didn't wait for us to enter the next car. The door slid open and all of them rushed through, weapons shouldered, firing. A burning pain shot through my side as the second man in the stack lit me up with a P90 submachine gun. As I fell, Lorenzo dropped to a knee and opened fire with the shotgun, blowing the lead man's head off in a spray of blood and buckshot. Stumbling backwards, I landed hard on the armrest of one of the economy-class seats, lost my carbine, and flopped to the floor. I rolled onto my side, pulled the .44 from its holster on my hip and jabbed it outward, rocking the trigger, firing up the aisle toward the man who was now trying to retreat. He didn't make it.

"You good?" Lorenzo asked as he dragged me up.

I nodded jerkily. It burned, and I could feet something hot and wet under my armor vest. A round must've gotten through.

It didn't matter. We couldn't stop now. "I'm good. Let's go."

LORENZO

Entering each new car was a nightmare, but we had to keep pushing.

The doors were a fatal funnel, but there was no other way to go around. I couldn't tell how fast we were going, but judging by how quickly the countryside was flying past the window, it was *really* fast. If this had been a normal train I could have taken to the side or the roof to bypass the choke points and ambush the ambushers, but on this thing that would've been like trying to walk across the wing of a jet plane. Despite that the ride was remarkably smooth. If we hadn't been fighting to the death this would be a pleasant way to travel.

Valentine was leaning against the huge, flexible rubber gasket that served as the bridge between cars, waiting for me while I hurried and looted a corpse. He still had that eerie *Calm* thing going on, but he was breathing too hard.

"You hit?" I asked as I took the dead man's FN P90. The magazine was translucent and looked almost full. Good. I was out of .45 and had dropped the old 1911. I flipped it over and checked the chamber. *Hot.*

"Vest stopped it." But I think he was lying. He went back to trying to get a peek through the glass door into the next car to see how many of them were waiting to kill us. "I don't see anyone."

I risked a glimpse through the glass door. The next car was the food car, with rounded couches instead of packed seats like our current economy car, and a bar down the opposite side, but I didn't see anybody waiting for us. "They're there."

"I know." He'd picked up a SCAR off one of the men we'd killed, and kept that at his left shoulder while he put his right hand on the door to pull it open for me. I got into position, and when I nodded back, Valentine yanked the handle.

I dove through, hit the floor, and rolled behind the end of the bar. Somebody must have shown themselves because Valentine started shooting over my head. I crawled forward as bottles and glasses shattered above me. I flinched when I stuck my palm on something sharp, but I was too occupied to care. By the time I popped up, there was a bunch of stuffing floating in the air, as Valentine tried to peg one of Kat's men hiding behind a couch. There was another man hiding at the opposite end of the bar, so I opened up on him. He ducked further down as he was pelted with splinters and flying glass.

"Moving," Valentine shouted as he came through the door. I kept hammering the boxy little subgun at the two men, alternating between them, fast semi-auto shots, trying to keep them pinned. Apparently there was some sort of solid metal frame beneath the rounded couch, because I couldn't seem to hit the bastard through it, but from the swearing and shouting, I was pretty sure I'd gotten the one behind the bar.

Valentine went right down the middle, gun shouldered, aggressive as could be, and by the time the men realized he had an angle on them, it was too late. He pumped half a dozen 5.56 rounds into the one behind the couch. The barman leapt up to engage Valentine, but I put a bullet through the side of his skull on the way up. He jerked the trigger as he fell, shooting through the side wall and spraying rounds across the French countryside. Valentine reached him and put one more into his head to be sure.

"Clear!"

I ran up to him. It wasn't until I looked down to see how much ammo I had left that I realized I was bleeding all over the P90. I'd cut my hands on broken glass. But that wasn't as important as the fact that the gun was almost empty. Fifty rounds went fast when you were really motivated.

The glass door had been struck and broken during our firefight. Valentine had an unobstructed view into the next car. He took a knee by the wall and signaled for me to stay low. There were more waiting for us. And as if to punctuate that, somebody started randomly launching bullets through the wall. Valentine hunkered down as I crawled toward the nearest body.

While I was searching for another weapon, a voice came over the intercom.

"This is your captain speaking," Katarina said. *"Apparently we have some uninvited stowaways on our five-thirty nonstop to London. Whichever one of you kills these annoyances will receive a ten-million-dollar bonus. That is all."*

The man we'd nearly decapitated had been armed with a P90 as well, so I started rifling through his stupid contractor vest looking for more magazines. Valentine fired back through the door. "Just one shooter. He's retreating," he reported.

Fresh magazine in the gun and another one stuffed in my back pocket, I got up. "Keep pushing." The two of us rushed into the next car. We both had to pause and take cover as the man we were chasing decided to start firing indiscriminately through the walls again.

"Are they dead yet? I'm getting impatient up here. Is that you, Lorenzo? Valentine? I knew it. You just couldn't let it go." Kat was getting agitated. *"Bonuses be damned, if you idiots don't hurry up and take care of them, they're going to kill you all."*

We reached the next wall. There were brass casings rolling beneath our boots. The glass between the two cars was already shattered. Valentine did a quick peek through the hole, then pulled back and held up one finger. The shooter was waiting for us. Another fucking fatal funnel.

I didn't know who her security was. They looked more like PMCs than typical Montalban criminal stooges. They probably didn't even know they were protecting a maniac with a nuclear bomb. Not that they'd be inclined to believe us over their current employer, since we had just killed a bunch of them, but what the hell? It was worth a shot.

Signaling for Valentine to hold, I shouted, "Hey, asshole. Do you know what's in that box you're protecting?"

There was a brief pause, and then somebody shouted back. "Why don't you tell us then?"

Valentine's eyes narrowed. He slowly moved his weapon along the wall, estimating where the voice came from.

"It's a nuclear bomb. Kat intends to blow up London with it and I don't think she's going to stop and let you morons off first!"

He must not have believed me, because he opened fire, punching holes through the rubberized walls. I nearly got my head blown off. Valentine emptied his magazine through the wall in response.

Except for the ringing in my ears, it was quiet. "Fuck diplomacy!" I shouted.

"You're really bad at it," Valentine stated flatly. We both looked in. The gunman was flat on his back, dead. He'd been hiding behind a table, but Valentine had shredded it and his body. "Go." We moved in, leaping over the dead man, and headed for the next car.

There couldn't be many left. I didn't see anyone inside the next one. This car must have been intended for business meetings and taking calls. There were little glass privacy enclosures inside, each one crowded with comfy chairs and tables. It was all very fancy. It was a good thing the maglev line didn't actually have passengers yet, because we'd indiscriminately fired so many rounds through this place we would have accidentally killed a bunch of them.

There was movement at the far end of the car. *Anders!* Unfortunately, he saw us coming and jumped down the stairs before I could get a shot off. I'd forgotten just how freaking fast he was for a big dude. Val had seen him at the same time, and both of us instinctively rushed inside, hoping to take him out fast. Since the glass partitions ran down the middle with aisles on the sides, Valentine automatically veered left and I went right. Anders was a high-value target. He had to die.

It wasn't until the gunshot went off that I realized we'd walked right into a trap. Valentine shouted a warning as he caught a bullet in the back. I spun around to see the shooter, but I was too late. He'd been lurking in a corner, hiding behind a shelf, and since we'd focused on Anders we'd gone right past him.

We fired at the same time. The glass partition between us exploded. I know I hit him, but then it was like a fiery fist punched me right in the sternum. He punched a few holes in the glass behind me before there was a flash of heat down my forearm and the P90 was torn from my grasp. I crashed against the heavy window hard enough to crack it, and then launched myself at the floor before he could shoot me again.

I know I'd plugged him repeatedly, but the stubborn gunman was still up and coming my way. He lined up the sights of his subgun on my face and I knew I was going to die.

But then Valentine rolled over, pulled his .44 and blew the back of his head off.

My chest was on fire. Because I'd needed to be mobile and stealthy low crawling through the weeds all night, I'd only worn an old Level II soft vest beneath my shirt. I put my bloody hand on my sternum and found the slug flattened there, still hot to the touch. Then I realized his other bullet had cut a shallow bloody line down my arm before it had smacked the FN, but like Gideon had always said, the wound wasn't squirting . . . So I crawled forward, trying to find a gun so I could finish off Anders before he could—

Anders came out of nowhere and kicked me so hard in the ribs that it launched me through another glass partition.

It was like being mule kicked. I'd broken the glass with my head. I lay there on the floor, stunned, cut, in a pile of broken glass, trying desperately to breathe, as Anders crunched after me. He had that little suppressed shotgun pointed toward where Valentine had been. Apparently Anders didn't have a shot at him through the furniture separating us, but that didn't stop him. He simply switched the shotgun to his other hand, aimed it at me, and ordered "don't move" as he pulled a pistol from beneath his jacket to keep pointed toward where Valentine was hiding.

"Yo, Valentine, show yourself or I'm killing your partner here."

"You think he cares?" I gasped.

"Shut up." The 12 gauge hole on the end of the boxy shotgun remained pointed at my mouth. His finger was on the trigger.

"What are you doing, Anders?" Valentine shouted back. He sounded like he was in a lot of pain, but he was smart enough not to show himself. Anders didn't miss much. "You're not suicidal."

"You think I wanted to end up on this train? That's your fault. From here on Kat can see her glorious dreams come to fruition without me. I'm getting off here."

We were riding the world's fastest train, how in the hell did he think that was going to happen without turning into paste? But then I remembered that he'd been doing something in the floor between the train cars.

"He's decoupled the cars!" I shouted. "You've got to reach that bomb, Valentine!"

Anders just scowled and dropped one big boot down on my chest, stomping the remaining air right out of my lungs. *Damn. That hurt.* But shutting me up had been a mistake. Anders was now in reach.

"Hell, it wouldn't be the first time. Valentine helped us retrieve this bomb. Isn't that right, kid? We couldn't have done Project Blue without you."

Fuck it. He was going to kill me anyway, and we couldn't afford to let that bomb go off. I had to go for it. Only before I could make a grab for Anders' shotgun, I saw something silver sliding across the floor, beneath the couches, directly toward me.

It was Valentine's .44 Magnum.

Valentine leapt up, not heading for Anders, but rather sprinting for the next car. I went for the shotgun.

Anders reacted and pulled both triggers, firing his pistol at Valentine and his shotgun at me. I *barely* knocked the muzzle aside as it blasted a dozen holes in the floor next to my head.

Glass shattered between Anders and Valentine. Blood spatter decorated the walls, but Valentine just put his head down and kept running.

With one hand pushing the shotgun's muzzle away from my face, I desperately reached for Valentine's revolver with my other. Only to discover that the .44 had stopped just out of range. *Damn it, Valentine. Good idea, shitty execution.*

Anders was still trying to shoot both of us, only the instant he wasn't busy aiming at Valentine's moving target, I was dead meat. I gave up on trying to grab the .44 and went after the suppressed shotgun with both hands, this time trying to pull Anders down toward me to twist it from his grip. That was even harder than it sounded considering he was stepping on my chest and was twice my size. I managed to pull him off balance, and his next few shots at Valentine went wide. Snarling, Anders turned his pistol on me.

Only Anders didn't realize I hadn't been trying to take his shotgun away. I'd been trying to *aim* it. I shoved my thumb inside the trigger guard on top of his finger and fired the shotgun directly into the closest interior window. The buckshot hit the already damaged safety glass—

FOOOOOOOOOOOOOM!

And a three hundred mile an hour wind came ripping through the cabin. It was like stepping into a tornado.

Everything that wasn't bolted down was hurled around the car. Anders instinctively raised his arms to cover his face as he was pelted with debris. He stumbled aside, trying to protect his eyes. I rolled over and went for Valentine's gun, only to discover that it had been blown away. I scrambled and rolled behind a couch before Anders could get his bearings.

I had to hand it to Anders, he was one committed son of a bitch. He fired wildly toward where he thought I was, then still managed to try and kill Valentine again one last time. Anders dropped his pistol and pulled out a radio detonator. I could only hope that Valentine had made it through the gasket before Anders mashed the button. There was a bright flash at the front of the car, but I couldn't hear the little explosive over the rushing wind.

The cars separated. Within seconds the engine was leaving us behind. Kat was getting away.

I'd failed. Valentine was now London's only hope.

As for me? I was still on a train car with the bastard who had shot Jill. I was determined to find that .44 and kill this fucker once and for all. Only my search was interrupted by an incredibly loud noise, and I suddenly found myself flying through the air.

One thing I hadn't known about high speed maglev trains: when a car gets decoupled, it has some *serious* emergency brakes.

VALENTINE

I had barely made it through the gasket before the explosion, but Anders had clipped me on the way. There was a shallow tear through the skin and muscle along my hip. It burned. I could feel sticky wet blood under my shirt from where I'd been hit earlier. I was dizzy and weakening. *Gotta keep moving.* I was only down for a few seconds, but by the time I looked back, the rest of the train cars were a shrinking dot in the distance. Lorenzo hadn't made it across. I was on my own.

Anders had used an explosive device to separate the coupling. It had cracked the safety glass of the next door, but hadn't blown it out. The next car only had one big floor with a tall ceiling, but it appeared clear. I went through. When I slid the door closed behind me, it was all at once eerily quiet. Out the window, we were passing through what appeared to be a seaside town. Then suddenly everything out there was black. At first I thought we were going through a tunnel, but then I realized this was the Chunnel. We were travelling beneath the ocean. Outside, safety lights flew past at a frightening speed. I didn't know how long we had until we emerged on the English side of the channel, but certainly not long aboard this thing.

Sweating, breathing hard, and bleeding, I limped down the stairs. This was a luxury car, and it was decked out in sleek, ultramodern décor. There were even potted plants and a crystal chandelier. The car was divided into several alcoves, providing privacy to passengers as they sat on plush couches. There was an information screen mounted on the wall but now it was just flashing an error message. There was no bomb on this car.

You can't just stand here and bleed. As if to drive the point home, the doors at the front of the train car slid open. I took cover in an alcove, then risked a peek down the aisle. Two men entered, pistols drawn, and they moved down the stairs cautiously. I pulled back. I'd lost the carbine in the last car. I'd given my .44 to Lorenzo. All I had left was the hideous, plastic Taurus .357 snubby that I'd been carrying since the Crossroads. It only held five shots.

Unlike the guys in tac gear we'd faced when we first boarded the train, these guys looked like Kat's regular bodyguards. *What the hell are you people still fighting for?* Maybe she told them they'd have time to escape before the bomb detonated. Maybe they were just that fanatically loyal to the woman. Maybe they didn't know what Kat was doing and thought they were just protecting her.

I shouted at them. "Do you know what this train is carrying? Do you have any idea what you're doing? You're protecting a nuclear fucking bomb, and when this train gets to London you, me, your lunatic boss, and a million innocent people are gonna die! Whatever she offered you, whatever she pays you, it isn't going to matter when we're all dead!"

One of the men said something to the other in a language I didn't understand. The other answered him harshly, and my plea was answered with a hail of gunfire. Bullets tore up the seat, the floor, and punched holes in my cover. One of them fired shot after shot, not letting up, but the other held his fire, waiting for me to make a move. I scrunched down lower, trying to merge with the floor. The gunfire ceased as suddenly as it had started. All that shooting and he hadn't hit a damned thing. But they knew where I was, so all they had to do was wait for me to pop out. I wasn't playing that game.

Only they were moving up on me, leapfrogging forward. One covering my position while the other moved to the next alcove. Next time they opened up, my bullet riddled cover would be insufficient. Except they stopped when the door to the last car slid open again. Kat was staying behind cover, but I could hear her clearly as she asked her men something. One of them answered. Then she raised her voice. "So there's only one of you left? Which one is it?"

"Give it up, Katarina. This is insane."

"Valentine? Disappointing. After everything we've been through together I thought Lorenzo would come through for me at the end."

"He's busy murdering your boyfriend."

"Anders is a strong man, but he does not share my level of commitment. Very few do."

"So you're going to ride this nuke to London and go out in a blaze of glory." I still hoped that her men were in the dark, and they would balk when they realized what was happening.

"I would rather not. The train is programmed to slow when it enters the metro area. I'll be getting off there with plenty of time to get out of the blast radius and seek shelter."

"I hope you like radioactive fallout."

"I'm not entirely happy about how this is working out, but that is your fault. I should be on my way home right now to enjoy some wine and a relaxing bath while I watch news reports of how my rivals perished in cleansing fire."

One of the guards said something then. He must have caught

enough of our exchange to realize what was going on. *That's right, morons. Your boss is insane.*

"So tell me, Valentine. Have you met Mr. Perkins yet?"

I was bleeding out, so the name didn't immediately ring any bells. I risked a peek, only to see Kat aiming a cut-down M79 grenade launcher at us.

One of Kat's men began shouting something in French. I didn't need to speak the language to understand that he was begging her not to use that thing in here. A panicked *you're going to kill us all* sounds the same everywhere.

"But, if you die, I don't have to pay you," Katarina told him. Then she blew up the train.

LORENZO

The sudden stop had been hell on the furniture. Whatever hadn't been bolted down ended up in a pile at one end of the car, including me. Unlike a regular train coming to a surprise stop, there weren't any sparks or screeching noises followed by a violent derailment. This was more of a *whoosh*, like when an airplane lands, but a whole lot more abrupt. I ended up pressed against a broken table, up to my eyeballs in broken glass, and as the G forces subsided, the table toppled over and fell on top of me.

I was having one hell of a night.

As we came to a shuddering halt, I heard Anders coughing. He'd landed ten feet away, only he wasn't crushed beneath a bunch of debris. I struggled to get out from under the table, and of course, it weighed a ton. I tried to do a push up, but the stupid table was somehow wedged on top of me. It was stuck. I started clawing my way through the glass, grabbing handfuls of carpet, trying to wiggle out from beneath it.

"Damn, Lorenzo, you're one obnoxiously hard-to-kill son of a bitch. No wonder you screwed up so many of our operations in Zubara." Anders must have lost hold of his guns, because if he still had one, he'd be shooting rather than talking. Not that a monster like Anders needed a gun to kill me, and he proved that when he stomped the table and knocked the ever living shit out of me beneath it.

I was screwed. He kicked the table several times, but it was enough of a shield that he grew frustrated.

"I told Kat I should have just murdered you when I had the chance at the Crossroads, but oh no, she said you had to suffer first! She loved the idea of Sala Jihan catching you." Anders was like two hundred and seventy pounds of solid muscle, so when he reached down and grabbed the wreckage, he flipped it off of me like it was a card table.

I sprung up. The instant my Benchmade knife snapped open in my hand, I slashed for his guts. But he'd been waiting for that, and his open palm hit my forearm so hard that it felt like I'd bashed my bones on a pipe. Anders caught the back of my knife hand and twisted, trying to snap my wrist. Once he had me off balance he swung me against a window. I tried to twist out of it, but his grip was as hard as the Pale Man's shackles. I lost my knife as I dropped all my weight on his thumb, but I broke free. Luckily I accomplished that the microsecond before his fist put a dent in the wall where my head had been.

I launched myself at his legs. I got an arm around one ankle and threw my shoulder against his knee, trying to lever him down. It would have worked against most people, but Anders just kicked his back leg out to steady himself. I couldn't topple him. He dropped a hammer blow on my back, then encircled my torso in his massive arms, hoisted me off the floor, and flung me against the wall.

Damn, he was strong, but I'd fought a lot of men a lot bigger than I was, and no matter how tough they were, anybody could be crippled. I came off the wall, swinging. Anders blocked my arm, but he'd known that was just a feint and easily dodged the snap kick I'd aimed at his knee. I ducked beneath his jab and then danced back.

"Slippery little bastard," Anders growled as he went after me.

I met him in the middle of the train car, doing everything I could to hurt him. We collided, knees and elbows flying. I'm a damned good fighter, but physics were unforgiving, and he was one big, powerful motherfucker. The only advantage I had was speed.

And it turned out I didn't have nearly enough of that when he swatted my arms out of the way, slugged me in the side of the head, kneed me in stomach hard enough to lift me off the ground, and spun me around into a couch. I went over the top, rolled across the floor, and only stopped my momentum by carpet burning my face.

"You know all that fucked-up shit Silvers did to Valentine? I wasn't interested in her mental games, but I *volunteered* for the physical part."

I got up, far slower that time, remembering Valentine telling me about how Anders had singlehandedly beaten the hell out of an entire Dead Six chalk. That story didn't seem very far-fetched right now. My chest was on fire. It was like I couldn't breathe fast enough. My head was swimming, but he was already charging me again.

There was no finesse this time. Anders just tackled me, swept me off the floor, and drove us back into the wall. Another window broke out of its frame. Then we were sliding down as he got on top of me, slamming his fists into my face. His knuckles dented bone and split skin. Each impact put a lightning bolt through my skull. I tried to get my hands up to stop him, but he had me, and just kept punching down through my defenses. I tried to lift my body to close the gap, but he just kept on striking.

With perfect rational clarity, I knew that he was going to render me unconscious, and then cave my skull in, and I had no idea how to stop him.

The better question is, Lorenzo, why won't you die?

It was like the Pale Man's voice awakened all the savagery I'd learned in the dark. The son of murder doesn't die. He kills.

I caught one of Anders' hands before he could retract it, pulled it close, and bit down on his wrist as hard as I could. Blood filled my mouth. Anders screamed in my ear and tried to pull away, but I wouldn't let go. I jerked my knee into his crotch. Anders shouted as he clubbed me with his other hand, but he didn't have as good an angle now, and I'd gnaw his damned hand off before I'd give up.

Anders flung himself backwards to escape. I think I might have left one of my teeth embedded in his wrist, but I was too dazed to tell. Anders was waving his bloody hand, spasmodically clenching and unclenching his fingers as I pulled myself up the wall. I must have bit through a tendon. *Good.*

I spit out a mouthful of blood. This time I charged him. He hadn't been expecting that. He was so much taller than I was that I practically had to jump to strike him in the face, but I still sunk my knuckles deep into one eye socket. Anders reeled back. I kept on hitting him, trying to tear him down. I don't think I've ever hit anybody that hard, that many times, and it still didn't seem to do shit.

Anders clocked me again. The only reason his fist didn't break any ribs was that my bulletproof vest spread out the impact. He struck me with a shockingly quick jab that split my lips open, then he got a handful of my shirt, rolled me over his hip, and tossed me hard on the floor.

I landed in a pile of broken glass and debris. The back of my head struck something round and metallic. I rolled off it, only to discover that it was Valentine's Smith & Wesson.

Anders was on his way over to finish me off, blood and snot leaking down his chin. His face was contorted with rage, but he froze when he saw what I was reaching for. Realizing he was unable to close the distance between us in time, he lurched desperately toward the broken window as my hand fell on the grip.

My eyes were nearly swollen shut. My hands were shaking so badly I couldn't even find the front sight. Anders was a blurry mass climbing through the window. I jerked the double action trigger. My first round punched a useless hole in the wall next to him. My second shot, I think I missed again, as Anders fell out the window and disappeared.

It took me a few seconds to get up, and a few more to wobble to the window. I was so dizzy that I tripped over my own feet, fell down, and then had to catch my breath before trying again. I probably had a concussion.

When I pulled myself up I saw the orange vapor lights of an industrial park. It was nearly dawn. The train cars had come to a stop on a small rise. Squinting, I looked down, hoping to see Anders lying next to the tracks in a pool of blood, but there was nothing but gravel and litter. There was a gentle slope of dried grass down to a chain link fence fifty yards away . . . Which was shaking back and forth because Anders was climbing over it. I'd only grazed him.

The front sight was wobbling badly as I pulled the heavy trigger.

I missed. "Fuck this thing!" I snarled, and fired again. Another miss.

Anders landed on the ground on the other side, glaring at me, and then he took off running across a parking lot.

I hate revolvers. I always have. Even back when Gideon Lorenzo had tried to teach me how to use one of the old-fashioned things, I had sucked with them. It didn't help that this particular gun had offed my business associates, wrecked my hearing in one ear, and shot me in the chest, *twice*. Valentine's gun really had it in for me.

But this time I slowed down, braced my arms against the window to steady myself, and thumb cocked the hammer. That took the trigger pull weight down to nothing. Blood was running into my eyes, but I just squinted through it and kept tracking Anders through the red haze. He was running between parked cars. I led him a tiny bit, and exhaled as I squeezed the trigger.

BOOM!

Anders spun around and crashed against a parked car. He slid down the hood and fell from view.

That was more like it.

Then I realized there had been multiple witnesses to my shooting an unarmed, fleeing man in the back. A few men and women, most of them in coveralls and work clothes, had come out of the nearby buildings to see why a train had stopped here. Some of them had gotten close enough to hear our fight, which certainly explained why they'd been hesitant to cross the fence. When they saw me, ragged and bloodsoaked, with a big stainless cannon dangling from one hand, hopping down from the train, the smart ones fled back inside, while the dumb ones pulled out their phones to call the police.

Well, shit.

My survival instinct told me to get the hell out of there, but I was too damned angry and started limping down the hill anyway. I'd just survived a knock-down, drag-out, literal tooth and nail fight, and I wasn't leaving until I was one hundred percent sure Anders was dead. It took my rattled brain a moment to remember that this fucker still had two more bombs out there unaccounted for, and suddenly I found myself in the weird position of hoping that I *hadn't* actually killed Anders. If I could find out what the other targets were, the authorities might still be able to stop them.

My radio was missing, probably somewhere back in the train. I still had my phone, but when I checked I had no service, probably because of Kat's cyber-attack. On the bright side, it looked like the witnesses trying to call the *gendarmes* weren't having much luck getting through either. By the time I reached the fence, the remaining witnesses had retreated. As pissed off and messed up as I was right then, I probably looked like death incarnate.

I clambered over the fence and practically fell over the side. My balance was all screwed up, but I got right back up and wobbled after

Anders. Gun leveled, I approached the car, and sliced the pie around the trunk. There was blood there, but Anders was already gone.

He was out of sight, but had left a red trail for me to follow. I could tell by the smears he'd crawled across the asphalt, keeping the car between us. Then it turned to droplets as he'd stood up again. The dots got farther apart as he'd started running—I glanced around—into a construction site. He was bleeding bad, but Anders was slippery. If I gave him too much of a lead he'd hijack a vehicle or find some other way to escape, which meant I needed to hurry. Only he was also a malicious, clever bastard, he'd know I was thinking that, and he could be lying in wait to ambush me, which meant I was better off taking my time while his blood pressure kept dropping.

Except I wasn't exactly in good shape either. I just wanted to lie down and pass out. Plus, for all I knew somebody had gotten through and the cops were on their way, and oh yeah . . . don't forget the nuclear bombs speeding toward their targets. So I set out at a run toward the construction site. It wasn't much of a run, but it was the best I could do since my chest felt like it was on fire and my legs were made of lead.

The construction site was still laying a foundation. It was nothing but dirt holes, footings, and rebar. If there were any workers here this early, they had better have seen Anders coming and gotten out of his way. Which was good, because if he'd taken a hostage, I was in a bad enough mood I probably would have just shot through them, and I had enough baggage already.

There was some shouting ahead of me, followed by a meaty impact. I moved around a stack of concrete forms and spotted Anders at the edge of a drainage ditch filled with muddy yellow water. He'd just brained a construction worker over the head with a stout length of rebar and was in the process of stealing his car keys. Anders looked like shit. He'd been cut by glass, fists, and teeth. The bullet had hit him low, through the side of his abdomen. It looked too shallow to have punched any vital organs, mostly just muscle and subcutaneous fat, but that wound was bleeding profusely and running down his leg. I'd been aiming at his center of mass, but in my defense, I could barely see my distant moving target, and Valentine's gun hated me, so it had been good enough.

I stopped twenty feet away and aimed the revolver right between his shoulder blades. I cocked the hammer. It was just for dramatic effect. Even I couldn't miss with this damned thing at conversational distance.

Anders slowly turned. His chest was heaving from the exertion. I wouldn't say he looked defeated—I don't know if a warrior like him could even understand the concept of defeat—but he knew I had him dead to rights.

"Do it then."

"Tell me where the other bombs are, and I'll let you walk."

He laughed. Even I'm not that good of a liar. But the fact I'd not simply just blown him away told Anders he had something to bargain with. He pressed one hand against his bloody torso. "How about this, Lorenzo? I give you two targets, you let me drive away, then I'll call and give you the other two."

"I already know two."

"Fuck it then." Anders grimaced, as the blood continued to roll between his fingers. "I'm not that committed. I only wanted to take over Kat's empire . . . I would've made a great crime lord." Anders was acting cooperative, but he hadn't let go of that piece of rebar or those car keys. "Then I'll give you one more. You'd better decide fast. Paris, London, and Brussels, they're rigged for a simultaneous detonation, and you're running out of time."

Exodus had stopped one at Evangeline. That had to be the Paris bomb. I could only hope Reaper and Bob had figured out the Belgian one. "And the fourth?"

Anders gave me a malicious grin. "Kat's primary target, the council. That one left hours ago. Hell, I think some of the Illuminati leaders were actually riding on board with it. Those clueless fucks were heading to their fancy secret meeting. The whole cabal, all her competition, all in one spot, and the best part is they're all there just to talk about what to do about her. Kat has a sick sense of humor that way. Toss your piece and I'll tell you how to disarm all of those bombs."

It had to be a trick. "You think I'm stupid?"

"You think I ever would have tried to escape on that train with one if I didn't have a way to stop the countdown? I can transmit a code that will shut them all down." Anders was hard to read at the best of times. Bleeding, in pain, and with nothing to lose, it was even harder to tell. "Let me go, and the code is yours."

My gut told me he was jerking me around. He'd ended up on that train because they'd been surrounded, taking fire, and it was the one way out. "You're lying."

"You willing to take that chance, cowboy?"

I had to follow my gut. "You might not be that committed, but Kat is. With her there's no backing down. No second thoughts, no cold feet. When she launched, that was it. There's no magic code to take it back, because Kat knew if there was, then someone close to her might be tempted to use it. She's willing to burn the world to get what she wants, but someone else involved might turn out to have a soul." I shook my head. "No. There's no code. She wouldn't allow it."

Anders eyes narrowed. Damn it, I had been right. "How'd you know all that, Lorenzo?"

"I made her that way."

Cool as could be, Anders lifted the big chunk of rebar like it was a club. He was done playing games. He was going to go for it.

I pulled the trigger.

Click.

It was the loudest sound in the world.

Click. Click.

Valentine's revolver was empty.

I hate this fucking gun.

Anders smiled. His teeth were stained red. It was the most murderous, bloodthirsty, confident expression I'd ever seen. And then he came over to beat me to death.

VALENTINE

There was an angel standing over me when I opened my eyes. She was speaking but I could barely hear her. Every sound was muffled, as if I were underwater, except for the rapid pounding of my heart. *Am I dreaming? Am I dead?*

I knew I had been here before, only that angel had turned out to be Ling, and she had saved my life. Not just there, but ever since. That had been Mexico, where we had saved Ariel. Now I was beneath the English Channel and had to save London.

This time the angel was speaking with Ariel's voice, urging me to wake up, to get back in the fight.

Please, get up.

Then the angel was gone, swept away in the wind.

Groaning, I sat up. The main lights were out in the train car, but there were small orange emergency lights on the floor. From the screaming noise whipping past, all the windows had been blown out. The air tasted like smoke and copper. My clothing was hanging in tatters, and then I realized that some of that was my skin. I realized that there was a big chunk of metal embedded in my vest, and it was still hot. When I tried to pull it out, my right hand wouldn't work. My fingers couldn't close around the slick piece of frag hard enough to get it out. I had to put my gun down to pull it out with my left. Blood came welling out of the hole. That was bad. Probably should've left it in.

Then I noticed my right leg was worse. From the knee down, the flesh was shredded. My calf was a pulverized mess. I could actually see the bone. I was sitting in an expanding pool of red.

It doesn't matter. Get up. You're almost there. I was beyond *Calm;* I was serene.

Everything hurt. I'd been flayed. There was so much pain that I should have passed out, but instead it just faded into a sort of background noise as I calmly opened the first aid kit in my cargo pocket and pulled out a tourniquet. I tied it just below my knee, cinched it up, twisted the windlass—spitting blood and spittle through gritted teeth at the agonizing bolt of pain—and locked it in place. That would keep me from bleeding out in the next few minutes. *Long enough.*

I picked up my gun and began to crawl onward. The interior of the car was a twisted mess. Kat's last two men were dead, their bodies mangled and bloody. Above, the Chunnel flashed by at frightening speeds, as I followed the orange lights to my destiny.

Hurry, Michael. You are going to be a father. Don't you want to meet her?

I shook my head. I kept hearing voices. I had lost a lot of blood. I was in shock. Soon I would lose consciousness, and then I would die. I was okay with that. It didn't matter, so long as I stopped the bomb. As I dragged myself along, beneath the English Channel, alone and bleeding, I was at peace.

The bomb had to be in the next car, where Kat was waiting for me with that damned grenade launcher. I pulled myself up the stairs, trying to keep the snubby pointed ahead of me, hoping that I'd get a shot off at her fast enough. If nothing else, I was inside the arming distance of a typical 40mm grenade round. It wouldn't detonate at such close range, a safety feature designed to prevent grenadiers from accidentally blowing themselves up.

She wasn't waiting for me at the door, so I pulled myself up and looked through the glass. The lights were on in this car. It was similar to the other luxury car, except in the middle of the room was a big, green metal box. Katarina was pacing back and forth next to her bomb. I could tell she was scared, that she didn't want to die and was trying to think of a way out. She hadn't come to terms like I had. I thought that her line about getting off in London had been a lie. She had a ring of keys in her hand, and the safety lock on the side door was green instead of red.

Startled, she looked up when I slid the door open. Before she could do anything, I shot her.

Katarina Montalban took a couple halting steps. There was a red hole in her shirt, about where her belly button would be.

"It's over." It was a strain to say every word. "Now open the box and disarm that bomb or I swear to God I'll kill you."

"Nothing's over!" she shrieked. Katarina put her hands on her stomach. They were quickly covered in blood. Grimacing, she walked to the side and sat on one of the couches. "You shot me. It's not supposed to be like this."

"Shut it off."

"I can't stop the timer." She was obviously in terrible pain. *Good.* "The train's failsafe mechanisms have been overridden, and the controls are locked out. Even if we stopped, once in motion, if the bomb remains stationary for too long, it'll detonate. I win no matter what."

"There has to be a way!"

"No." Blood was spurting from her body, and had rapidly formed a puddle on the couch cushions. Katarina was dying, just like I was. "This *is* the way. These men have controlled the world for too long. It is time for someone else to have a turn."

Using the seats to brace myself, I hobbled to the case. The locks and latches on the box were heavy duty. Bullets would have bounced right off. Even if I had known how to disarm it, I couldn't get to it in time. The box weighed a ton. It had probably taken two or three men to lift it off the cart.

Kat kept rambling. "But it was supposed to be my turn. All I ever wanted was what was mine. I worked so hard, sacrificed so much. Why couldn't they just let me have what was mine? My father, Rafael, Eduard. None of them. Why couldn't Lorenzo? Why couldn't *you*?" Katarina stared at me. Her eyes were filled with anger, hate, but then her expression softened. She turned her head to look out the window. Her reflection stared back. "I'm tired."

Anders had decoupled the cars, maybe I could find a way to separate us from the engine? Better for the bomb to detonate under the ocean than on land. Except Anders had used explosives. Just the metal-on-metal friction, at the speed we were travelling, would mean the cars wouldn't separate without being forced. Even if there was a way to stop the train, or decouple the cars, I didn't know what it was and I didn't have time to figure it out.

Wincing at the almost unbearable pain, I undid the Velcro fasteners and lifted my armor vest off my head tossing it into the aisle. I was too weak to keep it on; it was slowing me down. My shirt was soaked with blood. Blood was running down my legs. I was so cold as I lurched to the door control and the now-green button.

Katarina's voice was a whisper. "Look, a light . . . a light at the end of the tunnel. Watch the end of the world with me, Valentine?"

It was too late to make a difference, but no matter what happened, she wouldn't get the satisfaction of seeing her plans fulfilled. I raised the .357 and shot her in the side of the head.

There was only one way left to stop this bomb. I hit the button. The doors began to hiss open, but they had never been intended to open at this speed, and with a screech of metal, were violently torn open. Cold tunnel wind blasted into the car. I fell on my back.

I crawled to the bomb. The physics package from the Topol warhead we had recovered in Yemen was heavy, the metal case added even more weight. I put my shoulder against it and shoved hard. It barely scraped an inch across the carpet, but it *moved*.

My body was shutting down, but I kept pushing. My blood was all over the metal, making it slick. I drew myself back, and then flung my body against it, again and again. It slid further and further. There was more blood, but the wind was closer. The end of the case was through the gap. I was freezing, shivering, but sweat was pouring out of me, cutting tracks through the blood.

I could see the light now, too. I didn't know if it was the end of the tunnel, a hallucination, or the afterlife waiting for me, but I kept pushing. The case began to tilt. Everything was fading into oblivion. My vision went dark, and I drifted away.

LORENZO
France

The first blow hit me in the upper arm. I tried to get out of the way, but Anders still hit me with the chunk of rebar across the shoulder. It sent me spinning over the edge. I landed in the mud and rolled, splashing into the drainage ditch.

Desperate, I tried to stand in the knee-deep slippery muck, but Anders was already sliding down the bank after me. He was bleeding badly from the gunshot wound, so with his heart pumping this hard, he'd weaken eventually. I just needed to stay alive however long that took.

Anders brought the rebar down hard. I barely got out of the way as it sent up a plume of yellow water. He had a reach advantage on me anyway, giving him a three-foot length of metal wasn't helping. In the muck, I couldn't move fast enough to get out of the way, and he caught me flat on the chest on the back swing.

I hit the water again. That had to have broken a rib, but I thrashed my way back up beneath a pouring drainage pipe. He was splashing after me. Trying to negate that length advantage, I threw myself at him, and wrapped my arms around his waist. He kneed me in the chest, and now I was sure that rib wasn't just broken, but might actually have just punctured a lung. He broke away and shoved me back. I ducked as the rebar whistled past my head.

As I tried to get up, Anders brought the rebar down across my back. I can't even begin to explain how badly that hurt. Then he kicked me in the stomach, flipping me over, deeper into the ditch.

"You should have let me go, Lorenzo!" Anders swung his club, barely catching the edge of my scalp. It split my head open, but my skull escaped in one piece. I was down. He put his boot on my chest and shoved me beneath the surface. The water was hip deep here, but pinned beneath him, it might as well have been at the bottom of the ocean.

He was still shouting, but I couldn't hear him. There were only bubbles and the sound of my own heart pounding. I thrashed and fought, clawing at his leg, trying to get free. He was going to drown me in a few feet of water.

Desperate for air, the sound of my pounding heart was replaced by something else. *Incomprehensible whispers.* The whispers wanted me to give up. They had always wanted me to fail. My damaged vision was turning black as the Pale Man's prison. I'd been to hell once before, and I was about go back, only there wouldn't be any escape this time.

Why won't you die, Lorenzo?

Because *fuck you* is why.

I'd forgotten something, probably because I thought of it as a souvenir, merely a letter opener, or toy, more than a weapon, but at that brief moment in time, my life hanging in the balance, it might as well have been Excalibur. I let go of Anders' leg, reached for my pocket, and by some miracle, the little switchblade Decker had gifted me in Africa all those years ago was still there. I got it free, pushed the button to release the blade—I could only hope that it would still pop open under water—and then I slammed it upward into Anders' leg.

I ran the blade up his thigh.

The boot came off my neck. The pressure was gone. I sat up, bursting out of the water, and gasping for air.

Anders was standing there, staring in disgust at the blood *pumping* out of his leg. I'd been right about the cheap little Italian knife. The blade had broken clean off the first time it had gotten some serious use . . . but not before it had sliced through several inches of muscle and his femoral artery. There was no stopping that here. Sever the femoral and unless it was clamped off, it meant death in a matter of minutes.

He knew it. I knew it. Anders was a dead man walking.

"You killed me," he stated, so matter-of-factly, it was like we were talking about the weather. "Fuck."

I could only cough my response. "You deserve it."

Bleed a man, a clock begins to run. When it reaches zero, it's over. Anders lifted the rebar. He could still take me with him.

And he tried damned hard. I was too messed up to even dodge. All I could do was make sure it hit my shoulder instead of my head. But Anders was weakening, slowing, and his next shot only broke the surface of the water. He fell to his knees. We were face to face, breathing hard, as he shifted the rebar so he could try to stab me in the throat with it. I shoved it away. He fell on his face with a splash.

Anders was still struggling. He got his hands beneath his body and pushed himself out of the water. Give him an inch and he'd find a way to kill me with it. He'd remain deadly until his heart quit beating. So I climbed onto his back and wrapped my arms around his face.

But I wasn't going to try to choke him. *Oh no.*

I clamped down with all the strength I had left. The tough son of a bitch still tried to bite a chunk out of my bicep. But I twisted hard, straining against his thick neck, craning his head around until his chin was pointed at his shoulder. Then I put all my weight into it and flung myself back.

SNAP.

I lay there against the muddy bank. Gasping for air as my chest filled with fire instead of air. Anders floated to the top of the yellow water, face down, but with his head at a horribly unnatural angle. I got to my feet as Anders' body slowly began to float away. I was pretty sure there was a bone sticking into my lung, but the horrible choking noise I made right then was actually supposed to be a laugh. I was in so much pain that I wasn't sure if I was going to die or not, but for just a moment, I was triumphant. The darkness had come to take me away again, but I'd won.

There was light on the horizon.

I looked toward the sunrise.

It was in the wrong direction.

Chapter 17: The New World Order

VALENTINE
Location Unknown
Date Unknown

The first thing I remember was a muted rattling sound. After a while, I realized it was rain on a window. It took some doing, but I forced my eyes open. After a few moments, things came into focus, and I found myself surrounded by medical equipment.

"I'm not dead," I said, my voice little more than a raspy croak. "How about that?"

I tried to sit up, but it only brought me pain, so relaxed and stayed down. I wasn't in a hospital. It seemed like a bedroom in a nice house somewhere. I had IV tubes running into my arms, and my body had been bandaged. I remembered the train, I remembered shooting Kat, and I remembered pushing the bomb off. Somehow, I had survived, but I had no idea where I was.

My leg ached with a dull, but relentless throb. I remembered how badly it had been mangled. I was scared to look, but forced myself to sit up enough to see. There was an empty flat spot beneath the sheets where my right leg should have been. My leg was gone from just below the knee.

My leg is gone. I laid back down, surprisingly calm about the whole thing. I guess it hadn't really sunk in yet.

There was a TV on the wall. It was on BBC news, but it had been muted. A tired-looking anchor had a grim look on his face. The crawl along the bottom of the screen said something about thousands still missing. The screen changed, and it was a picture of a mushroom cloud.

My heart dropped into my stomach. I was dizzy. I felt like I was going to throw up. We'd failed. God forgive me, we'd failed.

"Hey," someone said then, startling me. It was Tailor. I hadn't noticed him sitting in a chair in the corner. He looked exhausted, his clothes wrinkly, with dark circles under his eyes. He hadn't shaved in a couple of days, and was smoking a cigarette. He dragged his chair over and parked himself at the edge of my bed. "How you feeling, man?"

How the fuck do you think I'm feeling? I pointed at the TV screen. "Is that London?"

"No. London is safe. You stopped the bomb."

"Where is that, then? What happened?" I tried to sit up.

"Just relax, man. I'll catch you up."

"What about Ling? Is Ling okay?"

"I don't know. We haven't been able to contact anyone from Exodus, or your buddy Lorenzo." He nodded at the TV; now the video was of buildings in flames. "We got three out of four. The London one detonated at the English end of the Chunnel. It's gone. The Chunnel, I mean. It collapsed and flooded. But the explosion was underground and the radiation was mostly contained. Casualties were, well, minimal, all things considered. A lot of traffic had been stopped because of the cyber-attack. The normal trains weren't running. It could've been a lot worse. Anyway, you were found passed out on the train at a station in London. The thing blew right through the stops it would have made under normal circumstances and went straight to the city. It was a miracle you survived that long. You lost a lot of blood."

"How? How did you find me?"

"London was in chaos. A nuclear bomb just went off in the Chunnel, man. They were trying to evacuate the city and they hadn't realized where that train had come from yet. Our people knew where it was going, though, and snatched you up before the British authorities found you. Probably did you a favor, since they'd think you were the terrorist who blew up the Chunnel."

"What about the other bombs?"

"You guys caught the one headed to Paris. The other was intercepted on the way to Brussels, and a NATO special ops team took care of it. We can thank your little girl for reasoning out that target and putting us on it. She saved a lot of lives."

I was staring at the TV, lost. Now they were showing video of the wounded, people badly burned, and children crying for their parents. "Where is that?"

"It detonated on the rail line between Saint-Omer and Calais." Tailor sounded incredibly weary just then. "It's bad, but it could have been way worse. The government is saying that the terrorists had probably intended it to go off in a different city, but it detonated prematurely."

That wasn't true. The bomb had gone off right when it was supposed to. The cities weren't the main targets. They were secondary targets, intended to sow chaos, clean up loose ends, and further damage Kat's rivals. The primary objective had always been to cut the head off the snake. "That was where the Illuminati meeting was, wasn't it?"

Tailor nodded slowly.

"What happened? We warned you! I thought you warned your boss?"

"I did. I don't know what happened. The estate they were meeting at was wiped off the map. They're all dead. The leadership of the other families is gone."

"What about Romefeller?"

Tailor took a long drag off his cigarette. His hands were shaking badly. "Romefeller got held up. He hadn't arrived yet. He's the only one left."

That son of a bitch. "You told him, but he didn't warn his associates to get out in time. He didn't find some way to stop the train like they did in Brussels. You don't find that suspicious?"

Tailor took a deep breath. "Listen, you need to stow that line of thinking for now. Romefeller wanted to talk to you when you woke up. Don't go pointing fingers. It'll just make this harder on you."

"Am I a prisoner?"

"No, Val. You're a hero."

I sure as hell didn't feel like a hero. "I need to rest now."

"Hey, listen . . ."

I didn't let him finish. "Just get out."

"Okay, man. Get some rest. I'll talk to you later." He left the room and closed the door behind him. The TV continued to show images of horror and destruction. I closed my eyes and tried not to cry.

The next time I woke up, Alistair Romefeller was sitting next to the bed. Tailor was wearing a fresh suit and standing in the corner like a dutiful toady. He looked like worn out shit. Romefeller seemed as cool and collected as ever. Why not? Everything had worked out for him, and he hadn't gotten his hands dirty.

"Welcome back, Mr. Valentine. I apologize for the loss of your leg. I promise you'll get the best prosthetic available. I owe you a great deal, and millions of people owe you their lives."

"We didn't stop all the bombs." Tailor was standing behind Romefeller, so his boss couldn't see him. He quietly shook his head in the negative, like I should shut up.

Romefeller sighed. "What happened was a dreadful tragedy, simply dreadful. We did the best we could, but Katarina was too well prepared. Her disruptions of communications and emergency response protocols were just too thorough. I, personally, lost many friends and colleagues to her madness. But we are still here, and we will rebuild, and together we can manage real global problems. Resource inequality, climate change, overpopulation, conflict, poverty . . . these are real problems that are causing real suffering. My peers talked about building a better world, but they were little more than a . . . how did you put it? Model United Nations? A debate club. No more. Things will start to change, now, and I owe all of this to you and your friends. In the end, the whole *world* will owe you a debt of gratitude."

I looked him in the eye. "Right. Tell me, when did you figure out that Blue was intended to target an Illuminati council meeting? Because it seems mighty convenient that that's the one bomb that got through, and even more so that you're the only one left. Things really broke your way, huh?"

Romefeller was quiet for a long time. The billionaire bit his lip as he mulled that over. Tailor was distressed, but didn't say anything. "That is a serious allegation, young man, especially after my surgeons saved your life. You are here, enjoying my hospitality as a guest, rather than being turned over to the British government for questioning. You have to know that had that happened, your own government would take you back into custody, and your former employers would undoubtedly acquire you again. You should feel grateful."

Grateful. "You're a cold son of a bitch, I'll give you that. You told me you people liked to pull strings, and you sure as hell played me. Your rivals are gone, you're in charge, European governments will be panicked and vulnerable. Either a rogue American organization or one of your dead rivals planned and set up the whole thing, depending on who you care to blame. A few thousand people had to die, but you won, didn't you? You got your new world order, and you come out looking squeaky clean."

Romefeller leaned forward, put his elbows on his knees, and rubbed his face with both hands. "Ah, I see. Very well." Tailor looked crestfallen, like I had just signed my own death warrant. "I was worried it would come to this." Romefeller finally lowered his hands and looked me in the eye. "You're reckless, but you're no fool. So let's dispense with the pleasantries and get down to it, shall we? Your survival depends on your cooperation, so I suggest you consider your words very carefully before you speak."

"What do you want from me?"

"Two things, Mr. Valentine. First, what did those Exodus fanatics do with the nuclear weapon intended for Paris?"

"It was still at the train station, last time I saw it." That much was true. "What, you couldn't even take care of that without me? I left the bomb sitting there and it disappeared?" I shook my head. "Unbelievable."

Romefeller scowled, but ignored my defiant sarcasm. "Enough. Tell me about the Oracle."

I laughed at him. "I don't know enough to tell you anything. Besides that, fuck you."

Tailor looked aghast, silently pleading with me to keep my mouth shut, but his boss also ignored my insult. "She is special, isn't she? After the bombings, I sent someone to collect her. She was alone in the residence we'd provided for you, after all, and in danger. She's much too valuable to be left alone like that. I sent one of my best, someone who I knew would see her to me safely." Romefeller reached into his breast pocket and removed a folded, yellow piece of paper. "Later, a second team found her, my operative, I mean. She was alive, but in a coma. She'd had an aneurism. The girl was nowhere to be found."

"What's that?" I asked, nodding at the piece of paper.

"We also found this. It's a note from the Oracle herself, addressed to you. Would you like to read it?"

I lurched up. "Give it to me, you son of a bitch!"

Romefeller actually smirked and tossed the folded piece of paper onto the bed. I snatched it up and opened it. It was written in neat cursive, with a purple ink pen. The I's were dotted with little circles.

Michael,

For better or for worse, it's done. By the time you get this, I'll be long gone. Please, don't worry about me, and don't try to find me. It's not safe for either one of us. Too many bad people are looking for you and me both for us to stay together. I know you'd die to protect me, but I don't want you to ever been in that position. You've done enough for me. You deserve to be free of all these burdens, and to live a happy life.

I have to follow my own path now. I don't belong anywhere now. I need time. I need to find myself. I need to find out who I really am, what I really am, and where I really belong. There are so many things I wanted to tell you, but I just couldn't, and I'm sorry about that. I was afraid you wouldn't understand, and I guess I was afraid you wouldn't believe me. I know better, now. I know you'd stay with me no matter what, and that's why I have to go. They're coming for me, and I'm done being a pawn in someone else's game.

I don't know what the future holds now. The old constants are gone, leaving only variables like you. I can make guesses, but there is no certainty anymore, just probabilities. I guess this means humanity is on its own now. No more puppet masters, but that's for the best. That's the way it's supposed to be. Those who want to force a certain order on the world have brought more death and suffering than anything else. Now the world has a fresh start, and a chance to do better.

Please don't be sad. I will miss you so much, but I promise I'll see you again. I just have a lot of things I need to do, and I need to do them on my own. Thank you for being my family. Thank you for showing me what it means to be human. Say hi to your little girl for me, when she's born.

I love you.

—Ariel

My hands were shaking as I lowered the note. My eyes teared up as I carefully folded it back up.

"Imagine the good that I could accomplish, with a mind like that in my employ." Romefeller said. "I've learned much about your young oracle, and I understand now why so many have fought for her. Tell me, where do you think she would go? You can't tell me that she really just disappeared, a teenage girl, in an unfamiliar country."

"Wherever she is, she's out of your grasp."

The smug bastard chuckled at me. "I assure you, *nothing* is out of my grasp. Either you're lying, or you really don't know. In either case, I'm afraid that makes you a liability."

I said nothing. I clutched Ariel's note and stared the old Illuminatus down.

Romefeller looked over shoulder. "Mr. Tailor?"

Tailor's face was a mask as he stepped forward. Without a word, he reached under his suit jacket and drew his pistol.

I looked him in the eye. "I told you it would come to this."

"Val . . ." he trailed off.

I shook my head, but didn't avert my gaze. "Do what you have to do, man. You should know something, though: she told me that humanity is on its own, now. No more puppet masters."

Tailor looked at me, but said nothing else. He looked over at Romefeller, then back down at me.

"Mr. *Tailor*," Romefeller repeated, his very tone a threat.

After another couple seconds, Tailor nodded to himself. In a flash, he turned and cracked Romefeller in the mouth with the butt of his gun. I saw a tooth go flying as the billionaire stumbled backward, stunned and in pain. Tailor then grabbed him by the lapels of his expensive suit, spun him around, and pushed him down onto my bed. The old man kicked and thrashed, but my friend didn't hesitate. Grabbing a pillow with his free hand, he stuck it over Romefeller's face, stuck the muzzle of his pistol into it, and pulled the trigger.

With a muffled pop and a puff of feathers, Romefeller stopped kicking. Tailor stood up, straightening his suit jacket as the dead billionaire slid off the bed, leaving a bloody mess on the sheets, and crumpled to the floor in an undignified heap.

It was suddenly intensely quiet in the room. Tailor and I stared at each other for a moment, not saying anything.

"Jesus Christ!" I finally blurted, breaking the silence. My heart was racing. "God *damn*, dude."

Tailor crossed the room and returned with a wheelchair that had been parked against a wall. "Yeah, well, he can consider that my two weeks' notice. Come on, Val, we're getting the fuck out of here. We don't have a lot of time."

He helped me out of bed and into the wheelchair. My right leg ended at a stump, just below the knee, so it wasn't like I was getting out on my own. "Where are we going to go?"

"Bob Lorenzo went to the U.S. embassy in Paris and gave them everything your people have collected on both Majestic and the Illuminati over the last couple years, all the evidence you've recorded, all the puzzle pieces that your girl put together. Here." He dropped a Glock 26 into my lap before unlocking the brakes on the chair. "Hide that, don't pull it out unless I tell you to. I can still talk my way out of here. The shit's hitting the fan all over. Two nukes went off in Europe. NATO is on full alert. The U.S. is at DEFCON 2. I really don't want to be here when the French government puts everything together."

He started to wheel me out of the room. As he asked, I concealed the little pistol in my lap, along with Ariel's note. "Where are we going to go?" I repeated.

"I've got a contact with the CIA. Don't freak out, it's the CIA, not Majestic. Believe me, I did some digging. Majestic has a lot of reach, but they're not everywhere, and they're on the run now. Things are going to change, fast. Now shut up and let me get us out of here."

"Tailor?" I said, as he rolled me down a quiet hallway. "Thank you."

"Yeah, well, it's only fair, I guess. If it weren't for me you'd still be a security guard in Vegas, and you'd still have both your legs."

I actually chuckled.

LORENZO
Ostrava, Czech Republic
Three weeks later . . .

Europe was in chaos. It was like Kat's bomb had set off every simmering bit of built-up anger and resentment on the whole continent. There were riots in every major city. And then there were counterprotests that turned violent because people were sick of the rioters' bullshit. Militant assholes used the chaos to strike. Governments cracked down on threats, both real and imagined. In my old life it was exactly the kind of volatile situation that I would have found a way to take advantage of.

But I was retired. And this time, I meant it.

I hadn't seen Exodus since the night everything fell apart. Antoine had gotten hurt, but Skunky had taken a bullet to the chest at Evangeline, and had been touch and go for several days. Reaper's war-criminal doctor network had gotten a little richer, but Skunky had pulled through. Exodus had gotten out of France their own way after that. As for my brother, I had not even gotten to tell him goodbye before he'd gone to the U.S. Embassy and started raising hell. Before he had turned himself in, he had made a bunch of calls, so there were enough law enforcement and intelligence VIPs there watching like hawks to make sure Majestic didn't just murder him.

After I had gotten patched up, Jill and I had fled the country too. I told myself if I hadn't just been used as Anders' punching bag I might have felt up to trying to relieve the decapitated Illuminati of some of their wealth, but to be honest, my heart just wasn't in it. So we had headed east until the rioting stopped and we found a quiet place to hide out. Jill and I were both still a mess, and we spent most of our time lying in bed and healing. Reaper caught up a few days later, and tried to take care of us. He was a terrible nurse.

Jill kept healing, and one day while she was watching the news, and they were showing something about London—and it wasn't a smoking radioactive crater—it finally sank in what we had accomplished, what she had spent a year fighting for. She looked over, tears in her eyes, and didn't have to say a word. I went over and held her, and that was the day she began to forgive herself for being human and having to make a call.

She was going to be okay. We were going to be okay.

It kind of blew my mind thinking about it. Valentine, Skunky, his buddy Tailor, and me; four former Switchblade mercenaries, all trained by Hawk, brought together by crazy coincidence, and we'd changed the course of history. I knew Hawk would be proud. Hell, I think even Decker would have been proud, if he knew. If nothing else, it demonstrated how capable his guys really were.

Reaper was being even more jittery than usual, and that was saying something. But it wasn't the pensive, mopey, afraid of the dark Reaper I had been dealing with recently. He was excited about something, and after a couple weeks of relative quiet, he finally let me in on his secret.

Wincing at every step because of my ribs, Reaper had led me down the narrow stairs to the private lane behind the house we were renting. There was an unremarkable van parked there.

"Okay, Lorenzo, before you freak out, I just want you to know that this is a little scary, but I think it is the best idea I've ever had."

"I have no idea what you're talking about."

"Sala Jihan is still out there. It's about that burn on your chest. Yeah, you've been talking in your sleep ever since you got out. I know about the nightmares. I know you can still hear stuff occasionally, just like I can still see stuff once in a while when I close my eyes, and it scares the hell out of me, you know?"

"Sadly, I do." I had fulfilled my part of the bargain, but I still wore the devil's mark. One day he might decide to reclaim what he owned. "Wait, have you been watching me in my sleep?"

"Don't worry about it. I got a message from the Oracle. She said because some of the bombs came from him, he'll be hiding for a bit, but after that he'll start rebuilding his empire. She said that with time she could figure out how to get him, that *you* could get to him."

I still didn't know what that girl was, but she was on the opposite side of the Pale Man, and that was good enough. "Reaper, I just want to find a home, and go there. Just me and Jill. No more of this . . . whatever it is."

"And what if the Pale Man decides he's not done with you?"

"I can only hope we're done with him."

Then, grinning like a maniac, Reaper opened the van doors and showed me his souvenir from France. "What if this time we could make *sure*?"

Epilogue: The Blood of Patriots, and Tyrants

VALENTINE

Hays, Kansas
Three Months Later . . .

Kansas was cold and windy in January, but today was a pretty nice day. The sky was blue, the sun was shining, and I was sitting on the back porch of an old farmhouse, bundled up, sipping hot chocolate as I talked with my visitor. Tailor and I had been moved from safehouse to safehouse ever since we'd been brought back to the United States. We'd been smuggled into our own country on an Air Force C-17, and hadn't stayed in one place for too long since. The old farmhouse was heavily guarded.

Bob Lorenzo was leaning on the railing, looking out over the snow-covered field behind the house, awkwardly trying to make small talk. "So how's Ling?"

"She's fine," I said tersely. She was out of the country, far away and safe, and Bob didn't need to know where she was.

"How's your kid-to-be?"

Ling had told me in an encrypted email that she'd been examined by Dr. Bundt. The pregnancy was going fine so far. It was too early to tell if it was a boy or a girl. "Fine."

"Parenthood is great. It changes everything. I sure missed my kids while I was locked up. Still do, but at least I know they're safe. And they know I'm alive. Having children really puts things in perspective. It makes you realize the importance of leaving them a future."

"I already agreed to testify about Majestic in exchange for a pardon, Bob. What else do you want? I'm giving my full cooperation."

"First things first. I have something to give you. Here." He handed me an ornate wooden case that he retrieved from an attaché case.

"What is this?" I asked. I undid the brass clasp and opened it. The case was lined with silk padding and contained some kind of medal. It hung from a long red neck ribbon, connected to an ornate badge by an enamel laurel and oak wreath. At the very center of the badge was an engraved image of a woman's head. The inscription on the badge read, *République Française.* The inside of the lid had a plaque affixed to it, which read, *On Behalf of The French Republic,* in both English and French.

"You've been inducted into the National Order of the Legion of Honour, at the rank of *Commandeur.* It's the same award they gave General Patton. There are similar awards, though ones of lesser rank, available to your former teammates if you ever to decide to give the French their names."

"I don't think that would be a good idea."

"I understand your caution, but you saved Paris from a nuclear bomb. The whole thing is being kept secret for the time being, but they love you more than Jerry Lewis now. There's rumblings that the British want to grant you a knighthood, too, for saving London."

"You'd think they'd be mad I collapsed the Chunnel."

Bob shrugged. "We've briefed the Ministry of Defense on everything that went down, and gave them your sworn statements. Nobody who matters thinks there was anything more you could have done. You need to quit beating yourself up."

"Fine," I said again. "Is this why you came all the way out here?"

"No, Valentine, it's not. Listen, we both know that a cancer like Majestic isn't something that can be rooted out with just hearings. They're still out there, sinking their claws into everything, trying to rebuild their shadow government. But they're on the ropes. This is our chance to root them out, once and for all."

"Did the FBI give you your old job back or something?"

"No. This is bigger than the FBI. The president gets it now. He knows how dangerous Majestic is, and he wants them gone. He's created a special task force. Since he wanted somebody motivated, and somebody he thought trustworthy, he put me in charge. Now I'm recruiting people that *I* can trust." He turned around and gave me a very solemn look. "Your country needs you again, Valentine."

I scoffed and sipped my hot chocolate. "You know, Gordon Willis told me the same damn thing. You know how that worked out for me."

"I need people who hate Majestic just as much as I do, who know what they're capable of, who can't be corrupted by them."

Is he for real right now? "So you get a secret government task force, to fight the last secret government task force that went out of control?"

"I've got men who can follow orders and pull a trigger, Val. I want people like you running it specifically so we don't turn into the very thing we're fighting against. It isn't about just building an operation; it's about having the courage to tear it down when we're done."

I looked up at him incredulously. "Do you have any idea what you're asking me? I've lost friends. I was tortured. They screwed with my mind in ways I still don't understand, I should be with the woman I love while she's carrying my child, and let's not forget," I knocked on my prosthetic right leg, "I'm crippled. You want me to do *more*?"

"Yes," he said, so earnestly I wanted to punch him in his big, stupid face. "I know the gravity of what I'm asking, but I also know what's at stake. I think you do, too. Are you willing to do what it takes, or will you sit back and hope things work out for the best?"

"The question isn't whether or not I'm willing to do what it takes. The question is, how far are *you* willing to go? What needs to be done won't be pretty. It won't be within the confines of the law. It can't be, because *they* don't operate within the law. We can't use due process when they can corrupt the process itself so easily. In order to do what you're suggesting, we will have to do things that are illegal, unconstitutional, and unacceptable to the American people. We're going to have to hunt down and probably kill American citizens, and there's no guarantee that we'll succeed. Sure, this president says he's on board, but as soon as things get ugly he's liable to change his mind. Politicians won't have the stomach for what needs to be done, and God only knows how many of them Majestic has its hooks in. Even if we do pull it off, even if we uproot Majestic from the ground up and wipe it out, then what? Now that the dirty work is done, we're a liability. We're a liability and sooner or later they'll be tempted to come after us."

Bob nodded. "I know."

"Then why are you doing this? Why should *I*? What is the point if we do all of this, only to end up in prison or in an unmarked grave someplace?"

He was quiet for a long time. "Project Red tore China in half. Project Blue was supposed to do the same thing to Europe. Those aren't the only such projects out there. There are rumors of another one, aimed at the United States itself."

My titanium and polymer leg creaked as I leaned forward on it. "What are you talking about?"

"Project Black is the Majestic contingency plan to overthrow of the government of the United States. It was originally cooked up, way back in the 1950s, as a hypothetical failsafe in case the government was compromised by Communist agents. Well, more than half a century later, we've backed a rabid dog into a corner. We have no way of knowing how much of this contingency was set up, how many assets are in place, or what all it would involve. But you know what they were willing to do to China, and you saw what they were willing to do to Europe. These are the same people that left you all to die in Zubara as soon as you became a liability. These are the same people that use American citizens for science projects. You *know* what they're capable of. You know what kind of state the country is in already. Something like this? It could be the end, Valentine. Your country is at stake."

"I'll think about it."

"The Tree of Liberty must be refreshed, from time to time . . ."

I didn't let him finish the quote. "Yeah, yeah, I took American History too. I said I'll think about it."

"I'm confident you'll make the right choice. Mr. Tailor is already on board, and we've got other leads we're chasing down. He's trying to contact your teammate, Hudson, I think, from Dead Six. I want you to know, too, that if you do this, I'll guarantee the safety of your family. They'll be given the same protection as mine. So please, think it over." He turned to leave. "Oh, there was another package for you. I left it on the table. I'll be in touch." He zipped up his jacket. "Stay warm. It's a cold one, this year."

I waited until I heard his car leave, then I limped to the kitchen. I was still going through a lot of physical therapy, learning to walk all over again. It made me glad Ling couldn't see me like this. Standing over the package, I hesitated for just a moment. It was a plain cardboard box. *No.* No more fear. I snapped open my automatic knife, and cut the tape holding it closed. Bob wasn't the type to leave a bomb or anything for turning down his offer, and the house had his people in it, guarding me. It was stupid paranoia, and some days it was a struggle to overcome it.

The box contained my Smith & Wesson 629 revolver, my custom sidearm, my lucky sixgun, completely caked in dried mud. Knocking hardened clay off of the frame, I got the cylinder open. It still had six fired brass cases in it. I was going to have to detail-strip the gun to get all the crud out.

There was also a note.

Thanks for the loaner. I used it on our mutual friend. I heard you dealt with my ex. Thanks.

I saw my brother. He made me the same offer he's going to make you. I told him no. Any organization that would hire me is too disreputable to work for. Besides, I've got my own business to handle. But I know you won't say no. You'll take his job. I don't know how you'll justify it, but you will, and then you'll go ruin some assholes' day, because that's what you do best. A warrior needs a war.

This time, I'll try and stay out of your way. You need me for something, you can figure out how to reach me. I don't say that lightly. I don't have many friends. I consider you one of them.

I set the letter down, looked at my gunked-up gun, and sighed. I had a revolver to clean. Then I needed to call Ling, tell her I love her, and hope she wouldn't be mad at me for taking a new job.

LORENZO
Altay Mountains, Russia
Three Years Later . . .

My message had been delivered. The face that haunted my nightmares appeared on the screen. Sala Jihan stared through me with his unnatural black eyes. Even though I was sitting in the back of a truck, upwind, twenty miles away, his gaze was still unnerving. It was like he could reach through the glass and rip out my soul. Maybe he could, I didn't actually know.

"I warned you never to return."

The scars on my chest burned as he said that. "The two of us had some unfinished business."

"You have made a grave error." He must have been holding the device too close to his face, because now all I could see was his teeth. That was somehow even worse. *"You will pay for this trespass."*

"Probably."

"Why has the son of murder called upon the Pale Man?" As he said that, he turned the camera enough that I could see the concrete walls of the missile silo he called home.

Location confirmed. "I'm returning something you lost."

When Reaper had shown me what he had taken from France, I hadn't believed it, at first. It was hard to comprehend the fact that my friend had stolen one of the four horsemen of the apocalypse. Guided by the Oracle, it had still taken a long time and a lot of meticulous planning to get the nuclear warhead buried into the mountainside next to Sala Jihan's fortress. Ariel had insisted on that to minimize fallout to the regional villages. I had been all in favor of an underground detonation, because it didn't matter if he lived at the bottom of an impenetrable missile silo, if I dropped a whole mountain on top of him.

I opened the control box, and turned the key, and placed my finger on the red button.

"What do you think you are doing?" the Pale Man demanded.

"You once told me you like digging in the earth. Dig your way out of *this*." I pushed the button. There was a roar like thunder. The earthquake hit a moment later. The screen went black.

Reaper's voice was in my headset. "Detonation confirmed, Chief."

VALENTINE
Flagstaff, Arizona

I leaned in the doorway of my daughter's bedroom, watching her sleep. Sarah Mei Song-Valentine was an energetic toddler, to say the least, and she wore me out. Even after running around the house all morning, she stubbornly refused to take a nap until she was so tired she fell asleep on the floor in the middle of her toys.

My wife appeared next to me, leaned her head on my shoulder, and looked in on our daughter. "You finally got her to go to bed," she said, quietly.

"It was a struggle today," I said, smiling.

"It will be a struggle tomorrow," Ling agreed. "She's so full of energy."

"I hope you got in a nap yourself." She had taken Sarah to the park that morning, and apparently there were a bunch of screaming toddlers there. I was gone a lot, so I tried to do as much parenting as I could while I was home. Raising a kid was a full-time job, and I felt guilty about Ling doing it by herself so much.

Task Force 151 had kept me busy for the past three years. When Bob first approached me, on the porch of that old farmhouse in Kansas, I'd never have imagined that his proposal would grow into what the task force had become. What started as a handful of patriots grew into over a hundred, backed up clandestinely by the FBI, the CIA, the NSA, and the military. The tentacles of Majestic and its subsidiaries went farther and deeper than we ever would have guessed, too. We'd made a lot of progress in the first three years, and Majestic was on the run. Many of its key personnel were in witness protection, prison, or buried out in the desert. The president had kept his word to let us do what needed to be done, and we kept our part of the bargain by keeping him in the dark about it.

Someday, the country would know the truth. Someday, these stories would be told. Until then, we worked in secret, trying to undo decades' worth of damage without turning into the very thing we were fighting. It was a fine line to walk, and we'd had some pretty major successes. We'd gone deep into the base popularly known as Area 51, tracking down a Majestic supercomputer/AI called Prometheus. This machine had given our information warfare guys all sorts of hell, but in the end, Reaper helped us pin down the physical location of the AI, hidden in the DOD black budget, in a bunker that few had access to. After we pulled its drives to comb for intelligence, I dropped a Thermite grenade in its CPU and burned it to slag.

No, I'm not at liberty to discuss anything regarding extraterrestrials that may or may not have been there.

After a year-long operation, we were able to find and secure a pair of nuclear weapons that had officially been missing since 1961. The two hydrogen bombs had supposedly never been found after a B-52 carrying them crashed in a North Carolina swamp. Information from Prometheus' drives led to the realization that an arm of what became Majestic had clandestinely secured the weapons, and later held them in reserve. Tailor and I oversaw the capture of these weapons and their long-overdue return to the Air Force. They were eventually sent to Oak Ridge and decommissioned. Each one had a yield of 24 megatons, far bigger than the warheads used in Project Blue. Getting those out of Majestic's hands was one of our greatest accomplishments to date.

There were setbacks, too, of course, and the matter was anything but settled. But three years in, I felt that the tide had turned. Majestic was on the run, and for the first time in my adult life, I was cautiously optimistic about the future of my country. Oh, don't get me wrong, politicians are still crooks, Washington, DC is a sewer of cronyism and corruption, and the nation is still polarized, but I didn't go into this expecting to fix any of that.

Lorenzo had been right about me, though. A warrior needs a war, and this was *my* war. It felt good to be fighting for something I believed in, for my daughter's future, when I had spent so much of my career fighting for a paycheck.

"I slept for a while," Ling said with a yawn, "until your phone went off. Your work phone."

"Oh, God," I said, taking the plastic rectangle from her. "What is it now?"

She smiled. "Go see what they want. Don't forget, it's your turn to make dinner tonight."

"Okay. Do we have any hamburger left?"

"We're not having hamburgers again."

"Okay. Do we have hamburger so I can make tacos?"

Ling shook her head.

"Well . . . how about I order a pizza?"

"Just go," she said. "I'll get dinner started."

"Love you!" I said, walking into my office with my phone. Once inside, I unlocked it and checked my messages. There were a bunch, as usual, but an urgent one from Tailor.

Val, check this out. That seismic disturbance the other day was definitely a subterranean nuclear blast. It was located in the Altay Mountains, right on the border of Russia and China. Bob is sending Dragic's team in to assess the situation on the ground, but it looks like the old Russian missile base there was destroyed. A mountain fell on it. Will keep you posted. Sorry to bug you when you're on leave.

I opened the files Tailor had sent with the message. Satellite imagery, wind analysis, seismic activity recordings, things like that. What was left at the Crossroads was now gone. I had no way of knowing for sure what happened, but I had a pretty good idea. *Lorenzo, you amazing son of a bitch.* I was just glad he didn't accidentally start World War Three.

There was a second message, this one from an unknown sender. That immediately set off alarm bells in my head. This was my work phone, and it was supposed to be secure. I wasn't supposed to get spam. *I swear to God, if this is random junk mail I'm going to tear someone a new asshole over at tech division.*

It was a picture of a lovely young woman, a selfie. It took me a moment to recognize Ariel, but when I did, I almost dropped the phone. She had purple streaks in her platinum blonde hair now, and had on a pair of those big sunglasses that girls like to wear, but there was no mistaking her. With the image there was a brief message.

Michael:

I'm sorry you haven't heard from me. I had something I needed to do. Tell Ling that the Pale Man is gone, for good this time. Also tell her I miss you guys, and I love you both, and I can't wait to meet Sarah. I just knew you were going to name her Sarah! Oh, and happy birthday, Merry Christmas, etc., times three. I hope I can see you soon. Until then, please don't worry. I'm okay.

Love, Ariel

"Michael?" Ling startled me when she said my name. I'd been engrossed in my phone and hadn't heard her come in. "What's the matter?"

I looked up at her, smiling, and handed her the phone.

END